The
Orchard

Books by Beverly Lewis

The Orchard • The Beginning
The Stone Wall
The Tinderbox • The Timepiece
The First Love • The Road Home
The Proving • The Ebb Tide
The Wish
The Atonement • The Photograph
The Love Letters • The River

HOME TO HICKORY HOLLOW

The Fiddler • The Bridesmaid
The Guardian
The Secret Keeper • The Last Bride

THE ROSE TRILOGY

The Thorn • The Judgment
The Mercy

ABRAM'S DAUGHTERS

The Covenant • The Betrayal
The Sacrifice
The Prodigal • The Revelation

THE HERITAGE OF LANCASTER
COUNTY

The Shunning
The Confession • The Reckoning

ANNIE'S PEOPLE

The Preacher's Daughter
The Englisher • The Brethren

THE COURTSHIP OF NELLIE FISHER

The Parting • The Forbidden
The Longing

SEASONS OF GRACE

The Secret • The Missing
The Telling

The Postcard • The Crossroad

The Redemption of Sarah Cain
Sanctuary (with David Lewis)
Child of Mine (with David Lewis)
The Sunroom • October Song
Beverly Lewis Amish Romance
Collection

Amish Prayers
The Beverly Lewis Amish Heritage
Cookbook

www.beverlylewis.com

The
Orchard

BEVERLY
LEWIS

BETHANYHOUSE
a division of Baker Publishing Group
Minneapolis, Minnesota

© 2022 by Beverly M. Lewis, Inc.

Published by Bethany House Publishers
11400 Hampshire Avenue South
Minneapolis, Minnesota 55438
www.bethanyhouse.com

Bethany House Publishers is a division of
Baker Publishing Group, Grand Rapids, Michigan

Printed in the United States of America

ISBN 978-0-7642-3753-9 (paperback)
ISBN 978-0-7642-3754-6 (cloth)
ISBN 978-0-7642-3755-3 (large print)
ISBN 978-1-4934-3910-2 (ebook)

Scripture quotations are from the King James Version of the Bible.

This story is a work of fiction. Names, characters, incidents, and dialogues are products of the author's imagination and are not to be construed as real. Any resemblance to any person, living or dead, is purely coincidental.

Cover design by Dan Thornberg, Design Source Creative Services
Art direction by Paul Higdon

Baker Publishing Group publications use paper produced from sustainable forestry practices and post-consumer waste whenever possible.

22 23 24 25 26 27 28   7 6 5 4 3 2 1

To
Darla Demahy
for your faithful prayers
and sweet encouragement—
despite two back-to-back hurricanes!

Who loves a garden still his Eden keeps;
Perennial pleasures plants, and wholesome harvests
reaps.

—Amos Bronson Alcott, "The Garden," *Tablets*, 1868

Prologue

APRIL 16, 1970

In the early morning light, I looked out one of my third-floor dormer windows and treasured the springtime rebirth taking place as far as my eyes could see. The orchard was a sea of frilly pink peach blossoms, fifty rolling acres of fruit trees. I wondered how the garden of Eden could have been any more lovely, and I thanked God for the beauty below.

Eager to breathe in the familiar fragrance of the orchard, I raised the window as birdsong beckoned to me. But I also wanted to feel the cool morning dew on my bare feet before doing chores. So, already dressed, I gave my waist-length, light brown hair a good brushing, then twisted and pinned it into a thick bun—not bothering to put on a bandanna.

I slipped down the two flights of stairs in my family's home, then walked out the side door and across the yard and beyond. Unhurried, I wandered past the blooming peach trees, along the grassy strips that separated their rows. Time seemed to slow to the easy ticking of a heavenly clock. Honestly, I was so thankful not to live like our few English neighbors scattered here and there amongst us. Such a racket came from their big tractors and other farming equipment! *Ach*, it was bad enough that planes streaked our skies, trucks and cars crowded the highways, and folk in the city of Lancaster rushed helter-skelter.

But here? My heart drank in the peace of this lovely place, the soft blossoms dusting the atmosphere with their sweet peachy scent—like honey. As a young girl, I'd declared that the Lord God himself must surely dwell in our orchard—the most splendid spot on earth.

"If I could, I'd stay here forever," I whispered, ever so content.

From behind me, I heard swift footsteps and assumed it was my oldest brother coming to check on the swath of newly planted semi-dwarf apple trees down near Harvest Drive. But to my surprise it wasn't Jonah but Evan, my twin.

"Whatcha doin' up so early, Ellie?" he asked, stopping to roll up his black pant legs. "You nearly beat the dawn." He straightened, a whole head taller than me, almost as tall as our older brothers, Jonah and Rudy—both married with growing families and places of their own.

"It's so fresh and dewy this time of day," I said. "Ain't so?"

Evan nodded, a sparkle in his blue eyes the same shade as mine. "No wonder Adam and Eve walked with God in the garden in the cool of the day—and no better place for a Hostetler to be on such a fine Thursday morning."

"I'm sad for everyone who doesn't have an orchard to come home to!"

"You remind me of *Dawdi* Hezekiah, comin' out here to ramble through the rows."

"*Jah*." I smiled, happy that *Dat*'s elderly father lived in the small *Dawdi Haus* addition to our home just as he had for nearly two decades—since well before *Mammi* passed away three years ago. "Well, he's the one who planted most of these trees back when. They're his children, in a way."

Evan gave me a look that suggested I was *ferhoodled.* "Do ya realize how many of these trees'll be gone and new ones planted by the time I'm as old as Dawdi is now? The smaller trees bear fruit only up to twenty-five years, ya know."

"Well, since Dat's handin' these acres over to your care when he retires, it'll be up to you to see to all that someday." I didn't need to remind Evan that being the youngest son was a truly special blessing when it came to taking over the land—and in our case, an orchard, too. *A blessing for sure,* I thought, envying my brother a little. If I'd been born the younger twin and a boy, *I'd* have been chosen to run the orchard in the future. But alas, women didn't have much say in those matters. It had always been that way amongst the People.

We walked for a while, and Evan kept glancing at the sky, now brushed with golden streaks. Something had to be on his mind for him to come out here before breakfast.

At last he said, "I'm plannin' to go to Jack Herr's burial service tomorrow afternoon in Carlisle, at the Ashland Cemetery Soldiers' Lot."

I had known who Jack was—our farm neighbor's son—but hearing Evan talk like this confirmed what I'd long suspected. He and Jack had become friends. "I'm surprised, I guess . . . ya wanting to go . . . since that would be frowned on, *jah?*" We both knew that anything related to the military was forbidden.

Evan halted between the rows of new apple trees. "And for that reason, you must keep mum."

"I won't say anything, but are ya sure you oughta go?" I'd heard of Jack's death from *Mamm* several days earlier, but I hadn't read his obituary for myself. Too many young men were dying in Vietnam. It was heartbreaking.

Evan frowned and nodded. "Well, Jack was my best English friend, so I wanna be there." He sighed loudly, walking a bit farther without saying more. Then when he spoke again, it was nearly in a whisper. "I still can't believe he's gone." He glanced toward the road beyond the orchard. "Jack gave up his life for our country—for people like you and me—so I'm gonna pay my respects," he said flatly.

So many families round Lancaster County had lost sons or brothers, even husbands, to this dreadful war. But none had been Amish. Our father, like all Old Order Amishmen here in Lancaster County, Pennsylvania, held a strong belief in non-resistance, which meant he didn't approve of going to war under any circumstances. Dat said it went against the Lord's ways for the People to choose violence, and this fight wasn't ours anyway since America wasn't our true home. We were only passing through. *"We're pilgrims and sojourners whose final destination is heaven,"* he liked to say.

"Dat *will* be displeased if he finds out, though," Evan added, his expression melting into misery, "so just remember to keep this to yourself."

I bobbed my head in agreement, then impulsively asked, "But why must ya be friends with outsiders, anyway?"

"Aw, Ellie, just 'cause you don't have any English friends doesn't mean I can't have a few." He pushed his straw hat down on his corn-yellow hair.

"I don't understand why ya need fancy friends, though. You used to be *gut* friends with Solomon Bontrager, remember?"

"I was curious, so I dipped my toe in the outside world even before I turned fifteen. Wanted to know what I was missin'."

For quite a while now, I'd pondered Evan's desire to spend time with a handful of English fellows—mostly Jack and his friends. At nineteen, and unlike me, my brother hadn't started baptismal instruction, deciding instead to stay in *Rumschpringe*, the season prior to baptism when our youth began to socialize with their friends, sometimes outside the confines of the church. I had no idea why Evan wanted to continue with this stage of his life. Even so, he knew Dat had always advised us to choose our friends wisely, which naturally meant amongst the People. Some teens were known to push the boundaries, though, causing heartache for their parents.

"Take Jack's younger sister, Cheryl, for instance," Evan said now. "She's real nice, and you'd know it, too, if ya ever wanted to give her half a chance. Neighbor that she is." He paused. "I really like her."

This surprised me. Evan had shown only a smidgen of interest in the Amish girls in our church community, but he'd never said much about Cheryl Herr, either. And though I was sure she was fine for an *Englischer*, what did she and I have in common except for having older brothers?

"I have my own friends, Evan."

"Only two that I know of—Leah Bontrager and Cousin Ruthann."

"Well, I'm not as outgoin' as you, so I don't need a bunch of friends."

Stealing a glance at my grieving brother, I wished I hadn't pushed myself into the conversation. After all, we'd been talking about Jack's burial service. *"Killed in a hopeless war,"* I'd heard some womenfolk murmur. It was such a tragedy. "I'm awful sorry, Evan. I should've kept my thoughts to myself."

He leaned down and picked up a handful of freshly fallen

pink blossoms. For a moment, he appeared to be pondering something.

"What're ya doin'?" I asked him.

He looked at me without saying. Then at last, he smiled. "Hold out your hands."

I stepped closer, opening my palms, and he placed the few blossoms there like he did when we were little, knowing how much I loved them and everything about the orchard.

"Remember when I'd put them in my hair?" I asked.

"Wasn't that long ago, really," he said, eyes soft and gentle.

For fun, I sprinkled a few on my head, glad I hadn't worn my bandanna yet today.

"Now you're the pertiest Amish girl in Bird-in-Hand," Evan said. "I daresay you could have any fella your heart desires."

I broke into a smile. "*Ach*, Evan, I only care 'bout one boy."

"And who would that be?"

"Ain't tellin'."

Evan chuckled, shaking his head.

"Anyway," I said wistfully, "the day I marry is the day I leave the orchard behind."

Evan nodded, a look of empathy on his face.

"Kinda strange that it'll be the best day *and* the worst," I added.

He looked at me. "For your sake, I wish it could be different, Ellie. Maybe we could manage the orchard together . . . if things work out that way."

And miss out on love and having my own family? I thought, though I was moved by his caring. Truly, I couldn't have asked for a better brother. If anyone deserved to inherit the orchard, it was Evan.

"All of this'll be in your capable hands," I replied.

"Remember, you can always visit," he said, a twinkle in his eyes.

He reached for the blossoms in my hair, but I ducked and scooted away. Laughing, he patted his straw hat. "I'll be seein' ya at breakfast." He gestured toward the right, then went on ahead up the walkway of thick grass between the trees.

Already missing the banter, I watched him go as I imagined him running the orchard when Dat retired in a few years. No one loved the orchard and the work involved quite as much as Evan—except, of course, me. Through the years, we'd spent long hours together out here, especially during the springtime and the harvest, talking and laughing as we worked from sunrise to sundown.

I thought then of my best friend, Leah, who lived two farms up from us. I couldn't imagine losing her like Evan had lost his friend Jack. Goodness, I'd known Leah was meant to be my friend clear back when we met as youngsters. At recess that first day of school, she'd whispered to me that her favorite thing to do was sit on her covered porch while it rained. It was as if lightning had struck, because there was no way she could've known one of *my* favorite things was exactly that, too.

Shaking the remaining blossoms from my hair, I walked back to the house and looked toward our newly painted white barn and the carriage shed nearby. A plump red robin flew across to its nest high in one of the two oak trees Dat planted the day Evan and I were born, and in that moment a frightening thought crossed my mind—something else Leah had told me in a whisper.

On July first there'd be a military draft lottery drawing for nineteen-year-old boys. Even for our Amish fellows, although I was sure most if not all of them had registered as conscientious objectors. I shuddered to think of it. How many more young men would have to die like Jack Herr?

I hurried past our family's fruit store and up the walkway toward the house, my heart filled with dread.

1

From Ellie's spot in the backyard, where she was hanging a quilt on the clothesline, she could see her twin trudging home from Jack Herr's burial service. He was meandering this way through the north side of the orchard, out of view from the house, his shoulders stooped and head bowed. The sight of him made her sad.

Evan's carrying a weight of sorrow, she thought, her heart soft toward him.

She glanced back at the house and wondered if it was safe for her to run out and say something kind to lift her brother's spirits. But she certainly didn't want to call attention to him. Only a few minutes ago, she'd heard a car in the near distance, and still up in her sewing room, Mamm might have heard it, too. No doubt Evan had traveled to and from Carlisle with one of the English neighbor boys.

Her back and neck muscles tense, she kept on with the task of draping bed quilts over the clothesline for their springtime airing. She wished Evan would glance up so she could at least wave or give him a thoughtful smile, but he proceeded to slog toward the yard, eyes on the ground.

My poor brother.

Evan turned toward the barn, and Ellie inhaled with relief. *Surely he'll pull off his black coat and nice shoes and slip Dat's overalls on to groom Nelly or Captain.* That chore helped him unwind sometimes.

It wasn't long now till suppertime, and Dat and Dawdi Hezekiah would be arriving home from the horse auction. Far as she knew, she was the only one aware Evan had left. Jonah would know, though, since he and Evan worked in the orchard together. But that didn't mean Evan had told their brother where he was going.

She slipped off to the stable and found Evan sitting on a three-legged stool in the farthest corner from the stable door, leaning forward, hands covering his face.

"*Bruder?*" she whispered as she crept in. "You *allrecht?*"

He looked up to reveal a tearstained face and removed his straw hat. Then he pulled a white handkerchief from his pocket and wiped his nose. "*Ach*, ya caught me blubberin' my eyes out."

"Maybe splash some cold water on your face at the well pump before ya go inside the house?"

"*Jah*, and I'll get out of these here *gut* clothes, too," he muttered, looking somewhat dazed as he stood. "Honestly, the burial service was the worst thing ever. Jack's family was so solemn. Some were crying. An American flag was draped over the casket, and the military men removed it and folded it real special-like into a tight triangle. And after a bugle played a sad tune, one of the men handed the flag to Jack's weeping mother." Evan swallowed hard.

At the thought of Jack's grieving mother, Ellie pressed her lips together to keep her composure, then drew a deep breath. "My thoughts were with ya the whole time you were gone."

Evan looked at her, eyes rimmed in red. "Kind of ya, Ellie, but my sorrow's nothin' compared to the Herr family's." His voice broke. Then, coughing, he seemed to gather himself. He told her about Jack's great sense of humor and how he always finished his farm chores quickly and was kind to his younger brother, Chuck. "And he was a loyal friend, to be sure. Never seemed to mind that I was Plain and he was fancy when we were out together."

Ellie listened, saying nothing.

"Jack sent me letters in care of the post office, and he told me he was mighty proud of his ability to fight for this country. He wanted to be a help to his fellow soldiers." Shaking his head, Evan slowly walked past Nelly's and Captain's stalls, then pushed open the stable door and headed for the house.

Feeling ever so sad, Ellie hoped Mamm wasn't in the kitchen checking on the roast beef in the cookstove. Evan was in no frame of mind for a talking-to from either parent. Not today.

During the meal that evening, Ellie was thankful for Dawdi's animated talk about the auction. She tried not to fidget or let her thoughts give her away as she recalled her conversation in the barn with Evan earlier. Now and then, she glanced across the table at him, conscious of his unusual silence. *Has Dat or Mamm noticed?*

Evan's eyes met hers, and she sensed his own relief at Dawdi's talking just now.

Dat sat erect in his chair at the head of the table, an obvious indentation in his graying brown hair where he'd worn his straw hat all day. When he passed Mamm's roast beef platter to

Evan for seconds, his gaze lingered on her quiet brother. She held her breath as Dawdi continued describing one of the frisky thoroughbred horses he'd had his eye on "for your Dat here to purchase."

Evan cracked a quick smile, more than likely for Dat's benefit.

When Dawdi stopped talking to dig into the meat on his plate, Mamm said, "Anyone savin' room for dessert? I made a butterscotch pie." She lived for desserts—making and eating them—which Ellie appreciated, having a sweet tooth of her own.

"Oh *jah*. Always," Ellie said, her mouth already watering at the sight of the pie on the counter. *Evan's favorite*, she thought, glad Mamm had made it today.

"I'll make extra-big slices," Mamm said to the obvious pleasure of Ellie's brother, whose dour expression brightened slightly. Now Dawdi was clapping his big calloused hands and grinning at Evan as Mamm rose to cut the pie.

"What all'd yous accomplish in the orchard today, son?" Dat asked, looking straight at him.

"Jonah and I spread fertilizer round the new trees," Evan said, glancing at Ellie.

Dat nodded slowly, studying Evan but good. "How far'd ya get?"

"Far as we could. Was a lot of work."

Dat looked puzzled, making Ellie want to change the subject so he wouldn't ask further questions. But Dawdi chimed in before she could.

"Keepin' an orchard healthy is always a lot of work."

"And mighty worth it," Dat said before taking another bite of his beef.

A clatter of carriage wheels came from the lane, and Ellie

turned to look out the window. There was her closest cousin, strawberry blond Ruthann Kurtz. Moments later she was tying up Bullwhip, her father's road horse, at the hitching post. She liked to drop by in the evening, and Ellie was always happy to see her.

Evan excused himself to go to the side door and step out. He called "Hullo, cousin," which he typically did whenever Ruthann arrived at the tail end of their supper. Her family ate earlier, and besides, their plump cousin loved Mamm's desserts as much as the rest of them did.

Dat moved his chair back from the head of the table, locking eyes with Mamm, still looking befuddled.

Whew, Ellie thought, *Ruthann's come in the nick of time.*

2

Ellie reckoned Mamm would invite Cousin Ruthann to join them at the table like she usually did. Dawdi Hezekiah, as if delighted by a fresh set of ears, wasted no time in beginning to entertain her while Mamm served Ruthann a piece of the butterscotch pie.

"What with Ascension Day comin' up on May seventh, I'm reminded of my *Aendi* Rosanna. She always cooked a big spread and invited us youngsters over for a picnic at her *Haus*," Dawdi said, gray eyes alight and a smile on his wrinkled face. "*Ach*, she had the greenest thumb ever—well, two of 'em. My Mamm always said I inherited my own green thumb from her." Here, he stopped to chuckle. "Seemed like Rosanna could encourage a wilting daisy to perk up with a mere whisper."

"No one's ever told me that 'bout her," Ruthann said.

"'Tis true!" Dawdi insisted, straight-faced. "Saw it with these here eyes," he added as he pointed to them.

"Did she always have a watering can with her, maybe?" Mamm asked, smiling at Ellie. "Was that how she perked up the daisies?"

"Couldn't've been *just* a whisper," Dat said, and Dawdi laughed with him.

"Have ya thought of getting these little anecdotes down on paper?" Ruthann asked Dawdi when all the chuckling quieted down. "I doubt everyone in the family has heard 'em," she said, her pale green eyes sparkling as she forked another bite of the splendid pie.

This seemed to encourage Dawdi all the more. "Well, now that ya mention it . . ."

Dat was nodding in agreement. "Might be a *gut* idea. Family stories—and tall tales—to enjoy and pass down."

Mamm smiled broadly.

Meanwhile, Evan got up to pour more ice water from Mamm's pitcher. Ellie could tell he was restless, but he sat back down. *He's got to be worried Dat'll find out he went to Jack's burial.*

Later, as Ellie and Ruthann cleared the table, Ruthann mentioned going for a walk after dishes were done. "I have somethin' amazing to tell ya," she whispered.

"*Ach,* such a tease!" Ellie said as she turned on the sink's hot water spigot.

The minute Ellie and her cousin headed down the treed lane toward Harvest Drive, Ruthann began talking animatedly about seeing Solomon Bontrager at market that morning.

"Did he ask ya out?" Ellie said. Ruthann had been holding her breath for a date with Sol for some time now.

"*Nee,* but he was quite talkative," she said, grinning. "So I guess there's still hope."

Ellie was happy for Ruthann, as her cousin had waited awhile for a breakthrough like this. "What did yous talk 'bout, or shouldn't I ask?" She was dying to know.

"Sure, but ya might not care to hear it." Ruthann's blue

bandanna billowed out from her head as they turned right onto the road. A market wagon rumbled past, the horse galloping.

"Why wouldn't I wanna hear it?"

Ruthann glanced at Ellie. "Okay, then." She drew a breath. "Sol told me he heard Chuck Herr wants to attend a protest with a bunch of other guys at the square in downtown Lancaster. They're angry 'bout Jack's death . . . don't want the same thing to happen to them or anyone else they know."

Sol worked with Evan in the orchard six days a week, so Ellie wondered if her brother knew anything about this. Many marches and protests calling for the withdrawal of American troops had taken place throughout the war in both Lancaster and other areas of the country, including at the White House in Washington, DC. Like the rest of her family, Ellie had read multiple newspaper accounts of people gathered in these large groups, handing out antiwar flyers, carrying peace signs, and holding candlelight vigils.

"People are upset, Ellie. I mean, *really* upset. Did ya know that close to twelve thousand American soldiers were killed over there just last year? And that was only *one* year!" Ruthann's voice broke.

"Sol told you this?"

Ruthann nodded, slowing her pace now. "'Tween you and me, I'm so relieved he registered as a conscientious objector last year when he turned eighteen."

Ellie immediately thought of Evan. Like Sol, he was the wrong age at the wrong time. *Surely Evan registered as a CO, too.*

"I'm glad Sol spent some time with ya," Ellie said. "It must've made your day."

"And then some." Ruthann's expression brightened. "I'll let ya know if—or when—he invites me out ridin'."

"Maybe he will at the next Singing. Or will ya see him some-where on Ascension Day, maybe? Several picnics are planned for *die Youngie* that day."

"Sol didn't say anything 'bout that, so I'll just go wherever my brother wants to. Yonnie can decide."

"Well, if ya want to get Sol's attention, maybe see if you can find out which picnic he's goin' to."

"That's a great idea." Ruthann paused. "But how can I fish around without him knowin'?"

"I'm sure ya can find a way."

They were coming up on the Bontragers' beef farm now, and Ellie could see her slender brunette friend, Leah, out sweeping the walkway. Then as Ellie and Ruthann were passing the fam-ily's mailbox, Ellie noticed blond-headed Sol himself walking out of the shed in back, carrying a load of wood—for their cookstove, she assumed.

Ruthann must have spotted him, too, because she let out a little gasp. "*Ach*, I should've worn a nicer dress and apron."

"Well, we could just walk over and say hullo to Leah. Maybe then you could wave to Sol."

"But my hair's not very tidy," Ruthann said, shaking her head. "I think we oughta head back to your house."

"But ya wanna get married at some point perty soon, don't ya? Gotta get a fella's eyes on ya somehow."

As they headed back down the hill, Ruthann was quiet. Was she thinking about Sol and the draft lottery? Ellie wondered if her cousin worried about him the way she worried about Evan. If their numbers were called and they refused to go, *Englischers* around here might bully them.

When will this awful war end?

The next morning Lyle Hostetler walked with his eldest son, Jonah, out to the northernmost end of the orchard, where the new apple trees had been planted last month. He was mighty pleased with the thriving orchard his father planted many years before. He remembered walking between the many varieties of fruit trees as a lad, holding his *Daed's* callused hand.

"An orchard is a reminder of God's hand at work on the earth, creating these trees to bear fruit each and every year," Daed would say.

Lyle had come to appreciate God's faithfulness and the seasons that led to the harvest and then repeated the cycle year after year. Working in the orchard was not only his life but his responsibility, though at fifty-six he wasn't quite as spry as a youth. But he could hold his own, even around Evan, who worked the hardest of all.

And then there's Ellie, he thought fondly. It was quite possible his daughter loved the orchard more than any of them. In fact, when it came to working there, she was often the first to volunteer—if her household duties were done.

"Say, did Evan work a full day yesterday?" Lyle asked.

Jonah looked confused. *"Nee,* but I assumed ya knew that."

"Oh?"

"Jah, he got himself all dressed up and hurried out toward the road. He didn't say why he was taking the afternoon off, but I figured he was headed to Jack Herr's burial." He paused. "Didn't ya know they spent time together?"

Lyle shook his head. *"Nee,* and Evan never said a word 'bout goin'." Perplexed, he puffed his cheeks and then blew out the air. He'd read Jack's obituary in the newspaper and heard talk in the community about how devastated the Herr family was. "If that's where he went, though, Evan must've known Jack fairly well."

"Must have." Jonah began working along the drip line of the new trees, spreading fertilizer.

"I'm sure he knows better," Lyle said as he helped. "I mean, the church takes a firm stand on bein' connected in any way to the military. Even burials are off-limits." Lyle clenched his jaw. "Honestly, I suspected Evan was runnin' round with *Englischers*, comin' home all hours as he does sometimes. Once when I bumped into him while returning from checking on ailin' Nelly, he smelled of cigarette smoke, too."

A time or two he'd wondered if Jack and Evan had exchanged letters during the nearly two years Jack was overseas, but he'd never seen any evidence of that. He pulled on his beard. "I have big plans for Evan, so I can't let this slide."

Jonah grimaced. "Evan's of age, Dat, and makin' his own decisions. Under God, you've done your part as a father."

"Yet I wonder where I failed," he said softly.

"Plenty-a fellas did far worse than this during *Rumschpringe* and later got themselves straightened out. I don't think you have to worry 'bout Evan too much."

The sound of a tractor in an English farmer's field down the way caught Lyle's attention as he removed his blue paisley kerchief from his pants pocket to mop his brow. He was mighty disturbed by Evan's apparent interest in fancy folk. How much had they influenced him? Truth be told, Lyle disliked the very idea of *Rumschpringe*, though the running-around years were a coming-of-age tradition for their Amish youth.

Only the Good Lord knows my son's heart, Lyle thought, stuffing his kerchief back into his pocket.

"Has Evan talked yet of bein' baptized?" Jonah asked suddenly, as if he'd been thinking along the same lines.

"Not to me he hasn't." Lyle wasn't too surprised Jonah brought this up. His eldest son had wasted no time joining the church at eighteen, a year before marrying sweet-spirited Priscilla from their local church district.

Inhaling deeply, Lyle tried to reassure himself. Evan had always been devout in the faith, never questioning his upbringing. *Once he's a little older, surely he'll settle down again.*

After supper dishes were done, Ellie strode out to the barn to check on the livestock's water levels. Inside, she could see the large lantern lit on the table Dat and Jonah used for a desk in the office around the corner from the feed bin, and she heard her father talking to someone. Was it Evan?

Her brother had been nowhere to be seen following Mamm's supper of tender pork chops and scalloped potatoes. He hadn't even made an appearance when Rudy, paid to farm the homestead for Dat, had dropped by with feed invoices. And when Mamm told Rudy that Dat was *"quite occupied at the moment,"* Ellie thought something was up. Then Rudy said he was in too big a hurry to stick around, so Dat couldn't be talking to him.

From what she thought was a safe distance, Ellie could hear Dat's voice rising and falling, like he was making a strong point. She cringed at the thought of Evan getting a talking-to, although he'd certainly known better than to go to Jack's burial. It was impossible to make out Dat's words, though, and Ellie didn't want to eavesdrop, so when she'd finished her chore, she slipped out the door and headed toward the house.

On the way, she prayed silently, trusting that if Dat's conversation had indeed been with Evan, he might help steer him back on the straight and narrow. *Surely Evan will tell me 'bout it later,* she thought, almost sensing her brother's distress as she hurried into the house and up the long staircase beyond the kitchen door.

She was thankful the stairs had been constructed at this far end of the house, making it easy for her to slip out to enjoy a breeze on hot summer nights or during a rainstorm—or to stare at the stars and think. Sometimes she talked to God out there, not just limiting herself to the usual rote prayers but silently sharing her private hopes, even though the ministers preached that He already knew them.

When Ellie turned twelve, Mamm had suggested she move from her second-floor bedroom to her sister Lydia's old room on the third floor. Seventeen years older than Ellie, Lydia had married Titus and moved out some years earlier. Jonah had the third-floor room till he married, too, leaving Rudy a room of his own on the second floor, where he stayed till he married and left as well. Ellie's old room, down the hall from Evan's, became Mamm's sewing room.

Ellie had felt honored to be allowed to take the large bedroom on the top floor, nearly as large as Mamm and Dat's own.

The space was rather warm during the months of July and August, but she wouldn't have traded anyone back for her old room. From her two dormer windows, she could view the orchard she loved. And from the north-facing window, she could also see the Bontragers' farmhouse in the distance, where the lantern's yellow glow in Leah's bedroom was snuffed out each night at nine o'clock sharp except on Saturday date nights.

Leah must be excited 'bout seeing Josh Lantz again tonight, Ellie mused, knowing they were seriously courting. Ellie wondered when *her* someone special might ask her out riding. Unfortunately, she was fairly certain that particular fellow didn't even know how much she liked him.

After pinning the washing to the clothesline with Mamm early Monday morning, Ellie carried the food waste out to the compost pile. She spotted Rudy tilling up the large kitchen garden plot for Mamm and looked forward to helping plant all the usual vegetables when it was time.

Over in the orchard, Evan was working with Jonah, Solomon, and Dat, all of them applying liquid soil drench to keep the trees healthy as well as to resist disease. *Makes for very tasty fruit*, Ellie thought.

She wondered when—and if—Evan might tell her about Dat's talk with him, assuming that had taken place. Since the new year, Evan had been working closely with their father, and it crossed her mind that her twin might already be in training to manage the orchard. Dat was known to plan way ahead, a valuable trait in an orchardist. They had to look ten to twenty years into the future for production and plantings. But Evan would have to change his ways.

Ellie sometimes wondered what her life would look like years from now . . . and what kind of work her future husband would do. *Likely a farmer. He wouldn't be an orchardist, not if he's from this church district.* Theirs was the only orchard in Bird-in-Hand.

Ellie walked back to the house, giving thanks to the Lord, grateful for her father's devotion to God and family . . . and his meticulous tending to the orchard.

Still fretting over his talk with Evan two nights ago, Lyle took time after evening chores to select several verses and place bookmarks in his Bible so he could easily find them. He was hoping that reading them during family devotions might underscore what he'd told Evan. His own father had read these verses to him as he was growing up.

At the appointed time, the family gathered in the front room—except for Daed, who'd returned to his *Dawdi Haus* after he mentioned feeling weary.

How full this room had always been before the older boys and Lydia married! It struck Lyle that his two youngest were no longer children. And so far, three out of five had followed the Lord in holy baptism and were walking in the Old Ways. *And now Ellie will be joining church soon,* he thought, at the same time wishing Evan had joined her in taking baptismal classes.

He opened the Good Book.

"Let us remember the importance of this nightly devotional time together as a family," he began, looking at Ellie and then Evan, noticing his son seemed distracted. *Is he pondering what we discussed? Or eager to get on with his evening?*

"Instead of reading a chapter, I've chosen three verses for each of us to think 'bout," he added, wondering if Evan might feel singled out. Still, he felt led to do things this way. "The first is Second Corinthians, chapter six, verse seventeen. 'Wherefore come out from among them, and be ye separate, saith the Lord, and touch not the unclean thing; and I will receive you.'"

Lyle glanced up at Ellie, who was paying close attention, and now Evan was sitting more erect, too, his eyes on him as well. *Is he finally taking this to heart?*

The room was still as he located his next bookmark. "Verse seven in Proverbs chapter four focuses on wisdom, which each of us needs every single day," Lyle said, again primarily for Evan's benefit. "'Wisdom is the principal thing; therefore get wisdom: and with all thy getting get understanding.'"

Praying that his son was still listening, Lyle went on to read the last verse he'd chosen. "Our final verse to consider is found in First Peter, chapter five, verse five. 'Likewise, ye younger, submit yourselves unto the elder. Yea, all of you be subject one to another.'"

His wife fidgeted next to him on the settee. Doubtless Elisabeth was thinking he'd read enough verses tonight for one young man to ponder. "Let's kneel in reverence and thankfulness," Lyle said, trusting the Lord would add His blessing, if not conviction, to the readings.

O Lord, in Thy great kindness and mercy, draw our son Evan into the fold, he prayed silently.

After their prayer time, Lyle wandered out to the kitchen for some coffee. Evan walked past him with Ellie following close behind, and the two headed into the kitchen hallway leading to the side door.

What're they up to? Lyle thought, wondering if he should be worried.

3

"S ure seemed like Dat was preachin' at me tonight," Evan said over his shoulder as Ellie stepped down the porch steps behind him. Then he headed toward the carriage shed.

"Well, he *has* read all those verses to us before," she replied, glad she'd followed her brother out of the house as she caught up to him.

"Not one after the other, though."

He's right.

"Dat had a lot of things to say to me Saturday evening, too," Evan said, removing the straw hat he'd snatched off its hook before they left.

"I wondered who he was talkin' to."

"So ya heard, then?"

"Only from across the barn. Whatever Dat was sayin', he sounded intent on makin' his point."

Evan sighed as they walked out toward the far south end of the meadow, where he stopped and stared at the sky. It was nearly sunset now, and crickets were already chirping in the underbrush near a grove of trees.

"I know you're upset, Evan. You're goin' through a lot right now. But you can talk to me, like always."

Evan seemed to contemplate that, then said, "Dat told me to end my friendships with outsiders."

"Are ya takin' things further than ya should during *Rumschpringe*, maybe?"

Evan hesitated a moment before answering. "Well, Dat wants me to hurry an' get baptized, then settle down with a nice Amish girl."

"Don't ya plan to eventually?" Suddenly Ellie remembered what Evan had said about Cheryl Herr, and a shiver ran through her. "What's so bad 'bout that?"

Evan started walking again. "Think how *you'd* feel if Dat told ya which of your friends were okay and which weren't."

Right then she knew it wouldn't go over well if she said Dat approved of *her* friends, not with the mood Evan was in. "Maybe you can sleep on it some more—and pray 'bout it, too. Prayin' always helps me." She glanced at him. "Remember what Dawdi Hezekiah likes to say: 'You'll be smarter in the mornin'.'"

Evan walked a few more steps before he turned to her. "I wasn't gonna tell ya what I told Dat, Ellie." He looked up at the sky again, squinting now, like he wasn't sure if he should say it at all. "But now, maybe . . ."

"What is it?"

After inhaling slowly, he said, "When I went to the local draft board on my eighteenth birthday, I didn't register as a conscientious objector."

Ellie was stunned. "But you could be drafted and sent off to war!"

Evan shrugged. "The chances of my getting a low lottery number are prob'ly slim."

"Ach, Evan. Won't ya think more 'bout this? Seems awful risky. I mean, if ya went, you'd be goin' against everything we believe in as peacemakers." *And you could die in combat, like Jack.*

"I'm sorry, Ellie. I shouldn't have told ya. But if other men are willing to fight against the spread of communism, why shouldn't I?"

"Ain't sure I understand, but I'm glad ya told me."

"Please don't worry, though."

How can I not? she thought, sad as they started back to the house.

The days passed, and soon it was Thursday, May seventh—Ascension Day—when all the Amish businesses in Lancaster County closed to commemorate Christ's return to heaven after His resurrection.

Ellie's parents and Dawdi Hezekiah had taken time to dress like they were going to Preaching service, then left with Captain, their fastest road horse, hitched to the family carriage to visit relatives in Bird-in-Hand for the day, not far away.

Evan had chosen which special event for the youth he and Ellie should attend and decided on the one at Zeke Mast's farm on Weavertown Road. Zeke was the bishop's oldest son, and a barbecue was planned as well as a volleyball tournament. Ellie was glad they didn't have to ride past the Herr farm on the way. Maybe not having another reminder of Jack would keep her brother's mood light today.

"You ever gonna tell me who ya like, Ellie?" Evan's blue eyes sparkled with amusement as he held the driving lines to Cupcake, the mare Dat bought him three years ago.

"I told ya, I'm not tellin'." She was a little tired from lying awake last night, still worried over what Evan had revealed to her more than two weeks ago. She really just wanted to pretend that conversation hadn't happened. It did feel good to see her brother smiling again, though.

"What if I try an' guess his name?" he teased.

"*Nee!*"

He chuckled now. "It's Menno Bontrager, ain't?"

"Evan!"

He glanced at her, his expression full of mirth. "I guessed, didn't I?"

Ellie folded her arms and pretended to ignore him.

"C'mon," Evan said, pressing again. "I've told ya who *I* like."

She shook her head. "I wish ya hadn't. It makes no sense to date an *Englischer*." Frustrated, she puffed out a breath. She'd prayed that Evan might tire of his penchant for outsiders. "I know at least three Amish girls who'd love to be asked out ridin' with ya. Why not give one a chance?"

Round the bend, they came up on *Onkel* Omar's rambling white clapboard house on the left, set on a wide spread of land with a woodworking shop out back. Ellie looked to see if Aendi Marla was outdoors with their school-age children, but she didn't see anyone. *Maybe they've gone visiting, too.* The way this ride was going with Evan, she wished she'd gone with her parents and Dawdi Hezekiah.

After what seemed like a long pause, Evan said, "Don't fret 'bout so many things, Ellie. Who I see doesn't affect us. We're twins, so we'll always be close."

Ellie sighed. "I care 'bout ya, Evan, and Dat does, too. I know ya like Cheryl, but surely you're not backing away from the faith." She paused for a second. "Maybe you could seek out Deacon Lapp if you have questions."

Evan became quiet, and Ellie felt sure she'd spoiled the rest of their ride together.

Immediately after unhitching the mare and leading her to the big water tank with the other horses, Evan took off to play volleyball. Ellie was pleased to discover that Leah had just arrived with her brother Solomon. She and Leah decided to sit with several other girls on the back porch, including the deacon's niece, seventeen-year-old Arie Ann, and her same-age cousin, Sally. Ellie noted the two girls, both wearing royal blue, were nicely dressed for the occasion. So was Leah, who wore her tan dress and black apron, while Ellie wore her newest plum-colored dress and matching apron.

A folding table placed out on the wide porch held two pitchers of iced meadow tea, drinking glasses, and bowls of popcorn and peeled orange slices.

Ellie glanced around for Cousin Ruthann but didn't see her on the porch or over playing volleyball. How she wished she'd come, since Sol was there. She guessed her cousin hadn't bothered to check on his plans like she'd suggested. *She'll be so disappointed when she finds out.*

While she and Leah sat with the others, Ellie couldn't help noticing that her friend wasn't her usual perky self. Her expression was drawn and serious, and she hardly said a word when spoken to. *Is she feeling under the weather?*

"Say, Ellie," Arie Ann said conspiratorially in a lowered voice, "did ya notice who's here?" The pretty brunette bobbed her head toward the side yard, where both guys and girls were playing volleyball.

Ellie glanced at her. *First Evan and now Arie Ann. Does everyone think they know who I like?*

"Maybe ya missed seein' him when he arrived," Arie Ann added.

"For goodness' sake." Leah surprised Ellie by speaking up.

"It's just us girls," Sally said. "Who're ya talkin' 'bout?"

Ellie held her breath, hoping Arie Ann wouldn't take the bait. But right then the volleyball came flying onto the porch, and all the girls ducked. Ellie got up and tossed the ball back toward the net, thankful for the distraction.

Leah continued to be so quiet, if not solemn, that Ellie was befuddled. *Is she sick, or is it something else?* she wondered as she watched her brother leap into the air to spike the ball.

Evan's team cheered, and Ellie smiled momentarily. But she continued to fret. *What'll happen to my brother if his lottery number is low?*

During the ride back from visiting Elisabeth's older brother Jesse and his family on Leacock Road, near the shoe store, Lyle's father brought up a niggling topic discussed during their time there.

"So many deaths from the war, all of them unnecessary," Daed said from the second buggy seat. "Makes me sick to my stomach. I hate to think we'll never see some young men like Jack Herr round the area again."

Seated up front next to Lyle, Elisabeth let out a long sigh.

"Fighting's displeasin' to God. Such a senseless way to meet one's end."

"*En Sin un e Schand,*" Lyle said, agreeing with her.

"A sin and a shame is right," Daed declared.

Lyle recalled what Jesse had told them during the noon meal. Evidently, the son of his English neighbor had come home from Vietnam seriously wounded, and Lyle had been troubled by Jesse's description of the helicopter crash that caused the young man's terrible injuries. *He's fortunate to be alive,* he thought as Daed continued to talk about the war.

"Just ain't right," Daed was saying. "So many family trees with broken-off branches. Even the young men who do make it home aren't the same."

Elisabeth looked over at Lyle. "I don't wanna be critical, but the military lottery just seems wrong to me. Like gamblin' with lives . . . as if war itself isn't bad enough," she said, a quaver in her voice. "How am I s'posed to feel? How is any parent s'posed to feel? And now that Evan's told you he didn't register as a CO, I wonder every day what's to happen if he gets called up."

"*Ach,* love, ya mustn't stew." Lyle wanted to reassure her. "We'll live each day as it comes."

Elisabeth folded her hands in her lap and stared at them.

Lyle felt guilty for giving her advice he himself found hard to follow. To think that their youngest son—"sweet Evan," as his mother had called him when he was a child—had seemingly hardened his heart against the Old Ways.

Lyle blamed *Rumschpringe* as the culprit. *Like playing with fire!*

4

That Sunday was Mother's Day. Ellie made a large skillet omelet for everyone at breakfast and gave Mamm a hand-crafted card, Evan presented her with a card he'd purchased in town, and Dat marked the day with a large tray of her favorite pansies for her flower garden. They weren't for making much fuss over either Mother's Day or Father's Day, but Dat had always led the way in doing a little something special for Mamm.

Later that morning, Ellie enjoyed attending the baptismal instruction class and then the Preaching service, where she noticed several families absent. Of course, they might have been visiting other church districts in Bird-in-Hand or Ronks, spending the day with elderly mothers.

By the time Singing rolled around that evening, Ellie couldn't have been happier when Evan, as he often did, offered to take her there in his black open carriage. The sky was still light and the day warm as they rode to the big two-story barn a mile and a half away. Busy as Evan had been in the orchard, they'd spent little time with each other these past three days since the barbecue on Ascension Day, and she was pleased at how talkative he was.

When they arrived at the farm hosting the Singing, Evan pulled partway into the long dirt lane and halted the horse right there, the driving lines still in his hands. "Have yourself a *gut* evening, Ellie."

She was startled, if not confused. "Ain't ya comin'?"

Evan shook his head slowly. "Meeting someone."

"Oh," she said softly.

"I already asked Sol to give ya a ride home if you don't go out ridin' with someone. Figured since he lives up the road from us, he wouldn't mind."

"Well, what if he asks someone out, though?" She was thinking of Cousin Ruthann.

"Sol seemed fine with it, so I wouldn't worry 'bout that."

Leah's younger brother had always been neighborly toward Ellie—and they'd played together as children, especially when Evan was around—so she guessed it was all right.

"*Denki* for not askin' Menno," she said, indirectly admitting he was indeed the boy she liked. When and if the time came, she preferred it be Menno's idea to offer her a ride home.

Evan nodded and smiled. "Oh, and I'd appreciate it if ya didn't tell Dat I didn't stay. It would only worry him all the more," he said as Ellie stepped down from the buggy. "I'll be home at the usual hour."

"Okay." Ellie nodded in agreement but felt strange about it, realizing Evan was likely going against Dat's wishes even after that stern talk last month. Concern snaked through her as she made her way up toward the dirt lane leading to the back of the bank barn.

Inside the newly swept haymow, *die Youngie* talked and mingled about. Leah spotted Ellie as she entered and hurried over to sit with her on one of the wood benches beside the long tables.

"I've been wanting to tell ya somethin'," Leah said in a hushed tone, her dark eyes serious.

Ellie was hungry for some good news, but the way Leah's mouth turned downward, she wasn't sure she should expect any. "You okay?"

Leah leaned closer. "My beau an' I won't be seein' each other anymore."

"*Ach*, no." Ellie was shocked.

"Josh and I broke up Thursday morning." Leah looked down at her folded hands.

So that was why she seemed so glum at the barbecue? "I'm sorry to hear it," she said, feeling so sad for Leah. She'd been sweet on Josh since the fifth-grade spelling bee.

"And there's somethin' else." Leah paused and glanced away, like what she had to say next was harder than what she'd just revealed. "*Ach*, I hope ya won't be too upset, Ellie."

What could be worse?

"I've decided to accept a live-in job with a young English mother who really needs the help. Her husband left her after returning from the war, maimed and very troubled." Leah paused and chewed the inside of her lip. "The thing is, though, it's in Chambersburg."

Ellie couldn't make her lips move to speak. Leah had never showed any interest in moving away, let alone so far. And to live with an *Englischer*!

Leah gave her a faint smile. "I know it seems like a sudden decision, but the timing seems right to me. And I've already met the woman—Carolyn Madison, a cousin of Cheryl Herr's. Carolyn's parents live in Tennessee, so she's alone with the children. With her husband gone, it's more than she can handle. She needs to go back to her nursing job."

Ellie was still too flabbergasted to speak.

"When I heard about it from Cheryl recently at the fabric store, I had a strong feeling I was s'posed to contact Carolyn." Leah's brown eyes glinted in the corners. "Have ya ever felt like that?"

Nee. And the only thing Ellie could think about at the moment was Leah's going away. It felt like a bee sting to her heart.

"It's the saddest thing, really," Leah continued. "She has three small children—a four-year-old boy and three-year-old twin girls."

Ellie's stomach knotted. "You'll be so far away," she said in protest as words came to her at last.

"I know, but we'll write to each other, *jah?*" Leah looked more cheerful now, but Ellie knew her well enough to suspect she was only trying to make this easier on her.

Don't be so selfish, Ellie scolded herself, thinking of the plight of the young woman and her children. But she couldn't pretend it would be easy with Leah so far away, and it would be hard to think of her living with an *Englischer,* considering the attachment Evan had obviously developed with a non-Amish family.

"You'll always be my dearest friend," Leah said, attempting to reassure her.

Yet Ellie wondered how that would be possible now. "We were gonna be baptized together this fall, remember?"

"Believe me, I thought of that. Guess I'll be continuing with *Rumschpringe* for a while yet."

Like Evan. "Did ya forget our childhood dreams for a double wedding?" she whispered.

"We still might have that. Who knows?"

But how? Ellie sighed.

Ellie really needed a drink of water, but she didn't want to go over to the refreshment table. So instead, she walked to the barn door and slid it open. Leah followed her out and down the long slope toward the well pump in the backyard.

"I tried to think when would be best to tell ya," Leah was saying as she hurried to keep up with Ellie. "I guess I should've waited till after Singing, but I figured you'd go ridin' with one of the fellas, and then there'd be no time to talk much before I leave."

Ellie realized Leah must have already been thinking this through during the Ascension Day barbecue. And she cared too much to cause her friend more distress. "How soon must ya go?" she asked, pumping the handle hard. When the water came, she cupped her hands and drank.

"Day after tomorrow."

"Tuesday? *Ach,* so soon? When will ya return home?"

Leah's lip quivered. "Not sure. Could be months. But it's a *gut* opportunity to bring in some extra money for the family."

Ellie lightly shook her hands in the air to dry them. "I wish things could stay the same."

"You always say that, Ellie." Leah touched her arm. "You hate change."

She's right, she thought, still trying to make sense of all this as she wrapped her arms around herself. "S'pose you've already talked to Bishop Mast 'bout not continuing on with baptism classes."

"Not yet, but I will. And please keep this a secret—at least for now."

The parent sponsors were coming across the yard toward the barn, and Leah waved at them. "*Denki* for hostin' Singing tonight," she had the manners to say.

Ellie waved, too, not wanting to seem aloof or ungrateful.

But she felt sick at the thought of losing Leah. *This wasn't supposed to happen!*

They headed back up the hill and around to the haymow door, where Leah's very handsome twenty-year-old cousin Menno Bontrager was about to enter. Seeing them, he quickly stepped aside and waited.

"*Denki*," Ellie said, finding her voice at last. She recalled the first time the rather shy Menno had ever spoken to her—maybe five years ago now. She'd been waiting in the rain for Dat to pick her up from market when Menno came running outside and handed her a big black umbrella. "*I don't need it,*" he'd said before dashing across the field toward home in the drenching downpour.

She smiled at the memory—ah, those golden-brown eyes!

"Nice night, ain't?" Menno said presently, his light brown bangs all fluffy and clean beneath his straw hat.

Ellie nodded, surprised he'd spoken to her.

"You're practically late," Leah said, scolding him.

"Well, I stopped to give a hitchhiker a lift."

"Oh," Leah said kindly, like she regretted chiding him.

"That was *gut* of ya," Ellie said, wondering if the hitchhiker was one of the many wounded soldiers all over the county. They were everywhere across Lancaster, it seemed, military boys who'd returned home injured. *And then there are those like Jack Herr who never made it home at all.*

Ellie followed Leah inside and sat at the long table with her. *Our last Singing together for now,* she thought wistfully, remembering how she'd felt at their first-ever Singing three years ago. She'd been nervous at the thought of being invited to ride with one of the fellows in his courting carriage. She would have preferred to stay home, actually, spending the evening talking with Mamm or reading a good book. Over time, though, she'd become accustomed to attending Singings and other youth activities. Having Leah there most of the time helped.

Now the fellows were wandering over to the table, preparing to stop visiting and sing. But Ellie's heart—and her singing voice—was far from ready to join in. With Evan skipping out tonight and Leah suddenly moving away, Ellie felt as limp as days-old lettuce.

5

Ellie stood with Cousin Ruthann near the refreshment table after Singing, planning to bake cookies for two elderly shut-ins in the church district. "*Kumme en mei Haus* on Thursday morning," Ellie suggested, wanting something to look forward to after Leah's leaving.

"*Ach*, what's wrong?" Ruthann said, stepping closer and adjusting the shoulder strap on her purse. "You look discouraged."

Struggling with what to say since Leah had asked her to keep her news quiet for the time being, Ellie said with a heavy exhale, "I'm a little out of sorts."

"Oh? Why's that?"

Just then Ellie spotted Sol and his younger brother, Aaron, coming toward them. Maybe when Sol took her home, he would take Ruthann home, too. Ellie could almost feel the pent-up hope in her cousin. But before Sol reached them, Menno wandered over and paused at the table like he was deciding which type of cookie to eat on the way out.

Then he glanced in Ellie and Ruthann's direction. "Might yous need a ride home?"

Ruthann looked at Ellie expectantly. *Does she realize I like Menno?*

Then Sol waved at Ellie like he was telling her to go, so she said, "*Jah. Denki,*" and then followed Menno out the haymow door, Ruthann behind her.

This'll work fine, she thought, thrilled Menno had volunteered. *Ruthann will just have to find a way to spend more time with Sol on her own.*

"Nice of ya to offer," Ruthann said, making small talk.

"We really appreciate it," Ellie added, wanting to express her gratitude, too, but trying not to show her excitement.

"Glad to help," Menno said. He hurried around to the right side of the open buggy and stepped in, his long legs scarcely fitting beneath the dashboard.

Ellie sat next to Menno, and Ruthann got in next, a tight squeeze in the two-seater courting carriage.

During the ride, Menno surprisingly asked Ellie whether the orchard hired any seasonal workers.

"Well, since we're not a pick-your-own kind of orchard, we do have part-time and seasonal workers. You'd have to talk to my brother Jonah or Dat 'bout that."

"I know my cousin Sol works there durin' the apple and peach harvests," Menno said with a glance at Ellie.

"*Jah,* Solomon's worked quite a few years now for us." She didn't know what more to tell him, since it wasn't her responsibility to take job applications. But she did think that as quiet and kind as Menno was, he'd likely be a diligent worker.

"I could use a part-time job around that time," Menno said. "Besides, I'm curious 'bout orchard work and what it involves."

Ellie's ears perked up. "Ya can't go wrong workin' in the best place on earth," she declared.

"Can ya tell she's partial to her orchard?" Ruthann said, laughing a little.

"My orchard?" Ellie smiled. *Don't I wish.*

Menno smiled but didn't comment.

Ellie could hear crickets in the grass along the roadside and an owl hooting in a tree as they passed.

Ruthann spoke up again. "Say, Menno, did ya happen to know Jack Herr?"

Ellie was surprised her cousin would bring up Jack—and out of the blue, too. But maybe after what Sol told her about Chuck, she was just curious.

"Well, I ran into Jack here and there around town a couple of times before he left for boot camp. I wouldn't call myself a friend of his, but he was a nice fella. I feel terrible for his family. And Jack spoke highly of Evan the few times I was around him."

"I'm not surprised," Ruthann said. "After all, Evan's one of my best cousins." She smiled at Ellie. "Well, next to this one, of course."

Menno smiled, eyes focused on the road.

A few moments later, a courting carriage tried to pass them, and Menno courteously slowed the horse to allow them to get by. His thoughtful manner stuck in Ellie's head even after Menno dropped her off and left to take Ruthann home.

Dat would be impressed with him, she mused as she headed around to the side door. But she couldn't help wondering who Menno had actually wanted to ride with tonight. *Is he interested in Ruthann? Or in me?*

Indoors, she found Mamm reading their German Bible, the King James Bible open on the kitchen table next to it. Dat was around on the back section of the wraparound porch, talking with Dawdi Hezekiah, and she remembered Menno's apparent interest in orchard work.

What would it be like seeing him every day during harvest? she wondered, smiling.

By the time Ellie came downstairs again after breakfast on Monday morning, Mamm had already rinsed their clothes and run them through the wringer. Mamm was particular about how she did things, and she liked to have time alone to pray while sorting and washing the clothes. It fell to Ellie, then, to shake out the flattened clothes and carry them outside to the clothesline. She and Mamm had done it this way ever since Lydia married and left home more than a dozen years ago.

The day was already warming up with an occasional breeze, ideal for drying. Ellie squinted into the sky, cupping her hands over her eyes. "Leah's comin' over tomorrow after breakfast," she told Mamm.

"To help with your chores?" Mamm reached into the clothespin bag hanging off the line.

Ellie glanced at her, certain if Leah's news had made its way to her mother through the grapevine, she wouldn't have asked. "*Nee*, just to visit a short while," she said, turning her head toward the carriage shed. She wondered when Evan had come in last night, because earlier she'd noticed dark circles under his eyes. Despite that, he seemed to be in a better mood at breakfast. Helpful, too, offering to carry several boxes of canning jars to the cellar for Mamm.

"*Don't even think 'bout pickin' them up, Mamm,*" he'd said, humorously flexing his muscles. "*That's my job.*"

Mamm had chortled. As far as Mamm was concerned, it was like Evan could do no wrong. Of course, she would never be pleased to know he'd been friends with Jack Herr and hadn't registered as a CO. Had Dat told her about all of that? Ellie was very sure they didn't keep secrets from each other.

Ellie got up a little earlier than usual the next day to make cinnamon rolls for Leah's visit. Given that Mamm still didn't seem to know anything about Leah's plan to live and work in Chambersburg, she felt awkward about it and was glad to be alone in the kitchen. *Ninety-eight long miles away,* she thought, having determined the distance using Dat's old atlas in the tall bookcase in the front room. She wasn't looking forward to saying good-bye today and felt sad to see Leah off.

After the family's breakfast of homemade waffles and German sausage, which Ellie had only picked at, she washed the dishes while waiting for Leah to arrive. Mamm had gone upstairs to iron and to give the girls some time alone to talk, something she often did when Leah came to visit.

At last, the Bontrager family carriage pulled into the lane. When Leah arrived at the screen door, Ellie swallowed hard at the sight of her closest friend. *"Kumme en,"* she said, wiping her hands on her white work apron.

"Smells *gut*." Leah looked a little tired.

Ellie uncovered the cinnamon rolls. "I made your favorite."

"You didn't have to," Leah said, sitting at the table.

Ellie felt a lump in her throat. "Would ya like some coffee to wash it down?"

"Sure, but I can't stay too long, really. I still have a few things to do at home, and I don't want to miss the bus to Chambersburg."

For pity's sake, thought Ellie. While she'd suggested to Mamm that Leah might stay for only a short while, she'd mistakenly assumed they'd have time for a leisurely visit.

"*Es dutt mir leed*," Leah said.

I'm sorry, too, thought Ellie.

"I know you're probably disappointed, 'specially after going to all this fuss," Leah said, taking a roll. "Leavin' like this is just as hard on me, honestly. I don't want to draw it out."

Then don't go, Ellie thought, pouring coffee into two mugs.

"Is your Mamm home?" Leah asked.

"She's upstairs. Doesn't seem to know 'bout your plans."

"Hardly anyone does at this point."

Ellie frowned, puzzled. "Is it still a secret, then?"

"Not really." Leah glanced out the window, blinking. "Guess I don't want anyone tryin' to talk me out of it."

Ellie gave Leah a wry smile. "Knowin' how you set your mind to do things, do ya think they'd try?"

Leah shrugged. "My parents sure did."

Ellie understood now, though she couldn't say she disagreed with Leah's parents. Since Leah wasn't baptized yet, going to work for an *Englischer*—and someone none of them really knew—was a huge step for her. And that Carolyn Madison lived so far away made it all the more worrisome. "This is a drastic move for ya, Leah. I'm concerned. Are ya sure you should go?" It was hard getting the words out, but she'd never known her friend to be so impulsive.

Leah sniffled and pulled out a hankie from beneath her dress sleeve to dab at her eyes. "Like I said, it's a *gut* opportunity to bring in some extra money for the family . . . and, well, it seems like the right time."

"Because of the breakup with Josh?" She hated to bring this up, but Leah seemed quite emotional, and it didn't seem like her friend had thought everything through.

"*Nee*, it's not about Josh."

Ellie listened, struggling to believe that Leah knew her own mind. "Couldn't ya take some time to think it over . . . pray 'bout it, too?"

"Oh, I've done that." Sighing, Leah pulled a slip of paper from her dress pocket and set it on the table. "Here's my new address. Sol says he'll write me, but I don't know how often. I'd love if *you'd* write whenever ya can."

"I will." Ellie took another sip of coffee, then a small bite of her roll.

They locked eyes for the longest time without speaking. Ellie remained convinced Leah's breakup with Josh had something to do with her emotional response today. She didn't want to make things worse by asking again, but she hoped Leah might tell her more in a letter after she was settled in Chambersburg.

"By the way, I noticed my cousin Menno gave you a ride home after Singing," Leah said, unexpectedly changing the subject.

"Well, it wasn't only me," she said. "Ruthann was along, too."

"But it's a start, *jah*?" Leah's eyes twinkled for a brief moment.

So she's figured out I like Menno—Ruthann probably has, as well, thought Ellie, blushing.

But it was too soon to know what Menno was thinking, though she did feel a sliver of hope.

"Let me know what comes of it, okay?" Leah said.

"I will." Ellie could hear Mamm walking around upstairs. "What should I tell Mamm 'bout your leavin'?"

"Once I'm gone, feel free to tell her or anyone else what I told ya."

"All right."

Leah reached across the table for Ellie's hand. "Please don't cry . . . or I won't be able to go through with it."

Ellie clasped her hand, gazing into the expressive brown eyes she knew so well. They'd not only encouraged her through the years but could read her like an unlocked diary. "I'll pray for ya every day, Leah," she said softly. "And I'll miss our long walks and talks."

"It's prob'ly not for too long. Besides, I'll be in touch, I promise." Leah's eyes glistened.

"I'll count on that."

When it was time for Leah to leave, Ellie walked her out to the buggy, where she untied the horse and readied the driving lines. "The Lord be with ya, Leah," she said, stepping back from the wheels.

"*Da Herr sei mit du,*" Leah replied, waving and then picking up the lines. "I'll be sure to write."

Ellie smiled, and in a minute Leah was gone.

Ellie plodded back to the house and sat on the side of the porch, where Mamm had put out some pots with the purple and yellow pansies Dat gave her for Mother's Day. And for a good fifteen minutes or more, Ellie pondered what had happened.

I can't believe she's leaving.

All the years they'd planned out their lives together—double-dating, family homes within an easy walk, their children growing up to be best friends just like *they* were. Was any of that going to happen now?

She sighed deeply. *No one'll ever take Leah's place.*

6

Wednesday morning, Lyle recognized Frank Herr at the historic Old Village Store in Bird-in-Hand. Jack's father had aged significantly, even lost weight, since Lyle had seen him out riding his lawnmower last summer. *Grief can do that,* Lyle thought as he caught the man's eye.

Dressed in dark blue bib overalls and a white undershirt like many of the Yankee farmers in the area wore, Frank was waiting to pay the cashier. Suddenly, he stepped out of line and came toward Lyle in the hardware section of the store. "Your son Evan has been a wonderful encouragement to our family since Jack's death." He paused, seemingly to collect himself. "Thanks for allowing him to spend time with us."

Speechless, Lyle nodded.

"And if I'm not mistaken, our Cheryl has a little crush on him."

Lyle quickly found his tongue. "Oh?"

"They're young yet. I'm sure it's simply friendship."

Better be, Lyle thought, recalling how attractive Cheryl was. "Well, once Evan's baptized, I 'spect he'll stay closer to home."

He could tell the man wanted to engage him in conversation. The pain behind his eyes was quite apparent.

"To be clear, we wouldn't think of stepping on any toes when it comes to that," Frank was quick to reply.

Now Lyle was embarrassed at his awkward response, but he thought it might be better to leave things at that. Besides, he wasn't sure what more to say, except "My wife and I are mighty sorry for your loss."

"That's very kind." Frank reached out to shake his hand. "I appreciate it."

Nodding again, Lyle excused himself and returned to looking for the metal brackets he needed for an extra shelf in the barn office.

The sun was peeking in and out of thick layers of clouds as Ellie walked out to get the mail that afternoon. As she carried the letters indoors and up to the sewing room, where Mamm was mending Dat's older britches, her mind was on Leah. Now that her dear friend was gone, it was okay to tell Mamm what Leah was up to.

Placing the mail on top of the oak spool cabinet, Ellie said, "Looks like a couple of letters for you."

"*Denki*, dear." Mamm glanced at her. "You seem a bit sad."

"I am," Ellie said, and told her all that Leah had shared.

"So she's already left?" Mamm looked flabbergasted.

"Yesterday, *jah*." She paused. "There was no talkin' her out of it, and she didn't seem troubled by the fact she's bound to be influenced by the world. She said she really wants to help this young English mother."

"I can't imagine what the poor woman's goin' through."

"Such a tragedy."

Mamm nodded her agreement. "And Leah's your closest friend. I'm truly sorry to hear this."

Ellie sighed. "To be honest, I'm disappointed we won't be finishing baptismal instruction together."

"I'm sure her parents are worried 'bout that, too. And to think she'll be that far away." Mamm shook her head sadly.

"Even so, Leah will surely be baptized in a year or so, when she returns."

"We'll keep her in prayer, for certain."

Ellie nodded her agreement. "She'll need it."

Before bedtime that evening, Ellie looked out over at the Bontrager farmhouse. Leah's window was ever so dark now. She wondered how Leah would feel if Sol, *her* close brother, hadn't registered as a CO. *Wouldn't she be as worried about him as I am about Evan?* she pondered. She hadn't wanted to tell her friend about Evan's troubling news before she left for Chambersburg and was feeling wrung out and needing to pray just now.

Ellie knelt beside the bed and folded her hands in front of her face.

Dear Lord in heaven, I thank Thee for all the years of my friendship with Leah. Please, I pray, keep her from straying from the Old Ways and from Thy plan for her life. Bless her for being willing to help the troubled family in Chambersburg. Be ever near her and remind her of Thy great love, O Lord. And give Evan wisdom to realize he is not doing Thy will—not even close. I pray these things in Thy holy name. Amen.

Ellie awoke the next day, looking forward to Ruthann's visit and baking with her. But her cousin had a way of sensing things, and if Ellie wasn't bright and cheery, she'd ask what was bothering her. Not ready to talk about Leah's departure just yet—still feeling numb about it—she was determined to keep a pleasant attitude.

After making scrambled egg muffins for breakfast with Mamm, she cut the lawn with the push mower. When she stopped to wipe her brow with her hankie, she heard the familiar song of a black-capped chickadee—a whistled *fee-bee-ee*. Looking around, she saw its black-and-white head as it scavenged amongst the bushes near the cider-making shed, a few yards from the small family fruit store where she waited on customers four days a week, trading off with Dat and sometimes Mamm, too.

Again, Ellie heard the chickadee singing its heart out. *Maybe we need another birdhouse round here.* She glanced at the side yard, where Evan had erected two tall purple martin birdhouses several years ago. *Was he spending time with Jack Herr and other worldly fellows even then?* she wondered. She was upset with herself for not guessing sooner, if that was the case.

But wasn't it? On the day Evan told her that he was going to Jack's burial, he'd also mentioned he had started exploring what he might be missing before he was even fifteen.

When Cousin Ruthann arrived, the two of them set to work making butterscotch cookies, another of Evan's favorites. Ruthann told her she'd heard through the grapevine that Sol had attended the Ascension Day barbecue at Zeke Mast's farm. "I can't tell ya how upset I am about not goin' to the *right* picnic," she said. "It's annoying."

"Well, you were with Sol at Singing last Sunday," Ellie said, reminding her. "He talked to ya during refreshments, ain't so?"

Ruthann shrugged. "He said hi to me, but that was mostly it. And then Menno offered us a ride. . . ." She grimaced. "Anyway, I still can't believe Sol was at the barbecue where you and Evan were . . . and I wasn't."

"You should've come with *us*," Ellie said, teasing now.

"Oh, next time I will."

Ellie suggested she should be sure to smile at Sol next time she saw him at market or after Preaching. "Don't be shy, okay?"

Later, when the cookies had cooled, Ruthann insisted on their taking her father's carriage to deliver the cookies to two women—one who'd broken her right wrist and the other grieving her close friend's recent passing. Between houses, Ruthann looked over at Ellie and said, "I think you should know somethin'."

Will this be gut news? Ellie wasn't sure she could take more sadness.

"After Menno dropped you off Sunday night, he asked if you were seein' anyone."

Ellie's ears perked up. "You wouldn't fib to me, would ya?"

"Never." She nudged Ellie with her elbow. "It seemed very clear why he was askin'."

Ellie was grinning now. "I'm glad ya told me."

"I knew you'd be happy."

"Why'd ya wait this long to say somethin'?" she asked, eager to write to Leah about this.

"Guess I wanted to spread out the joy."

Ellie laughed. "For mercy's sake!"

"Hey, wouldn't it be nice if Sol and I could double-date with you and Menno sometime?" Ruthann asked.

"Sure would." Ellie tried not to get her hopes up, though. Menno, after all, was the most attractive fella around Bird-in-Hand. Shy as he was, he still must know lots of girls who would like to date him.

"Of course, Sol would have to ask ya out, too, *jah?*" Ellie said, teasing her cousin again.

During the next week and a half, Ellie worked in the orchard alongside Evan whenever she had a spare moment. She didn't mind carrying a shovel to tamp down the soil around the newly planted trees or using a sickle to cut grass near the trunks of trees before the fruit store opened in the morning. Dat had insisted she didn't have to help with "men's work" after her indoor chores with Mamm were finished, but Ellie merely smiled. *Dat should know by now I'd rather be here than anywhere else.*

On May twenty-third, the Saturday before the next Singing, Sol stopped to talk to Ellie near the easternmost border of the orchard near Leacock Road. She was assessing the shape of several larger trees, trying to decide which ones might require further pruning.

"I don't want to jump ahead of Menno if he hasn't asked ya yet, but . . ."

"Asked me what?"

A sheepish expression crept onto Sol's face. "Well, about doubling up with Ruthann and me after Singing tomorrow night."

"If he'd like to, that's fine." Ellie tried to keep her tone casual despite her excitement for both her and her cousin.

"*Gut.* I already asked Ruthann, and we're both lookin' forward to it."

Ellie smiled. She couldn't believe it, and she was sure her cousin was as happy as she was. *At last!*

Midway through Singing the next evening, Ellie was delighted when Menno approached her about doubling up with Sol and Ruthann. Not letting on that Sol had already revealed the idea to her, Ellie smiled in agreement.

"We'll ride around in Sol's father's buggy, then head over to my older brother's place for ice cream," Menno said as they stood by the refreshment table. He looked handsome in the black dress trousers, vest, and coat he'd worn to Preaching that morning, and his exceptional eyes captured her attention yet again.

"That'll be nice." She was somewhat relieved that their first time out together wouldn't be a solo date.

It was starting to rain when she and Menno climbed into the back seat of Sol's buggy, and he commented on how good it was that they had an enclosed one.

"A little rain wouldn't hurt, though," she said.

"Well, in late May, it can make down real *gut* sometimes."

"I s'pose. Besides, we wouldn't all fit in a courting carriage anyway," she added with a laugh.

"No kiddin'," Sol said from the front seat as he picked up the driving lines. Ruthann smiled at them over her shoulder.

The ride took them past the southernmost tip of the orchard, then over to East Gordon Road and on to Belmont Road. A train whistled in the near distance, but Ellie paid it little mind since they'd already passed the railroad crossing.

Sol was more talkative than Menno, which wasn't a surprise to Ellie. Menno had always been more reserved, though from observing him stand around with the fellows at youth activities, she was aware he could be quite talkative with people he knew.

Ruthann, on the other hand, was fully engaged in conversation with Sol. They were talking about the upcoming chicken barbecue to raise money to support the work of the volunteer Hand-in-Hand Fire Company firefighters that served the Bird-in-Hand community.

While Menno glanced at Ellie to smile occasionally, he didn't say much unless Sol asked him a question, and Ellie felt too shy to talk much herself. Later, though, Menno told her he'd arranged to help his father's cousin with haying and other tasks in the Big Valley area until mid-July.

"So you won't be able to work in the orchard, then?" she asked.

"Oh, I'll be back for the peach and apple harvest, if help is needed." He paused to look at her. "And I'll write ya, too, when I can."

Ellie was happy to hear the latter, but a little sad that she wouldn't be seeing much of him for weeks on end.

During their visit to Menno's brother's farm, Menno talked quietly with Ellie as they ate homemade chocolate chip ice cream. He hesitantly mentioned hearing that Evan hadn't registered as a conscientious objector.

Ellie nodded. "*Jah*, Evan told me that, too."

"Well, it wonders me," Menno said, frowning. "Doesn't he know he could be drafted if he gets a low lottery number?"

While Menno was right, she wasn't going to be disloyal to

her brother. "I s'pose you'd have to ask him," she replied, aware that Menno didn't have to think about this year's lottery since he'd turned twenty last November.

"I'm sorry, Ellie," Menno said now. "Don't mean to bring up a sore point."

"Honestly, it's in the back of my mind all the time."

"I'm sure it is." Menno gave her an endearing smile, those golden-brown eyes twinkling, and her heart fluttered.

7

On the first of July, Lyle had to keep himself occupied so he wouldn't be anxious about that day's annual lottery draft drawing. He worked either in the orchard or in the office he shared with Jonah in the barn, and he even went back out to the orchard after supper. There, he found his father walking amongst the apple trees.

"Best time of the day, *jah?*" Daed glanced at him. "Even on such a night."

Lyle knew what he meant. They'd all been on edge about the lottery drawing. "How far do ya expect to walk?" he asked, thankful they still had a few more hours of daylight.

"Oh, maybe down to Leacock Road and back," Daed said flatly. "Been sayin' a prayer for Evan, to tell the truth. 'Tis all I can think of here lately."

Lyle nodded. "Hard not to, ain't?"

His father reached through a low branch to pick a Yellow Transparent apple, which fell right off the stem. He wiped it off on his black work trousers and took a bite.

Lyle really wished Evan would give up his *Rumschpringe*, his excuse for running around with outsiders. It was exasperating the way he clung to it.

They walked farther, enjoying the quiet evening. His father's apple was so ripe that juice ran down his chin, onto his long white beard. But he didn't seem to mind. There was something childlike about his enjoyment.

"Here," Lyle said, offering his blue paisley handkerchief.

Daed quietly wiped his chin.

They continued to walk in silence, and Lyle sensed that his father wanted to be alone with his thoughts. So after a time, Lyle said he was ready to head back to the house. Daed waved him on nonchalantly, and Lyle decided to go around to the front porch, since Elisabeth and Ellie were shelling peas out back. *Probably trying to keep busy,* he thought, needing to sit alone for a while and watch the horses and buggies pass by. The soothing *clip-clop-clip* of hooves would keep him focused on the here and now.

A few minutes later, a car pulled up and parked on the road near the front lawn. The driver was a young man Lyle didn't recognize, but the windows were rolled down enough for him to spot Evan on the passenger side. For a few minutes, he could hear the two of them discussing something, and rather heatedly at that. Then abruptly, Evan opened his door and got out. A few seconds later, the car took off again, shooting away from the shoulder and onto the road.

Evan plodded up the maple-lined lane, shaking his head, eyes cast down.

Lyle rose from the brown wicker chair and called to him. "Son!"

Seemingly startled, Evan looked up, then forced a smile. He gestured toward the house, obviously not wanting to talk.

Tempted to say more, Lyle let it go, hard as it was.

Evan stuffed his hands into his trouser pockets and hurried on his way across the yard.

Lyle's heart throbbed with sudden dread.

———

As Ellie was coming down the stairs with a pillowcase she had been embroidering a few minutes earlier, she heard the screen door slap. By the time she'd turned past the small pantry at the far end of the kitchen, Evan was at the sink, turning on the spigot, his neck and face red.

"*Bruder?*" she said. "You all right?"

He splashed water on his face, then reached for the hand towel and dried it off. "Heard the lottery drawing on Chuck Herr's car radio," he said, looking at her. "Mine's twenty-five."

"That low?" she whispered, pulse pounding. She set the pillowcase on the counter, her threaded needle pushed into the fabric.

Evan placed the towel on the counter near a bunch of ripe peaches ready to be made into jam and headed into the front room.

Ellie couldn't help herself; she followed him in there and took a seat across the room from him. "Do Dat and Mamm know?"

Evan grimaced. "Not yet."

She groaned softly.

Evan rubbed his hands over his face, then folded his arms and looked out the window, expressionless.

———

Lyle waited a while before heading into the house to gather his thoughts. He reached for the back screen door and stepped inside. Elisabeth was making a fresh pot of coffee on the stove. "Where's Evan?" he asked before sitting at the table. "I thought he came inside."

"He went to the barn a little while ago, just as I came up from the cellar." She reached for coffee mugs from the cupboard. "I'll put out some chocolate chip meringue bars in case he wants to join us later."

"*Gut* idea," Lyle said, determined to talk to their son. "Did he say anything?"

"Nary a word. He looked mighty discouraged, though. I saw it in his eyes."

This added to Lyle's concern. But curious though he was, it was better to give Evan some leeway. *Best not borrow trouble.*

He was already on his second cup of coffee when Evan eventually wandered in and sat down in front of the plate of chocolate bars.

Not daring to bring up the lottery yet, Lyle asked, "How'd your deliveries go this afternoon, son?"

"Oh fine." Evan reached for one of the bars. "By the way, the customer in Conestoga wants another bushel of Yellow Transparent apples next week. I let Jonah know so we can schedule another delivery." Saying no more, Evan munched on the bar.

Elisabeth glanced at Lyle as though wanting him to proceed to the thing that was burning a hole in both their hearts.

Lyle nodded, inhaling deeply. Then, as calmly as he could, he said, "Did ya happen to go somewhere to listen to the lottery drawing today, son?"

Evan picked up the salt and pepper shakers, then moved them around as if in a daze before taking a second bar from the plate.

"Reckon it's a mighty tense evening for many families," Lyle said, trying again to engage him.

Evan said nothing as he rose to go to the gas-powered refrigerator, removed a bottle of milk, and returned to the table with a glass.

This was starting to feel like pulling teeth. "What is your lottery number, son?"

At that moment, Ellie came down the stairs. She halted when she saw them and stood at the end of the kitchen, frowning. "Am I interrupting?" she said at last.

Elisabeth waved her over. "*Kumme.* Have some sweets."

Ellie moved quickly to the table and took a seat beside her mother, her usual spot. "Have ya told them, Evan?" she asked, her eyes on her brother across the table.

Stalling like before, Evan ran a hand through his thick blond hair and then took a drink. "Not yet," he murmured.

Lyle's heart dropped.

"Why not just say it, *Bruder?*" Ellie said, tears welling up.

Evan set down his glass. "All right, then." His shoulders rose and fell, like he was worried about their reaction. "Twenty-five's my lottery number. If I pass the military physical, I'll be inducted into the army."

A pang flashed through Lyle's chest as Elisabeth bowed her head. He waited a moment lest Evan might say more. But Evan simply got up, made his way to the side door, and walked out of the house, leaving Ellie to slip her arm around her mother, who was breathing mighty fast.

Surely now he'll talk to the bishop about trying to qualify for a religious exemption, Lyle thought, hoping so with everything in him.

It was late when Lyle retired for the night. Bible reading and prayer time with the family was a dim memory now as he closed the bedroom door behind him.

In the lantern's light, he leaned back against the dresser and looked at his wife, all curled up beneath the sheets. As emotionally spent as he was, it was beyond him how she could sleep.

Still contemplating what had transpired earlier, Lyle turned to pull open a drawer and find his pajama bottoms. Thankfully, Ellie had pushed her brother to say something, or they might all still be at that kitchen table.

Lyle said his rote prayers, then pleaded with God to help them through this rough patch with Evan. *We need Thy strength, O Lord . . . and Thy mercy.*

8

The next morning, Ellie couldn't help noticing hardly any-one spoke at breakfast. She hadn't slept well, finding it impossible to get comfortable, then rising to pace the floor in her room. Eventually, she'd opened the windows at each end of the narrow hall outside her room. All the while, she'd prayed, asking God for the right words to say to her brother, who seemed downright conflicted. *He needs guidance from someone who'll take him under his wing. But who?* Would either Jonah or Rudy step forward to lead their ill-advised brother back onto the right path? But they had their own small farms to tend to, juggling their work at home with the orchard work with Dat. And they had families to look after.

Even Dawdi Hezekiah was uncharacteristically quiet as he ate, glancing every so often at Evan, who looked as solemn as when he'd returned from Jack Herr's funeral more than two months ago. Evan drank his coffee and moved his scrambled eggs around with a fork, sporadically taking a bite.

Poor, weary Mamm slumped in her chair to the right of Dat. At one point, she started to speak but instead shook her head and reached for a glass of water, then her coffee, and then her water again.

To Ellie, it felt like the calm before a storm, and by the way her father's jaw twitched, surely one was coming.

At noon, Mamm served a corned beef and cabbage casserole to all the family members who'd been working in the orchard. As with breakfast, Ellie said barely a word except to compliment her mother on the delicious meal.

Meanwhile, unlike his behavior earlier, Evan had piled food on his plate and was making quick work of it. Frankly, she had assumed he'd lost his appetite following yesterday's lottery drawing. But now he didn't seem bothered by the outcome.

She felt tense there at the table as Jonah, Rudy, and Titus began to rehash the details of the draft lottery, which they'd surely read about in the morning newspaper, *The Intelligencer Journal.*

"Sol's lottery number is eight," Jonah said, raking his hand through his bushy brown beard. "He told us the minute he arrived at work, mighty relieved that he registered as a CO last year."

"Sol could share what he knows 'bout all of that with Evan," Titus remarked as he buttered his bread roll.

It struck Ellie as odd that Titus was talking as if Evan wasn't sitting right there with them.

Jonah leaned forward to look at Evan. "All ya have to do, little brother, is contact the local Amish Steering Committee. They'll represent ya to the state officials and walk ya through everything ya need to do."

Dawdi Hezekiah spoke up. "Of course, for that to work, ya'd

have to be in right standin' with the church—a baptized member or preparing to be. That's for certain."

Instead of replying, Evan reached for his tumbler of water and took a long drink.

Ellie wondered why her brothers hadn't already discussed this with Evan this morning. Then she remembered he'd been out running errands for Dat in Paradise and Smoketown. *It's good he's getting this advice now.* She hoped he'd take it to heart—and soon. Time was running out for him to catch up on baptismal instruction.

"Son, are ya still leanin' toward not registering as a conscientious objector?" Dat asked, his voice a bit husky. He didn't wait for Evan to reply. "If you've changed your mind, you need to make immediate arrangements. As I understand it, the bishop will have to vouch for ya first." He paused. "I'd be happy to go with ya to talk to him."

Evan seemed to study Dat, paying close attention. "I'm in *Rumschpringe*, though, Dat," he said quietly. "I'm not ready to take that step."

"*Rumschpringe!* Are ya nuts?" Jonah scowled. "Haven't ya run around long enough? I mean, Evan, you've got a *gut* head on your shoulders, so wake up and do the right thing. It could spare your life!"

Mamm nodded her agreement, her expression anxious. "You'll think on all of this, won't ya, son?"

Evan looked at her. He always took it seriously when Mamm spoke up.

"We love ya, *Bruder* . . . all of us," Ellie said, having a hard time getting the words out. Her twin looked like he felt cornered, and though he'd brought this on himself, she felt strangely sorry for him.

Sitting up straighter, Evan reached for the casserole dish. He helped himself to generous seconds, and Ellie knew for sure the conversation was over.

At Friday market, Ellie couldn't stop thinking about Evan's demeanor at yesterday's noon meal. The men around the table had certainly explained what he had to do if he'd changed his mind. She'd fallen asleep last night thinking of him, and even dreamed about him, though now she couldn't remember what the dream was—something about Evan getting lost overseas.

She still wondered why he hadn't responded to Dat and the others' advice—or at least to Dawdi Hezekiah's. Their grandfather had always had a soft spot in his heart for Evan. All the same, she worked diligently with Mamm at market, serving every customer. By the end of the afternoon, they'd sold all the homemade Dutch apple pies and apple fritters they'd brought, some of which Ruthann's mother, Aendi Cora—Mamm's sister—had purchased since she didn't have time to bake for company she hadn't been expecting.

When they returned home, Ellie hurried out to check the mailbox as a reprieve from her thoughts of Evan. She was glad to find a letter from Leah, but she and Mamm needed to get busy cooking. She waited till after supper and Bible reading with the family to read it, hardly able to keep her attention on her silent prayers while they all knelt together in the front room.

The minute they were finished, she excused herself and went up the stairs to her bedroom. Closing the door behind her, she sat on her bed, opened the envelope, and was surprised to see a photo of the three children Leah looked after while their mother worked as a nurse. The inscription on the back of the photo listed their names—Bobby, Lisa, and Kimberly. Ellie could see how pretty the three-year-old twin girls were with their auburn hair and blue eyes, alongside their handsome four-year-old brother, Bobby.

Dear Ellie,

Thanks for your long and interesting letter. I'm so glad you make sure I know what's going on back home, and I always read your letters more than once when they arrive. To be honest, they help to ease my homesickness. Mamma writes faithfully, too, as does Sol—to my surprise—and two of my sisters-in-law sometimes send postcards. It's nothing like being face-to-face with my family or my best friend, but I'm doing okay here, so don't worry.

So, how are you this week? I'm sure you're as busy as I am, except in a different way.

Oh, I must tell you about something that happened at market recently. I met some Amish folk, and it was such fun to talk with them in Pennsylvania Dutch. Anyway, the Amishwoman and her courting-age daughter invited me to come to their Preaching service sometime. Unfortunately, it's too far for me to walk there, and I wouldn't think of asking Carolyn to drive me on a Sunday. She likes to rest and spend the day with the children after working long hours all week at the hospital. So for now, at least, I'll continue to enjoy reading my devotional book and the Bible instead.

As you know, I've also been teaching Bobby to say the Lord's Prayer, like our Mammas taught us when we were little. It's still hard to believe he had never heard of Jesus before I came! Little Lisa and Kimberly have started to wander over and listen when I read Bible stories to Bobby, who likes to sit right next to me on the sofa. The twins sit on the floor, peering up at me. It's the sweetest thing.

Well, how's the year's first crop of apples? I remember walking in the orchard with you last July as we picked the ripe yellow apples off the trees. I'll never forget all the secrets we shared through the years in that most beautiful place. I'm sure you remember, too.

Ellie leaned back on her headboard, holding the letter against her heart. "I'm happy for her," she murmured, thankful Leah was making friends with other Amish there. *She isn't just spending time with* Englischers *after all.*

Ellie savored every word as she read the rest of the letter, then placed it in her second dresser drawer with the others. Through the years, Ellie had also saved cards from her family, especially from Lydia, who lived two miles away with Titus and their five children and loved to keep in touch that way, as well as visits.

Ellie glanced at her wall calendar and wished she could mark the day, or at least the month, when Leah would return. *But she doesn't know how long she'll be gone,* Ellie thought, reminding herself to retain a grateful spirit. *I'm thankful to you, Lord, for giving me the kind of friend who's hard to say good-bye to.*

She prepared for bed, then carefully pulled back the top quilt. Although it was a summer cover, tonight the room was much too warm for anything but her cotton nightgown. She checked to make sure all the windows were wide open, then sat on the room's only chair and brushed her long hair as she prayed for each of her family members by name, beginning with Evan and lingering there before moving on to her other siblings and their families. She prayed for Dawdi Hezekiah, too. It was a blessing to have so many loved ones to pray for, she thought, then suddenly remembered Jack Herr's family would always have a son missing.

When she came to Leah's name, she prayed for Carolyn Madison and her children, too, since it seemed like they needed a special prayer just for them. And with her eyes closed, Ellie had a growing sense that God really had led Leah to be with this family.

The next morning—pulling the red wagon Dat purchased for her and Evan when they were little—Ellie took thermoses of cold water out to the orchard. Solomon was picking Yellow Transparent apples while standing on metal stilts. She could see that he was being careful not to bruise the branches or the fruit. His striking golden-blond hair, so like Evan's, stood out from that of the other workers, who were over emptying their harvest crates into the waiting market wagon.

As always, Sol was kind as he thanked her for the water.

"Happy to help," she said, wondering if now was a good time to ask him something. "Say, has Evan talked to ya at all 'bout the draft lottery?"

"*Nee*, but I've heard about his number from Jonah, Rudy, and Titus."

"It's strange, really—not sure what Evan's thinkin'."

"Seems to me he's preoccupied with the outside world." He gave her a sidelong glance. "Sure hope I'm not speakin' out of turn."

"*Nee*, you're right. He's got at least one foot there."

After a momentary pause, Sol said, "Leah says she's been keepin' in touch with you at least once a week by mail."

"*Jah.* In fact, I got a letter from her just yesterday."

Sol nodded pensively from where he was still perched on his metal stilts. His half-full harvest crate was strapped securely to his brawny shoulders and around his waist. "I have to say it's still strange with Leah gone," he told her. "Her place next to Mamm is empty at meals, left that way on purpose for when she returns."

Ellie noticed Sol's tone soften, and she understood how close he was to his sister. *Like I am to Evan.* "It's sad not seein' Leah at Singings and the summer gatherings—and knowin' she's not just up the road anymore."

Sol removed a kerchief from his pocket and wiped his brow. "My parents are hopin' she won't be gone too long, but that's up to Leah to decide."

"She wrote that she's still homesick, so maybe that means she'll be ready to come home soon." Even though it was the honest truth, she didn't add that there was no better friend for her than Leah. Cousin Ruthann was a close second, for certain, but Ellie had never fully shared her heart with her. *No reason to when I always had Leah to talk to,* she thought as Sol opened the thermos and took a long drink.

"I thought there'd be a trial period, but she seems to love working there. Says she feels called to help this woman."

Ellie smiled. "She was rather insistent 'bout that very thing when she first told me about goin'."

Sol didn't respond to that, and there was a lull between them. "By the way," he said, his hazel eyes squinting in the sunlight, "it was fun double-dating with you and Menno that time we all went out the end of May."

"It was," Ellie replied, wishing Menno had been more talkative that evening, the last time she'd seen him before he left town.

Sol took another swig. "Maybe once Menno returns from the Big Valley, he'll want to do it again."

Ellie didn't know enough to comment since she'd received only two postcards from Menno. She'd replied with a short letter and was looking forward to his return.

"Ya might also be interested to hear that Jonah has Menno on the alternate list for part-time peach pickers," Sol said, then chuckled. "Say that fast five times."

"Menno must be glad."

"I would guess so."

Ellie appreciated that Sol had told her this about his cousin. "Well, I should deliver the rest of these," she said, glancing at the thermoses still lying in the wagon.

"Okay. See ya, Ellie."

She smiled at how friendly Sol was and wondered if he'd asked Cousin Ruthann out again after that double-date. But then again, if he had, Ruthann wouldn't have been able to hide her excitement.

While redding up her room later that morning, Ellie opened the hope chest that had belonged to her mother as a teen. The lid was as solid as the rest of the oak chest handcrafted by Mamm's eldest brother, Jesse.

Ellie reorganized the contents, then placed inside the new set of pillowcases she'd embroidered recently. As far as linens and blankets and such, she now had practically everything she would need to set up housekeeping as a newlywed. The only thing missing was an honest-to-goodness steady beau. Might Menno be that person? He was very nice and as polite as he was strong—she'd heard he could toss a bale of hay like it was a feather. But she didn't know him all that well yet, since they'd had only that one double-date before he left for the Big Valley. All the same, she would be patient. *If Menno even considers me a potential sweetheart . . .*

She lowered the lid on the chest and turned to look out one of the windows at the orchard below, still one of the main reasons she liked having her room up here. She could see her mother walking across the side yard to the fruit store. *Mamm was already betrothed to Dat at my age,* she thought, wondering what God had planned for her own future.

In the near distance, an early firecracker exploded, then three more—*pop, pop, pop!* The sounds startled her out of her musing. *Someone must be in a hurry to celebrate Independence Day,* she thought, looking forward to her sister and family coming for ice cream after supper. There wouldn't be any firecrackers here, but there would be candy sprinkles and chocolate syrup to drizzle over Dat's creamy, homemade vanilla ice cream. Hopefully, Evan would be on hand to enjoy the celebration with them, too.

That evening at supper, Dawdi Hezekiah seemed more like himself for the first time since Evan's announcement, telling one story after another. Ellie enjoyed his lighthearted demeanor and perked up when he started talking about how, since boyhood, he'd always sought to be prepared for anything.

"Like what?" Evan asked between bites.

"Well, for the unavoidable, for instance." Dawdi gave a nod of his white head. "That's why I've decided to build my own coffin," he said, a twinkle in his eyes.

"Dawdi . . ." Ellie said.

"I measured myself from head to toe and located some used pine wood. Should be all ready to start."

"Oh for goodness' sake," Mamm said, eyebrows aloft.

"Several of my uncles did this very thing," Dawdi said. "So I'll be prepared like they were, and yous won't have to bother havin' one built at the last minute." Dawdi reached for another dinner roll and slathered butter and some thick strawberry jam on it, seemingly untroubled at the thought of his own end.

Evan was clearly paying attention to the conversation now. "Never heard of such a thing."

"*Puh!* Folks said the selfsame thing back when I planted my big orchard," Dawdi retorted.

"And the orchard worked out fine," Dat said with a smile. "And continues to."

Ellie disliked thinking about Dawdi's passing. "I wish ya wouldn't talk about coffin building." She glanced at Evan, who nodded in agreement.

Dawdi waved the comment away. "Well, as the Good Book says, 'It is appointed unto men once to die.'"

"Still, it's too soon for ya to talk this way, Dawdi." Ellie wished for a different topic.

"All in *Gott's* time," he replied. "And no need to weep for me when I'm gone, Ellie-girl. I'll be home with the Lord who made me, who planned for me to be born Amish and live a right *gut* life . . . well, 'cept for that long-ago trial I had durin' the Great War."

Dat frowned and coughed a little, and Ellie wondered what on earth Dawdi meant.

9

Lyle was turning the hand-crank ice cream maker on the walkway out back when Evan hurried down the porch steps and out to the carriage shed. When he pushed his open courting carriage out to the lane, Lyle wondered what was up.

He asked his father, who was sitting on the glider, to crank for a while, then headed over to Evan. "Did ya forget Lydia and her family are comin' over?"

Evan rubbed his chin. "That's tonight? I already made plans," he said right quick. "I'll have to see Lydia another time . . . and Titus'll be workin' with me in the orchard tomorrow, so . . ."

"This is *family* time, son." Lyle's words flew out faster than he could stop them.

Evan bobbed his head. "I'll make it up to them." Then he stepped toward the stable, no doubt to get Cupcake.

He's going to celebrate the Fourth somewhere else, Lyle assumed, walking back to where Daed was steadily cranking.

His father frowned. "Your face is mighty red."

Lyle ignored the comment. "I'll take it from here," he said, and his father went back up to the glider and sat with a groan.

"Evan has developed a mind of his own, Lyle," Daed said from where he was rocking now.

Lyle glanced at him. "Seems that way."

"The harder ya question and push, the worse it'll get."

Lyle shook his head. "I hate to see Evan ruin his life. And his future." He thought how, during World War I, his father had endured so much to preserve his pacifist values by refusing all forms of service. And now, here was his grandson, willing to set that aside and act as if he was an *Englischer*. Truth be known, Lyle was furious. Yet he was also worried for Evan, who didn't have any idea what he was getting into. *He could end up dead.*

"Remember, we rely on *Gott* to keep goin' no matter what's happening round us," Daed said. "'Tis hard to stand back and watch, I know," he added. "But we'll keep Evan in our prayers."

Daed was right . . . and wise. Lyle turned the crank all the faster as he watched Evan hitch Cupcake to the courting carriage. He offered a silent prayer for divine protection over his unbaptized son.

Ellie stepped out the side door to greet Lydia and her family while Titus tied their horse to the hitching post near the carriage shed. The evening was beginning to cool, not nearly as hot and muggy as it had been all day. Twelve-year-old Pete and nine-year-old Sammy followed Dawdi and Dat out to the barn, while Ida, eight, Verna, seven, and five-year-old Alma scurried into the house to greet Mamm.

Once Ellie was in the kitchen as well, towheaded Alma hugged her tightly around her waist and grinned up at her, revealing a missing front tooth. "I couldn't wait to see you, Aendi," she said in *Deitsch*.

"I'm glad yous came for ice cream," Ellie said, heading to the sink to show Alma the hand-crank ice cream maker.

"Dat has one like this, too. I help him turn the handle sometimes."

"Your Mamma says you're a *gut* helper."

Alma smiled, seeming to take it all in. "When I'm all grown up like you, I want to make lots of ice cream."

Ellie cupped her niece's little chin with her hand. "I'm sure you will."

"And have lots of children," Alma added.

Ellie grinned. "You and your future husband will have as many as God gives ya."

She and Alma stepped back outside to walk barefoot through the rows of tall sweet corn, as the little girl liked to do this time of year.

Later, when the sun was lower in the sky, they all assembled indoors while Ellie and Mamm dished up the vanilla ice cream in bowls and placed the sprinkles and chocolate syrup on the counter so everyone could help themselves. Mamm had also laid out thinly sliced canned peaches and peach preserves for toppings. Dat bowed his head in a silent prayer over the dessert, and everyone else did the same.

After the prayer, while most of the family stayed inside, Ellie headed to the porch steps to sit with Lydia for a few minutes. Mamm's spider plant dangled nearby nestled in macramé, moving slightly in the breeze across from the long flypaper.

"Where's Evan tonight?" Lydia asked, dipping her spoon into her ice cream.

"Wish I knew."

Lydia's eyes searched hers. "Everything all right?"

Ellie simply shook her head, too emotional to say.

"Is it the draft? Jonah told Titus about it, and he told me."

"That, and other things." She didn't know for sure, but she wondered if Evan had gone to spend the evening with Cheryl Herr again.

"Mamm does seem a bit worried," Lydia replied.

Ellie nodded. "But she has a way of putting on a *gut* face . . . most times."

Lydia scooped up another spoonful of her ice cream, not saying more about that. After a time, she said more softly, "I hate the thought of Evan spendin' all his time with *Englischers* like he does."

So Lydia knew about that, too. "Well, he's been minglin' with them plenty while still livin' at home," Ellie said glumly. *Seems like we're spinning our wheels about Evan. He's all anyone wants to talk about.*

After eating their ice cream, all the adults visited on the porch while the children took turns sitting on the glider, then played hide-and-seek. After a while, they played catch with a large ball Dat had purchased for gatherings like this.

Later, Ellie and little Alma walked hand in hand out to see Nelly and Captain in the stable.

"I miss Onkel Evan," the little girl said. "Where is he?"

It *was* so unlike Evan to slip out of a family get-together. "Don't worry, honey. I'm sure you'll see him again soon."

"I hope so," Alma said in her adorable little voice. "He makes me giggle, like Dawdi Hezekiah does."

"Dawdi does have a *gut* sense of humor."

Alma nodded as she reached up to touch Nelly's nose over the stall door. "My Dat makes up silly stories, too."

Ellie hugged her. "Our family does have some interesting storytellers."

Alma's words echoed in Ellie's mind long after Lydia and her family had left for home. Then after Dat and Mamm headed for bed, she decided to stay dressed and wait on the porch steps for Evan's return. Besides, it was so hot in her top-floor room.

It was almost midnight when he pulled into the lane. Quickly, he unhitched and led Cupcake to the stable, then pushed his buggy into the carriage shed. Ellie could hear him whistling as he made his way across the yard toward the house. When he looked up, she waved to him.

"Still awake?" he asked, sounding a little hoarse as he sat down next to her.

Evan's breath smelled strange, but she tried to ignore it. "Can't a girl wait up for her brother?"

He smiled. "Did ya have a nice time with the family?"

She said she did and told him what little Alma had said about him.

"Alma's a sweetie," he said, then leaned forward, staring at the ground.

"You okay?"

"Prob'ly had a little too much to drink after we left the Herr place."

So that's what she'd smelled on his breath. "Oh, Evan. What were ya thinkin'?"

"There were drinks at the Herrs', too."

"You spent time with Jack's family, then?"

"Not long, really." Evan sat up straighter now. "Chuck Herr

83

talked me into tagging along with him and a few other guys to Long's Park in Lancaster, where a live band was playing antiwar songs. Chuck's so mad 'bout Jack's death that he said he needed to march around with others protesting, so I went with him for somethin' to do. He was chanting with that crowd till his voice nearly gave out."

"Chanting what?" She wondered why her brother had gone at all, especially if he wasn't going to register as a conscientious objector.

"Just some stuff 'bout Tricky Dick and a no-reason war."

"'Bout who?" Ellie asked, puzzled.

"President Nixon. He keeps tryin' to end the war but can't pull it off—or so Chuck says." Evan rubbed his chin. "There must've been a thousand people at the park tonight, maybe more. And policemen everywhere." He sighed. "Some guys were burnin' American flags. Several were arrested for it—I saw 'em being handcuffed and taken away."

Ellie shuddered. "Arrested? That's awful."

Evan nodded.

"You took a big risk by goin', don't ya think?"

"It was pure chaos, but I wasn't anywhere near those arrested. Stayed clear of that."

"Well, I'm so glad you're home safe now." She sighed. "It was nice and quiet here 'cept for the children runnin' around and playing. Oh, and Pete and Sammy had fun in the haymow. Sammy finally got brave enough to try the rope swing," she said, trying to change the subject.

"It's about time he got some courage. Too many cowards in the world right now."

She sensed he was talking about something completely different. "Little Sammy's not a coward, Evan."

"*Nee*, but a lot my age are. . . . Yankee guys talking 'bout driving up to Canada to avoid the draft. Get this: The day of the lottery, Chuck yelled at me for not seeking CO status—called me *plain stupid*. He did it again tonight. Said he'd be quick to sign up for it if he were in my place. I was tempted to shout back at him that he and his friends are nothin' but scared chickens."

Ellie shook her head. Did Evan think the peacemaker Amish were chickens? "I just wonder why ya went with Chuck tonight . . . if ya didn't want to. Ya would have had more fun here."

"I told you, he twisted my arm. Sure, it's *gut* for any war to end—or never start—but I'm not protesting this one. It's not won yet." Evan got up from the step. "Well, it's late, and I need to be up early tomorrow."

"*Jah*," she said, rising to follow him into the house. "What'll ya tell Dat and Mamm 'bout where ya went?"

"As little as possible."

Again, Ellie was at a loss for words. Baffled, really.

Sure ain't the brother I used to know.

10

Following Preaching service and the fellowship meal the next day, Ellie sat near one of her open bedroom windows at the small desk Dat had built for her years ago. She was trying to decide how to start her latest letter to Leah. A house wren perched conspicuously on a nearby tree branch, and Ellie paused to listen to its familiar chatter. Peering through the window screen, she heard a similar bird calling back and smiled wistfully, remembering once more how she and Leah would always look across the meadow to see each other's bedroom windows lit up at night.

Birds of a feather, she thought fondly of her friend as she fanned herself with a spare piece of stationery, then started to write.

Hard as it was, she chose not to tell Leah about the news of Sol's and Evan's low draft lottery numbers. After all, her Mamm or Sol himself would surely let her know about his situation. And besides, Evan's response to receiving a low number was too perplexing to share. So she began by mentioning the upcoming youth activities, especially the volleyball tournament scheduled for next Saturday evening at her brother Rudy's small goat farm.

He and Lovina were having a cookout for all the district's youth. *It'll be nice*, Ellie wrote, *with roasting ears, hot dogs, and my sister-in-law's homemade relish. I really wish you could be there, too!*

Putting down the pen, Ellie struggled with how much to share about the youth events here. She didn't want Leah to feel left out. On the other hand, she wanted her to know how very much she was missed.

Sighing, Ellie leaned forward, her elbows on the desk, and heard male voices floating up from the front of the house. A car door slammed, and she went to the other window, where she observed her brother below. Evan was shaking his head and frowning something fierce.

"Evan?" she called, surprised he'd gone riding in a car on the Lord's Day, something they weren't permitted to do. Then again, her brother had pushed so many other boundaries, why was she surprised by this one?

He glanced up at her. "I'm not the best company right now, Ellie."

"*Ach, Bruder.* Can't we talk?"

He sighed. "Nothin' to say . . . not now." He hurried up the lane, and Ellie leaned against the windowsill and made herself take a deep breath. *O Lord, my brother needs Thy help—and quick.*

Sitting in the glider with his wife while drinking iced meadow tea on the back porch, Lyle had been staring out at the wide meadow where wildflowers bloomed, trying to relax. But then he'd suddenly heard Evan's voice. "I think I'd better talk to him," he told Elisabeth.

He headed down the steps to the walkway, where he waited for his son to come around. When Evan appeared, Lyle asked him to go with him into the house.

"It's so hot. I'm burnin' up." Evan pressed his lips together and wiped his forehead with his hand.

"Some cold tea'll do ya *gut*," Lyle said, motioning toward the side door.

Surprisingly, Evan led the way. In the kitchen, he went directly to the refrigerator and poured a tall tumbler of cold tea for himself. Then he crossed the kitchen to sit near the open window at the foot of the table, where he'd sat when he was young, long before his older siblings married and left home.

Lyle could guess why he'd chosen to sit so far away. "I heard ya talkin' to someone," he said. "Ellie, maybe?"

Evan nodded. "Just comin' back from a drive with Chuck after church." He took another sip, working the tumbler in his hands, smoothing the condensation away with his fingers.

"*Ach*, son . . . ya didn't."

Frowning, Evan repeated that he had.

"Wanna talk about it?" Lyle wished he were as wise as Daed in dealing with something like this. He recalled what his father had said about praying more than talking.

"Chuck's still tryin' to get me to apply to be a CO," Evan told him. "Asks why should I fight in an *unjust war* and get myself killed like Jack did."

Couldn't have said it better myself, Lyle thought, hoping perhaps Evan would listen to Chuck since he didn't seem to be listening to his own family.

Evan continued. "Chuck doesn't understand. I was Jack's loyal friend," he said, his voice breaking. "He said so in his last letter. The one I got after he died."

So Jack and Evan did exchange letters somehow.

Lyle couldn't make sense of any of this. "What does that have to do with your decision, son?"

88

"I want to honor Jack and do my part for this country. Ain't right to leave it up to others to fight for the freedoms we enjoy. Jack himself mentioned this in one of his letters to me."

Baffled, Lyle asked, "So for that you're willin' to go against everything right and *gut* you've been taught?" He stopped to breathe and tried to calm himself. "Have ya even thought of talkin' to the bishop 'bout this?"

"We've already discussed this, Dat. How can I qualify for a religious exemption when I'm not baptized, and not even takin' classes? It's the chance I took when I registered for the draft."

"But won't ya at least try? See if Bishop will allow ya to get caught up with the baptismal instruction. Maybe Ellie can help ya, too."

"Dat . . ." Evan paused as if trying to formulate his words, and for the first time, he met his father's eyes. "I'm not even sure I want to be Plain anymore."

Lyle's stomach clenched. *So that's where this has been leading.*

Evan stared out the window. "I'm not ready, Dat. I may *never* be ready."

Lyle could not comprehend this, not coming from one of his own children. Evan would rather go to war than be baptized? It made no sense. "Well, Plain's how ya were raised. Doesn't that count for something?" Lyle said, grasping for more to say, another means for his son to escape what he seemed to already accept as inevitable.

He shuffled his feet under the table, feeling desperate. Truth be told, he wanted to demand that Evan start behaving like an Amishman and honor God, above all else. Yet he feared that would have his son walking out the door right now.

"Would ya want me to be baptized just to avoid the draft?" Evan asked.

"*Nee*, it'd be wrong to pretend to be ready to join church—that'd be downright dishonest." Lyle's heart was beating mighty hard.

Evan took a drink of his iced tea and then sighed deeply. "Listen, Dat, I'd appreciate it if *you* told Mamm I've made a final decision not to avoid the draft."

"Won't ya think more 'bout this, son? Remember, we're peace-loving people. We oppose all manner of violence. While that might not mean much to ya now, it might someday. And as your father, it's my job to keep ya on the right path."

"Dat, I'm not changin' my mind."

Lyle was perspiring heavily now. "Think how much better it would be to reflect God's love in this troubled world—with a wiser choice—and maybe bring about some positive change that doesn't take lives?" He tugged on his beard, relieved Elisabeth wasn't here to observe their son's open resistance.

Evan drank the rest of his tea straight down and then set the tumbler on the table hard. "All it takes for evil to triumph is for *gut* men to do nothin'."

"*Ach*, son."

"I'm sorry, Dat. I wish this wasn't such a disappointment to ya, but it's what I want to do . . . what I need to do." With that, he left the kitchen and disappeared upstairs.

Stunned at how stubborn Evan had become—and how hardened against the Old Ways of the People—Lyle felt his anger rise. He trembled, but try as he might, he could not quell his frustration—and fear.

If Evan were younger, I'd put my foot down on all this and spare him harm. But he's no longer a child.

90

Knowing he'd be up from his Sunday afternoon nap by now, Ellie walked over to visit Dawdi Hezekiah with a big jar of cold homemade root beer. She couldn't help noticing the pretty pink and white petunias he'd planted along either side of the short walkway leading to his *Dawdi Haus.*

"Thought ya might want something cold to drink," she said, entering his little kitchen and setting the jar on the counter.

From the table where he sat with his old German *Biewel,* Dawdi gave her a big smile, his spectacles on the tip of his shiny nose. "Always nice to see ya, Ellie-girl." He rose and went to the cupboard to take out two drinking glasses, then set them on the counter. "Can ya stay for a little while?"

"Sure," she said, pouring some root beer into each glass.

"There's some chipped ice in the icebox," he said, motioning to it.

"This is nice and cold already."

"All right, then." Dawdi accepted the full glass and again sat at the small round table in the corner of the room near the windows. "Want some sweets to go with it?"

"Do you?" she asked, guessing he was hoping for some from Mamm's constant supply.

"S'pose I had my fill at the fellowship meal earlier, so I'll be content with this *wunnerbaar-gut* root beer your Mamm makes." Dawdi eyed her like he sensed something was up. "I daresay you're not yourself." Studying her, he tilted his silvery-white head.

"Actually, Evan's the one who's not himself anymore," she said, going on to share that her own twin didn't seem interested in listening to her.

"Well, it ain't like Evan to dismiss his sister."

She shook her head. "Or anyone."

"Lest ya forget, this is the same young fella who, as just a lad, would go round the orchard lookin' up and thankin' the trees for their fruit and the birds for their song, filled with gratitude to *Gott.*"

Ellie sighed. "I remember that, too."

"That same young boy is still in there, somewhere. We may not see it right now, but we're not givin' up on him, 'cause the Good Lord sure hasn't."

"It's so hard to recognize any of that in *this* Evan."

Dawdi nodded slowly, his gray eyes misty. "I s'pect he might need to know that your love for him is constant in spite of his poor behavior."

She felt so softhearted around Dawdi. "Do ya think you might be able to talk to him? Would ya?"

"Straighten him out, ya mean?"

"Seems like Dat's been tryin', but nothin's worked. I thought you might be able to get his attention."

"Well, I could try, but Evan's grown now and has to make his own decisions under *Gott.* There's no forcin' the heart to shift in a direction it ain't ready to go in." Dawdi took a drink, then set his glass down in front of him, his fingers still wrapped around its base. "You remember the proverb 'Train up a child in the way he should go: and when he is old, he will not depart from it.'"

"I know it well."

"Hard as it might seem to ya, we have to believe that the godly instruction your Dat and Mamm have given Evan all these years will carry him through."

"What if that means waitin' till Evan's old, like the verse says?" She'd sometimes wondered about that. "And if he makes bad choices, will he have to suffer the consequences?"

"Our Lord is sovereign," Dawdi said, his expression serious. "Come what may, we should never second-guess Him."

Ellie drank some root beer, pondering all that Dawdi had said. "What if my parents' teaching doesn't hold for Evan? I mean, he's not interested in bein' baptized yet."

"As long as Evan has breath, there's still time."

"Guess I want to hurry him up."

"You'd like to fix him, ain't so?"

She had to smile. "You know me, *jah?*"

"Well now, I believe I do." Dawdi sat back and folded his arms, grinning at her. "You're a peach of a girl with a tender heart toward your twin. It's always been thataway. But the best thing ya can do for your Bruder now is to pray for him . . . and let him know ya care."

They each drank another glass of root beer, and later she said good-bye and walked back to the main house, somewhat encouraged. Dawdi always seemed to understand whatever she was going through.

11

After her chores Tuesday morning, Ellie headed across the yard to the family fruit store, then down to the cold cellar to get a crate of ripened Sentry peaches. She and Mamm planned to bake more pies for Rudy to sell at market tomorrow.

As she was returning to the house, Ellie overheard Dawdi talking to Evan over near the woodshed about the importance of "following God's way of peace, come what may." Ellie held her breath and even paused to hear if Evan might respond, but she heard nothing.

Will Evan heed Dawdi's wisdom? she wondered as she went around to the side door of the house, past the long rope to the dinner bell high above.

"Have ya found some ready for pie making?" Mamm asked when Ellie appeared in the kitchen.

"Ain't many left. Customers are buyin' them up quick-like."

"We're always thankful for that."

Ellie peeled the peaches while Mamm rolled out the pie dough.

"I s'pose you're still prayin' for Evan," Mamm said quietly.

"Dawdi said God won't give up on Evan, so we shouldn't either."

Ellie glanced at her Mamm, who was silent for a moment. Then Mamm said, "Your Dawdi Hezekiah often says that the person who's most blessed is too busy to fret in the daylight and too tired to fret at night."

"*Jah*, I've heard him say that very thing."

"But to be honest, it's been a challenge for me not to worry 'bout your brother."

Ellie nodded. "Because you're his mother."

"Well, and *you*, Ellie, are his twin sister." Mamm stopped, a quaver in her voice.

"I know it's awful hard, Mamm."

"I'll be all right. I'm relying on God for each day . . . for all of us. Even if that means simply stepping back and accepting that Evan's goin' to do things his way, disappointing as that may be."

"I just overheard Dawdi outside talkin' with Evan about following God's way," Ellie said, gathering up the peach skins. "But I didn't hear Evan responding."

Mamm sighed. "Your Dat says Evan's standin' firm in his decision not to fight the draft. I guess he sees it as having the courage his friend Jack had. Or so he told your father." She shook her head. "Wish he understood that sometimes it takes more courage to walk away from a fight."

"Evan can be so stubborn sometimes. But like ya said, we must trust the Lord for his comin's and goin's. Worry doesn't fix a thing . . . but I sure wish it did."

Mamm placed the rolled-out pie dough into the first of nine tin pie plates. "'Tween you and me, I dread what the rest of the community will say once Evan leaves for his physical and basic training. I don't want anyone's pity."

Ellie looked at her mother with concern, for the first time realizing that their whole family would have to endure the scrutiny of the People once that awful day arrived.

"Not that I don't dread what could happen to Evan overseas even more." Mamm paused a moment. "He's never even held a gun—not even for small game hunting."

Like some men amongst the People, Dat and Ellie's brothers had always used a bow and arrow for hunting.

"We can't let ourselves imagine what's ahead for Evan," replied Ellie, knowing that was easier said than done.

That Saturday was exceptionally warm and humid. When Evan took Ellie to Rudy's farm at five-thirty for the volleyball tournament and wiener roast, the sun was still bright. A number of the youth were already gathering, and Lovina's male cousins were just leaving in their spring wagon—James and Ephraim worked for Rudy on his goat farm.

Ellie expected Evan to simply drop her off, as aloof toward everyone as he'd become. But he surprised her by getting out of the open buggy and tying Cupcake to the hitching post.

"You're stayin'?" she asked, glad to see it.

"Can't pass up Lovina's *gut* cookin', now, can I?"

It's impossible to know anymore, she thought, shrugging.

In the meadow, several goats bleated as Cousin Ruthann called to her from the backyard. Joining her, Ellie saw Sol motioning to Evan from the back porch. *They used to be the best of friends*, she thought as the two fellows headed to the side yard, most likely to help Rudy put up the second volleyball net.

At the screen door, Ellie's sister-in-law waved to her and

Ruthann with three-month-old Mary asleep in her arms. They headed up the porch steps to talk to Lovina, who said she'd latched the screen door to keep three-year-old Caleb corralled in the kitchen. "So far, I think we've got things under control," she said, laughing. "Rudy's gonna do some of the cookin' on the outdoor fireplace over yonder."

"Well, let us know if ya need help with the little ones," Ellie said. "Or with anything else."

"Ach, wouldn't think of it." Lovina looked down at her sleeping infant. "You'll have plenty of time to hold babies once you're married. You're here to have fun tonight."

"And maybe get acquainted with a potential mate," Ruthann declared.

Ellie's mouth dropped open. "Ach, cousin!"

"Well, what do ya think these youth gatherings are for?" Ruthann laughed as she bobbed her head toward Menno, who was helping Rudy along with Sol and Evan. This was the first time Ellie had seen him since his return from the Big Valley.

Now Lovina was grinning through the screen. "She's right. So go and enjoy yourselves."

Ellie waved farewell to Lovina, then headed to the backyard, where several of the boys were setting up tables with benches for the meal.

Later, after everyone had eaten their fill, Rudy had the youth count off in fours for the volleyball teams—eight young people per team, which accommodated all thirty-two in attendance. Ellie was separated from Ruthann and ended up on a team with Sol. *Sol's the best spiker*, Ellie thought, seeing Menno talking with Ruthann. *How'd they get on the same team?* she thought, glad Menno was back.

As daylight faded after the tournament, Rudy brought out

two large ice cream makers, and Evan and Menno offered to crank them. Ellie was fanning herself with her long apron hem, standing under a tree, when Solomon wandered over.

"Do ya mind if I join ya?" he asked, undoubtedly aware that others were observing them.

Ellie shook her head. "It's okay."

"Menno and I were talkin' with Evan earlier," he said, glancing toward her brother, clear across the yard near the driveway, talking to three of their guy cousins. "It's unbelievable what he's decided to do 'bout the draft."

Ellie nodded empathetically. "*Jah*, it's breakin' our hearts."

Sol raked his hand through his fair hair. "I tried to talk him out of it, but he seems resigned to goin' and getting it over with."

Ellie looked at Sol and realized how much he cared about her brother, and it touched her deeply.

"It's like he prefers to stay in *Rumschpringe* for the time he has left before boot camp," Sol added.

It's more than that, she thought sadly. *He acts like he doesn't even want to be Plain anymore.*

Sol shifted his weight from one bare foot to the other. "Honestly, if Evan knew anything about what war's really like, he'd want no part of it. You'd think Jack's death would've impressed on him how dangerous it is. I mean, doesn't he see the front-page headlines in the newspaper every day, like the rest of us?"

"Evan just reads the sports page, I think."

"You're sure? I almost wonder if he just chooses not to read things about the war. Here lately, there was an article about some local attacks on Amish and Mennonite young men."

Ellie's hand flew to her chest in surprise. "Attacks?"

Sol explained that an Amish teen had been shot in the arm while riding in his courting buggy with his girlfriend, who only narrowly escaped being hit as well. "Evidently, the shooter was angry because he thought the Amish fella was just usin' his CO status to avoid bein' drafted. They don't understand that not fightin' is part of who we are . . . what sets us apart."

Ellie shivered.

"Sorry. Didn't mean to alarm ya." Sol's eyes searched hers. "The world has turned upside down."

Right then, one of the fellows called to Sol, and he excused himself and headed off.

Ellie resumed fanning herself with her apron, surprised that Solomon had sought her out like that, in front of all the youth. And she also realized that, in spite of being observed just now, she didn't mind. It was the second time she and Sol had spoken somewhat privately. Even so, she should be cautious not to give the wrong impression, since Ruthann had gone out with him at least once after the double-date, and her cousin remained optimistic about being courted by him. *I wouldn't want to interfere.*

Lovina stepped outdoors at that moment, so Ellie walked across the yard to where she'd taken a seat on the porch swing. "Want some company?"

Lovina stopped the swing with her bare toes and patted the seat. "The children are finally tucked in for the night."

"You can relax now," Ellie said, glad to sit with her. "It's been a *wunnerbaar-gut* evening."

"And your team ended up in first place, ain't so?"

Ellie was surprised she'd kept up with that. "Rudy must've told ya."

Lovina nodded. "He's been lookin' forward to hosting the youth for some time. He remembers what it was like bein' a teen—wasn't too terribly long ago." She laughed softly, then paused. "He's so confused 'bout Evan refusing to pursue religious exemption."

"I don't think anyone in the family can understand. But whatever his reasons are, Evan seems fixed on the idea of goin' when he's called."

Lovina patted Ellie's knee. "Perhaps there's still time for him to come around." For a lingering moment, Lovina was quiet. "I remember bein' nineteen," she said, lowering her voice as the swing slowed. "Some days I felt mature, and other days almost childlike . . . slippin' back and forth." She turned to look at Ellie. "But one thing was always clear in my mind: I knew I wanted to join church and be Amish for the rest of my life."

Ellie nodded, wishing Evan felt the same way.

12

Early Thursday morning, Ellie was picking peaches from the same tree as Menno, who had asked her to join him. She was quick to do so.

"The volleyball tournament sure was loads of fun last Saturday," Menno said with a grin. "I wish we played volleyball at every youth gathering, 'specially during the warm weather."

"*Jah*, I've always enjoyed playin'." Ellie placed the peaches carefully into the harvesting crate she'd strapped around her shoulders and waist. "Maybe the girls could play against the boys sometime."

"*Gut* idea."

Ellie realized how nice it was to spend time with Menno beneath the shade of the tree like this.

"Say, Ellie. I wonder if you'd like to double-date with Yonnie Kurtz and his girlfriend, Katie, on Sunday. I'd suggest doubling with Sol, but Ruthann and her parents are goin' to visit relatives down in Quarryville, and won't be back in time for her to get to Singing."

Pleased, Ellie nodded. "Sure, that'll be fun."

"Yonnie and I thought it'd be nice to take you girls for some ice cream at my cousin's place," he said, his golden-brown eyes twinkling.

"*Wunnerbaar*," she replied, looking forward to it.

He smiled, and they moved around to the other side of the tree. It was the first time they'd picked together, and she was delighted.

Pinch yourself. You're goin' out again with Menno Bontrager, she thought, inwardly sighing. *Every girl's dream . . .*

That Sunday evening, Dat dropped Ellie off for Singing since Evan had left after the post-Preaching fellowship meal and hadn't yet returned. More and more, it seemed like he was too eager to spend extra time away from home.

Things are so different between Evan and me, she thought. *He lives and works at home, but I can almost see the walls he's building around him.*

When it was time for refreshments halfway through Singing, Ellie noticed Menno over in the corner, talking with his cousin Yonnie. She was excited for another double-date but sorry it couldn't be with Sol and Ruthann.

She picked up a sugar cookie just as Sol wandered over for a can of cold pop. He seemed hesitant at first, then said, "Leah wrote me a short note and said to tell ya she's awful sorry to hear 'bout Evan's low draft number—she must've heard it from the grapevine, 'cause I didn't tell her. She'll be writin' a long letter to ya soon."

Leah must wonder why I didn't tell her, Ellie thought.

"But the best part—she's comin' home for Thanksgiving," Sol added.

"That's great news. Oh, I can hardly wait to see her."

"Believe me, she feels the same way."

Ellie looked at her cookie, "Ya know, I feel sad 'bout joining church without her."

Sol nodded. "You and Leah were two peas in a pod. Well, *are*."

"It's somethin' I think about a lot. Not that I don't want to be baptized—I just wish Leah could be there, too." She could imagine that sacred moment, shared by her family, all the People, and her precious friend. It was a day she'd looked forward to for a while now.

"You know you can share whatever's on your mind with me, like Leah does." He paused and glanced at her. "*Ach,* maybe I shouldn't've said that. You've got plenty of other people to talk to."

There was an awkwardness in their silence, and Ellie wished she'd kept her thoughts to herself. *He must think you're ferhoodled, sayin' such a thing.* After a time, she ventured to say, "I'm glad you and Leah are close siblings, like Evan and I used to be."

"I suspect any change isn't your doing. Evan's nothin' like he was a few years ago. Back then, he talked with me 'bout joining church early."

With everything that had transpired, it felt so long ago now. "It's puzzlin' what happened to change his mind on that, other than becoming too interested in the world." She sighed. "I wish Even were like you, following the path of peace."

Sol took a swig of his pop. "Evan will certainly regret being non-resistant."

"How could he not?" She stared at her last piece of cookie. "I think my parents are worried 'bout the shame it'll bring on our family. But even more so 'bout the possibility of losin' Evan in battle." Her voice broke.

"I'm so sorry, Ellie. I shouldn't have brought him up."

She shook her head, unable to speak.

Sol stood there with her at the refreshment table as Ellie finished eating her cookie. Then he excused himself, still looking concerned as he left for the other side of the haymow to hang out with the fellows. His seeking her out here at Singing was another surprise—the first time they'd talked since their conversation at the volleyball game. But it seemed obvious he wanted to discuss their mutual loss of Leah and the family heartache over Evan's painful decision.

She could see Yonnie and Katie waiting over near the barn entrance, as Menno walked toward her smiling. *We'll have a nice time*, she thought.

The following evening, Ruthann arrived in her father's gray carriage in time for dessert. Since Evan hadn't stayed around for dessert, Ellie went into the hallway to the side door to greet her like Evan usually did.

"Hullo there, cousin," Ruthann said, smiling. "These'll melt if we don't eat 'em right away."

"*Kumme en*," Ellie said. "Dawdi will be so happy to see ya . . . and have some of your amazing fudge!"

"He does enjoy sweets," Ruthann said, heading inside as Ellie held the screen door.

Mamm's eyes lit up to see Ruthann with her tasty offering. Since the house had been much too warm to bake today, Mamm had brought out only a few leftover cookies. "It's so *gut* to see ya," she said, and Dawdi's eyes suddenly brightened.

"Evan will be sorry he didn't stay around," Dat said in a flat tone.

Ruthann frowned empathetically but said nothing.

"I'll get some milk for us," Mamm said, rising. "It would've been nice to have ice cream ready, but . . . this'll do."

"No apologies necessary," Ruthann said, then sat across the table from Ellie, next to Evan's vacant spot.

"Say now, Ruthann," said Dawdi, "did I ever tell ya 'bout the time when, as a youngster, I painted horseshoes and sold 'em at our roadside stand for a little bit of nothin'?"

Ruthann shook her head. "I don't think so."

Ellie couldn't help but smile. Here was another story from Dawdi's brimming memory bank.

"Well, one year at Christmastime," he began, "I made a wreath for the schoolteacher out of painted red and green horseshoes. Bless her heart, bein' the city girl she was, I doubt she knew what to think." Dawdi paused to laugh. "All the same, she held it up for the class to see and announced to all, '*Somebody's horse is trotting around in his socks.*'"

Ruthann burst out laughing, and Mamm shook her head, smiling.

Ellie asked, "Dawdi, are ya sure you're not just pullin' our legs?"

"Say now, I know this one's true," Dat said, vouching for Dawdi. "I heard 'bout it many times from your Mammi Hostetler growin' up."

"Come to think of it, I might still have one of 'em horseshoe wreaths lying round in the attic somewheres," Dawdi said, looking more serious now. "*Jah,* 'tis every bit true."

Ellie wished Evan was present to hear this. She was grateful Dawdi's incomparable humor remained intact despite the perpetual cloud hanging over their family.

13

After picking peaches all day Thursday, Ellie saw a fat envelope waiting for her when she came into the house for supper. She waited till she'd dried the dishes, then opened the envelope and found the longest letter Leah had ever written to her.

Out on the back porch, Ellie settled into the comfortable glider and began to read.

Dear Ellie,

I love hearing from you every week. It's one of the sweet connections I have to home. I'm so thankful for you and Mamma and Sol and everyone who continues to answer my letters.

I've been thinking a lot about the likelihood Evan will have to join the army, so I'm praying more often now for your family. Please keep me updated!

Also, I think it's time to share with you just what happened between Josh and me back before I came here. No one except Josh knows that I was the one who broke things off. I was heartbroken, like I told you, but things couldn't go on as they

106

were. Josh had privately told me that he wasn't sure he could be Amish for life—he'd actually had a few discussions with Evan about that, all without anyone else knowing, Josh said. I'm sure that'll come as a surprise to you, too.

Difficult as it was to break up with him, how could we keep courting once I was aware of his true feelings? And many of the youth—and maybe even you—probably thought I took this job so far from home because I was jilted. Between you and me, I still do care for Josh, but I'll have to get over him sooner or later. There just isn't a way forward for us.

With Baptism Sunday coming up soon, just know that it makes me sad to miss out on witnessing you make your lifelong vow to God and the church. And, honestly, I wish I could follow through with the instruction and be baptized alongside you, like we'd always planned, instead of waiting till I return home. Even so, I do believe I did the right thing by coming to help Carolyn and the children, who've become nearly like family to me.

Every day I read the verses we were studying in baptism class, and I pray faithfully, too, so don't worry that my time here is pulling me away from the People.

You'll also be happy to hear that little Bobby can say the Lord's Prayer without help now. And he's been teaching it to his mother and wee sisters. I've taught him to sing "Jesus Loves the Little Children," too.

Ellie's face broke into a smile. "That's *wunnerbaar*," she said out loud.

By the way, Carolyn has been very respectful about the fact that I'm Plain—she's never asked me to dress fancy, and the children don't seem to mind, either. Can you imagine me in Englischers' clothing? I certainly can't!

I also want you to know that I can definitely get away for a Thanksgiving visit—if only for a few days. Carolyn's parents are traveling from Tennessee to celebrate with her and the children here, so I'll be free to come home, at last! I'm afraid it'll be hard to leave again, though.

"She's comin' for sure," Ellie whispered, delighted. She read the last pages, which focused mainly on Leah's activities with the children—shopping for fall clothes and shoes, visiting the library every other week, and playing at a nearby park. And Leah had recently helped the children make cards for their mother's upcoming birthday.

Ellie finished reading the letter, then headed around to the side door. The screen door flew open, and Evan rushed out.

"*Ach*, such a hurry! *Dummel dich net!*" she said.

"Sorry. Runnin' late," he called over his shoulder after hurrying past her.

"To see Cheryl again?"

Evan stopped in his tracks and turned around. "She's become very special to me, Ellie."

"But she ain't Amish."

Evan shook his head.

"Is she interested in the Plain life?"

"Are ya kidding?" He grimaced. "She won't even ride in my buggy!"

Ellie briefly wondered how they got around or if they only visited at her house.

"She wants to see me as much as possible before I leave for boot camp."

"How will ya know when you'll be goin'?"

"Well, Cheryl said Jack had to leave about a month after he received his induction notice."

"So you'll be around for a while yet. That's *gut*." Ellie felt a measure of relief. "We'll get to spend some time together."

Evan frowned. "Maybe not so much as ya want. Dat thinks I'm a bad influence."

"He said that?"

"I can just tell."

"But you're *mei* Bruder."

"We're a world apart now, Ellie." He sounded almost sad.

"Well, who's responsible for that?" She barely got the words out.

"You're joinin' church, and I'm joinin' the army." He looked at the ground and scuffed his shoe against the grass. "Don't hate me for spreadin' my wings."

"I could never hate ya," she whispered. "But I still don't understand." She gritted her teeth so she wouldn't cry as he turned and hurried toward the carriage shed.

After Bible reading and prayers with her parents and Dawdi that evening, Ellie stayed in the front room and told Mamm about Leah's letter. "When she said she hated missing my baptism vow, it brought tears to my eyes."

Her mother listened, nodding. "Her heart will be with yours on that day, I'm sure."

"It just feels like I'm movin' ahead without her."

Mamm blinked slowly as she studied her. "Baptism is a result of your *own* heart's desire to follow the Lord, Ellie. Not Leah's, nor anyone else's. When you kneel before Bishop Mast in front of the congregation, your vow will be between you and almighty God."

Ellie dabbed at her eyes.

"I pray this will be a testimony to Evan, if he hasn't already left for military training by then," Mamm added.

Hearing this, Ellie fished for a hankie in her pocket. "I hope he's still home, Mamm," she said. "But will he even attend if he is?"

Her mother reached to hold her, soothing her.

Lyle had settled into bed, pillows behind him as he sat listening to Elisabeth talk about Ellie's upcoming baptism. It was clear his wife was concerned about their daughter's sadness as she missed Leah and fretted about the possibility Evan wouldn't even go if he was still home by then.

"Ellie has reason to worry 'bout Evan," Elisabeth said while brushing out her long hair. "My sister Miriam saw him walking along the road with the young Herr girl the other evening."

Lyle groaned. *It goes from bad to worse.*

Elisabeth looked away, tearing up as worry seemed to consume her.

It pained him to see his wife like this. Her concerns about Evan kept her up at night, causing her to toss about in bed. Sometimes she even got up and went downstairs for a few hours.

"Evan's like a branch in the wind, swept about in all directions," Lyle said, struggling to say the right thing. "And mighty confused, too, is what I think."

Elisabeth slipped on her bathrobe and then sat in one of the chairs near their window.

"Not tired yet, dear?" Lyle asked.

"Think I'll sit a while and look out at the stars and pray."

"Want some company?" he asked, swinging his legs over the side of the bed.

She murmured and shook her head.

Sighing, he got back under the sheet. He would comfort her later, when she was ready. "We'll get through this with God's help," he said softly, closing his eyes in prayer.

14

At their father's request, Ellie went with Evan to make peach deliveries in the market wagon. These trips were one of her brother's regular responsibilities, and though he didn't say, Ellie imagined Dat was thinking she might be able to make them once Evan was gone. Maybe Evan thought so, too. It was already the twentieth of August, so it probably wouldn't be much longer before he had to leave.

This was the first she'd done this, though, so at each location Evan introduced her as his sister.

"Do ya ever wish we could purchase more land to expand the orchard?" she asked him between two of their stops.

"Can't say I have." Her twin glanced at her from the driver's seat, the reins practically resting on his knees as he held on. "Why do ya ask?"

"I've been thinkin' how nice it'd be to plant plum and cherry trees . . . if some land became available."

"All our surrounding neighbors are Amish farmers."

Which means they'll pass the land down to their children, she thought, still wishing Evan might toss the idea around with her. But he remained silent, his mind apparently on other things.

"S'pose you'll be seein' Cheryl Herr again this weekend," she said in an attempt to draw him out.

"I want to see her as often as I can before I leave."

Ellie was still surprised at his strong attachment to Cheryl, fancy as the young woman was. She compared it to her and Menno's experience of double-dating with not only Sol and Ruthann but Yonnie and Katie, too.

"She says she'll wait for me till I return in two years."

"Two years is a big commitment."

"For sure, and no girl's ever cared for me like that."

"Well, you've never gone to war before."

"*Nee*, but just think of what she's doin' . . . for me."

Ellie pondered that. "So you're sure Cheryl has absolutely no interest in becomin' Amish?"

"*Puh!* Never! I told ya already."

"Our parents aren't going to like it if ya continue on with an *Englischer*, Evan. And ya know that Dat's expectin' you to take over as the orchard's manager when he retires."

"He won't let me forget. Another big challenge."

Ellie shook her head, ever so sad for him—yet frustrated, too.

"Dawdi, Dat, our siblings . . . nearly everyone I know 'cept Cheryl has tried to steer me in a different direction."

"Doesn't Cheryl worry 'bout you goin' to fight in the war?"

Evan glanced at Ellie. "Actually, she wishes I'd asked for CO status like Chuck urged me to. But she's not poundin' away at it like everyone else seems to. She's not like that."

Miserable, Ellie sighed. What more could she say?

Two days later, while taking a quick break from picking peaches, Ellie strolled down their shady lane to get the mail. As she retrieved the letters from their big black mailbox, she noticed at the very top an important-looking envelope with the words *Official Business* in the upper left-hand corner and *Selective Service Board* written beneath that. It was addressed to Mr. Evan Hostetler. She felt like she'd been kicked in the stomach as she strode back to the house, suspecting what might be inside. How long before her brother had to leave?

She chose not to take the letter out to the orchard for Evan. For one thing, she didn't know precisely where he was picking peaches, and for another, she didn't want to be the one to give it to him.

Once inside the house, Ellie placed the mail on the kitchen table and returned to the orchard, strapping on her harvesting crate. She was thankful for the cloud cover now, hot as it had been. She could hear Midnight and Shadow, Benjamin Bontrager's German shepherds, barking two farms away, and her thoughts flew to Leah. *I'll write her a letter later tonight*, she thought, needing to share her thoughts with her friend.

Lyle was thankful that numerous customers had purchased the day's fresh peaches and freshly baked pies and cobblers at their family's store. At closing, he hurried across the side yard and into the kitchen hallway, where he removed his shoes and socks in the utility room he'd built years ago at Elisabeth's request. The outer room with a deep sink and ample space for shoes and outerwear was one way to keep the orchard dirt from tracking into the kitchen. For good measure, he'd also put in a bathroom just steps away.

Once the Saturday clientele had begun to thin out, Elisabeth had returned to the house to prepare supper. He watched her now as she placed a large bowl of cold macaroni salad on the table before returning to the woodstove. She had grilled ham and cheese sandwiches with help from Ellie, who was slicing fresh tomatoes from their garden. Meanwhile, Evan stood at the opposite end of the kitchen, opening a letter.

Observing his son with some trepidation—Evan rarely received mail—Lyle took his seat at the head of the table and folded his hands, waiting for his family to be seated.

Elisabeth wiped her hands on her work apron and reached behind her to untie it, then came to sit on Lyle's right.

"Isn't Daed eating with us tonight?" he asked her.

"Oh, he's havin' supper with Enos."

Lyle knew that Daed was fond of his recently widowed younger brother. Anytime he was invited for a meal, or for the day, he was more than happy to go.

Ellie sat down to the right of her mother. "Supper's on the table," she announced, looking over at her brother.

Bringing the letter to the table, Evan placed it near Lyle's plate. "Well, guess it's official. I've been drafted into the United States Army," he said as he took his seat to Lyle's left.

"Let's bow for prayer," Lyle said, frustrated that Evan had practically pushed the draft notice under his nose. Nevertheless, he somehow managed to direct thoughts of gratitude to God for this provision of food set before them.

When the prayer was finished, he cleared his throat and raised his head to see Evan staring at the induction notice.

"Son?"

"*Ach,* sorry." Evan tapped the letter. "I'm to report for my physical on Monday, September twenty-first, at the Military

Entrance Processing Station in Harrisburg," he said casually. "If I'm fit enough, I'll go directly to basic training from there."

Lyle couldn't respond immediately, light-headed as he felt. This was the last thing he wanted to discuss during supper.

Seemingly unfazed, Evan picked up his hot sandwich and leaned over his plate to bite into it.

At last, Lyle said, "We'll be lookin' to hear from ya as soon as you can get word home to us, son."

"At least you have another whole month here with us," Elisabeth added.

Ellie was staring at Evan now. "I still can't believe this is happening."

Elisabeth looked like she might cry.

In a short while, Evan slid off the bench and headed upstairs.

Lyle couldn't help seeing Ellie's lower lip quiver.

Elisabeth slipped her arm around her. "May the dear Lord help our family," his wife whispered, her eyes filling with tears.

Upstairs, a door closed, and Lyle reached for Elisabeth's free hand, shut his eyes, and breathed a prayer very different from the table blessing.

Later, after supper, Lyle picked up the letter with the ominous and official-looking letterhead. *Correspondence from the world*, he thought as his eyes fell on the date for Evan's military physical and induction in Harrisburg. Then, leaving the letter where he'd found it, he exited the stifling kitchen, needing some fresh air. Much as he wanted to, he wouldn't go upstairs to talk to Evan, secluded in his room and likely as resistant to conversation as he'd been since the night of the lottery drawing.

No point in it, Lyle thought.

He plodded outdoors and headed toward the orchard, gazing at the sky, still bright. *How did we get here, Lord?*

After a time, he returned to the side yard and wondered if Daed might be back from his brother's place. Going to the *Dawdi Haus*, Lyle opened the screen door and called to him, but there was no answer. Then walking over to the carriage shed, Lyle saw that the spot for the spring wagon was still vacant.

Looking up the hill toward the Bontrager farm, Lyle was drawn to it. He wanted to talk to another man—a father who'd successfully reared his sons in the faith. Sighing several times, he meandered through his own meadow as if in a stupor. He tried to keep his wits enough to pray a significant prayer, but when that became a struggle, he realized he was already tramping through the next neighbor's cornfield. At all costs, he wanted to avoid walking along the road, weary of church members averting their gaze as they passed by, even a few of his and Elisabeth's kinfolk here lately.

The breeze at that moment was a welcome respite from the heat, and Lyle pushed his straw hat forward to shield his face from the sun's rays as the clouds moved in.

Ellie had seen her Dat wandering through the pasture, his shoulders slumped and his gait heavy and slow. She'd asked her mother if he was all right, and Mamm had shaken her head. "I daresay we're all in pieces" came her reply.

Ellie recalled what Dawdi had said about Evan while they drank root beer at his house. *"He might need to know that your love for him is constant in spite of his poor behavior."* She mentioned this to Mamm.

"He's quite right, I daresay. And I believe your Dat is torn between that and wanting to make Evan see the folly of his ways."

"Seems to be takin' its toll on poor Dat. I wish there was somethin' I could do to make all of this better."

Mamm opened her arms to hug her. "We'll stick together and cast this burden on the Lord."

Later, after Dat had returned and led family Bible reading and prayer—without Evan, who'd once again left the house—Ellie slipped off to her room and opened her heart to Leah, ever so far away.

Dear Leah,

How are you doing?

I know it's been a short while since my last letter, but I need to tell you some troubling things. Honestly, I wish I could talk to you face-to-face. While I was thinking about everything that's happened today, I knew I should write to you right away. If I wait too long, the gloom of it all might make me feel like burrowing into a hole somewhere. I really don't know how else to describe what I'm feeling.

You see, Evan received his draft notice from the army today. I've said all I can think of to him, so I'm plain numb now.

I hope that for your sake and mine, you have happier news when you write, Leah. For one thing, you must be relieved that your brother Sol is a devout young man and already baptized, following God and the Old Ways of our forefathers. If only Evan was that earnest.

Ellie set down her pen and rose from the desk, then meandered down the two flights of stairs to the kitchen. From the open window, she could hear Dat talking on the back porch as she poured cold water from the faucet into a tumbler and then drank nearly half of it.

She recognized Evan's voice now, and it sounded like they

were discussing orchard-related things. She wondered at their apparent calmness.

Who will take Evan's place while he's gone? she thought as she headed back to her room. She picked up the pen and letter she'd written to Leah and sat on the bed to read through it. Without enough pleasant news to share this time, she decided to simply sign off.

After closing her door, she removed the bobby pins from her hair bun and let it down. She shook out her lengthy tresses and brushed them with long strokes, watching the reddish half moon rise on the horizon line.

15

In the fourth week of August, the peach harvest coincided for ten days with the start of Golden Supreme apples, and a week or so after that, the sweet Galas. This was "the overlap," as Ellie's father often referred to those hectic days, which meant a new crew of apple pickers joined the crew of peach pickers who had been working for weeks. Menno was one of those who showed up just after dawn, and while Ellie had her own chores making apple pies, fritters, and cider for the family store and market, she was aware of Menno's attentive gaze each time she glanced his way. This made her smile, as she enjoyed her time with him, though they were still only double-dating.

During one of the overlap days, Ellie was driving the smaller horse-drawn wagon with bushels of apples to the cider shed, and Sol was coming from the other end of the orchard in the spring wagon with more bushels to unload. He halted Nelly and jumped out to tie the mare to the hitching post in front of the shed.

Spotting Ellie, Sol came around and looked up at her. "Let me haul them in for ya."

"*Denki*, but ain't necessary." She walked along with him to deposit the first bushel with Rudy, who was already turning the cast-iron wheel and grinding another big batch of apples Dat and his crew had brought in earlier. Mamm had hosed them off and was feeding the newly washed apples into the hopper.

Sol headed back down the wood ramp for more bushels and quickly returned.

Ellie thanked him again.

"Anytime," Sol said before turning to go out for more.

"Someone's mighty attentive," Rudy said, grinning at her.

"He just likes to help" was all Ellie said. She sure didn't want to get tongues wagging about her and Sol being too friendly. It wouldn't be right. And besides, it wasn't true. Not really.

Ellie suddenly awakened during the night and heard the patter of rain on the roof. Often when rain showers came, she relished the comforting sound in her room. And sometimes, if it was warm enough outdoors, she'd creep downstairs and sit on the porch in her bathrobe, breathing in the wonderful earthy scent of the rain.

Once, soon after moving into this uppermost bedroom, she'd spotted a leak and hurried downstairs to get a bucket from the utility room, then fell asleep to the steady *drip, drip*. In the morning, she let Dat know, and he and Evan got out the extension ladder and patched the roof.

Now she drowsily sat up in bed and contemplated Leah's thoughtful letter from a while back, her heart reaching across the miles to her friend. *Leah wishes she could have continued with baptism instruction*, she thought, getting out of bed. On bare tiptoes, she crossed the hardwood floor, where she paced the length of her room and back to the steady rhythm of the thrumming rain.

A few minutes later, she saw a light flash outside and moved to a dormer window to check. Over near the carriage shed, she could see Evan leading Cupcake to the stable, his flashlight pointing the way.

It's so late, she thought, recalling his surprising comment that Cheryl Herr said she would wait for him to return home.

After Ellie's morning chores, she put on her harvest bag to help pick apples and spotted Menno working with Evan and Titus farther up the row. Menno smiled at her broadly, and she smiled back, glad things had worked out for him to be a part-time picker again.

Later, when she was emptying her apples into bushel baskets, she noticed Dawdi Hezekiah heading her way. "Are ya comin' to pick with me?" she asked.

"For a while," he said, his shoulder straps already hooked to a long gray harvesting bag like those the other pickers used. His silver-white bangs peeked out from beneath his straw hat, and he was wearing his old frayed black suspenders. "Remember when I first showed ya how to know when an apple's close to its peak of ripeness?"

"*Jah*. I was only four. You told me to hold the bottom of the apple, then lift it up against the stem and twist. If it comes off, it's ready. If not, it needs more time to ripen."

Dawdi chuckled. "'Tis a mighty happy memory, teachin' ya that day."

"I was the same age as the young boy Leah Bontrager takes care of in Chambersburg."

"Really, now?"

Ellie mentioned that Leah had taught Bobby to say the Lord's Prayer and sing "Jesus Loves the Little Children." "Isn't that *wunnerbaar?*"

Dawdi was quiet for a moment, then said, "Well, that prayer and the little song might just change the youngster's life."

"Maybe his family's, too, opening their hearts to God," Ellie added, thankful for Leah's strong faith.

"We can pray so."

Ellie's cloth bag was getting heavy again, so she walked up to the spring wagon, breathing in the fresh, fruity scent of the pretty red and green apples, and carefully emptied her harvest into a partially filled box. Then she returned to Dawdi.

After picking for a while longer, Dawdi poured his bagful into one of the many bushel baskets, then placed the basket on the spring wagon. When he returned with his empty harvest bag, he wiped his brow with his blue paisley handkerchief.

"What have you been up to lately, Dawdi? I've noticed you've been heading out some evenings."

He gave a nod. "*Jah.* I've been building my coffin over at Rudy's place, and it's nearly done."

"*Ach,* I'd hoped ya'd forgotten 'bout that."

"Figured ya might." Dawdi gave her a little smile as he reached for the empty bag and hooked his shoulder straps into it. "The undertaker is scheduled to come for it in a few days and store it for me. Or maybe one of my brothers'll need it— we're all 'bout the same height, ya know—whoever the Lord calls home first."

"Aww, Dawdi. It's just hard for me to joke 'bout. Ain't 'cause I don't care. It's 'cause I *do.*"

He reached to pick an especially large apple, then placed it gently in his bag. "Preparation for *life* is just as important. And also what you'll be doin' on Baptism Sunday next month, makin' the most precious and holy vow there is."

Captured by the urgency in his voice, she looked at him, this kindhearted and compassionate man who would do anything for her. *And anything for the Lord and His people.*

"Just think what our Savior gave up—all the glory of heaven—to come to this old world. And like you and me, He came as a newborn babe. To think He lived a mighty short thirty-three-year life and then willingly surrendered it up to Calvary's cross . . ." Dawdi inhaled slowly. "Makes ya want to give all your days to Him. Every breath till the very last."

"I certainly do, Dawdi."

"Just remember, when ya take your kneeling vow before *Gott* and the People, I'll be relivin' my own baptism, so long ago." He paused to look at her with tender eyes.

Nodding solemnly, she gazed at the trees laden with beautiful apples—this orchard that had always pointed her toward the heavenly Father. *His presence is ever near*, she thought. *How blessed I am . . . and so grateful!*

After breakfast dishes were done the next morning, Ellie hurried through her household chores of dusting, sweeping, and redding up, wanting to pick the last of the peaches with Evan.

She remembered the verse in Hebrews she'd read during her devotions that morning: *Jesus Christ the same yesterday, and to day, and for ever.*

Our faithful Savior doesn't change, she thought, heartened. *I can depend on Him.*

Later, when she found Evan working with Menno, Ellie kept walking up the grassy pathway, searching for a tree that needed harvesting.

"Ellie!" Menno called to her. "I'll trade places with ya, if you wanna pick with Evan."

Surprised that he seemed to know why she'd come, she turned around. "Okay." She headed back toward them. "*Denki.*"

"Anytime," Menno said, then scooted away.

He understands I want to spend as much time with Evan as possible, she thought, smiling at her brother as he reached for a high branch. She waited for him to speak first, keeping her focus on the harvesting for a good ten minutes before he finally did.

"I came off rude the day we went to town makin' deliveries together. I'm sorry, Ellie."

She nodded her acceptance. "It was *gut* we could talk even for a little while."

Evan smiled. "*Jah,* and I *do* think it'd be nice to have plum and cherry trees, so ya should talk to Dat 'bout it."

"I'll sure miss pickin' with ya out here," she said, feeling the urge to tell him important things before he left instead of waiting to write them in a letter.

"I'll miss ya, too, Ellie." Her twin placed two peaches in the harvesting box strapped to his shoulders. "But I won't be gone forever."

She dared not ask if he meant he'd be coming home to live, concerned he might instead continue his relationship with Cheryl Herr and join the ranks of the fancy folk.

"Remember, we have right now," Evan surprised her by saying.

"I'm so glad." She moved around the other side of the peach tree. "And I wanna make the best of it."

She paused to take in God's masterful work of fruit trees and sun and sky as a gentle breeze stirred the leaves. She realized there was peace right here in the midst of this heavenly sort of place, despite the unpredictable storm churning around her family.

16

Lyle opened the door to his barn office the next morning and headed outside, across the yard to the side entrance of the house. Elisabeth had been on his mind ever since he'd noticed how withdrawn she was at breakfast, not herself at all. So he'd suggested Ellie go to market with Rudy in her stead.

He found his wife chopping celery in the kitchen, looking a bit pale. When she glanced up, he noticed puffy little pockets under her blue eyes. She offered him something cold to drink, but he declined and sat at the head of the table. "*Kumme*, sit with me," he said. "Rest a little."

She set down the knife and wandered over.

"I'm concerned 'bout ya," he said as she sat and leaned her elbows on the table, sighing.

"I'd be fine if I could just get a full night's sleep," she replied softly.

He nodded, in tune with his bride of thirty-eight years. "Evan's on your mind, ain't?" Lyle reached for her hand. "The Lord knows the beginning and the end, and He'll take care of our boy."

"Even though Evan's outside the fold?" Her eyes were gleaming as tears threatened.

"Like Daed says, we must give this to God." He squeezed her hand. "Worryin' could make ya sick, love."

She smiled weakly. "No time for that round here."

"Well, listen, you just take whatever time ya need to rest. I'll massage your feet and your back tonight at bedtime."

Elisabeth nodded. "All right, and I'll take some honey beforehand. Maybe drink some warm milk, too."

"*Gut* idea." He glanced at the chopping block. "Now, how 'bout I finish cuttin' up that celery for ya."

"That's all right, dear. I'll do it."

"After the noon meal, a short nap might do ya *gut*."

"Then I won't sleep for sure tonight."

"Well, when the twins were babies, remember how you had to sleep whenever you could?"

"Such a long time ago." Elisabeth smiled with a sweet sigh. "I'd give almost anything to have them snuggled in my arms again."

"I know ya would," he said, wishing there was something more he could do for her right now.

They heard the side door open. "The vet's in the stable ready to check on Nelly and Captain," Rudy called in. "Got my work boots on, so I won't come in."

"I'll be right there. Almost forgot." Lyle rose and offered his hand to Elisabeth, who took it and stood. "*Ich liebe dich*," he whispered, then kissed her cheek.

"I love ya, too." She embraced him, and he wrapped his arms around her.

The day before Baptism Sunday in mid-September had been very busy, and Ellie was ready to settle in for the night. She walked up the two long flights of stairs to prepare for bed. Then, closing the door behind her, she noticed a note lying on her pillow. When she picked it up, she saw it was Mamm's handwriting.

Dear Ellie,
    Your Dat and I are so thankful you want to join the family of God. May you always remember how blessed you are to serve our Lord and Savior Jesus Christ.

                        We love you dearly,
                        Mamma and Dat

Ellie pressed the note to her chest and then carried it to the dresser, where she placed it next to her handheld mirror. *Mamm's so thoughtful.*

After an early breakfast of cold cereal and fruit, Ellie was delighted to see Evan hurry downstairs after chores, dressed for church. *He's coming after all,* she thought, truly grateful.

Evan said nothing as he headed out to help Dat hitch up Captain to the family carriage, but she'd noticed the dark circles under his eyes. Was he out late again last night? Then she remembered what Dat often said—that they must take each day as it comes.

O Lord in heaven, let my baptism today be a witness to my brother, Ellie prayed silently as she placed her crisp white *Kapp* on her head.

Turning, she saw her mother coming through the kitchen with the loveliest smile and wearing her for-good black dress, cape, and apron. Together, they made their way outside.

Lyle kept his head bowed during the long second sermon, praying something the minister was saying might strike a chord in Evan's hardened heart. He'd prayed similarly during each and every Sunday Preaching since Evan had declared he wouldn't fight the draft.

Following that sermon, Bishop Mast called for the baptismal candidates to kneel in front of the congregation—five young women and nine young men in all. Each candidate was addressed by the bishop, who asked if, with the eunuch in Acts chapter eight, they confessed that Jesus Christ is the Son of God.

When Ellie answered, Lyle could hear the emotion in her voice. He had to cough to keep from tearing up, so touched was he by his youngest daughter's meek and tenderhearted response.

The bishop then asked, "Do you acknowledge and submit to this church and its fellowship of believers?"

Ellie answered in the affirmative, as did the other candidates.

"And from this day forward, do you renounce the world, your own flesh, and the devil, and desire to live in obedience to only Jesus Christ, who gave His very lifeblood for you?"

When Ellie and each of the other candidates had responded again, Bishop Mast recited from the prayer book as the People rose to their feet. "These young people desire to live for the Lord in this consecrated and godly fellowship." He ended by saying that they had consented with gladness to put their faith in the holy Gospel and to obey its teachings.

Later, after the congregation was again seated, the time came for Ellie's actual baptism. The bishop cupped his hands on the hair just in front of her *Kapp* while the deacon poured a small amount of water into them. The bishop released the water and pronounced, "I baptize you in the name of the Father, the Son, and the Holy Ghost."

Again, Lyle was deeply moved. He hadn't been this emotional during any of his older children's baptisms.

He thought again of Evan's rebellion. *When we're young, life tricks us into thinking we have plenty of time.* Lyle shuddered at the thought.

After helping Mamm pin the washing to the line the next morning, Ellie mailed the letter to Leah she'd written the day before. In it, she had shared every detail of her baptism and how close to the Lord she'd felt.

While she cared for other chores, she thought about Evan asking her how it felt to kneel before the bishop.

"I felt so warm all over . . . and tears came to my eyes," she'd answered. "I know I belong to Jesus now. It's such a blessin' to me."

Quiet, Evan had seemed to study her.

The following Saturday afternoon, a long, newsy letter arrived from Leah, thanking Ellie for writing about that never-to-be-forgotten Baptism Sunday. *You made it so easy to picture*

everything you shared about joining church. Leah also wrote that an Amish family from market had volunteered to pick her up for their Preaching service every other week, so she was finally able to attend church again.

I'm so glad, Ellie thought, happy to hear that Leah was enjoying fellowship with some of the People out there.

17

The following Monday, Ellie rose early to kneel beside her bed as usual. It was the day of Evan's scheduled departure for his physical and induction, and like on each of the days leading up to this one, she asked God to help her brother survive the war.

After the prayer, she read from her Bible, then dressed and raised her window shades to look out at the acres of fruit trees while winding her hair neatly into its usual thick bun. "Two long years without Evan," she murmured.

His future role as orchard manager was "up in the air now," Mamm had told her yesterday with a somber look. Ellie had assumed Dat and Jonah would oversee things, though with the recent huddles she'd seen between the two, she had to wonder what would be decided. *I have some ideas to discuss with Dat, too.*

Downstairs, Ellie discovered a hot breakfast casserole made with ham, scrambled eggs, shredded potatoes, and cheese topped by a hearty white sauce. It didn't surprise her that Mamm had risen extra early to make this special farewell breakfast. Despite their concern, her parents had not changed one iota in showing compassion toward their wayward son.

After the tasty breakfast, Ellie asked Evan to go into the front room with her. There, she handed him an envelope. "Open it when ya get settled in at Fort Polk, okay?"

He grimaced. "I didn't write anything for you."

"It's just some late-night thoughts," she told him. "You'll write me when ya can."

"Well, there won't be much time for letter writing the first two weeks of boot camp, I'm afraid."

"I can wait." She nodded, a lump in her throat. "I'll be prayin' for you every day."

He smiled fleetingly and placed the envelope in a zippered pouch on the outside of his duffel bag. "Take care of yourself, Ellie."

"You too." She'd barely eked out the words.

He frowned suddenly. "I'm not too sure how an Amish guy's gonna fit in with . . ." He pressed his lips together hard.

"Oh, Evan . . ." She reached to quickly hug him.

He straightened and seemed to gather his wits. "S'pose I should go say good-bye to the rest of the family."

She bit her lip, staying there as Evan left the front room. Then, hearing him talking to their parents and Dawdi out in the kitchen, she moved to the front windows and stared out at the sad gray sky, waiting. Evan had let them know Cheryl was coming to drive him to the bus station.

How will our days be without him?

While Evan was saying good-bye to his mother and grandfather in the kitchen, Lyle grabbed his sweater from the utility room and pulled it on. Then he buttoned it up as he headed out the side door with his youngest son, down the porch steps, and across the yard.

Unexpectedly, Evan paused and turned to face him. "I don't want ya worried 'bout me, Dat."

"*Nee*," Lyle said, even though he felt a tearing in his heart. "I'll be prayin', though . . . never doubt it." With that, he clamped his hand solidly on Evan's shoulder. "Every day, son, I'll ask the Lord for your safe homecomin' and for Him to help ya find your way back to Him and the People."

Straight-faced, Evan gave a swift nod, then turned toward the lane tall and erect, his shoulders squared.

Lyle drew a ragged breath and stared at his son's back, stamping the image on his memory. "Keep in touch when ya can," he called.

When a car pulled up, Evan turned briefly and raised his hand to wave. Then he opened the back door and threw in his bag before slipping in to the front passenger seat. The car sped away.

Clenching his teeth, Lyle stood there, heart pounding. When he turned toward the house, he saw Ellie at the front window, her forehead pressed against the pane. He looked away lest she was crying and trudged up the porch steps to the side entrance.

He found Elisabeth not in the kitchen but sitting in the front room, one hand covering her face. He went to her and, leaning over, kissed her cheek. "Evan's on his way." He assumed Daed had returned to the *Dawdi Haus*.

Elisabeth looked up at him, her face marked with tears.

"How's Ellie?" he asked. "Saw her at the window." He knelt beside her chair.

"She ran upstairs just now." Elisabeth leaned her head against his for the longest time. "*Gut* thing I'm caught up on my chores," she said. "I have not a speck of energy left."

"What can I get for you? Anything from the kitchen? Warm tea, maybe?"

She wiped tears away. "I'll just sit here a while."

"Well, if you're sure . . ."

Nodding, she smiled weakly. "Why not let the others do the harvesting today, Lyle? They'll understand."

"It'll do me *gut* to do my share." Slowly, he rose and left the room, then made his way through the length of the house, pausing to look at Evan's spot at the kitchen table.

Three days had passed with no word from Evan. Lyle hadn't really expected any, but as each day ticked by, the silence began to weigh on him. How was Evan holding up? What was he experiencing?

Curious, Lyle had visited the library a few days ago to read about what took place during army basic training. Getting into physical shape was one priority, and Evan was certainly already that. But the tactical and survival skills, the marching and rappelling, the military customs, and the shooting—it would all be foreign to his son. Really, Lyle would rather not ponder any of it for long.

He hadn't checked the book out to bring home lest Elisabeth fret when she saw it. Sometimes what a person didn't know was easier, he'd decided. Especially when, in the case of his wife, certain concerns tended to play over and over in the deep of night, causing sleeplessness—something she'd been struggling with for too long. So Lyle had read as much as he could at the library—a stop while in town to pick up more bushel baskets for this harvest season and next year's.

No one need know how heavyhearted he felt, most of all his precious wife.

Ellie was thankful her time was taken up with the autumn apple harvest, including helping to wash apples and jug cider with Mamm and Rudy and sometimes Dat, too. They wanted to have plenty of gallons in the cold cellar for their store customers.

But Evan's leaving remained heavy on her mind, and when she found a letter in the mailbox from him addressed to Dat and Mamm, she ran up the long driveway and into the house.

A big smile spread across Mamm's rosy cheeks when Ellie handed it to her, and she quickly opened the envelope, standing right there at the sink to read the few lines he'd written.

"Evan says he arrived and is just fine," Mamm finally told her. "Says he'll write more later . . . and he thanks you for your thoughtful send-off note."

At this news, Ellie was eager to write to Evan, grateful to now have his return address. Truth be known, she was still pondering the strangeness of his final words to her, when he suddenly wondered how he'd fit in with the other men.

Ellie hadn't told anyone about her and Evan's private good-bye, although there had been an opportunity to share it with Cousin Ruthann. She'd dropped by the evening of Evan's departure, bringing an angel food cake with strawberry preserves for the topping. Ellie had also talked briefly with Sol earlier that evening, after he'd brought in the spring wagon filled with ladders and empty crates. Sol had asked how she was doing, but he never mentioned Evan's parting.

That was implied, she thought as she looked back to their conversation now.

She *had* managed to keep how she'd felt that morning to herself, shielding others from knowing it seemed nearly like a betrayal to her for Evan to have abandoned the teaching of his childhood. *Leaving Amish life behind . . .*

Ellie mailed a letter to Evan the following Monday. She wondered when she might hear from him. How busy was he at basic training?

Only recently had Jonah told her that when Dat paid Evan for his work just before he left, he had included a generous amount extra. *Another kind deed from Dat in spite of the circumstances,* she thought, glad for her father's kind heart.

18

A full week later, October fifth, Ellie still had no reply from Evan. But she had decided to try something new.

Without telling her father, she headed to town with a dozen bushels of apples, making a beeline for a restaurant that had been open less than a year. She prayed that God would help her have a winning way with the owner, like Evan always seemed to with their accounts. Once she got over her nerves and even offered apple samples to taste, the amenable middle-aged man purchased three bushels on the spot. He also asked to be on their regular customer list, then suggested another larger restaurant she might want to stop by. "My cousin's place," he said. "Be sure to tell him I sent you."

Greatly encouraged, she drove the spring wagon straight to the next restaurant, ever so thankful and excited to tell Dat the news.

When she returned home, Ellie found her longed-for letter from Evan. Tears of joy sprang to her eyes as she hurried to the house to announce it to Mamm, who smiled and placed her hand on her chest.

"Praise be to God!" she whispered.

Ellie sat at the table and opened the envelope, wishing there was another letter from Evan for Dat and Mamm.

"Why don't ya read it first, then tell me what you'd like to share," Mamm said.

Ellie nodded at the suggestion and began to read, her hands trembling a little.

Dear Ellie,

Thanks for your great letter! I enjoyed getting it—read every word. I'll try to answer quicker next time. Since I don't have a lot of time right now, I probably won't be able to write Mamm and Dat today, too, so go ahead and pass on whatever I've written here that you think won't alarm them.

Nearly within the first hour after I arrived at camp, my head was shaved down to my scalp and all my personal possessions were taken away and replaced with army-issued items like toothpaste, a toothbrush, and a comb. Then came a whole batch of required shots in my arm and more tests. I didn't feel like myself at all.

Since we all wear the same brown uniform, everyone in my platoon looks alike. And we march everywhere—to eat, to class, to our drilling activities, to the barracks. We're up each morning around four o'clock—something I've adjusted to more easily than most thanks to the hours I kept back home—and we eat whatever they give us without complaining (how I miss Mamm's cooking!) and speak the way we're told to. Too often for my liking, we do long-distance runs till we're either told to stop or drop from exhaustion, which happened to several guys the first few days here. Two of them are no longer with our platoon, and I'm not sure what happened to them.

Copies of the UCMJ (Uniform Code of Military Justice) are

posted everywhere in the barracks, at the mess hall (huge room where we eat), the classrooms, and in the latrines (bathrooms). We're required to know it inside and out, and the same with the Code of Conduct. If we're called on (hollered at) by the drill sergeant, we must recite the exact section of it he asks for, stating it perfectly.

I'm sure by now you can tell that my life here is very different from anything you've ever experienced, Ellie. We're even told how to think! Honestly, between you and me, I'm still trying to figure out this strange world called the U.S. Army. Plenty of days I wonder if I've made a mistake, but it's too late for me to back out.

That last line haunted her, but Ellie continued reading the remainder of the letter, thankful Mamm had busied herself with making beef stew for supper, putting a pot of it on the woodstove to cook. She had no idea which part of Evan's letter wouldn't alarm Mamm. Now, Dat was a different story. Ellie wasn't sure what he knew about military life, but she guessed he might know a tad more than Mamm even though all of this was so new to them. *New even to Evan.*

"He's happy to receive letters from home," she told Mamm, sharing something he'd written close to the bottom of the second page. "He also hopes we've passed along his address to Lydia and the boys and anyone else amongst the People who'd like to write him . . . if any aren't still too upset." She paused. "Maybe Sol would like to write him," she said more to herself than to Mamm.

"So . . . Evan's okay?" Mamm turned around to ask.

"He's just getting used to things." Ellie didn't want to paint a rosy picture, but she certainly wasn't going to upset Mamm with details about all the strenuous activities, or the part about learning to carry and shoot a gun, which Evan had also mentioned close to the end of the letter. It would never do to bring that up.

"I'll write him again," Mamm said.

"So will I."

Later, while making a tossed salad, it struck her that Evan had never been one to complain. Not that she could remember. Yet this letter seemed to be all about complaints. She wondered if he'd just been out of sorts or if everything he'd described was starting to affect him negatively.

He's not even halfway through boot camp.

At supper, Ellie told her father about the two restaurant managers she'd visited.

"What a *schmaert* thing to do," he replied, grinning and glancing at Mamm. "*Denki*, Ellie."

Mamm nodded approvingly. "You are truly your father's daughter."

Ellie was happy to hear it, since working hard, especially for the orchard, made her happy. "I'm glad to help wherever I can."

"I'll say," her father replied. He looked at Dawdi Hezekiah, whose smile lines deepened as he grinned, too.

They kept the cider press busy even as the late apple varieties began to come at the end of October and into November. Ellie, Mamm, and Rudy worked together, using three hand-cranked apple peelers, while Jonah, Dat, Titus, and some of the crew turned to spreading the fall fertilizer. Sol, Menno, and others continued with the apple harvest, and whenever they could, she and Menno stood and talked together.

It wouldn't be long until Thanksgiving, after which the enormous process of pruning the fruit trees would begin, encompassing all the months till April. As was their usual tradition, Dat, Dawdi, and her brothers took a day off to go bow hunting for wild turkeys in Gobbler's Knob southeast of Strasburg, and Ellie couldn't help wondering how strange it must be for them with Evan absent.

To Ellie's surprise, Sol occasionally sought her out, as if keeping an eye on her, and she had to wonder if Evan had anything to do with that. Sol mentioned Leah at times and her upcoming visit for Thanksgiving. She, too, could hardly wait to see Leah again, though the visit would be short. At every opportunity, Ellie slipped in a comment about Ruthann, wanting Sol to know she fully understood how fond he and her cousin were of each other, though Ruthann had been rather mum on that lately.

Very early Thanksgiving morning, Ellie helped Mamm set the table and make side dishes while Dat brought in some firewood for the cookstove. Since Jonah and his family were the only relatives coming for the noontime feast this year, the turkey Dat had bagged recently was just right.

After the meal, followed by coffee, dessert, and lingering conversation, Dawdi excused himself and headed to the *Dawdi Haus* for his afternoon nap. Dat and Jonah continued talking in the front room. Every now and then, a word or phrase about the future of the orchard drifted to the kitchen and caught Ellie's attention. *What will Dat do?*

Once the kitchen was all redded up and the children had run outdoors to play, she, Mamm, and Priscilla sat in the kitchen, sipping more coffee. Ellie enjoyed hearing her sister-in-law talk about patching her grandmother's old quilt.

After Jonah and his family left for home, Ellie decided to walk up and see if Leah was free to visit now. The day's high temperature was supposed to be thirty-nine degrees, but the air felt a little warmer due to the sunshine and lack of wind. Even so, Ellie was glad for her black coat and warm headscarf.

She felt fidgety as she strolled along, going out of her way to walk in the fallen leaves, the crunching sound a sweet reminder of her and Evan's jaunts up to see Sol and Leah when they were children, kicking the leaves and laughing as they went.

Oh, she could hardly wait to lay eyes on Leah again. She recalled how, nearly every Thanksgiving Day since she was school-age, she and Leah had met halfway between their homes after the family meal to walk together—sun, rain, or snow. Afterward, they usually returned by way of the orchard, which for Ellie was like the frosting on a cake any time of the year.

Ellie heard quick footsteps coming this way, and when she glanced up, there was Leah walking on the opposite side of the road. Her face shone with delight. "Happy Thanksgiving, friend!"

"I was just headin' up to see ya," Ellie replied, grinning as she crossed the road.

Leah's laughter rang out in the chilly air. "And I was on my way down to visit *you*."

Ellie fell in step with her friend as they walked hand in hand back toward the orchard. "I'm so glad you could get home."

"Me too. It's been the best Thanksgiving. I've missed bein' here ever so much. And I've missed you, Ellie."

"Could ya stay longer, maybe?"

"Oh, I wish." Leah sighed. "But I'll be home longer at Christmas." She glanced at Ellie like she had something more to say.

They were nearly to the orchard when Leah finally said, "How're ya doin' . . . I mean, with Evan gone?"

"Well, it's not easy, but it helps that he's writing to us."

"*Des gut.*"

"Honestly, I'm not sure how we'd bear it otherwise."

"I'm so sorry." Leah squeezed her hand. "I truly am."

Ellie didn't want to dwell on this with such a short time to spend with Leah, so she changed the subject. "Tell me what it's like at the church in Chambersburg."

"It's a joy, actually—and similar to our church here. I was startin' to feel lost not being able to attend Preaching for so long."

Ellie nodded. "There's just something about joining your voice with everyone's and hearin' the sermons, ain't?"

"And visitin' with folk at the common meal."

Ellie laughed softly. "*Gut* fellowship, *jah.*"

Leah suggested taking a shortcut through the orchard, and Ellie agreed, wondering how often they'd done this on their many walks. "Mamm'll wanna see ya, I'm sure."

"I was hopin' to visit with her. And how's your Dawdi? Still tellin' his stories?"

"He's all right. Still has his sense of humor, for sure." Ellie mentioned their frequent jaunts to inspect the trees for pests.

When Ellie and Leah arrived at the house, Mamm greeted them at the side door. "*Willkumm!* I'm glad ya stopped by, Leah." She ushered them in through the hallway to the warm kitchen. "There's hot cider waitin' and some dessert leftovers," she said, giving Leah a hug, tears welling up.

Ellie took Leah's coat and scarf and hung them beside hers, then returned to the kitchen, so thankful her friend had come, helping to dispel some of the sadness on this special day.

The final days of November brought milder weather, and Ellie often encountered both Menno and Sol while out pruning the apple trees. Menno and the other seasonal workers would soon be let go for the winter, which meant Ellie would only see Menno regularly at church and Singings every other week. She rather lamented that—though it wasn't as if he was leaving town again like Leah had.

Lyle was relaxing with Elisabeth in their bedroom as she read him the letter Evan had written to them on Thanksgiving. Evan said he'd "somehow lived through" basic training, with its five-to-six-mile runs before breakfast every day and obstacle courses. Presently, he'd start eight weeks of Advanced Infantry Training. Today was November thirtieth, and Lyle made the calculation in his head for when that would end.

When Evan made a point of saying he'd still have time to read letters from home at night, Lyle realized their son had spared them any comments about combat practice and other preparations for war. He appreciated that for Elisabeth's sake. Anymore, these letters had a tendency to give him heartburn, and it disturbed him to think that Evan was likely marching with a rifle on his shoulder. Sometimes he wondered if he would even recognize his youngest son if he ran into him on the street somewhere.

Elisabeth, on the other hand, seemed to pour her worries into baking cookies, including some of Evan's favorite bars, and sending a fresh batch nearly every week. And because he'd written that his platoon buddies were "going bananas over the treats," she now baked extra to mail.

As the days came and went, Ellie continued to write to Evan, sometimes twice a week. Every so often, late at night when she came downstairs for a drink of water or some milk, she'd find Mamm sitting at the kitchen table writing by candlelight. It wasn't Ellie's place to know what her mother was sharing with Evan, but she was curious all the same. One thing was surely apparent to her brother by now: He was greatly loved and prayed for in spite of his worldly stance. Even Dawdi Hezekiah occasionally added a handwritten note to him in Ellie's letters, which was rare for Dawdi to do, considering he wasn't fond of writing much of anything. In one of the notes, he'd written, *God's presence is real even in the most difficult times. I know this firsthand, Evan.*

Ellie wondered what he'd meant by "firsthand," but if he wanted her to know, he would tell her eventually.

At the smithy's, Lyle ran into his younger brother, Omar, who'd been treating him as if he were to be pitied for Evan's lack of interest in upholding their peace-loving ways. Since Evan's shortcomings were already evident to Lyle, he merely nodded when Omar frowned at him. He didn't expect Omar to speak to him, but Lyle asked about his best driving horse all the same, trying to break the ice. "Any improvement after the vet's visit?"

Omar shrugged. "Some."

"*Des gut.*"

Omar looked at him askance. "I'm curious. Does your Evan have the decency to keep in touch?"

"He has been." Lyle nodded. "And he could use more prayer."

Acting skittish at that, Omar quickly said, "Ain't like we're not prayin' for him."

"I appreciate that."

This sort of thing had happened a few times before—even after the common meal following Preaching, of all places. Each time, Lyle had silently asked God for a spirit of meekness, much as he wanted to speak up. Truth be told, he was still smarting from his son's desire to forge ahead with joining the army.

"How was your Thanksgiving?" Lyle asked Omar now.

"*Gut.* Half the kids were home. You know how it is: The married ones must juggle the in-laws." He actually chuckled.

"'Tis true."

When Lyle finished making an appointment with the smithy, he waved at Omar, who bobbed his head slightly.

None of his boys have given him a speck of trouble, Lyle thought as he headed for his waiting horse and buggy.

19

The annual Christmas supper for *die Youngie* was held on Tuesday, December twenty-second, at Bishop Mast's farmhouse. His wife, Tessie, had strung up red and green paper chains over the doorways of their large basement, and handmade pinecone wreaths with red velvet bows hung in the windows all across one long wall.

Ellie was happy to double-date with Sol and Ruthann, who for some reason seemed especially pleased to welcome her and Menno along on the buggy ride. The four of them sat together at the table, too.

While they waited for others to arrive, Menno leaned forward and asked Sol, "Say, what would ya think of the four of us goin' sledding on Deacon Lapp's big hill tomorrow afternoon?"

"All right with you, Ruthann?" Sol asked.

"Sure, it'll be fun."

"I'll bring our big sled," Sol added.

Ruthann grinned. "We have a small one. Should I bring that?"

"We'll only need two large sleds—one per couple," Menno said. "I'll bring ours."

"And I'll ask to borrow our family sleigh and pick the three of yous up," Sol said. "Okay?"

Ellie looked forward to going sledding for the first time this season. And it was obvious how excited Ruthann and Sol were about it.

After the meal of savory meat loaf, baked potatoes, and cooked carrots had been capped off with a dessert of chocolate cake and ice cream, Ellie and Menno mingled for a while with her cousin Sarah Ann Hostetler and her date for the evening, Menno's longtime friend Chester Riehl.

The bishop came over and asked Ellie about Evan. "I've written to him several times," he told her.

"Evan mentioned that in a recent letter," Ellie said.

"I don't want him to think he's been forgotten."

"That's *gut* of ya, Bishop." *Especially after everything you've undoubtedly heard about him.*

Menno and Ellie wandered back to the spot where they'd sat at the table. "I wonder if ya checked the mail today?" Menno asked her, looking like he was trying to squelch a smile.

"I was busy getting ready for tonight," she said, smiling. "Why?"

He had a mischievous glint in his eyes. "If somethin' didn't arrive today, then it will tomorrow."

Since Menno only occasionally teased her, she enjoyed it all the more. "I'll look forward to whatever ya sent."

He chuckled under his breath, and Ellie could hardly wait to finish making her Christmas card for him.

Ellie had just finished making a big batch of fudge the next afternoon when she heard the mail truck. She hurried to the utility room and put on her coat and scarf, then rushed out to the road, eager to see if something from Menno had arrived. Sure enough, there was a package with her name on it.

Back indoors, even before removing her coat and scarf, she opened the box and discovered some floral stationery and two large Hershey chocolate bars with almonds, her favorite. *Menno knows what I like!*

After hanging up her coat and scarf inside, she made her way up the stairs to her room, where she found her homemade card for Menno and tucked it inside her shoulder purse. She looked forward to giving it to him in the horse-drawn sleigh later.

Ellie was glad to see her good friends when Sol arrived with Ruthann in the front of the sleigh and Menno waiting for her behind them. The horse's harness was bedecked with large metal bells, and some were even attached to the front of the sleigh.

"Hullo, Ellie!" they called. She hopped in and sat next to Menno, who smiled when she handed him the card and a tin of her fudge.

As Menno read the card, they rode along, the bells jingling prettily.

"I love the sound of bells," Ellie remarked.

"Aaron bought them and put them on," Sol said over his shoulder.

"Tell him *denki* for all of us," Ruthann said.

Sol nodded. "Aaron and I will take Leah out ridin' in the sleigh with my parents one of the days she's here for Christmas. Also, Dat's older brother and family are plannin' dinner at their place for all of us—my married siblings and their families. We'll prob'ly take the sleigh that day, too."

Ruthann spoke up. "Christmas will be the ideal time for your family to get caught up with Leah."

Menno looked at Ellie. "Thanks for the card and the fudge," he said quietly.

"*Du bischt willkumm! Denki* for the stationery and chocolate bars," she replied.

"Chocolate?" Ruthann said from up front. "Did I hear someone say chocolate?"

Ellie reached into her carryall and handed a tin of fudge up to Ruthann, then one for Sol.

Ruthann practically squealed with delight and pretended to keep Sol's tin away from him, but he just laughed.

Sol glanced over his shoulder. "What's everyone else doin' for Christmas?"

"Well, most of my siblings will be home for Christmas Eve supper," Ruthann said, opening her tin and taking out a piece of fudge. "Afterward, we'll all pull taffy."

"What 'bout you, Ellie?" Sol asked as a light snow began to fall.

She could see him glancing at his tin on Ruthann's lap. "My married siblings and their families will come over, but as yous can imagine, it'll be a very different year." She swallowed hard. *Without Evan.*

Menno reached over and placed his gloved hand over her mittened one. Surprised, Ellie glanced at him, and her face warmed in spite of the cold.

The tiny white flakes continued to drift down, making the atmosphere festive as Menno told of his immediate family getting together at noon on Christmas Day.

A few minutes later, Sol gave Ruthann packages to pass back to Menno and Ellie, keeping one for herself. Opening them, they discovered dark green homemade candles in jelly jars with narrow red ribbons tied around them.

"Ooh, these are nice," Ruthann cooed. "Did *you* make these, Sol?"

Menno laughed at that, and Sol explained that they were his mother's handiwork.

Ruthann held hers up and said, "It'll make the Christmas table even more cheerful."

"Be sure an' thank your Mamm," Menno said.

"*Jah*, from me, too," Ellie added. "It's so thoughtful."

Sol suggested they all sing "Jingle Bells," and he led out with a voice deep and clear.

Ellie observed the joy on Sol's face as he smiled over at Ruthann, his voice rising into the crisp and frosty air, the sky as gray as goose down.

But her thoughts were elsewhere. She could still feel the weight of Menno's gloved hand on hers. *Will our relationship pick up now?*

After baking pies and more cookies the next morning with Mamm and helping her plan the menu for Christmas dinner, Ellie took time to visit Leah with three dozen of her still-warm sand tarts along as a little surprise.

Leah's mother's eyes widened when Ellie placed the treats on the table. "I can never get them quite this thin," Nan said, taking a bite and smiling. "You have a knack, Ellie."

"They're my Christmas gift to your family," Ellie replied as Leah reached for a cookie, too. "And 'specially for Leah."

"*Denki*, and I'll be sure to share." Leah took a bite. "Oh, yummy."

"Sol certainly didn't share the fudge you gave him," Nan said, smiling.

"*Jah*, he took the tin to his bedroom and prob'ly hid it." Leah laughed.

Nan went to the cupboard and removed a saucepan. "I'll make some hot cocoa while you girls get comfortable by the coal stove in the front room."

"Oh, that'll be nice," Ellie said.

Leah tied her Mamm's apron in back for her, then led the way to the front room.

Thrilled to spend time with her friend again, Ellie sat with Leah on the sofa.

"Would ya like to go on a sleigh ride this evening?" Leah asked. "Sol and Aaron are takin' the sleigh to the caroling with *die Youngie*. It'll be a fun way for us to get there."

"Sure." Ellie recalled riding in the sleigh at Christmas with Leah and members of her family every few years. "For old times' sake," she said.

"We'll come down an' pick you up after supper," Leah added.

"I'm glad we can spend some time together like this."

"And tonight, too." Leah had a big smile on her face. "Unless you'd rather go with Menno."

"Oh, I'm sure I'll see him there, but I don't get to see you as much."

Leah nodded. "Be sure to bundle up."

"Okay, Mamm."

Leah laughed. "Remember when I'd always remind ya to wear your mittens at recess when we were little?"

Ellie smiled. "You were like a big sister to me."

"But not a bossy one, I hope." Leah smoothed her black apron over her green dress.

Ellie giggled mischievously. "Oh, *never* that!"

"Okay, maybe a *little* pushy."

Ellie laughed again.

The sleigh ride to the deacon's home, where the youth were gathering, was extra fun as Ellie sat with Leah. Sol and Aaron were up front chattering in *Deitsch* as Sol held the driving lines. They were both dressed in black church clothes, coats, and felt hats, and Aaron had on his black earmuffs as well. He was teasing Sol because he'd left his at home "on purpose."

Leah whispered that she thought Aaron was showing off for them.

"Maybe Sol wants to look nice for Ruthann."

"Could be." Leah adjusted her black woolen scarf at her neck. "I'm lookin' forward to seein' *die Youngie* again."

"It won't bother ya to see Josh, I hope."

"Not at all."

She's over him, Ellie thought, glad for Leah's sake.

"Say, Ellie, I've been enjoyin' your fudge," Sol said over his shoulder. "*Denki.*"

"Glad ya like it."

"Sol's still not sharing," Leah said, laughing.

Aaron nodded emphatically.

Sol glanced over his shoulder. "Well, it's *my* gift."

"I'll send some more for yous," Ellie replied.

Aaron turned around. "Ya would, really?"

Ellie nodded. "Sure, it's Christmas. All my favorite neighbors get some sweets!"

Leah giggled. "Can you believe these two, Ellie? Brothers!"

Ellie was amused, but it also made her remember how she and Evan bantered over trivial things. How she missed having him around for Christmas!

After a long day of clearing away clipped tree branches with his pitchfork and then burning them to thwart the spread of disease, Lyle was glad to simply listen to Elisabeth read Evan's recent letter at bedtime. Every so often, her voice quavered and she would stop to gather herself before starting again, but he was mighty thankful, if not relieved, that Evan continued to write to them as well as to Ellie.

It amazed him how appreciative Evan sounded about receiving their letters. *More like the way he used to be,* Lyle thought, watching his wife's dear face. According to Evan, the bishop had written him "yet another letter," and so had Sol Bontrager and others.

God's love comes in unexpected ways.

On Christmas Day, Ellie was eager to spend time with her family during Mamm's wonderful noon feast. Dat had added all the leaves to the table that morning and brought folding tables from the cellar for the grandchildren old enough to eat without assistance. Ellie placed two red tapers in antique glass holders on the long trestle table, a small sprig of holly around the base of each candle. Then she set it for the twelve adults and kept space for a high chair.

Ellie helped Mamm prepare the side dishes—sweet potatoes mashed with cream and butter, cut corn, lima beans, mashed potatoes with turkey gravy, tapioca pudding, chow chow, sweet and sour pickles, green olives, and two pies for dessert—pecan and cherry. All of this while the glazed ham roasted in the cookstove.

How many holidays will Evan miss? Ellie wondered, feeling twinges of sadness, as surely Mamm must be, too. *All of us are feeling it.*

When it came time for everyone to gather round the table, Dat placed young grandson Caleb on a Sears & Roebuck catalog in Evan's usual spot. Then Dat bowed his head for the silent table blessing for a noticeably longer time than usual.

After the prayer, the adults passed the serving dishes around. The older children took turns carrying their plates and their younger siblings' to their mothers, who dished up their food. Rudy and Lovina's dimple-faced Mary, now nine months old, sat in the wooden high chair while Dawdi Hezekiah made silly faces at her to make her giggle.

The kitchen was overflowing with wonderful-good food, jovial conversation, and most of the dear people in Ellie's life. Partway through the meal, she paused for a moment to look around and spotted Dawdi, his gray eyes gentle as he looked at her, as though sensing her thoughts.

Ellie doubted Dawdi would want to walk through the orchard in several inches of snow, so after her siblings and their families left around four-thirty, she headed over to his place. As she hurried up the porch steps, she noticed icicles dangling from the roof and sparkling like gems.

She opened the *Dawdi Haus* door. "It's Ellie," she said softly as she slipped inside.

"Was hopin' ya might come over," Dawdi said, sitting in his comfortable rocker near the black heater stove in the sitting room. "I'm movin' a little slow."

"Did ya have your nap?" Ellie asked as she hung her coat on one of the wooden pegs just inside the door. She headed into the warm room and sat on the sofa.

Dawdi chuckled. "*Jah*, this ol' body had to recover after that feast."

"I think I overate, too," she said, going on to say she'd played with her nephews and nieces after the leftovers were put away and the dishes were done. "You should've stayed round for the songs we sang."

"Did ya sing 'The First Noel'?" he asked, brightening. "I like the story that one tells. Your Mammi said it was the first carol she learned in English as a child . . . ever so long ago."

Ellie smiled, enjoying another of the family tidbits Dawdi liked to share.

"*Jah*, we sang all the verses, and 'Silent Night,' too. Evan used to say that carol made his eyes water."

Dawdi chuckled. "I'd have to say it makes mine water, too." He sighed. "It was a real nice time, seein' everyone round your Mamm's big table. But I guess I'm getting older . . . can't miss my daily nap."

"Far as I can tell, Dawdi, you're the same as yesterday and the day before."

"Nice of ya, Ellie-girl."

She smiled, always at ease around him.

Dawdi blinked several times, like he was fighting back emotion. "May the Lord above keep watch over our Evan this day and always."

"Amen to that," Ellie whispered.

20

Three days after Christmas, Ellie was making supper with Mamm and saying how good it was that Leah could get home for both Thanksgiving and Christmas.

Her mother nodded, listening as she cooked the chicken pieces with chopped potatoes, carrots, and celery in a large saucepan, preparing to make a pot pie. "According to your Dat, Sol and his family were thrilled 'bout that, too."

"Sol and Aaron seemed so happy to have her along for the sleigh ride over to caroling the other night," Ellie replied while rolling out half of the pie crust to press into a deep-dish pie pan.

"Because of her, Christmas was almost as special this year as other years, at least for you," Mamm said softly. She glanced at Ellie. "I know this one was difficult for your Dat, especially."

Ellie nodded. "Dawdi, too."

"So true." Mamm paused a moment, then added, "Your father has a lot on his mind. He's been contemplating his original intention for the management of the orchard."

Turning her head, Ellie asked, "Oh?"

"As you can imagine, he doesn't want to risk movin' forward

160

with the plan for Evan to take over, not with things so uncertain." Mamm sighed. "I'll just say he's grappling with it."

"Poor Dat," Ellie said quietly. "But I'm sure he'll do the right thing."

On the afternoon of New Year's Eve, a letter from Leah arrived, and Ellie, eager to read it, went straight into the house. She opened the envelope and began reading while standing at one end of the kitchen, waiting for the part of the floor she'd mopped earlier to dry.

Dear Ellie,

This is the first chance I've had to write since returning from Christmas—it's rare for the twins and Bobby to nap all at once. But I'd like you to know that my circle of friends at the Amish church here is growing, and I recently met someone.

His name is Reuben Miller, and his Dat is one of the preachers here. We haven't gone out yet, but he's talked with me several times after the common meal, and, well, I can tell he likes me. (You know when a fellow looks at you a certain way.) And the truth is, I like him, too.

Since Carolyn gives me Sundays off, I'll be able to go if Reuben ever asks me out riding after Singing. Of course, with my responsibilities, I can't attend any of the other youth activities, but that's all right. After all, I'm here to look after Carolyn's children, not to be courted.

I'd thought of telling you when I was home for Christmas, but I'd known Reuben just a little while, and I wasn't sure our relationship would go anywhere. But this past Sunday at

Singing, we talked quite a lot, so I'm more certain now about his interest.

"Oh goodness," Ellie whispered, a wave of despair threatening to wash over her. But thankfully, the rest of the letter said nothing more about Reuben Miller.

She returned the letter to the envelope and placed it on the counter. *I wonder if she's told Sol about this fellow,* she thought, not wanting to be the one to reveal the possibility that his sister might fall for a beau so far away.

At the end of the first Singing of the new year, and after he'd put his hand on hers in the sleigh, Ellie wondered if Menno might ask her to go riding with him alone. She really hoped so, although they'd had so much fun doubling with other couples, especially Sol and Ruthann.

Menno was standing in the corner of the hosts' large basement with the other fellows, all of them talking and laughing like the guys often did during refreshments.

Ruthann joined Ellie at the refreshment table for a cookie. "I wish we were goin' out with you and Menno again," she said softly. "But Sol didn't bring his father's enclosed carriage, so we must not be. I wonder why."

"Uh, maybe he wants to spend time with you alone sometimes?" Ellie smiled at her. "Be happy."

"I am, but 'tween you and me, Sol seems different when we're alone."

Ellie was surprised. "What do ya mean?"

"Not sure." Ruthann paused. "Just not as much fun, I guess."

162

"Well, double-dating is more lighthearted—everyone joins in the chatter, ya know. Serious dating is a completely different approach. And remember, there's courting to think 'bout, eventually."

Ruthann nodded. "*Jah.*" But she didn't look convinced.

The host blew the pitch pipe, signaling it was time to return to the tables and sing for another hour.

Ellie and Ruthann took their seats and waited as the others joined them. Menno caught Ellie's eye and smiled at her across the table, and she smiled back, though not too broadly— especially since Ruthann seemed disappointed that they weren't going out as couples.

When the last song had been sung, the youth milled around the basement, talking and pairing up. Menno walked over to Ellie and asked if she'd like to go out riding.

She agreed, and they headed up the stairs behind Ruthann and Sol. *She'll enjoy the evening,* Ellie thought, glad to have some time with just Menno at last. Hopefully, talking one-on-one tonight, they'd get to know each other better.

The night air was bitterly cold as they left the hosting farmhouse and walked to Menno's buggy. There, he unfolded the heavy lap blankets, and Ellie was extra glad for her woolen scarf and mittens.

Under the light of the near half-moon, Menno clicked his tongue and directed the horse onto the road. He couldn't have looked any more handsome holding the driving lines, sitting there next to her. She'd wondered how she might feel on such an outing, just the two of them.

"A real perty night," she said softly, looking at the stars.

"And real nippy." Menno chuckled.

Shivering, she waited for him to say more, wishing he might

put his arm around her, even just to keep her warm, yet knowing he probably wouldn't since they weren't officially courting.

"What do ya hear from your brother these days?" Menno asked.

"Oh, he'll be comin' up on the end of his two months of Advanced Infantry Training soon."

"Comin' home for his thirty-day leave?"

"I'm guessing so."

Menno bristled. "He hasn't told ya? That doesn't seem right."

She was surprised by his response. "I'm sure a lot's goin' through Evan's mind after more than three months away from home and all."

Menno nodded. "A long time to be in a foreign land."

"*Jah*, well, we all know Evan made a terrible choice," she replied, feeling uncomfortable.

"I wonder if he'll ever admit to makin' a mistake." Menno looked at her. "Has he ever said anything to you?"

The way Menno sounded just now, she really didn't care to share the personal things Evan had written to her. So she didn't answer his question.

"I guess it's none of my business," he finally said.

"Maybe we should talk 'bout something else." She wished he hadn't asked about Evan. It was hard enough, dealing with this strange time without her brother, and now to have to face such pointed questions from someone she liked . . . Well, it was disappointing.

"I prob'ly shouldn't say this, but Evan's like no other Amish fella I know. Seems awful selfish."

Ellie pressed her lips together. "We can't really know what another person is thinkin' or feelin', but he's my twin brother, and I care 'bout him."

Menno was quiet for a while, then said, "Must be hard for you, writing him and knowin' what he's putting you and your family through. I wouldn't do it."

She couldn't believe how judgmental Menno sounded. "Did ya know that the bishop and others are keepin' in touch with Evan?"

"But isn't that just to try an' keep him from turnin' his back on God and the People?"

"I'd like to think it's out of kindness and caring . . . for a young man who's lost his way. There's still hope, I believe." She pushed her hands beneath the heavy lap blankets, recalling Ruthann's peculiar remark about how things were different when she and Sol went out alone. *But this isn't only different,* Ellie realized. *Menno's spouting off his true feelings . . . and it's hurtful.*

For much too long, Menno said nothing, and Ellie felt all the more annoyed. At last, she said, "Ya know, if Evan's bad decision upsets ya so, maybe you'd rather not be around his sister."

"You mean . . ." Menno's tone held surprise.

She shrugged.

"Actually, Ellie, I've been wanting to talk to you for a while 'bout the shame Evan's put on not just himself and your family but on all the People here." Menno paused. "But I didn't think you'd react this way . . . defending him."

She shook her head, fuming inwardly. "Whatever he's done, I love my brother!"

Menno murmured under his breath, and she had a pretty clear picture of what he felt toward Evan and possibly toward her and her family. Now she couldn't wait for this evening to be over.

Another half mile, and they approached the front of her house. "Will ya let me out here?" she said.

"I'd like to walk ya to the door," Menno said as he signaled the horse to turn into the long driveway.

When they came to a stop, Ellie pushed the lap blankets back and stepped out of the buggy. She was met in front of the mare by Menno, who walked with her toward the steps leading to the side door. "Didn't mean to offend ya," he said.

"Wish you'd said somethin' before now."

Menno looked toward the sky, then back at her. "Still, I don't see how I can change my opinion."

How long has he felt such resentment toward Evan? she wondered, determined not to look back as she quickly climbed the porch steps, baffled this night had made such a sudden turn. Even so, it was better to know where Menno stood than to continue hoping they might end up courting.

"Well, *gut Nacht*, Ellie," she heard him say.

"S'posin' it should be good-bye." She opened the door and stepped inside.

Upstairs in her room, Ellie lit the lantern, took down her hair, and brushed it thoroughly, jittery with anger. "Calm down," she whispered to herself as she put on her white flannel nightgown.

She slipped into bed and pulled up the blankets and quilts, then stared at where the faintest light from the moon crept around the edge of a window shade. She yawned and reached over to outen the lantern, surprised she wasn't sorry her relationship with Menno had come to an end.

After a time, she got up and raised the shade on one of the dormer windows, then looked fondly at the expanse of orchard. Sighing with relief, she felt a surge of warmth, even contentment. "I'll get to stay round here for longer," she whispered.

Ellie worked alongside Dat all week, helping load the spring wagon with pruned branches on the ground beneath the apple trees. She was thankful for Evan's old work gloves, which were a little big for her but did the job.

She didn't tell anyone about the breakup with Menno, and she didn't say a word to Sol about Leah's recent letter about Reuben Miller, either. She had hoped Sol might hear about Reuben from Leah directly, considering how it could affect him and his family if she were to become serious with him. But if she *had* told Sol, it was a bit odd he didn't mention it.

Ellie contemplated the fact that she was now without a boyfriend—what an odd way to start the new year! Yet there was no second-guessing that. Menno's critical words still repeated in her memory, and she would tell Ruthann about it at some point—maybe even Sol, if he asked. After all, the grapevine would get out the news soon enough.

21

Ellie wasn't surprised when Ruthann dropped by Friday evening, a two-layer chocolate fudge cake in hand. And when she asked to go upstairs to talk "privately," Ellie knew what was coming.

Ruthann sat on the edge of Ellie's bed and removed her head-scarf. "I heard from Menno's older sister that he's no longer seein' you. You must be upset."

"*Nee.*" Ellie leaned back against the headboard. "'Tween you and me, I was the one who suggested we go our separate ways."

Ruthann glanced toward the window. "Well, I wanted to make sure you were okay."

"I am. And it's nice of ya to ask."

"I care, ya know." Ruthann then told her she was going to Somerset for the rest of the winter. "Mamm's youngest cousin needs a live-in helper during and after her upcoming back surgery. They have two children under the age of two."

"You do love takin' care of little ones."

"Which is why I volunteered." Ruthann paused a moment. "Honestly, I've been feelin' restless lately, so this'll keep me occupied till spring." She looked rather pensive now. "I've already told Sol 'bout it. I'm guessin' he'll write to me now and then."

"Of course he will."

"Well, he did say he'll be busy pruning the orchard. But I'll be busy, too."

Ellie was confused. This did not sound like either Sol or Ruthann.

When they finished talking, Ellie walked downstairs with her cousin, glad she'd dropped by. *It's heartening she's concerned about me, even though I'm fine*, she thought, actually more concerned about Sol and Ruthann's relationship.

The following week, Ellie gave Dat a list of six new customers in town, and he beamed.

"I was worried that Evan's absence would affect our sales," Dat said, "so it's a big help what you're doin', Ellie."

"Even though I'm not nearly as strong as Evan, I'm fillin' in wherever I can."

"But evidently, you're quite persuasive," her father replied, thanking her.

The next day, Mamm and Dat received another letter from Evan, who'd written that a good buddy from his platoon wanted him to go home with him during their thirty-day leave.

Ellie sat with her mother on the front room settee as she read Evan's letter for herself. *I've accepted his invitation. Honestly, I think it's for the better—I don't want to offend you with my military haircut and uniform. Let's face it: I'd get a lot of looks back there from anyone who knows me. I'll keep in touch, though, before I leave for Vietnam at the end of February.*

Ellie stared at the letter, trying to comprehend her brother's decision. Didn't Evan realize that nearly everything he'd done since leaving home was offensive to Mamm and Dat and their dearly held beliefs?

She handed the letter back to Mamm, whose lower lip trembled. "Aw, Mamm." She leaned her head on her mother's shoulder. "I know this makes ya sad."

"It just would've been so *gut* to see him again, no matter what he looks like." Mamm wiped her eyes. "Your poor father will take this mighty hard."

"*Jah*," Ellie whispered, knowing they all would.

After evening Bible reading and prayer with Dawdi and her parents, Ellie headed upstairs with the day's newspaper, wanting to look at the listings for land sales in the area. Again, she thought of how nice it would be to add cherry and plum trees to their orchard business, expanding their offerings. Following the news of Evan's decision not to come home for his leave, she needed something to keep her mind occupied.

At her writing desk, she scanned through the listings and found two properties of interest. She circled both a thirty-acre plot in Smoketown and a fifteen-acre plot in Ronks. Eager to have a look and nose around a bit, she imagined all the new fruit trees she so wished they could plant.

Ellie recalled sharing her secret desire with Evan before he left for basic training. He'd told her to talk to Dat about it.

I just need to get up the nerve.

A few days later, when Lyle returned to the house to fill up his coffee thermos, Elisabeth told him she'd found a shoebox of letters under Evan's bed when she was dry mopping that morning. "The letters are from Jack Herr during his months of basic training and then after he went overseas. I'm not sure how I missed seein' the box before," she said. "I left it on Evan's bed—"

"*Nee*, I won't violate Evan's privacy," Lyle said. "Next time I'm up there, I'll put the box under the bed and close the door."

"Thought you'd want to know." Elisabeth poured steaming hot coffee into the thermos.

"I appreciate it," he said, pulling on his work gloves, then carrying the thermos back to the orchard. It was time he paid the bishop a visit to share some things he'd had on his mind for a while now.

After supper, Lyle hitched up Captain to the family carriage and headed to the bishop's place. "Been meanin' to visit with ya," he said when the man of God came to the back door.

"*Kumme en*, Lyle." Bishop took his coat, scarf, and black felt hat. "Happy to talk with ya anytime."

Lyle followed him into the warm kitchen. Seeing Tessie at the sink washing dishes, he said, "It's a private matter."

"We'll go to the front room," Bishop replied.

Once they were seated across from each other, Lyle began to share how frustrated he was with their tradition of *Rumschpringe*. "Elisabeth found letters in Evan's room this mornin' from Jack Herr, our neighbor's son who was killed in the war."

Bishop nodded. "I recall hearin' word of his passing."

Lyle drew a long breath. "Our Evan was on the path to baptism.

171

Seems to me he wouldn't have taken up with Jack Herr and other worldly fellas if he hadn't felt the freedom to do so durin' *Rumschpringe*."

"You're questionin' the age-old tradition, then?" Bishop asked, his brow furrowed.

Lyle leaned forward, wanting to make his point clear. "There's just no way Evan would have ended up where he is without that." He paused. "Remember, Evan was close friends with Solomon Bontrager for all their growing-up years. So *jah*, I feel strongly that *Rumschpringe* changed everything."

Bishop looked at him solemnly. "*Die Youngie* are our community's treasure. And for three hundred years, *Rumschpringe* has worked for the vast majority of our sons and daughters. The boys, 'specially, tend to push the boundaries a bit—which they have the choice to do, just as you and I had a choice back when—and then they're usually willing to come forward and join church. Without that time of independence, they might wonder what they missed out on for the rest of their lives."

"But what if even one of our sons is lost because of this freedom?" Lyle asked respectfully.

Bishop's eyes were downcast for a moment. "That's the concern of every parent's heart, that their children might stray and not choose *Gott* after their running-round years." He ran his hand over his face. "He hears the cries of His People, Lyle. I'm not giving up on Evan."

"Neither will I."

"Under that hardened veneer, I believe Evan's heart is still soft toward the Lord." Bishop went on to mention that Evan had replied to two of his letters. "A *gut* sign, *jah*?"

"Well, but he's decided not to come home for his leave before goin' to war. So that's a *different* sign, and not a *gut* one." Lyle disliked contradicting the bishop, but he wanted him to know what he and Elisabeth and the family were up against.

"As you know, Lyle, Evan has the free will to make wise choices or poor ones, just as we do daily."

"And God is sovereign," Lyle said, assuming that was likely the next thing the bishop would state. Even so, the man had heard him out, and Lyle had only come to voice his objection to the practice. "I appreciate ya keepin' in touch with Evan."

Bishop folded his hands as he leaned forward. "I was ordained to be the shepherd of this little flock. And searching out the one who is lost is my responsibility under *Gott*."

Moved by that, Lyle rose and thanked him for his time, glad to have gotten this off his chest. He walked through the house to the utility room with Bishop close behind.

"I'll continue prayin' for Evan," Bishop told him as Lyle donned his outer clothing. "And for you and Elisabeth, too. I caused my parents a fair amount of heartache when I was seventeen, but their prayers made a difference in my choice to turn back to the faith of my childhood."

"I'll definitely share that with my wife." Lyle thanked him again and headed out to his horse and carriage.

The following Saturday morning, after filling the coal stove in the front room, Lyle and his father headed off to purchase three wheelbarrows from a farm auction west of them, in East Lampeter. While mingling with other Amish farmers, they overheard the local bishop telling about a barn that had burned nearby—arson, according to the police.

Perking up his ears, Lyle heard that the blaze was caused by teenage fellows who'd been stalking and taunting the young Amishmen living at that farm. "The Amish fellas were draft age," the bishop said somberly.

An older man accompanying the bishop said, "We've had several attacks on our teenage boys in the past weeks. One was hit with a brick while out on the field lane, mindin' his own business, chust bringin' his eight-mule team back for the night."

"Seems like these things keep a-happenin'," another farmer said, a large bag of homemade popcorn from the nearby food stand tucked under one arm. "And they ain't pickin' on just us Plain folk, neither. I've read in the newspaper about attacks on any young men who look to be draft age. Folks must assume they're COs or they wouldn't still be around."

Immediately, Lyle thought of Evan. Truth be told, he'd soon be in a far more dangerous place than right here in Amish country, even with the possibility of attacks.

22

Ellie stayed home during the second January Singing, not ready to answer questions about her and Menno parting ways. She figured Sol likely already knew, since he and Menno were cousins, but polite as he was, he hadn't mentioned it when they'd worked together pruning the apple trees with the orchard crew. She was relieved about that, since it might seem strange to Sol that she wasn't missing Menno much at all.

She also wasn't ready to start pairing up with a new fellow at Singings, although the day before she left for Somerset, Ruthann had suggested Ellie not wait too long. *"But that's up to you,"* she'd said. *"'Least you and Menno weren't seriously courting yet."*

Ellie had already shared about the breakup in a letter to Leah, not going into much detail except to say that Menno's disdainful attitude toward Evan had been at the root of it.

These days Lyle worked primarily in the barn offices. He'd had plenty to keep him busy till the annual three-day horticulture convention in Hershey took place. This year, he'd traveled there alone by bus to attend the large gathering, taking many notes during the sessions with industry leaders and university researchers. Lyle enjoyed meeting other Plain orchardists and comparing their experiences, though only a few Old Order Amish were present. But it certainly wasn't the same without Evan along.

Midway through February, Ellie penned what would be her last letter to Evan prior to his leaving for Vietnam. She was painfully aware that he might not receive any mail sent after this date for a long while. Mamm had already sent hers. But as far as Ellie knew, Dat himself had not written a single letter to Evan.

Ellie didn't think it was wise to tell Evan about Menno—she didn't want to distract him with such things. But she *did* write out a couple of Scripture passages, hoping they might encourage her brother in whatever he might face overseas. One especially she prayed would make him stop and think—Proverbs 3:5–6: *Trust in the* Lord *with all thine heart; and lean not unto thine own understanding. In all thy ways acknowledge him, and he shall direct thy paths.*

Oh, how she prayed he would take those verses to heart.

A few days later, Ellie rose extra early to accomplish her indoor chores before breakfast, then pulled on a pair of Evan's old trousers under her dress and apron and went out to help prune trees with the crew. The scratch brush from pruning the apple trees had finally been removed and piled into an enormous bonfire, an annual tradition for the workers. Once the fire burned down to embers, each person used a stick to cook a hot dog for fun. But now it was time to trim and shape the peach trees, with the goal to finish up by mid-April.

This morning, her thoughts were on a lengthy letter she'd received from Cousin Ruthann, revealing that she'd thought it over and wanted to call it quits with Sol—and of all things, she was asking Ellie for advice on how to do it by letter. *Do you think Sol will be hurt?* Ruthann had asked.

Goodness, how should I know? Ellie wondered, wishing her cousin hadn't put her on the spot. But sensing Ruthann's urgency, Ellie decided to write back that very afternoon.

As the work of the orchard overlapped with Ellie's indoor work, the days passed more quickly, and she was filled with expectation—she should soon be hearing from Evan again. To keep from fretting, she wrote two more letters, trusting they might eventually catch up with him wherever he was fighting.

Finally, she received a letter from her brother two weeks after she'd sent her last one.

I miss you, Ellie, he'd written on the first line. *I've been receiving your wonderful-good letters and look forward to them when they arrive at the army base in Long Binh Post once each week. The mail is delivered to us out here by a supply helicopter, and sometimes new troops joining our unit bring mail, too. I can't tell you exactly where I'm fighting, but I'm doing okay so far. Please let Mamm know . . . and Dat, if he's interested.*

She held back tears as she read, not wanting Mamm to know how blue she felt, trying not to picture Evan fighting in a flooded rice field, like was often described in the newspapers. Right there, she bowed her head and prayed, asking God for the thousandth time to bring him home alive.

Soon after Ruthann returned home near the end of March as planned, Ellie picked her up and took her to the fabric shop in Bird-in-Hand. On the way there, Ruthann revealed that she had, indeed, written Sol what she called "a gentle breakup letter."

"So ya prayed 'bout it?" Ellie asked, holding the driving lines, her eyes on the road.

"I sure did. And ya know what? He didn't seem to mind much, or so he indicated in his short letter back to me. I guess friendship was all Sol and I were ever gonna have," she said, a hint of a smile on her face. "And evidently, Sol told Menno 'bout it, 'cause next thing, Menno wrote to me. Ya don't mind, do ya?"

Ellie felt a tingle of surprise. *Menno wrote to her?* "Why should I mind? Menno and I aren't meant for each other."

"It's kinda funny, I think."

Ellie agreed, wondering why Sol hadn't told her any of this. But then, she had been tied up with vendors at market a lot, taking more orders as well as keeping an eye on land listings, though there wasn't much to choose from locally. *Maybe Sol figured it was better for Ruthann to tell me in person.*

"Have ya been at Singings at all since you and Menno broke up?" her cousin asked.

"Sure, and I had fun spendin' time with lots of my girl cousins, mostly."

"Mostly?" Ruthann's eyes brightened. "Someone asked ya out ridin'?"

"Two fellas did."

Ruthann frowned. "You didn't tell me."

"Well, 'cause I didn't go."

"Why not?" Ruthann looked baffled as they pulled into the fabric shop's parking lot.

Ellie shrugged. "Didn't feel like it." She got out to tie Nelly to the hitching post.

"*Two* guys, and ya turned them both down?" Ruthann asked as she met her there. "You must not care 'bout ever getting married."

"I'll trust God for that, when the time is right."

Ruthann nodded reluctantly. "You amaze me."

Inside the shop, Ellie headed over to look at the discounted spools of thread, and Ruthann made her way straight to the dress material.

After a short time, a pretty young woman wearing flared denim pants and a double-breasted navy-and-white-plaid coat came up to Ellie. "You're Evan's twin sister, aren't you?" she asked, a navy-colored headband in her shoulder-length blond hair. "You look just like him."

Nodding, Ellie realized this was Cheryl Herr, Evan's girlfriend. "*Jah.* I think we've met before, but it's been a while."

"Yes. At the farmers market. Soft pretzels are a weakness of mine."

"I think it's the salt—I love pretzels, too," Ellie said, face-to-face with the young woman who'd said she would wait for Evan before he left for boot camp.

"I'm sure you've heard from Evan now that he's overseas," Cheryl said. "I received a letter from him not long ago—written from the trenches." She shivered momentarily.

"*Jah*, he wrote 'bout the monsoons and how difficult it is to write letters with rain pouring on him and his unit."

Cheryl nodded. "I'm holding my breath until he's home safely."

Ellie felt the same. "And praying, too, ain't so?"

Cheryl smiled. "Maybe I'll do that."

Ellie mentioned the sale thread.

"That's what I came for, too," Cheryl said.

"Oh, what're ya makin'?"

"Two animal pillows for my cousin's twin girls, Lisa and Kimberly, in Chambersburg—birthday gifts."

"*Ach* . . . my friend Leah is their live-in mother's helper."

"Yes, I know. Carolyn mentioned that connection back last spring when Leah first moved there to help. As they say, it's a small world."

Ellie agreed.

"Well, it's nice to see you again, Ellie."

"You too, Cheryl," she replied, then made her way to the cash register.

What would Evan think of us running into each other? Ellie wondered as Ruthann joined her with an armful of royal blue and violet material.

Opening her window shades, Ellie was greeted by the most glorious sight. Many of the early apple trees were in full bloom this third week in April, as well as the remaining pink peach blossoms. Two days ago, she, Jonah, Rudy, Titus, and the other workers had placed honeybee hives on the apple side of the orchard—one hive for every two acres. It was essential to time this right as the blossoms were beginning to open.

Ellie felt sorry that Evan was missing out on this wondrous time in the orchard. She was fairly sure, though, that he hadn't forgotten the splendor of the blossoming trees even in the midst of combat. Thankfully, he hadn't gone into any detail about his fighting in his most recent letter.

23

Following the April twenty-fifth fellowship meal at church, Ellie wandered down a row of apple trees at home, breathing in the sweet fragrance and embracing the fluffy white beauty around her. She thanked God for it. In another few days, the apple blossoms would disappear, and the miniature fruitlets would start to develop.

She'd gone there alone, since Dawdi had fallen asleep in his willow rocker on his back porch, not far from the firewood bin. He firmly believed that the Good Lord had made Sunday afternoons for napping. Dat and Mamm, however, had taken the team over to Hunsecker Mill Road to visit Onkel Amos and Aendi Emma Lapp—Mamm's next-younger brother and his wife. It was the perfect time to slip away for a nice long walk.

She thought about Leah's most recent letter, describing Reuben Miller and even his family, including his nine siblings and quite a few nephews and nieces. Leah hadn't spelled it out, but it sounded like she was quite attracted to him and Reuben to her.

Ellie had replied with several questions about Reuben and

asked how Carolyn's children were doing, then mentioned meeting Cheryl Herr at the fabric shop. *Did Lisa and Kimberly like the animal pillows she made for their birthday?* Ellie had written.

She pondered Leah's moving away from Bird-in-Hand and the People here, making a new life for herself in Chambersburg and finding a potential beau among the Amish. "I wonder how Leah's family feels 'bout that," she whispered. "'Specially Sol." At least Leah hadn't abandoned the Plain life altogether. After all, she'd been living with fancy folk all this time.

Suddenly, in the midst of the flowering branches and the solitude, Ellie heard shouts of "Coward!" and "Draft dodger!" and then curses from the direction of the road. Never in her life had she heard so much hatred and anger in people's voices, and she felt sorry for whoever was their target. After a few nerve-racking minutes, an engine roared to life, and she heard the sound of tires spinning against gravel as a vehicle raced away.

Part of her didn't want to get anywhere near whatever had just taken place, but the other part felt compelled forward, though she took care to remain close to the apple trees as she went. A moment later she heard a deep moan. Hurrying to look, she saw Sol in his church clothes, struggling to sit up on the shoulder of the road, his black coat crumpled on the ground nearby, his left hand covering his left ear. He was breathing hard, rocking slowly. A nasty gash on the left side of his head had already stained his long-sleeved white shirt with blood.

"Sol!" she cried, her heart in her throat as she rushed across the road and knelt beside him. Several rocks lay scattered on the ground. "What happened?" Quickly, she removed her bandanna and pressed it against the gash to try to stop the flow of blood.

Sol gave her a dazed look. "Ellie," he mumbled, then glanced in confusion toward the road as if looking for whoever had attacked him.

"Can ya put your hand where mine is?" she asked, moving his left hand there. "Try an' keep a firm pressure on it, okay?"

He nodded slowly but winced at the motion.

"I can help you up," she said, lifting his coat from the ground and tucking it over an elbow. "If you can walk, I'll get ya to Dawdi's."

Slowly, he struggled to stand with her help, staggering some before she steadied him by slipping herself under his right arm and wrapping her arm around his waist. Sol leaned against her, his arm heavy around her shoulders as he groaned again, then gasped as if in terrible pain. "My right hand's throbbing," he murmured as it hung limp over Ellie's shoulder.

Gently, she guided him down from the road and into the paths of the orchard, praying for the strength to get him to Dawdi's, aware of his weight against her.

She remembered the vicious shouting minutes earlier. Had Sol been directly targeted? Or had his attackers been random passersby? But he was in no condition to answer the questions running through her mind, so she put all her energy into supporting him as they moved down the path between the rows of trees, sometimes stopping for Sol to catch his breath.

Surely Dawdi will know how to help him, she thought, hoping he would be within earshot once they reached the backyard. *O Lord, be with poor Sol*, she prayed, aware of his increasing unsteadiness and fearful he might faint.

They trudged across the orchard, struggling to stay upright as she led him slowly, step by step.

The minute the backyard came into view, she called, "Dawdi, I need your help! *Kumme schnell!*"

"Ellie?" Dawdi came around the porch, moving quickly. Then, laying eyes on Sol, he asked, "What's happened?" The bandanna was red with blood, yet what she could see of Sol's face was ghastly pale.

"Someone attacked him," she replied.

"Let's get him to *mei Haus*." Rushing into the yard to meet them, Dawdi took Ellie's place to Sol's right, and Ellie stepped to the other side, where Sol was still holding the bandanna against his head.

"His right hand is hurt, too," she said.

Sol leaned on Dawdi, coughing and heaving now as if he might retch.

"Chust a little farther," Dawdi said, encouraging Sol with a tone ever so kind.

The three of them plodded across the yard, past the two purple martin birdhouses to Dawdi's small porch. Ellie placed Sol's black suit coat on the banister and held the door open as Dawdi helped Sol into the spare bedroom not far from the sitting room. He helped Sol sit down on the bed, where Sol handed her the blood-soaked bandanna. Ellie could see a large goose egg on his head, directly above his battered left ear and the bloody gash. Dawdi elevated his bruised right hand on a pillow—there was some swelling there, too.

Ellie quickly stepped to the small closet near the spare room and found several clean cloths. Then in the kitchen, she dropped the soaked bandanna into the sink before removing a small basin from beneath the sink and filling it partway with cool water. She carried the basin to the spare room and set it on a small wooden table not far from the rocking chair. "This'll be cold," she told Sol, immersing one of the cloths and wringing out the excess water before handing it to him.

Gingerly, with his left hand, he placed the cloth over his injured ear, and when he did, Ellie could see a fresh bruise on his neck below.

"Somethin' must've struck ya," she said.

"Stones," he said, speaking ever so slowly. "Three Yankee fellas jumped out of their car. Didn't recognize any of 'em." He went on to murmur that he'd been walking home from visiting his older brother's family.

Removing the bloody cloth from his ear, he stared at it, and Ellie dropped it into the water basin.

Meanwhile, Dawdi was examining the wound on Sol's head. "The bleeding's slowin'."

"*Des gut,*" Ellie said, horrified to think that anyone would attack her friend.

"I pray they don't hurt anyone else," Sol said sadly.

"Let's have a look at your eyes . . . see if the pupils are dilated." Dawdi leaned over and gently placed his thumb on one eyelid, tugging it up. Then he made a small sound and said, "Looks like they are."

Ellie had guessed that Dawdi would be able to tell if Sol had a concussion. She was thankful that Sol's speech wasn't slurred, and he seemed to be making sense, but it wasn't a good sign that his eyes were dilated.

She carried the basin back to the kitchen, where she poured the water down the sink's drain and left both the bloodied bandanna and cloth in the sink for now. After she'd cleaned out the basin, she poured more cold water into it and carried it back to Sol. "Here's some fresh water," she said, but Sol was leaning over now, his head between his knees.

"Sol's *mir iwwel,*" Dawdi told her, worry lines between his gray eyebrows.

He's nauseated, she thought, hurrying outside to toss the fresh water over the banister, then returning to place the empty basin in Sol's good hand, just in case.

Dawdi asked for another clean, wet cloth, and Ellie rushed to the kitchen for another basin with some cold water. When she returned, Dawdi wet the cloth, rolled it, and placed it at the base of Sol's neck. "Lean back against this, if ya can," he said. Mamm always did this when Ellie felt queasy.

Moving carefully, Sol followed Dawdi's advice.

"That's right," Dawdi said quietly. "You're gonna be chust fine, son."

Mamm had always said the same thing to her when she was nauseated or light-headed. *To keep your mind off the suffering,* she thought.

After a few minutes, Sol reached to touch his left ear. "Ooh," he groaned, then said he felt dizzy again and put his head down once more. Dawdi placed the cold, wet cloth on Sol's neck as before.

"I'll get some ice," Ellie said, wishing there was more she could do.

When she returned with a bag of ice, Sol was telling Dawdi that he must get home to look after the herd of cattle and feed their dogs. "My family's . . . out of town."

"Son, you're in no condition for that. How about I go tend to your animals? Maybe I'll ask one of the other neighbors to help, too." Dawdi glanced at Ellie. "You'll stay here with him, ain't?"

Ellie nodded. "Of course."

"Someone needs to keep an eye on him for the next twelve hours." Then he said directly to Sol, "As a precaution, don't let yourself go to sleep."

Ellie was so glad Dawdi knew what to do.

"Oh, an' Ellie, his church clothes'll need a *gut* soakin' in cold water—just put them in the kitchen sink for now." He paused in the doorway, glancing over his shoulder. "Might be in shock, so if he starts shivering, put more quilts on him. And keep him awake, no matter what."

"You want me to sit with him?"

Dawdi nodded. "Pull the cane-back chair up close to the bed."

Ellie agreed, but she felt so inadequate, as if she wasn't up to the task. Still, Dawdi needed to take care of the livestock for Sol—knowing that was being done would certainly help give him some peace of mind.

Please, Lord, let Mamm and Dat return soon!

24

Ellie stepped back out onto the porch to get Sol's coat off the banister while he was slipping on one of Dawdi's work shirts. She shook out as much of the road dust as she could before hanging the coat on a wooden peg inside the doorway. Then before she went back to the spare room to make sure Sol stayed awake, she put his blood-stained shirt on one side of the deep double sink with his black vest, both in cold water and soap.

In the sitting room, she found Dawdi's black leather Bible next to his favorite chair and carried it with her into the spare room. She pulled the cane-back chair over near the bed and sat down.

"I'm s'posed to sit with ya till Dawdi's back," she said, noticing Sol's eyelids were already drooping. The ice bag was still perched on the goose egg. His hand was still elevated on the pillow, too, but she needed to get some ice for it as well.

"Sol? Can ya stay awake? Dawdi says it's important."

"Mm-m," he murmured, his eyes closed now. "Not sure . . . awful hard."

"What should I do if you fall asleep?"

"Poke . . . my foot," he said, moving it under the covers.

As exhausted as Sol looked, this was going to be a real challenge. "Now that you're more comfortable, let me take a moment to clean your face and ear," she offered, knowing that might help him remain conscious.

"If ya don't mind."

She set the Bible on the dresser across the room. "Please stay wide awake till I come back."

He said he would.

In the kitchen, she washed and dried her hands, then got some antiseptic and cotton balls from Dawdi's medicine cabinet before washing out the basin with hot water and swishing it around. After filling it with more clean water, she pulled her apron up to make a small pouch, then put the cotton balls and antiseptic there, and carried the basin to the spare room. She glanced at Sol to see that his eyes were open as she placed the items on the cane-back chair, then left to get two more cloths from the little closet nearby.

When she returned, Sol was lightly snapping his fingers next to his left ear. "I think my hearing's gone in this ear. Sounds are muffled."

Not sure how to react, she took the basin around to the other side of the bed and placed it on the small table there. She dropped one of the cloths into the basin to get it wet, then squeezed out the water. "You've had a bad beatin', Sol."

He sighed deeply and closed his eyes. "Don't worry . . . I'm awake."

"All right," she said, carefully patting the caked-on blood on his temple and down his face. Next, she gently dabbed at the gash on his head, which wasn't as deep as she'd thought it might be. He smelled of sweat and the metallic odor of blood. "How will I know if you're sleepin' or not, with your eyes closed?"

His eyes fluttered open again momentarily.

She continued to wash his face with care, wishing he were strong enough to shower. But the basin water would have to do, so she kept rinsing the cloth and wringing it out, the water turning a bright color of pink again.

After the head wound was clean, Ellie gently applied antiseptic with a cotton ball, feeling awful when Sol winced from the sting.

All the while, he kept observing her closely. "Could ya say something in my ear?" he asked when she was almost finished washing his face.

She put the cloth in the basin. "As soon as I return."

Back in the kitchen, she removed Sol's shirt and vest from one side of the sink, then poured the pink water down the drain in the other sink. Again, she washed her hands thoroughly and dried them on the hand towel hanging inside the cupboard door below.

Of all the Sundays for Dat and Mamm to be gone all afternoon, she thought as she turned to look out the kitchen window. And knowing how long it could take her grandfather to complete his tasks at the Bontrager farm, she asked the Lord to help her do the right things for Sol.

She walked back into the spare room, glad to see he was still awake as she came around to the left side of the bed.

"Will ya stay with me now?" he asked, sounding distressed, so unlike him.

She nodded. "Are ya ready for me to test your hurt ear?"

"*Jah.*"

Looking down into his swollen face, Ellie felt both sadness and compassion. She leaned closer and whispered, "Dawdi says you're gonna be just fine." She suddenly felt shy, being so near to him.

"Only muted sounds." His expression was glum. "Try again, a little louder this time."

Bending over, she said this time in a normal voice, "I'm awful sorry you're hurt." She straightened up again.

"I could tell you were talkin', but I couldn't make out what you were sayin'."

"Well, you must've heard something—which is *gut*. So you're not completely deaf in that ear." She sighed, so worried for him as she walked around the bed. She picked up the Bible, and to be sure he could hear her, she moved to the right side of the bed and sat in the chair. "Do ya have a favorite psalm?"

"The first one," he said almost inaudibly. "I think of the tree in verse three as one from the orchard."

Turning to Psalms, she read, "'Blessed is the man that walketh not in the counsel of the ungodly, nor standeth in the way of sinners, nor sitteth in the seat of the scornful. But his delight is in the law of the LORD; and in his law doth he meditate day and night.'"

She paused to look at Sol, and his eyes were shut again. Glancing where his feet were beneath the covers, she wondered if she should poke one, like he'd said to. She was about to do it when Sol's foot moved, so she assumed he was still awake.

Again, she began to read, a little louder than before. "'And he shall be like a tree planted by the rivers of water, that bringeth forth his fruit in his season; his leaf also shall not wither; and whatsoever he doeth shall prosper. The ungodly are not so: but are like the chaff which the wind driveth away.'" She stopped reading, because Sol's breathing had slowed, his eyes were still closed, and both his feet were motionless.

"Sol?" she said. "Can ya hear me?"

His eyelids lifted to half-mast. "So tired."

Don't fall asleep. She closed the Bible and rose to stand. "You need to stay awake, remember?" she said, feeling like she was repeating herself. But what else could she do?

Sol moaned. "I need more ice," he murmured.

"Okay." *This might be a losing battle,* she thought, going around the bed and lifting the ice bag off his goose egg, covered with his damp hair. She left the room, silently asking God to help her know what to do to keep Sol awake . . . and safe from a coma.

By the time Ellie returned, Sol was struggling to prop himself up with two pillows. "Here, I'll help ya," she said, carrying two ice bags, one for his head and one for his hand. She placed them on the bed.

With her help, Sol slowly sat up and scooted back closer to the headboard to elevate his head. He reached for her hand to help him gradually lower back against the pillows, then smiled faintly. "*Denki*, Ellie. That's better."

"I should've raised ya sooner," she said, then left the room to check for more pillows in another closet. She returned with two more. "Here we are," she said as he moved forward a little so she could push them down behind him.

Once he was settled, she placed one ice bag on his right hand and the other on his head, which he'd tilted back. Then, sitting in the cane-back chair again, she hoped he was more comfortable in this position.

Sol was quiet for a while, but soon he said he disliked bothering her again, but he needed relief from the throbbing in his head. "My Mamm uses cold vinegar on a cloth and wraps it around her head sometimes. Might that help?"

"I'm afraid that might sting, if not burn your wounds," she

told him. "But what 'bout just an ice-cold cloth around your head?"

He smiled faintly. "You could be a nurse, Ellie."

"S'pose so." She smiled as she headed out of the room. No one had ever said such a thing to her.

By the time Dawdi returned from the Bontrager farm and Ellie had bound Sol's forehead with cold cloths, it was suppertime. She asked Sol if he wanted anything to eat, but he asked only for some chamomile tea. *For comfort*, she thought, knowing he'd suffered trauma. So while Dawdi sat and talked with Sol, Ellie heated water in the teakettle to make some blended chamomile and lavender tea. Dawdi kept some in the cupboard next to his kitchen sink.

After making a hot sandwich for Dawdi with leftover roast beef, she located his tray and placed the sandwich and some coleslaw on it, along with a glass of lemonade and Sol's hot tea. As for herself, she would wait to eat once Dat and Mamm arrived home. They must have stayed longer to visit at Onkel Amos's than they'd planned, maybe even for supper.

Since Dawdi was in the midst of telling Sol he didn't have to worry about taking care of the animals for several days—he'd asked their neighbor to spread the word Sol needed help—Ellie waited in the doorway till Dawdi motioned for her to enter. She set the tray on his lap, then carried the teacup around to the left of the bed and gave it to Sol. The ice bag was balanced on his head.

"You've done so much, Ellie," he said as he took the cup in his good hand.

"Here, come sit in this chair," Dawdi said to her, handing the tray back when she came around. "I'll find another." And with that, he left the room.

"Hezekiah says he and I are both conscientious objectors," Sol said, stopping to sip some tea. He didn't sound as breathless now.

"That's true," she said. "He rejected any form of service in the First World War, including a non-combatant role as a worker in a Virginia psychiatric hospital."

Dawdi brought another cane-back chair into the room, lowered it next to the first, and sat down. "There, now," he said as Ellie placed the tray on his lap again. He bowed his head and silently asked the blessing on his meal, then reached for his lemonade and began to drink.

"Why are COs so despised?" Sol asked.

"Well, some people think they should be willin' to serve in the military no matter their beliefs. And in my day they weren't just hated for being pacifists; they were also used as guinea pigs for medical and pesticide studies. Imagine usin' people in such a way without their consent."

Ellie was stunned.

"Wow. I didn't know that," Sol said.

Dawdi continued. "Fortunately, I wasn't used in that way, but I was called every slur in the book, including some I can't repeat. People accused me of being a coward for my refusal to fight or even serve, and that got me sent to prison in Leavenworth, Kansas, for more than a year. Many COs then were put in military camps. Some felt sure 'twas a breach of their civil rights to have to serve the U.S. government in any way, shape, or form." He paused. "I felt it was wrong, too, but because of what the Good Book teaches . . . the path of non-resistance."

"Then this . . . is nothin' compared to *your* suffering," Sol said, seeming to pace his words.

"Well, I'd hate to think of *anyone* bein' chained to the bars in a prison cell eight hours a day," Dawdi said, then took a bite of his sandwich.

"That happened to you, Dawdi?" Ellie asked, horrified.

He nodded, still chewing.

"I never knew." Ellie was dumbfounded.

He drank more of his lemonade. "Ain't somethin' I care to talk about. But Sol here needs to know he's not alone. Many young men have been battered and even tortured for their stand for pacifism and non-resistance over the years. Plain men and others. Doin' the right thing can be an awful hard road."

Sol reached to set his teacup on the small table near the bed. "I'm sorry ya had to go through that."

"Well, now, in that war, sixteen thousand men refused to take up arms for either religious or political reasons. For many of us, it was about wantin' to obey the sixth commandment: 'Thou shalt not kill.'"

"I can't imagine carryin' a weapon meant to harm or kill another," Sol said, his voice weaker now. "I've been determined to keep the peace, no matter what. Guess that resolve was tested today."

Ellie looked at Sol, realizing that though he hadn't gone to war, he'd suffered serious injuries all the same—and in their own backyard.

"It's a blessing you live in this era, Sol, and are free to exercise your right to object to military service." Dawdi's eyes were moist. "I'm thankful, indeed, for how things have changed."

After hearing some of what Dawdi had endured, Ellie was, too.

Long after Dat and Mamm had returned and while Ellie was making a light supper for herself, she couldn't stop thinking about Sol and Dawdi's shared misery. Or the courage Sol had demonstrated by not striking back at his attackers.

After hearing about the attack, her father had gone right over to look in on Sol. When he came back to the house, Ellie heard him tell Mamm that he and Dawdi planned to take turns keeping Sol awake till sometime around three o'clock in the morning. *Twelve hours after he was hurt,* Ellie thought, truly sad for Sol, weary and hurting as he was.

Following Bible reading and prayers with her parents while Dawdi stayed with Sol next door, Ellie went up to her room and prayed some more. There was simply no way she felt up to going to Singing tonight.

25

The temperature was already approaching sixty degrees when Ellie and Mamm finished pinning the washing to the clothesline around six-thirty the next morning. They'd gotten up while it was still dark so they'd have time to make a nice hot breakfast for Ellie to take over to Dawdi and Sol. *If Sol's up to eating,* Ellie thought.

"Dawdi might ask ya to stay and eat with them," Mamm said as she covered the scrambled eggs and German sausage. The meal included orange slices, buttered toast, strawberry jam, and a small pitcher of apple juice.

"If he wants me to," Ellie said, looking forward to seeing how Sol was feeling this morning. In fact, she'd been so concerned last night that she'd given little thought to the Singing and all she was missing there. Undoubtedly, Ruthann and her other cousins had wondered where she was, since she'd been in attendance at Preaching that morning. By now, though, the youth would've heard about Sol's attack, since Dawdi had asked the neighbors for help. Such news would spread quickly.

When Ellie carried the large wood tray to the *Dawdi Haus,* Dawdi spotted her through the screen door and came to open it. "Yous hungry?" she asked, smiling at him as he led her into the small kitchen. There sat Sol, still rather pale but upright nonetheless, his right hand wrapped in a compression bandage. The gash on his head wasn't as visible as yesterday, likely because Sol had showered. "*Gut* to see ya at the table," she said, noticing he was wearing the white shirt she'd washed out yesterday, wrinkles and all.

"I'm still a little off-kilter," he told her as she placed the tray on the table.

"He survived half the night without sleep," Dawdi said. "Till the wee hours."

"And I have both of yous to thank for lookin' after me." Sol smiled at Ellie. "And your Dat, too. He didn't get much sleep last night, either."

Dawdi sat down with his coffee mug, across from Sol, who'd been sipping cold water. "Sit next to me, Ellie-girl," Dawdi said. He'd already set the table for three.

She took her seat, and Dawdi bowed his head for their table blessing. She added a silent thanks for Sol's improvement overnight.

After the prayer, Dawdi reached to uncover the eggs and sausage, and Ellie removed the foil over the plate of toast. "Smells mighty *gut*," Dawdi said.

Sol nodded. "I'm glad my smeller still works." He chuckled a little. "And my appetite's comin' back."

"How's your left ear?" Ellie asked even before thinking.

"Sounds are still real muffled."

Dawdi said, "Say, I took a look at your noggin while you were sleepin' and put more antiseptic on it. But since you've showered, we better apply it again."

"Mighty thankful." Sol gingerly poured apple juice into his

small glass with his left hand. He also dished up a medium-sized portion of scrambled eggs onto his plate, again with his good hand.

"I was happy to tend to ya," Dawdi said.

"Is your headache better?" Ellie asked Sol.

"Some. Honestly, thought I was done for."

"You should continue to rest here for several more days," Dawdi told him. "Even with a minor concussion, physical and mental rest will help the healin' process along. What with your folks gone and the neighbors pitchin' in to help, no need to rush that."

Ellie had to smile, hearing Dawdi talk so. It was obvious he cared about Sol.

Sol nodded. "Considerin' how dizzy I get when I stand up, I have no intention of goin' anywhere just yet." He paused a moment. "I hate to ask ya, but I'm thinkin' I'll need some fresh clothes."

"I'm sure Dat'll be glad to go up and get some at your house," Ellie told him.

"So it's settled, then," Dawdi said. "You'll stay put here till you're able to get back on your feet, then we'll take ya home to rest further."

"And no need worryin' 'bout missing work here," Ellie said. "I'll plan to spend more time in the orchard until you're feelin' better."

Sol's gaze lingered on her. Feeling a little shy again, she glanced away. Still, it felt pleasantly awkward.

Midmorning, Menno pulled into the lane riding in his father's spring wagon, evidently having heard of Sol's plight. Ellie was just returning from the orchard to wash up at the well pump. She shook her hands in the air to dry them and headed over to greet Menno. "Hullo," she said. "Didja come to see your cousin?"

"To check up on him, *jah*."

"He's over at Dawdi's," she said, pointing in that direction. She was glad he'd come. "He was really beat up . . . with stones, Sol said."

Menno frowned. "Ain't the first time somethin' like this has happened." He mentioned there'd recently been similar incidents in Quarryville, down where his uncle and aunt lived. "Sure wish it hadn't happened to Sol, of all people."

"I know. It's hard to see him like this."

"Deacon urged us fellas to walk in pairs or groups when we're out on the road."

"Wise idea." She wondered what would have happened if rocks had been hurled at Evan prior to his leaving for basic training. Would he have fought back, maybe?

"I'm glad Sol's not alone, with his folks away an' all," Menno said.

"Honestly, I don't see how he would've made it otherwise."

"Well, the Lord knew right where he needed to be for help, ain't?" Menno smiled, then excused himself and walked toward the *Dawdi Haus*.

No hard feelings, Ellie thought, relieved.

When Ellie went to pick up the breakfast tray and serving dishes at Dawdi's, she found he'd given in to a catnap right there in his sitting room chair. *He's sleep-deprived from his nighttime vigil with Sol. Bless his heart—and Dat's, too.*

"*Denki* for such a *gut* breakfast, Ellie," Sol said, reclining on the sofa. "And thank your Mamm, too."

"*Eenichmol*—anytime." She felt silly saying it quite like that.

"Nice of Menno to stop by," Sol said.

She nodded. "I'm sure everyone who's heard of the attack is concerned 'bout ya."

Sol smiled. "Well, I know you're busy, Ellie."

"Need any more aspirin before I go?"

"I think I'll be okay." He thanked her again.

"Try an' get some rest now." She opened the screen door and headed back to the main house.

The rest of the morning, Ellie caught herself brooding several times about Sol's condition, hoping he'd fully recover.

As Lyle poured hot coffee into his thermos, Elisabeth told him Daed had asked if Sol might join them for meals.

"Okay with me," he said.

"He's gotta eat somewhere," Elisabeth said while cleaning and scraping the skin of a whole chicken. "Too bad Sol's parents are gone when he's hurt."

"I'll say." Lyle headed for the back door. "But mighty glad Dawdi and Ellie were here to help him—and us when we returned."

"Even though you didn't get much sleep last night?" she asked.

"Well, I'd do the same for Evan . . . if he were here."

"I know you would, dear."

Lyle would give almost anything to have Evan back, and he couldn't imagine what he was experiencing in war-torn Vietnam. Some days, he had to give his youngest son over to the care of almighty God not only once but multiple times.

At noon, the table was filled with plenty of food, including cooked green beans with pieces of fatty ham, buttered cut corn, and the chicken Elisabeth had stuffed with breadcrumbs, onion, and celery. She'd also cooked a generous number of new potatoes.

Lyle couldn't help noticing Sol at the foot of the table near Titus. Ellie was seated between Daed and Elisabeth, across from the younger men, and she seemed more subdued, if not distracted. Sol frequently glanced at Ellie, although he hadn't spoken to her so far. It was curious, since earlier Daed had mentioned how chatty the two of them had been yesterday afternoon, after Sol had settled in next door.

Is Sol sweet on Ellie? wondered Lyle, continuing to observe him as discreetly as he could.

26

Ellie appreciated the cloud cover shielding her and the other workers from the sun that afternoon. She missed seeing Sol out there among the trees, but it was essential for him to rest in order to recover.

Earlier, after the noon meal and on the way back to the *Dawdi Haus*, Sol had asked her to help him by writing a letter to Leah on his behalf. He'd held up his injured hand and added, *"I'll tell ya what to write."*

Ellie had agreed but didn't know when he wanted to dictate the letter. The more she thought about it, the more she looked forward to helping with that, but she wondered why he hadn't asked Dawdi instead.

Jonah said something to her, and she realized she'd been day-dreaming as she tamped down the freshly fertilized soil around a new tree. "Sorry?"

"When did any of ya last hear from Evan?" Jonah repeated.

"Mamm and Dat got a short letter a few days ago, and I'm waiting for a reply—maybe sometime this week." She wondered why Jonah was asking and hoped he wanted to write to Evan, too—at last. It was, and had been, obvious that her brothers weren't happy with Evan. Mostly, though, like her parents, they were worried he might not survive combat. Terrible stories about the growing casualties were plastered on the front page of the newspaper nearly every day.

More and more, she was noticing how various people in the church district seemed to look askance at her and her family, likely because of Evan's decision. And she'd learned Dat and Mamm had stayed so long visiting Onkel Amos and Aendi Emma on Sunday because Amos had a bone to pick with Dat. He'd wanted to know why Evan had been permitted to go his own way even before he turned sixteen. Ellie was surprised that a close relative would talk like that to her father, who had certainly tried to steer Evan away from the world at large. *Dat didn't know Evan was sneakin' off to see Jack Herr back then.*

"Seems like Evan's thrown away everything," Jonah was saying as he poured the liquid fertilizer. "It's like he doesn't care one iota about his upbringing."

"It might look like that, but I'm clingin' to the hope that God will be merciful and bring him safely home to us." Ellie tugged on her bandanna, making sure her middle part was protected from the sun now that the clouds had moved away and the sun was beating down hard. "I'm sure you, Rudy, and Lydia are prayin' that way, too."

At supper, Ellie felt self-conscious with Sol at the table again. It was so different from when they were alone talking, but she tried to be more engaging with the family this time. When she passed the platter of porcupine meatballs, she commented to Mamm how nice and plump they were. And when the cornbread came around, she asked Dawdi if he'd like honey on his. Things like that, so she didn't just sit awkwardly, like a bump on a log.

But as was the case at dinner earlier, Sol didn't talk directly to her. Was he just shy around her family, maybe? Yet why would that be, considering he knew them all so well and worked closely with Dat and her brothers?

His muffled hearing might be the reason, she suddenly realized.

Dawdi Hezekiah spoke up just then to ask about the peanut butter pie on the counter. "Did ya use my wife's recipe?" His expression appeared hopeful.

"*Jah*, she let me copy it right off her tattered recipe card years ago."

"Oh goodness, that cream cheese and whipped cream, and a graham cracker crust . . ." Dawdi said in a sing-songy way.

Dat grinned. "That pie ain't for the faint of heart."

"I s'pose we really should finish our main meal first," Mamm said, laughing a little.

Dawdi nodded and winked at Ellie.

On his way to the side door after supper, Sol asked Ellie if tonight was a good time for him to dictate Leah's letter to her.

Ellie agreed and mentioned that she owed his sister a letter, too. "But she should hear 'bout the attack from you first, *jah*?"

"Sorry, I didn't quite hear the last part." He leaned toward her a little.

She repeated herself a bit louder.

Sol nodded slowly. "You're right."

"I'll be over after dishes are done," she said, still concerned he wasn't himself.

When Ellie arrived, Dawdi Hezekiah was sitting on his porch in one of his two willow rockers, wearing his dark blue sweater over his shirt and suspenders. "I found some lined writing paper for ya," he said when he saw her. "And a nice pen."

"We're all set, then," she replied as she reached for the screen door.

"Sol's real discouraged 'bout his difficulty hearing," he said. "Keep that in mind."

"I will."

He rose from the rocker, buttoned his sweater, and headed down the porch steps. "Well, I'll be out walkin' in the orchard if anyone needs me."

"You don't have to leave on my account," Ellie told him. "It'll get chilly soon."

"I'm wearin' my sweater." He chuckled. "How long's this letter gonna be?"

"That's up to Sol."

Dawdi started across the lawn. "I lit the big lantern in the kitchen," he called behind him.

"*Denki*," she said, then slipped inside to find Sol already at the table.

"I appreciate this, Ellie," he said as she sat across from him in the lantern light.

Sol scooted the paper across to her. "My brain's still a little hazy sometimes." He sighed and glanced at the ceiling. "I tried to read the Bible last night, and the words jumped around on the page. And this afternoon I tried to write with my left hand, but it was impossible to read." He grimaced.

"I'm glad to help," she said, realizing he might also have asked her to write the letter since she and Leah were close friends. "How do ya want to start?"

"Let's make it clear from the outset that you're writing for me because my hand's been injured, but not tell her how I injured it just yet."

Ellie wrote as quickly as she could, taking down precisely what he dictated—who was writing and why, his greeting, and then asking Leah how she was doing and if she was still seeing Reuben Miller.

"If so, have ya met any of his family yet, other than his preacher father?" Sol added. "And are ya getting serious with Reuben, or is it too soon to know?"

Ellie paused in her writing. "I was goin' to ask her that, too," she said softly.

He looked at her with confusion. "Sorry?"

Ellie repeated herself more loudly this time.

"Leah will know we both care 'bout her," Sol said. "Well, she already knows."

For the next few minutes, they forgot the letter and fell into their usual easy conversation, talking about their mutual concern that Leah hadn't known Reuben long, not to mention that he lived clear out there in Chambersburg, and Leah's family and all her relatives were *here*.

"'Tween you and me," Sol said, "I hope this is just a passing fancy."

"Leah's not given to crushes, though."

Sol frowned and cupped his left ear.

"I said, Leah's not given to crushes."

"Ah, true."

Ellie moved her chair closer to the table, thinking that might help Sol hear her better. "You and Leah are open with each other, so surely she'll tell ya how she feels 'bout Reuben."

He nodded, looking more thoughtful. "Now, the hard part. How should I tell her about what happened to me?"

Ellie sat with the pen poised.

Sol breathed deeply. "I don't want to frighten her with too many details."

"To be honest, she'll be worried with even the gist of it. I'm sure of it."

"I prob'ly shouldn't go into many details, then. I mean, by the time the letter arrives, I'll be on the mend . . . I pray." He smiled weakly. "It may take a while."

Ellie looked at him. "It's only been a day, Sol."

"Well, should I even tell her 'bout the attack, or wait?"

"Wouldn't you wanna know if *she* got hurt?" Ellie glanced down at the letter in progress. "Remember, I've already written that your hand's hurt enough that you couldn't write."

"*Puh!* I forgot that. See what I mean? I'm still fuzzy in the head." Sol frowned. "Okay, so what would you tell Evan if it was you?"

"Oh, I wouldn't tell him anything right now, considering he's scared to death over there."

Sol's head tilted as he looked over at her. "I thought he was itchin' to go."

Now she wasn't sure if Evan had told her about his concern in confidence, and she suddenly felt at a loss to remember exactly what he'd said. "I s'pose anyone would be nervous goin' into battle, but more so because Evan's never known a life with violence." She paused. "*Ach,* I've gone down a rabbit trail, I think. We were talking 'bout what to share with Leah."

Sol laughed softly. "That makes two of us."

Eventually, they came up with something that wouldn't cause Leah too much alarm, sketching out the basics of the attack but not all the aspects of his recovery. And for the next half hour or so, they worked together on the letter, stopping along the way to talk about this and that.

"Ya know, I feel pretty unsure of myself right now," Sol said thoughtfully, his gaze on the letter in front of them.

"What do ya mean?"

"Well, I can't help wonderin' how a young woman would respond to my deafness, if it lingers. And then there's all these injuries." He looked down at his wrapped right hand. "I'm all battered up."

His dejection was evident. "What's happened surely wouldn't lessen a young woman's regard for ya, Sol. Not if she cares for you."

He brightened as he looked at her, and Ellie realized that even if another girl didn't feel that way toward him, she certainly did. Her heart fluttered at the thought.

After they finished the letter, Dawdi came indoors, shuffled across the sitting room, and sat down in his chair. Before she noticed the time, Sol glanced up at the small clock above the sink and said he'd kept her much too long.

"Goodness, family Bible reading and prayer will be startin' soon," she said, looking over at Dawdi and seeing his slack jaw. "Looks like he'll be content right there for a while. I won't disturb him."

"He might be disappointed to miss out when he wakes up after his forty winks," Sol said as Ellie folded the letter.

The way Sol said it, Ellie almost wondered if he was wishing he might join her and her parents. "Well, I should go," she said, getting up, yet feeling strangely reluctant to leave.

"*Denki* again." He smiled. "I'll see ya, Ellie."

"At breakfast tomorrow."

"Lord willin'.'" He leaned back in the chair. "*Gut Nacht.*"

"Take care, Sol." She opened the inside door and then the screen door, wondering why she hadn't noticed how chilly it had become in the house.

The moon was scarcely visible, a waxing crescent so thin in the sky she stopped to stare at it. A barn cat meowed loudly across the lane from where she stood, and a crow *caw-cawed* overhead. She turned to look in the direction of the orchard, where she and Dawdi loved to walk in the late afternoon, but all she could see in her mind's eye was Sol picking fruit and occasionally stopping to talk to her. *All the while, I thought we were just friends.*

Sighing now, she felt *ferhoodled.* Thinking back to letter writing with Sol, she tried to understand what had happened between them. In just the space of . . . what? One evening? She'd revealed something of her interest when she'd implied that his injuries hadn't dimmed her regard for him. *And he seemed glad to hear that.*

Sitting on the porch steps, Ellie wondered about Sol's eagerness to have her write Leah's letter on his behalf. But if she continued to ponder it, her head would start to hurt like Sol's.

She rose to go inside, stopping at the kitchen sink for a drink of water, not sure what to do with these strange new feelings emerging for Sol. Was it simply his helpless state? *Maybe I just feel sorry for him.*

Making her way into the front room, Ellie sat in the chair across from Dat and Mamm on the settee while Dat read from his Bible. And once they had said their silent prayers and risen from kneeling, she told them she wanted to head for bed early.

Mamm gave her a little kiss on the cheek, and Dat said, "Sleep tight, Ellie."

"You too, Dat." She was suddenly too tired to even think of writing a letter to Leah now. Sol had suggested his letter should arrive first anyway, she remembered as she made her way up the stairs to her room. Once there, she looked at her Sunday dresses hanging on the wooden pegs across from the dresser and wondered which color she should wear to the next Preaching.

Catching herself, she turned to pick up the hand mirror on her dresser. "Am I falling for my cousin's former beau?"

27

A light but steady rain was falling the next evening. Ellie stood at the side door and stared out its screen. She'd sensed Sol's discouragement at both breakfast and the noon meal, and at supper he told her parents and Dawdi that he still couldn't hold a pen to write his name. He'd also admitted he wanted to return home to rest in his own bed, saying that his insomnia, though a side effect of a concussion, might lessen at home. *And his parents will be arriving home tonight, which will surely be a comfort,* Ellie thought.

So Dawdi Hezekiah had taken him home after supper and was already back enjoying seconds of Mamm's dessert—carrot cake with whipped cream.

Ellie thought it was probably a good idea for Sol to get settled in at home, even though she felt sad that he was so down about his condition.

Back in the kitchen, Ellie saw Mamm at one end of the table with her pen and stationery, which reminded her of last evening with Sol. Such thoughts had kept coming all day, and try as she might, she couldn't get them out of her mind.

"You all right?" Mamm asked, looking at her.

"I guess so."

Mamm continued to study her. "Thinking 'bout Sol?"

Sighing, Ellie pulled out the wood bench and sat down, leaning her elbows on the table much as she had last night while talking so comfortably with Sol. "Honestly—and I don't know when it happened—but I think I might like Sol as more than a friend."

Mamm pursed her lips. "He is rather *wunnerbaar.*"

Ellie was surprised at how quickly her mother spoke. "You think so?"

"Dawdi seems to, also. And we all know Dawdi's a *gut* barometer of many things."

Ellie smiled. "I'll say." She sighed. "Guess I'll just have to sort out my feelings," she said before Mamm could ask more.

She rose and headed into the front room with the family Bible, turning to the next chapter Dat would be reading and happy to wait for the rest of her family to arrive for their nightly routine.

At market the next day, Ellie happened to see Ruthann and Menno ordering peanut brittle together. It was obvious how very attentive Menno was, which was a good sign. The two of them hadn't even seemed to notice her, which was fine—and besides, she was carrying two tall lemonades back to their market stand, where Mamm was selling an excess of asparagus.

I couldn't be happier for Menno and Ruthann, she thought as she set the drinks on the table.

That Saturday, the first of May, dawned sunny, and Ellie continued to work extra hours in the orchard, checking trees to see if their pest management practices were working and reducing the need for pesticides.

More tired than usual at the end of the day, she took time to finally write to Leah nevertheless. She mentioned helping Dawdi look after Sol and how thankful she was to have been out walking in the orchard right when Sol needed assistance. She also shared that Ruthann was seeing Menno. *They're a good match*, she wrote.

She also made time to write to Evan earlier that week, afraid he'd wonder if she'd forgotten him, considering all the time she was putting in out in the orchard. But then he hadn't written in some weeks, either.

Ellie told him she had started to see some of the first benefits from the time she'd put in recruiting local restaurants and bakeries, many of which were signed up for the upcoming peach and apple season. *Our fruit will be everywhere*, she joked. Dat had taken notice, as well, which pleased Ellie no end.

The Lord's Day brought an early rain before dawn, "a *gut* soaker makin' plenty-a mud" as Lyle described it to his father as they sat at the table waiting for Elisabeth's hearty homemade granola and the fresh goat's milk purchased yesterday from Rudy's farm.

After they'd finished eating and the meal's second prayer, Lyle asked Ellie to go with him to check on Sol. They found him sitting on the wide back porch and petting Shadow, the Bontragers' beautiful gray and white German shepherd, whose front paws leaned on Sol's knees. Sol looked up when he heard them coming, and his face lit up like a full moon.

"Hullo there," Lyle said as he stepped onto the porch.

"Nice to see ya," Sol said, looking now at Ellie. "Have yourselves a seat."

Lyle sat next to him near several clay pots of aloe plants, and Ellie sat beside Lyle, who realized she was on the wrong side for Sol to hear her well. "We wondered how you've been doin'," he said louder than he normally spoke. "I know recovery isn't always a straight line."

"*Denki*," Sol replied. It looked like his thick blond hair had been recently trimmed, and he was without his straw hat. His face had a healthier glow, not nearly as pale.

The screen door opened and out came Sol's mother, Nan, her white work apron tied around her long black one. "*Willkumm*," she said, smiling as she came over to lean against the white porch post. "Benjamin's out in the barn."

"How was your trip?" Lyle asked.

"Oh fine, but it's always *gut* to be home again." Nan looked kindly at Ellie. "*Denki* ever so much for takin' care of our son. My goodness, yous were a godsend. He told us all 'bout it."

Sol smiled. "Today's one week since it happened," he said with a glance at Lyle. "I'm hopin' to get back to work in the orchard again soon."

"Only when ya know you're ready," Lyle said, and Ellie nodded.

Sol tilted his head, and Lyle could tell he hadn't quite followed him. So he repeated his comment more loudly.

"Oh, I'm doin' better. I still have insomnia, but the folk medicine book says to take one to two teaspoons of honey before bedtime, so I've been doin' that. To tell ya the truth, though, so far it hasn't helped all that much."

Nan looked at her son with concern. "His poor noggin took a poundin'," she said, pushing her blue bandanna back a little. "But he's drinking plenty of liquids and resting whenever he needs to. We don't want to make things worse by havin' him do much before his head's fully healed."

"*Des gut*," Lyle said, glad Nan was home, looking after Sol while Benjamin tended to the steers.

"Quite a few of *die Youngie* have dropped by to encourage Sol," Nan told them, smiling thoughtfully. "The bishop and all the ministers have, too, and of course our local kinfolk."

Sol seemed lost to the thread of the conversation, obviously still struggling to hear.

They talked a bit longer, and then Lyle and Ellie excused themselves to head home.

"*Kumme* anytime," Nan said warmly. "Sol enjoys seein' his favorite neighbors."

"Say hullo to Benjamin when he comes in from the barn," Lyle told her.

"I'll do that." Nan smiled broadly, as she often did. "Greet Elisabeth for me."

"I certainly will," Lyle replied, then said good-bye to Sol, waving along with it so he'd understand more readily.

"*Denki* for comin'," Sol said, suddenly sounding glum.

"Bye, Sol," said Ellie, but he didn't respond.

As they headed out to the waiting horse and buggy, Lyle couldn't help but feel sorry for Sol—and for Ellie, who hadn't had much chance to visit with him. At least she'd seen for herself that Sol was slightly better, though quite hard of hearing in his left ear.

She definitely cheered him up, Lyle thought, wondering if his daughter had noticed Sol's reaction to seeing her.

It was hard to think of much else but Sol as Ellie rode home with Dat. Thoughts of him hadn't quieted down much this whole past week, and now they were right back in the forefront of her mind. She'd have to be blind to have missed his big smile when she and Dat walked up the porch steps.

Does he light up like that for everyone?

Mamm was preparing a skillet dinner for the noon meal when Ellie walked into the kitchen for a cold drink of water. Small piles of chopped sausage, onions, and green peppers sat on the large cutting board, waiting for macaroni to boil. "I should've stayed home to help," Ellie said, feeling quite *ferhoodled*.

"Well, your father wanted ya along."

Ellie was curious why.

"So how's Sol?"

"Not back to normal yet. He said he's still not sleepin' much."

"With the injuries he suffered, that can go on for weeks, even years," Mamm said, lifting the lid on the big pot of macaroni. The steam rose instantly. She stepped back a moment, then began to stir.

"I wish something could be done for Sol—his deaf ear, 'specially," Ellie said. "He seemed to have an extra hard time hearing us today. Guess we'll need to sit on his right side when we visit next."

"*Gut* thinkin'."

"Seems like a real trial for him."

Ellie asked if there was anything she could do in the kitchen, but Mamm shook her head. So Ellie slipped outdoors, where she found Dat sitting on the back porch. Sitting in the rocker next to him, Ellie asked, "Do ya think Sol will fully recover, Dat?"

"We both know that's in God's hands."

"What're the chances he might not?"

Her father sighed. "I know of farmers who were kicked in the head by a horse or mule and died instantly, and I know of others who were knocked unconscious and suffered a much worse concussion than even Sol's and fully recovered. The thing is, it takes time and rest to heal a head injury."

"And his hearing?"

"That too."

"What 'bout his eyes blurring when he tries to read?"

"Could take a few weeks yet," Dat said, folding his arms across his chest. "But God's will is what we pray for in all situations."

"Sol seems to want to get back to work," she said, realizing she sounded impatient. *And I want an excuse to spend time with him.*

"Well, it's much too soon. Health is fragile—it can be altered in a moment's time."

"So true." She folded her hands and admitted quietly, "I'm fond of Sol."

Dat turned to smile at her. "We *all* are."

I'm glad, she thought.

28

Following a spaghetti-and-meatballs supper two days later, Mamm asked Ellie if she'd like to go with her to visit Nan Bontrager. "And to say hullo to Sol again," Mamm said, a twinkle in her eyes. "I baked a rhubarb pie to take along and some snickerdoodles, too."

"*Jah*, I'll go."

When they arrived on foot, Ellie saw Sol sitting on the front porch this time, his golden bangs shining beneath his straw hat. *There's more to watch on this side of the house*, she thought.

Sol waved, then rose to walk down the steps, waiting near the driveway for them. "Hullo again!" he said, smiling. He was dressed nicely in a pale blue long-sleeved shirt and black broadfall trousers and suspenders.

"Hope ya like rhubarb pie," Mamm said as they approached him.

"Ice cream'll make it extra tasty," Ellie said, observing him. *Is he feeling better?*

Mamm added, "It's nice to see ya getting some sunshine."

"It's such a nice day, I couldn't help it." Sol smiled again.

Ellie noticed he'd turned his head to favor his good ear.

Mamm glanced down at her quilted carryall. "Well, I'll be takin' this round to the back door. Oh, and we've brought snickerdoodles, too."

Sol chuckled. "I think you're tryin' to fatten me up."

Mamm laughed and went away with the pie and cookies, leaving Ellie there with Sol.

"Might as well go an' sit a while," Sol said, motioning toward the front porch.

She went with him up the walkway.

He offered her the rocking chair. "We'll watch the buggies go by."

"My Dat says it's relaxing," she replied as she sat to Sol's right, where he could hear her. "He waves at everyone as they pass by." She glanced at him. "Feelin' better since I last saw ya?"

He nodded. "Resting and learnin' to adjust a little more each day." He smiled again. "Between you and now my Mamm, I've been well taken care of."

"Have ya had more visitors lately?" Ellie asked, never guessing that she'd be talking with Sol alone like this when she'd said yes to Mamm.

"*Die Youngie* came over again Sunday afternoon to sing for me. Menno and Ruthann were with them." He paused a moment. "It was interesting to see them together, but I'm mighty happy for them."

"I saw them at market recently. They were laughin' and talkin' like they were the only two people in the world."

Sol stopped for a moment to look out at the sky like he was thinking hard. At last, he said, "Honestly, I'd often wondered if they might end up together."

"I was a little surprised at first. But the clues were there, *jah?*"

Sol nodded. "Things just weren't clickin' with her and me. I

221

guess it was complicated because the four of us were such great friends—all the double-dating we did." He leaned back in his chair and let out a sigh.

"We did all enjoy one another's company," she said, relieved they could talk freely about it.

"*Ach*," Sol said softly, catching her eye. "Though truth be told, Ellie, it's always been your company I prefer."

Surprised but delighted, Ellie's heart took wing. A few moments of silence passed before she found her voice. "We've been friends for a *gut* long time now."

"The best of friends," Sol said, almost in a whisper. He took a breath, as if fortifying himself with courage. "But I'd be mighty hesitant to ask ya to court, if I knew I wouldn't get any better."

Her heart beat more quickly at that. "Honestly, the Sol Bontrager I knew before the attack is the same Sol sitting right here. There's no difference to me."

"That's kind of you." He smiled again, then looked more somber. "Even so, I'd never want ya stuck with someone who might be a burden. Wouldn't be fair."

She had been concerned that he might think that. "Do ya remember what I said the night you dictated your letter to Leah?"

He nodded thoughtfully. "I haven't forgotten," he said, his eyes searching hers. "And you're right. *Abselutt.*"

She breathed deeply, content in this peaceful yet wonderful moment, knowing that Sol cared and wanted to regain his health for her. And as if to seal their words, they sat silently and watched the teams of horses and buggies *clip-clop* past, not caring who saw them together.

It was all Ellie could do to slow her pace enough to match Mamm's as they walked down the hill toward home. Oh, she wanted to run, to fly! But the spring in her step might give away the reason for her exhilaration, and Ellie wanted to keep this latest talk with Sol close to her heart for now. Besides, she and Sol wouldn't be going out as a couple till he was stronger, but knowing he wanted to court her made the evening sky seem brighter and the orchard in the near distance all the more beautiful.

The very next day in the mailbox, Ellie found the letter from Leah she'd been anticipating. Glancing at the postmark, she saw that Leah had sent the letter on Monday morning, two days ago.

So she's received both Sol's and my letters, Ellie thought, making her way back up their lane with its leafy green maples.

She had waited to check for mail just before suppertime since she'd worked in the orchard right up until then. Going up the side steps and around to the back part of the porch, she plopped down onto the glider and tore open the letter.

Dear Ellie,

You're such a good friend to me . . . and to Sol. When I saw your handwriting in his letter, my heart fell. It's a frightening and very sad world around us, ain't so? But I'm so glad there are kind and caring friends like you and your family. What would Sol have done otherwise? I'm so glad you can encourage him as he gets better. If I were there, I'd do the same, for sure.

Well, can you believe that it's been nearly a year since I left Bird-in-Hand? May twelfth it was, and you nearly cried when I came to say good-bye, I remember. You never knew it, but I wept all the way home that day, hating to leave my closest friend and my family behind. But if I hadn't taken that

223

risk, I probably never would have met Reuben. Oh, I wish you could meet him, Ellie. Goodness, I wish Sol could, too, and my parents. As you may have guessed, we've started to court now, and I enjoy spending time with him as much as anyone I've ever known.

As always, I can't wait to hear back from you.

Your friend,
Leah

Ellie pondered Leah's words. She'd sometimes imagined how she might feel when or if she received this sort of news from Leah. *She won't be moving back home,* Ellie thought, but it didn't bother her the way she'd expected. *She'll be so surprised when Sol and I start courting!*

The dinner bell was ringing, summoning her, Dawdi, and Dat inside for supper.

Ellie rose from the glider and went around to the side door, folding the letter and placing it in her dress pocket.

After Dat led in the silent mealtime prayer, Ellie thought more about Leah's letter . . . and Sol. It had sounded like he'd known he and Ruthann weren't meant to move forward in their relationship for a while before she ended it.

Meanwhile, Dawdi was talking about his childhood, reminiscing about how he'd sometimes played in the smithy's shop while the horses and mules were brought in to be shod. "I was prob'ly five, if that, when I decided I was gonna be the next Bird-in-Hand smithy," he said with a grin. "Never did I think I'd end up plantin' an orchard."

"Tell us the story 'bout what made ya want to plant fruit trees," Ellie said.

"Alrighty." He salted his sweet potato. "If it was written on the palms of these here callused hands, it couldn't've been any clearer to me." He told of staying overnight at his Mammi Hostetler's old farmhouse when he was around nine and opening the window that first morning to the beauty of God's creation. He said it was the first time he'd paid much attention to the two rows of fruit trees in his grandmother's side yard. "Well, I ran right outside in my nightclothes and stood under a tree with the tiniest fruitlets budding, staring up through the branches and leaves in astonishment."

"At breakfast, it was all I could talk 'bout," Dawdi said, his eyes alert. "Mammi said those trees were the best thing she and Dawdi had ever planted, and the happiest days of their lives had been takin' care of them together. 'God's wunnerbaar-gut *way to give us apples,*' she said." Dawdi paused, looking now at Ellie. "I've never forgotten that."

"No wonder it made a big impression on ya," Ellie said, enjoying hearing this story again.

"Oh, it did. And for years I daydreamed 'bout the queen of fruit, wanting to have apple trees right outside my own windows someday."

Ellie couldn't agree more. "Every spring when the trees blossom, I think of it as a gift from God. Did ya know?"

"Well now, Ellie-girl, we're cut from the same branch, ain't we?" He was grinning so big it made his wispy white beard move.

In that moment, she realized that she longed to tell Dawdi and her parents that Sol, who also loved the orchard, wanted to court her.

And I want to be his girl!

29

Ellie had always enjoyed the process of thinning out the apples once they were about the size of a dime, which they were now that it was May. She reached to cut off all but one tiny fruitlet in each cluster, taking note of the amount of space this created for the remaining apples to grow larger. *More air flow and sunlight for each branch*, she thought, appreciating how this process also made the tree healthier.

Nearly every afternoon, rain showers came for an hour or so. *Heaven's blessings.* Sometimes Ellie continued working through them under the tree canopy, wearing the raincoat and rain hat Dat had purchased for her several years ago. But whenever lightning appeared, she and the other workers immediately headed into the barn, staying till the storm blew over.

Evan loves thunderstorms, she recalled, wondering how he was. If only someone would hear from him.

The Saturday nearly three weeks after his attack, Sol showed up at work wearing a splint, his right hand still wrapped. Dat greeted him, shaking his left hand, and so did everyone else. Ellie hung back a little even though she and Dat, and sometimes Mamm, had visited him every few days during his recuperation. Somehow, each time they'd been able to talk alone for a while.

Still, Sol seemed a little bashful around her, like he sometimes was whenever they were around others. So she simply said, "*Willkumm* back, Sol," and he smiled.

Having visited Sol with Dat a couple of days ago, she knew Sol was still struggling with his hearing loss and doing everything with his left hand. But he'd also told them he was sleeping through the night, at last, which was making a big difference in his overall health.

Dat urged Sol not to use a ladder to thin apples just yet, and Ellie was glad of that. *Dat really is fond of him,* she thought, trying not to think too far ahead. *We must court first!* She wondered if Sol would attend Sunday Singing on the twenty-third.

That evening, Ellie slipped away to her room and wrote to Evan yet again.

It's a little complicated, but you might be happy to know that Sol wants to court me. I didn't tell you that Menno and I broke up back in January, but it was definitely for the best. Sol and I have been good friends for a long time, so I'm curious how it will be as we move into a serious relationship.

After she signed off, she searched both the newspaper ads and *Lancaster Farming* ads for land sales, her pen, as always, poised to mark one or two that stood out. So far, nothing had seemed quite right.

Setting the paper aside on her desk, Ellie thought of writing to Leah, but she decided to wait so she could tell her about the next Singing. *Leah will understand—and be excited—once she reads what I'll be telling her.*

The next morning after breakfast, Dat asked Ellie if she'd seen yesterday's paper.

"It's up in my room," she replied, setting down the tea towel. "Should I run an' get it?"

Dat waved it off. "It can wait."

But he looked puzzled, so she went ahead and told him her dream. "Been hopin' we might buy land somewhere nearby, so I've been readin' the land-sale ads."

Dat straightened, eyebrows raised. "Is that right? You've been a-hankerin' for cherries and plums?" he asked, running his hand through his beard.

Ellie nodded.

Dat glanced at Mamm as she offered him coffee in a thermos. "What do ya think, Elisabeth? Do we need more fruit trees, maybe?"

"Well, that's up to yous to decide." Mamm smiled.

"So there ya have it, Ellie. Keep on lookin' and let me know what ya find."

Ellie said she would, then picked up the towel to continue wiping the dishes, delighted that her father was on board.

The following Saturday afternoon, Ellie helped Dat wash down the family carriage and all its windows, too. She curried Captain, and Dat cleaned and oiled the horse's feet. When the harness was clean, Dawdi Hezekiah checked the battery for the lights and the fluid for the brakes—all this before suppertime.

Ellie could scarcely think of anything but seeing Sol at

Singing tomorrow evening. She didn't want to hold her breath, but they *had* talked quite a few times in the orchard during his first week back. Sol was still favoring his wounded ear and right hand, but he was able to do a few things with one hand— especially thinning apples, one at a time. It was apparent he was determined to do whatever he could, and Dat had noticed his perseverance, too.

She was sure Sol was feeling better as each day passed, and when he and Ellie were alone in the orchard, he'd mentioned that he no longer wanted to double-date—something he'd said with a twinkle in his eyes. Ellie had nodded her agreement, thinking how much she looked forward to their first real date.

Ellie was pleased that Mamm had invited Jonah, Rudy, Lydia, and their families over for homemade ice cream after Preaching and the fellowship meal the next day. It had been a while since they'd all come at once for a visit. She'd sensed that her mother missed Evan and needed the comfort of spending time with her family. Jonah must have picked up on it, too, because he volunteered to come directly rather than following their usual routine—heading home to get their younger children down for naps after the long morning of sermons.

The day was lovely, in the mid-seventies with a light breeze and partly cloudy—only one week till June. Rudy had suggested they all sit out on the back lawn, so he and the other men had brought out lawn chairs from the barn, and Ellie and Mamm gathered some old quilts to spread on the grass for the smallest children.

Dat and Dawdi had made several batches of strawberry

ice cream on Friday, so it was ready to serve. Ellie and her sisters-in-law helped dish it up so Mamm could sit outside enjoying the grandchildren. Lydia stayed out there, too, getting help with the little ones from her own daughters, Ida, now nine, and Verna, eight, as well as Jonah's oldest child, nine-year-old Lucy.

While the three younger women worked together in the kitchen, Lovina asked, "Is Mamm under the weather?"

"I think she's mostly missin' Evan," Ellie replied.

Lovina sighed. "*Ach*, no wonder."

Ellie handed the next bowl to Priscilla as she dug the serving spoon into the ice cream.

"We pray for Evan every day," Lovina told her. "Caleb and little Mary don't understand where he is, but they bow their heads and fold their hands. It's the most precious thing."

Ellie could imagine tiny Mary mimicking her older brother during prayer. She glanced out the window and spotted Rudy holding the drowsy child while he sat talking with Jonah. She smiled at the endearing sight and told Lovina, who seemed relieved.

"That's *gut*," she said. "Mary was awful fussy earlier because of teething, but she did nap a while in the buggy on the way over here." Ellie handed Lovina the next bowl, and after counting the bowls that were already full, she said, "We're getting close to enough now."

Priscilla found three trays in one of Mamm's cupboards and began placing some bowls on one of them. Lovina put the rest of the bowls on the other two trays, and Ellie held the side door open for all of them as they made their way out.

Ellie returned to the kitchen and found enough spoons in the utensil drawer for everyone, including the toddlers. Then she hurried back outside, carrying the spoons in her long white apron.

She sat in the only vacant chair left, next to Mamm, who thanked her for the help. Soon, Alma came over to sit in the grass near Ellie's bare feet.

"Was hopin' I could be near ya," Alma said, grinning.

"What ya been up to?"

"Mamm learned me how to do some stitchin'."

"For quilting?"

Alma nodded, big-eyed. "Gonna try an' make my first patchwork square."

"That'll be fun!"

"*Jah*, an' I'll show ya when it's done, okay?"

"You'd better." Ellie smiled, always enjoying how expressive Alma was. She reminded her of Cousin Ruthann.

Then while Alma dipped her spoon into her ice cream and continued eating, Ellie thought ahead to tonight's Singing, wondering again how the other youth would react when they saw her with Sol. It was hard not to break into a big smile.

30

No Singing in the past had caused the kind of excitement Ellie felt as she rode to this one with her father, who'd offered to take her there. Her pent-up anticipation pointed out the fact that she hadn't deeply cared for Menno or any other fellow she'd gone riding with, not the way she cared for Sol.

"You seem mighty happy tonight," Dat said, glancing at her as he held the driving lines. "I'm sure ya know your Mamm and I have put our faith in the Lord for the young man you'll marry one day, Ellie."

Dat had never said anything like this to her before, but she wasn't surprised to hear it. Trusting God was at the foundation of how they lived. "I'm thankful for that," she replied, "'cause I'd never wanna make a mistake in something as important as marriage."

Dat nodded thoughtfully. "Sadly, some young folks have been known to rush into it for the wrong reasons."

Ellie thought about Menno. Now that she'd had time to step back and think about their casual dates, she realized that she never could have married him—and not just because of his attitude at the time about Evan. *Was it merely his good looks that drew me?* she wondered. Yet what a shallow reason to continue going out with someone. "Marryin' for love is best," she replied to Dat. "With God's blessing."

Giving her a smile, he nodded, sitting so tall in the driver's seat that his straw hat nearly bumped the top of the carriage. "An unselfish, caring love that puts the other one first," he said. "That's a love worth waitin' for."

Ellie thought of Sol and the way she felt about him . . . and wholeheartedly agreed.

Heading into the large expanse of the cleared-off haymow in their hosts' barn, Ellie spotted several of her girl cousins. She made her way to the long wooden table and greeted them. Cousin Sarah Ann was talking animatedly to Ruthann.

Over on the other side of the barn, the young men stood chewing the fat after placing their straw hats in piles on some of the baled hay.

As Ellie stepped closer, Sarah Ann turned from Ruthann and asked Ellie, "How's Sol getting along now? You prob'ly see him workin' in the orchard, *jah*?"

"He's only been back for a week," Ellie said, trying to keep a lid on her feelings. "I think he's bein' careful not to overdo."

"Which he should be," Ruthann said, glancing knowingly at Ellie. "A concussion's nothin' to fool with."

"I wonder if he'll be here tonight," Sarah Ann said.

I wonder, too, Ellie thought, seeing Sol's younger brother, Aaron, enter the haymow door alone at that moment. She looked around but saw no sign of Sol. *Maybe he's not up to comin' to Singing quite yet*, she thought, saddened by the realization he might not be there.

Lyle took his time returning home, as he sometimes did after taking Ellie to Singing. He'd wanted to make sure she'd be free to accept a young fellow's invitation to ride in his courting buggy. Since Evan's leaving, this small responsibility had fallen to him, and he liked having the time alone to think.

Months ago, Lyle had presumed Ellie was seeing someone. He'd guessed Leah's cousin Menno, but he wasn't the type of parent to wait up to see who was bringing her home. Here lately, though, surely the love lights in Sol's eyes whenever Ellie was around were a giveaway. He and Elisabeth couldn't be more pleased if what they guessed about their daughter and Sol was the honest truth. And, of course, they'd done what they could to make certain the two of them had opportunities to visit during those first weeks of his recovery.

All the same, Ellie had been rather closed-lipped tonight, he thought, chuckling to himself. *Like I was back when I fell head over heels for Elisabeth. Ah, young love.*

With all the fellows and girls in their places, it was time to begin singing. The host and hostess had made their announcements, and the last of the stragglers had arrived and slid the barn door shut.

But Sol was not among them.

Ellie was disappointed but refused to feel glum. Sol hadn't actually mentioned taking her out tonight, but he *had* made it clear he was no longer in favor of double-dating with anyone.

As she sang with the others, Ellie anxiously wondered if something else had kept Sol from coming. Was he not feeling okay? Or was he uncertain about courting her with his limitations after all?

Then, just as quickly, she caught herself, even shaking her head in the middle of a song. Surely Sol understood that she cared about him just as he was. Hadn't she made that clear?

The last half of Singing was a test of Ellie's resolve as she tried not to let on how concerned she was about Sol. Thankfully, Ruthann never once asked what was wrong, so Ellie knew she'd managed to put on a pleasant face despite her troubled emotions.

———

After Singing was over and it was time to pair up, Ellie saw Menno and Ruthann slipping out together—no ride there. So she set out to walk home, thinking someone might offer her a lift along the way. She'd seen Aaron asking one of the preacher's nieces to go riding, though, so it was unlikely he would stop to offer her a ride. *Not on a first date.*

The tree frogs were especially noisy tonight, and the sound of their croaky song was somewhat of a comfort. As dark as it was, she was careful to walk close to the shoulder of the road. Tomorrow was the new moon, so there was no sign of it tonight. She wished she'd brought along a flashlight or even a small lantern.

After more than ten minutes of brisk walking, here came a buggy, slowing down.

"Ellie!" It was Cousin Sarah Ann's voice.

Relieved, Ellie turned to see the open carriage coming to a stop on the shoulder.

"Hurry around and hop in," Sarah Ann called. "You'll have to sit on my lap, though."

Ellie felt funny about it but went round the buggy and stepped inside, where Sarah Ann patted her lap. Fortunately, the distance home wasn't much farther, so Ellie sat lightly, glad for the ride yet sorry about intruding on Sarah Ann and Chester Riehl's date— though they'd been going out for quite a while now.

"Say, Ellie, I've been wondering 'bout Sol," Chester said. "I saw him out early in the mornin' the other day, walkin' down toward the orchard. He was on his way to work, I guess. I s'pose he hasn't heard that the deacon was warning us fellas not to walk alone along the road."

This was a surprise to Ellie. She'd thought Sol was coming down through the neighbor's cornfield each morning since his return. Hearing this from Chester made a shiver go up her spine.

"He's mighty courageous," Chester said. "Considerin' what he's suffered."

"Ever so brave," Sarah Ann said.

Contemplating what Chester said, Ellie was at a loss for words.

When they arrived at the house a few minutes later, Chester offered to pull all the way into the long lane so she wouldn't have to walk in the dark.

"Oh, I'll be fine," she said, still thinking of Sol's bravery. "*Denki*, though, Chester."

"We'll wait here till you're safely inside," he said.

"Mamm keeps a lantern lit in the kitchen near the window, so when I outen it, you'll know I'm in." She appreciated his kindness.

"*Gut* idea," Sarah Ann said.

Craning his neck, Chester stared at the house. "It looks to me like there's a lantern lit outside on the back porch."

"Really?" Ellie stepped out of the carriage. "Not sure why that would be. Well, *gut Nacht!*"

"Just wave that lantern," Chester replied, "and we'll be on our way."

"Okay." Very curious, she hurried up the lane toward the golden light near the side entrance, where she noticed someone sitting on the porch steps. At first, seeing the golden-blond hair beneath the straw hat, she thought it was Evan. *Is my mind playing tricks on me?*

"Ellie." This time she heard Sol's voice. "Didn't want to alarm ya." He lifted the lantern and rose.

"What a surprise," she said, never expecting to see him there.

"Hope it's a good one."

She smiled. "It surely is." She mentioned Chester had asked her to wave the lantern, so Sol raised it and moved it a little.

Soon she heard the *clip-clop-clip* of the horse heading away, and she decided not to mention what Chester had said about Sol walking along the road. "He and Sarah Ann kindly gave me a lift," she said, hoping it didn't sound like she'd been left in the lurch without Sol at Singing.

"Do ya mind if we talk?" he asked. He'd worn his nice black trousers and suspenders, rolling up the long sleeves of his white shirt.

"We can go round to the back and sit."

Sol carried the lantern as they walked to that part of the porch. Ellie was glad he'd brought it. Except for the dim light from the kitchen, it was as black as pitch outside.

"Let's sit in the glider," Sol said. "Okay with you?"

"Sure." She was so happy to see him . . . and to share the glider, too.

They got settled with her sitting on his right so he could hear better, and she realized they were as close as if they'd gone riding in his courting carriage.

"I should tell ya why I didn't go to Singing tonight," he said as they gently moved back and forth.

She tensed up a little. "*Jah?*"

"I spent some time tryin' to hitch my horse to the buggy this afternoon with just my left hand, but it didn't go too well. And it's too soon to try an' use my right hand—another ten days or so." He paused. "I figured if I couldn't hitch up my own horse, it wouldn't be safe to take ya out ridin'."

"Oh, Sol," she said, moved. And to think she'd fretted about why he hadn't come to Singing.

"Dat offered to help hitch up, but in the end he understood why I needed to do it myself and agreed that it wouldn't even be safe to hold the driving lines."

"I understand." She couldn't have been prouder of how hard he was working, and talking with him like this, she had no regrets at all about not being out for a ride.

"I'll keep my hand wrapped and in the splint till it's healed."

"Well, if need be, I'll help ya hitch up next time." She paused. "I mean it."

"Are ya gonna drive us, too?" He laughed softly.

"I would, if ya didn't mind."

"I'd mind, all right."

Now she was laughing.

"Goodness, you're not like any girl I know," he said, glancing at her in the soft, golden lantern light.

She shrugged, embarrassed. Had she overstated her caring, saying she'd hitch up for him . . . even drive his buggy? She remembered what Dat said on the way to Singing tonight, about putting the other person first in a relationship.

"So I guess our first official buggy date will have to wait," Sol said, his eyes still on her. "But I'm mighty happy you wanna be my girl, Ellie . . . if you're really sure. I want ya to know what you're getting into."

"I haven't changed my mind." She held his gaze there in the lantern light.

Sol nodded, seemingly relieved. "So next Singing, I want us to be out in my courtin' buggy for all *die Youngie* to see."

She felt so warm and contented hearing this.

"But if that Singing is held somewhere too far to walk home and my hand still isn't healed enough," Sol said, "we could skip goin', and I could come down here to visit. How'd that be?"

"I wouldn't mind that. We could walk in the orchard—where we first got to know each other."

"Where God brought us together," he said, leaning closer.

"True," she whispered.

"By then, the moon'll be out, hopefully . . . and lots brighter."

"We don't have to think too far ahead," she replied. "Your hand could improve a lot in two weeks . . . and your hearing." She recalled what Dawdi Hezekiah said about things taking time to heal.

"I knew you were real special when we first started talking," he said. "The way you stopped to chat with the orchard crew . . . and the love ya have for Evan even though he's gone against everything the People believe in. And Leah, too—you never said an unkind word about her when she up and left so suddenly."

"You seemed to understand how hard that was for me . . . what I was feelin'."

He was quiet for a time, the glider gradually slowing. "Seems to me like we've practically been a couple for a while already."

She nodded. "We've had something big in common, each of us missin' a sibling."

Over the last year, Sol had expressed so many of the same things she'd been feeling and struggling with. And now, here they were talking like a pair who'd known each other for a long time—which, of course, they had.

"Then when I was injured, I worried that I could never tell ya how I felt, and that I'd spent time dating someone I didn't care for like I care for you." He stopped talking for a moment, and she could hear him breathing. "It wondered me if I'd missed my chance to date ya, Ellie."

They were silent for a moment or two, surrounded by the night sounds she so loved. "Nothin' changed for me after you were hurt, Sol. Nothin' at all . . . except I realized how much I care for you."

"I like the sound of that," he replied, his eyes shining.

When Sol left to cut through the meadow and their neighbor's cornfield toward home, Ellie watched from her window high in the eaves, keeping her eyes on the bobbing yellow light of his lantern until it was no longer visible.

31

Ellie could scarcely wait to tell Leah what was happening with her and Sol. *It's the best feeling ever,* she wrote in a letter before the sun rose the next morning. *I dreamed the happiest dreams all night long!*

The days continued to warm, the rains came, and the new semi-dwarf apple trees thrived. Prior to that planting, the acre had been resting, covered with sorghum-Sudan grass, then plowed to nourish the quality of the soil and prevent disease. Since they'd stopped bearing fruit, some of the old trees Dawdi Hezekiah had named years ago had been removed, and it had been hard to bid them farewell—especially the one he called Methuselah.

Meanwhile, the orchard workers mowed the grass between the many rows of trees with the horse-drawn mower, a constant chore to keep pests from invading the low-growing branches. It wasn't something Sol could readily do with one hand just yet, though.

Ellie had started to occasionally work with her father in the barn office, helping take inventory of the harvesting tools and the right containers needed for the coming peach harvest in early July. They'd also discussed the fruit supply and the hoped-for demand for the next five years.

With some regular customers still backing away—likely due to Evan's going to war—Dat had seemed concerned about the profitability of the orchard. "Those new clients you contacted came along just in time," he told her. "*Denki*."

"Whatever I can do," she replied, grateful to be included. "I only wish all our Plain customers would realize that we're the exact same people we were before Evan left."

Dat gave her a smile. "Time will tell."

"And I'll keep makin' new contacts for the future."

Driving rain pelted the ground as Ellie ran out to get the mail in her raincoat and hat. Mamm had said she had the supper-making under control and to go ahead and make a dash for it.

On the way back, she noticed the column of woodsmoke billowing up from the chimney, then made her way around to the back of the porch, where she stood searching through the stack of mail for a letter from Evan. Instead, Leah had written, and Ellie quickly settled onto the glider to read her letter. Considering all the time she and Sol sat there talking privately these days, recently watching the sunset and enjoying every minute, she thought the glider had become one of the best investments Dat ever made. "*Our courting spot*," Sol had referred to it.

Smiling at that, Ellie began to read to the sound of pattering rain.

Dear Ellie,
How are you? Still smiling-happy?

I could tell by your last letter how pleased you are to be courted by Sol. It was the dearest thing to hear . . . and one of my secret desires, too, for you to become my sister-in-law someday!

I'm thrilled for Sol as well—two precious people have found each other. I couldn't be more excited. (I'll be writing to him right after I finish this letter.)

And in case you wondered, things are going along nicely between Reuben and me.

Ellie smiled at Leah's response, then read on and learned more about Bobby and his little twin sisters. All three of them had been asking Leah where she went off to on Preaching Sundays, dressed in her royal blue dress and white cape and apron. *Their mother, Carolyn, seemed* ferhoodled, *not knowing how to answer when Bobby wanted to know why* they *didn't go to Preaching, too.*

Ellie caught herself nodding, thinking back on what Dawdi Hezekiah had said some time ago—how Leah's influence on young Bobby might just change the little fellow's life. As hard as it had been not having Leah around, Ellie could see that good things were happening because of her willingness to work there.

Leah also mentioned Evan in her letter, saying she was committed to praying morning and evening for his safety. *The more who are praying, the better,* Ellie thought, finishing the letter and eager to show it to Sol when she saw him next.

Thankfully, a longed-for letter from Evan arrived in June.

I hope you don't think I've forgotten you, sister! he'd written. *The monsoons keep me from writing often, so please share this letter with*

243

Mamm and Dat. It'll rain cats and dogs practically around the clock till September, I've heard from guys who've been here long enough to know. Not sure I'll ever get used to that.

But I wanted you to know I'm safe for today.

The letter continued, inquiring about the family, but it was shorter than usual. *Even so, it's a relief to hear from him,* Ellie thought.

The month of August, just as sweltering and oppressive as July had been, was demanding, especially during "the overlap," when the tail end of the peach harvest coincided with the beginning of the apple harvest.

Ellie looked forward to seeing Sol at the house on weekend evenings. They took long walks together through the orchard, occasionally with Dawdi Hezekiah and sometimes with Shadow, too. Oh, how she lived for Sol's wonderful visits.

Though they had yet to join *die Youngie* at a Singing, on those nights they sang songs of praise while sitting on the glider, later munching popcorn and sipping homemade root beer or lemonade. Afterward, they played checkers and other games on a table on the porch. They missed the fellowship of *die Youngie*, yet they treasured the time they had alone to talk and open their hearts. And on the off-Sundays, Sol drove her around the back roads at twilight so they could at least have the experience of a buggy date now that his right hand was getting stronger.

When they finally attended Singing in mid-August, it was a treat to see everyone and confirm the grapevine's news that they were indeed a serious couple.

Sol had been able to pick peaches with his recovering hand

since late July, three months after his attack. Ellie was fairly certain he'd caught himself on his right hand when he'd fallen the day of the attack, but Sol couldn't remember exactly.

As for his bum ear, Ellie was mindful to be on Sol's right when they sat together or when they went walking in the meadow or orchard. And during one of their sunset strolls, Sol reached for her hand for the first time. It was unexpected, yet she'd longed for it. Even so, it took her breath away, and looking up at him, she couldn't help but grin as butterflies whirled in her stomach.

At that moment, she wanted to tell him how much she loved him but thought she should wait for him to be the first to say it. Although each and every day, she did take in many indications of his love—helping her attach her harvesting bag, assisting her with deliveries while she drove, and providing a listening ear when she felt sad, missing Evan.

Mamm invited Sol to join them on weekdays for the noon meal along with the rest of the family. Not long after that, Dat confided in Ellie that he hoped Sol knew how happy he and Mamm were about his becoming a serious beau.

Whenever the boys and their families came over for picnics or ice cream, Dat went out of his way to include Sol. And when little Alma brought her first nine-patch square to show Ellie, Sol made over it, too. In fact, Alma slid up on his knee and told him she wanted him to be her "Onkel Sol someday," which delighted Ellie no end but made Lydia's eyes pop with embarrassment.

There was no getting around that this was a very different kind of courtship than any Ellie had ever heard of, since most courting couples kept their relationships fairly private, even from family, until after their wedding dates were published following church in late October. Even so, she was thankful that her parents and siblings and their families enjoyed Sol's company so.

One Sunday evening, as Sol and Ellie stood near the porch steps quite reluctant to part ways for the night, Sol mentioned that, early on, he'd worried that he was somehow taking Evan's place in Ellie's heart. "Not that I ever could. I just didn't want to be a brother figure, ya know."

Ellie shook her head. "Never once did I think of ya that way," she said, assuring him.

Humorously, Sol wiped his brow. "Whew, that's a relief." They laughed together at his joshing, and then he took her into his arms for the first time.

Weary at day's end, Lyle removed his soiled work socks and placed them in the hamper near the closet. He wandered over to sit in his chair near the small table where the lantern glowed a perfect ring of light. He'd made the mistake of going into the back of the carriage shed before coming into the house, spotting the black courting carriage he'd purchased for Evan on his sixteenth birthday. *It just sits there*, he thought, recalling one of Evan's letters to Elisabeth where he'd admitted to often thinking about his Amish life there in Bird-in-Hand.

Lyle sighed.

Across from him in her pale pink robe, Elisabeth was reading *A Devoted Christian's Prayer Book*. He recalled a lot of interest in and a big push for this project among the Old Order Amish community when it was first published. One of his Indiana cousins was still involved with the publishing company, Pathway Publishers.

Lyle picked up the newspaper, which he hadn't read yet today. The number of reported war casualties set him back. The articles were bad enough, but oh, the horrific images. He'd considered canceling his subscription.

To think our Evan's over there . . .

He recalled what Ellie had told them back in early June. She'd said Evan had written he was "safe for today." *Evan must be terrified,* Lyle thought, still feeling concern, even dread, as well as bewilderment that a child of his would choose this life.

But that was more than two months ago, and Ellie hadn't shared anything more. He assumed she was still hearing from Evan occasionally, because he'd seen the APO address on the front of envelopes. When he did, it would hit him again, and mighty hard, that Evan was gone from the People, fighting in a war he should've never been a part of.

While he'd thought a few times of writing his son, he hadn't known where to start. But now he felt a sudden sense of urgency to sit down and share his thoughts with Evan.

He went to the front room, located a pad of paper and pen, and wrote.

Dear Evan,

I think of you and pray daily. But in case you wonder because of my silence, I want you to know how much I love you, son.

On Saturday evening, Sol came to visit Ellie with Shadow. Together, they strolled through the backyard, the air warm and breezy. The clouds opened up to let the sunshine through as they made their way past the *Dawdi Haus,* where Dawdi Hezekiah was watering multicolored petunias in his nearby flower bed. They waved, and Dawdi waved back, beaming.

"You've got yourselves a chaperone," Dawdi said, pointing at the dog.

Sol chuckled.

When they were deep into the orchard, he reached for Ellie's hand. "Anymore, I dislike our partings. I've been missin' ya," he said, "even though I see ya practically every day. I hate goin' home. Guess my heart's stuck right here."

She nodded, her heart in tune with his. Each time they said good-night, she longed to have more time together. "I feel the same way."

He stopped walking then, still holding her hand as he removed his straw hat. "I know how we'd never have to say good-bye again," he said, smiling down at her. "And I want that, if you do." He paused, his eyes sparkling. "That is, if you'll marry me." His eyes searched hers. "I love ya, Ellie."

She held his gaze. "*Jah*, I'll be your bride, Sol. I love you, too."

He raised her hand to his lips and kissed it. "I'm the happiest man on earth, here in this beautiful orchard where we first became friends." He opened his arms to her, and she moved toward him, her cheek resting against his shirt and suspender.

The dog nosed between them, tail wagging fast.

"Shadow approves," she said, laughing, then stepping back. "When shall we wed?" she asked, holding her breath now, the reality sinking in.

"How 'bout as soon as wedding season starts?"

"First Tuesday in November," she said, although he surely knew when that was.

He leaned down to kiss her cheek. "November second . . . two and a half months away," he whispered.

"Can we be ready in time?"

"Talk it over with your Dat and Mamm and decide," he said. "I'll wait to hear from ya, then tell my parents."

Ellie nodded and thought this night was the time to celebrate their love, to look ahead to becoming husband and wife. Her happiness knew no bounds, and she could hardly wait for Sol to hold her near once again.

Wisely, though, he turned to follow Shadow as the dog wagged its tail contentedly, and she and Sol talked hopefully about their future married life, where they might live, and the family God would give them, Lord willing.

"Will ya get to have one of the dogs once we're married?" she asked.

"I wouldn't wanna ask Dat."

She nodded. "That's up to you, but I think 'specially Shadow would miss ya."

Sol slipped his arm around her waist as they ambled along, and thoughts of dogs and nearly everything else flew out of her head. She was going to marry her darling beau!

32

Since today was a no-Preaching Sunday, Lyle could linger over a second cup of morning coffee in the kitchen. Elisabeth sat next to him with warm tea and the remainder of her half of the sticky bun she'd shared earlier with Ellie. "I don't know 'bout you, but I've been hopin' for some happy news like this," he said of Ellie's betrothal to Sol.

"*Jah*, and I wonder if Ellie slept at all last night, so excited she was after Sol left for home." Elisabeth's eyes glistened, and she reached for Lyle's hand. "Do ya remember how you felt back when we knew we were gonna be wed?"

Lyle nodded, squeezing her hand gently. "Young love's a powerful force, for sure." He looked out the window. "I believe Sol's had his eye on Ellie much longer than any of us realized."

"Honestly, I do, too."

Lyle released her hand and raised his coffee mug. "Won't Ellie be surprised to eventually take over this house—assuming Sol likes our plan, too?"

"I think she'll be quite pleased, to say the least."

"They'll spend their first few months as newlyweds here with us. Considerin' the apple harvest, there's no spare time to complete another addition bigger than Daed's before winter comes. But weather permitting, we can break ground and pour the foundation soon after the wedding. Most likely it will take three months to build."

"Sol and Ellie will have all the privacy they need up on the top floor till our new place is ready," Elisabeth replied, taking a small bite of the bun. "How soon will ya tell Sol 'bout his part in the future of the orchard?"

"Right away."

Elisabeth nodded. "He's the kind of man you can trust."

"And with his persistence and Ellie's creativity and dedication, they'll be a *gut* team."

Elisabeth broke into a grin. "I daresay you'll make Ellie the happiest woman alive."

Lyle chuckled. "Seems like Sol's already done that."

Elisabeth glanced at the calendar hanging on the cellar door and let out a long sigh. "*Ach,* poor Evan will be awful sorry to miss Ellie's wedding."

"I can only imagine how he'll feel when he hears."

"And I assume he would've been asked to be one of the wedding attendants, even though he and Sol haven't necessarily been close friends for a while."

Lyle wasn't so sure. "Remember, Evan isn't in *gut* standing with the church, so he couldn't be in his sister's wedding."

Elisabeth grimaced, and Lyle felt like a fool mentioning what they both knew—what they both would rather not remember.

Having just returned from walking through the orchard rows, Ellie was eager to write to Leah. She got right to the point and asked Leah to be one of her wedding attendants, sharing that she also intended to ask her cousin Ruthann. *Oh, Leah, I can't imagine being happier,* she wrote. *I hope you'll be able to come for Sol's and my wedding day.*

Without much pause, she also wrote a letter to Evan, sharing the happy news of her engagement. *Sol and I will marry this November,* she told him, wishing with all her heart that her brother could be present.

Later that afternoon, Ellie took the two-wheeled horse-drawn cart over to visit Ruthann, since her parents and grandfather had left in the family carriage to visit Dawdi's widowed brother, Enos.

Cousin Ruthann was ecstatic about being asked to be one of the wedding attendants. "I'd love to," she said, big-eyed as they walked together outdoors. "And do ya know who'll be Sol's?"

"He hasn't said yet, but I'm guessin' his brother Aaron might be one."

Smiling, Ruthann nodded.

"So how are you and Menno getting along?" Ellie asked.

"I think he might be close to proposin' marriage."

"Bein' in love is just *wunnerbaar,* ain't?"

Ruthann grinned now. "Absolutely." She sat on the stone springhouse steps and motioned for Ellie to join her. "Ach, I can't believe it, Ellie, how everything's turning out for us. And I'm so honored to be one of your weddin' attendants."

"Wouldn't have it any other way," Ellie replied.

Deciding to wait till after work the next day to talk with Sol and Ellie, Lyle had asked them to meet him in the barn office before Sol left for home. The three of them sat together now, Lyle having contemplated this moment.

"Now, then," he said, folding his hands, "I've been pondering somethin', and after praying for guidance and talking it over with Jonah, I'm ready to talk with yous."

Ellie's eyes were fixed on him, as she took in every word.

She might be expecting this, Lyle thought, suppressing a grin.

"I'd always intended for Evan to take over the management of the orchard, of course, but something had to be done, what with his leavin' the Amish life behind. So if you're interested"—he looked at Sol and then Ellie—"I'd like to train Sol to become manager in two to three years, in partnership with you, Ellie."

Ellie looked at Sol, whose jaw had dropped. "Are ya sure, Dat?" she asked, a little breathless and eyes wide with delight.

"Wow," Sol said. "I thought after Evan left, maybe Jonah would run things once you're retired."

"Well, Jonah doesn't want to be saddled with the day-to-day responsibilities of the orchard. And he and Priscilla like where they're living, but I want someone to live on-site. Ellie's always shown the greatest interest in the orchard of any of our children. I intend to give ya the opportunity to buy the house as well . . . make your home here. Elisabeth and I will move into a new, larger *Dawdi Haus* as soon as we can get it built after your wedding."

Tears welled in Ellie's eyes. "*Ach,* Dat, I don't know what to say."

Bursting with happiness at the joy this news had brought to his younger daughter's heart, Lyle looked to Sol for their answer.

"We would be honored," Sol replied. "And Ellie and I will be ever grateful to ya."

Lyle nodded, mighty pleased at their response—and relieved. "So Ellie'll partner with ya where she can, Sol, considering she'll have more household duties to attend to after Elisabeth and I move out of the main house. And eventually, Lord willin', you'll have a family, too."

"*Denki* for entrusting the orchard to us, Dat," Ellie said, now more sober. She frowned suddenly. "I'm wonderin', has Evan been told?"

"Not officially. But after some of the things he told me before leavin' for the army, I'm sure he suspects it."

Ellie nodded, listening.

"Of course, this is all a private family matter," Lyle added.

"We understand," Ellie said, glancing at Sol.

"I'll put my mind to learnin' quickly," Sol said, "and I'll do everything I can to make the transition a smooth one when you're ready to hang up your hat."

"It's a privilege to have ya onboard—and as a son-in-law come November." Lyle reached over to shake Sol's hand.

As for Ellie, she was clearly trying not to let out a whoop and a holler.

She's earned it, Lyle thought as Ellie and Sol left his office together, his daughter smiling up at her future husband.

On the walk across the backyard, Ellie squeezed Sol's hand. "Can ya believe it?"

"You'll never have to leave the orchard," Sol said with a grin.

She looked fondly at the main farmhouse. "We'll get to live in my childhood home, a real blessing. And our babies will be born here, just as I was, and grow up to love the orchard, too."

"Your father's givin' us a tremendous responsibility—and you're ahead of me on a lot of the business side." Sol chuckled.

"I'll share with ya what I know."

Sol slipped his arm around her waist. "We'll be *gut* partners, I believe."

"And not just for the orchard."

The bountiful apple harvest that fall took nearly every ounce of energy and focus for Ellie and Sol, but the Saturday and Sunday evenings belonged to them.

One evening Ellie showed Sol her latest letter from Evan. "Look what he wrote," she said, pointing to the words. "'I'm sending my warmest and best wishes for a happy wedding day.'"

It had taken her aback, the wording Evan used. It sounded so stiff, like they didn't really know each other.

"Evan's on my mind more than I realize, I think," Sol said. "I feel bad that we used to be friends but aren't any longer." He shook his head. "No one would expect an Amish guy to become a soldier."

Ellie was quiet for a moment, pondering something she'd thought about but hadn't voiced to anyone. *Will Dat's news about the orchard put a wedge between Evan and me once he finds out?*

33

Mid-October, Ellie was still over the moon that Dat wanted her and Sol to manage the orchard in a few years. *My not-so-secret desire*, she thought, snuggling against the pillows behind her as she sat up in bed long after her parents had retired for the night.

She took her time reading several psalms, then rose to open the windows as she often did when the night was mild. The wind had picked up considerably, and the lantern flickered as she headed back to outen it before slipping back into bed.

Another long day tomorrow, she thought, pulling up the home-made quilts and hoping for a soaking rain in the night.

Suddenly waking to the sound of tires squealing, Ellie bolted upright in bed. She'd heard that sound before, and she trembled, recalling the terrible day of Sol's attack. Rubbing her eyes in the dark, she soon recognized the smell of smoke and leaped out of bed, pushed her feet into her slippers, and pulled on her long robe as she hurried to a dormer window. Yellow-orange flames torched a number of trees in the southeast section of the orchard.

"Dat! Wake up! Fire in the orchard!" she yelled as she rushed down the stairs, then toward her parents' bedroom. "I'll call for help." Heart in her throat, she dashed down the next flight of stairs, out the side door, and across the windswept meadow to the shared phone shanty in the neighbor's field.

She shoved open the wooden door and reached for the phone, her hand trembling as she dialed. Breathing fast, she told the answering operator, "There's a fire in our orchard. Please get help!"

The woman asked for the address, but Ellie was so flustered, she explained where in the orchard she thought the fire had started instead of giving their street address.

"Is this the Hostetler orchard?"

"*Jah* . . . sorry," Ellie said, and the woman said the fire station would be notified immediately.

"*Denki*," she said, "ever so much," and hung up the phone, her heart pounding in her ears.

When she returned to the house, Ellie saw her father, still in his nightclothes, attaching a long hose to one of the outdoor spigots. "Help is on the way," she called to him.

How fast is the fire spreading? she worried, priming the well pump. She removed her long, thick robe and soaked it thoroughly before running with it toward the orchard.

How many of them have caught fire? she wondered, gasping for breath as the wind blew hard against her.

Swap! Swap! She beat the flames with her robe, repeatedly flinging it against the fiery trunk and branches. If she could spare even a few trees, she must. But the heat felt like needles on her forehead and cheeks, the smoke stinging her eyes.

O Lord, spare our orchard!

Breathlessly, she continued to thrash at the fire, slapping at the next tree's limbs and trunk, whatever she could do, going from tree to tree with her robe, smothering the snapping, hissing fire.

From behind her, she could hear the siren's wail in the distance and Dat and Dawdi calling back and forth to each other. Neighboring farmers, undoubtedly awakened by the siren, were coming quickly now.

Finishing with another tree, she stepped back to quickly appraise the situation. *How could so many trees catch fire at once?*

Then, detecting the unmistakable smell of gasoline, she knew.

"Keep away from the fire!" Dat was shouting at someone. She was certain he hadn't seen her run out here, though.

In a flash, Ellie decided where to head next, where she could do the most good. As she sprinted toward the farthest edge of the orchard, she imagined that, behind her, well water was flowing from the hose as Dat made his attempt to create a wet barrier against the fire.

Ellie's arms ached as she redoubled her efforts, determined to beat out the fierce blaze. Gasping in the dense smoke, she coughed so hard her lungs ached.

She could hear the sound of the siren coming closer, surely coming from the Hand-in-Hand Fire Company several miles away, but she kept up her pace.

Time seemed to speed up, and then out of the corner of her eye, she saw the fire truck arrive, saw the men hook up the hoses and come this way. She felt the mist of water caught and spread by the powerful wind and let herself go, overcome by smoke. She felt limp, fainted, and fell to the ground.

Not even the orchard is unscathed by this horrible war, she thought before sinking toward unconsciousness.

Somewhere in the corner of her brain, Ellie thought she heard a faint voice.

"Ellie, I'm here."

Exhausted, eyes closed, she tried to respond with a slow nod. Then strong arms gathered her up, and in the midst of the smoke and her own haziness, she realized the voice was Sol's. He must be carrying her.

"I . . . I'm . . ." she murmured, coughing, trying to squint at him.

"Just relax, Ellie. I've got ya."

Though she was unable to stop coughing, she felt snug and safe in his arms. "I can walk," she gasped, a burning sensation in her chest. It felt like he was carrying her a long way.

"We're almost to the house."

Once inside, Sol set her on the wooden bench in the kitchen. She was covered with soot, and she continued to cough as her mother wrapped a blanket around her. Then Mamm dabbed a cool, wet cloth on her face and neck.

Sol kissed the top of her head, frowning like he was worried sick. "My darling, ya put your life at risk," he said, touching her hair. With her long tresses unbound, she could see they were singed.

Ellie tried to speak but couldn't for the powerful urge to cough.

Mamm hovered near. Then to Sol she said, "I'll look after her now."

Sol nodded, and with another concerned look at Ellie, he left the house.

Ellie held the cool cloth on her forehead and over her eyes

and nose, wishing she could witness the fire truck's water hose drenching the flames with its mighty torrent.

Mamm sat beside her, soothing her with one hand on her back.

"I did everything I could." Ellie eked out the words. "But it wasn't enough."

"My dear, new trees can be replanted, but your life could never be replaced," Mamm said softly. "I'm so grateful Sol rescued you."

Ellie turned toward her mother and fell exhausted into her loving embrace.

A few minutes before dawn, Lyle turned over in bed and reached for Elisabeth, who was awake and restless. "Were ya able to get back to sleep?" he asked as she nestled against him.

"Had bad dreams," she said sleepily. "Who would do such a thing?"

"I'll keep my opinion on that to myself," he replied, unable to be certain and not wanting to judge. He exhaled. "But this—on top of Sol's attack."

Elisabeth nodded sadly. "I hate to think what would've happened if Ellie hadn't woken up to alert us."

"Mighty glad she did . . . and that she's all right."

"*Jah*, that's all I can think 'bout now—our Ellie's alive."

Lyle kissed her cheek. "God was gracious, indeed." He slipped on his bathrobe, then sat on the edge of the bed, pondering what might have been without divine intervention. "We have much to be thankful for."

Using her small mirror to examine her hair, Ellie shuddered. The ends were scorched and fell in several different lengths. "For pity's sake," she murmured, then noticed her eyebrows were nearly gone. She ran her fingers over the stubble.

The fire did this, she thought, but she'd been so intent on her task and trying to see through the smoke . . . Her last memory before Sol lifted her out of harm's way was of pounding the fiery trees with her damp and charred bathrobe.

Looking down at her hands now, she saw blisters on her knuckles. *Ach, Sol's bride looks a sight!*

She wondered if there was a home remedy that might help her eyebrows grow back more quickly. Gathering up her clean clothes, she hurried downstairs to find Mamm's folk medicine book and discovered that squeezing aloe vera juice on the eyebrow stubble and rubbing it in every day could encourage the hair to grow back. *I'll definitely try that.*

After she washed up in the small bathroom off the kitchen and dressed for the day, she headed back to her room and peered out the windows, curious about the fire's overall destruction. From what she could see, the area of the newest apple trees had suffered the most damage. But the vast majority of the orchard had been spared. *How many trees were lost?* she wondered, anxious to survey the damage with Dat.

After a quick breakfast of baked oatmeal and coffee, Ellie and her father took an account of the destroyed apple trees—charred black sticks now. They counted forty-five semi-dwarfs lost.

"Not as bad as it could've been," Dat said as they perused the acre together. "We'll need volunteers to help strip the scorched and fallen fruit." He leaned down to pick up the remains of a blackened apple.

"Won't some of the trees reflower next year?" Ellie asked.

"Some might." He pointed at the base of one of the trees. "But not if they look like this. See how badly burnt it is?"

She nodded, then followed him to check on similar-looking trees.

"If we just hope these'll reshoot next year, we could end up havin' apples growin' just very high on the tree . . . so much harder to manage. It's better to start over with fresh trees in a case like that."

Ellie was struck by how confident and knowledgeable her father sounded.

"Ya know, Ellie, all in all, we didn't suffer a big loss—and all 'cause of your quick response last night." He shook his head as though amazed.

"If my window hadn't been open, no tellin' what might've happened."

"I daresay the Lord caused ya to wake up." Dat looked heavenward.

"I think so, too."

Dat nodded, pushing his hands into his pockets. "There'll be a lot of extra work ahead of us, pullin' out the damaged trees and buyin' quality mulch—preferably natural compost—to gradually break down over time and add nutrition to the burnt soil."

"I'd like to help, Dat."

"We'll see 'bout that," her father said, chuckling. "You've been puttin' in many hours in the orchard already. And you've been itchin' to buy new land for some time, so Lord willin', now's the time."

They discussed the options she'd seen in the ads lately and made plans to look at some of them after the wedding.

"If we do purchase additional land, it won't help us this year," Dat said, "but it'll be a fine investment for the future."

Ellie agreed, though still rather dazed by the fire. And torn between sadness for what had been lost and what might be found.

34

Leah arrived home by bus three days before Ellie's wedding, and Ellie was eager to see her. Thankfully, Leah didn't make her wait long.

Spotting her out on the road from the front room window, Ellie rushed to open the side door. Then there she was, her precious friend, grinning as tears welled up.

"I almost rang the dinner bell, I'm so happy to see ya!" Leah said as she stepped inside and reached for Ellie's hands. "But I didn't want to alarm anyone."

Ellie embraced her. "It's *wunnerbaar-gut* you could get home. Mamm'll be so glad to see ya, too. All of us will." She laughed, looking at her friend. "You haven't changed one bit. But me . . . well, I've got no eyebrows, like I wrote ya."

"How much hair did your Mamm have to cut off to even it out?" Leah asked, hanging up her coat on one of the available wooden pegs around the corner. "In your letter, ya said you couldn't even look at the hair falling on the kitchen floor."

"I was actually holdin' my breath. Like yours, my hair had never been cut, ya know."

"Well sure."

"Let's just say that when I washed it and then brushed it out, it came to only partway down my back. Thank goodness I can still put it into a tidy hair bun." She sighed. "Let's talk about somethin' else, okay?"

"Oh, sorry. I'm just glad you weren't hurt." Leah went on to say that her coming home was possible only because Carolyn's parents agreed to travel to help with the children in Chambersburg for the week.

"I'm thankful for that," Ellie said, leading her into the front room, where the heater stove kept the large area warm and cozy.

Mamm looked up from her stitching, and a big smile burst across her face. "*Willkumm Heem*, Leah," she said, setting her handiwork aside.

"It's *gut* to be back," Leah said, sitting in a chair near Mamm. She expressed delight in seeing her, and they talked briefly about the pillowcase Mamm was cross-stitching. Then Leah said, "In my happiest dreams, Ellie was always my sister." She glanced at Ellie. "Sol's made a *wunnerbaar-gut* choice in a mate."

"And Lyle and I are very pleased with our soon-to-be son-in-law," Mamm said, which made Ellie equally glad. "He saved Ellie's life in the fire."

"He's so humble that he won't take credit for it," Leah replied. "Says the Lord led him to find her lyin' there."

Mamm nodded. "We believe that wholeheartedly."

Again, Ellie turned the conversation away from the fire. "Say, do ya need any help with finishing touches on your bridesmaid dress, maybe?"

"It just needs hemming, which I can do after Mamm pins it for me." She smiled. "You have no idea how eager I was to get here. Had to drop my bags and come right down to see ya, Ellie

. . . always the sister of my heart. Now part of our family in just three days."

Ellie nodded, gazing at her. "How long are ya here for?"

"Thursday mornin' I head back."

"Your family must be awful happy to see ya."

"I'm not so sure they'll let me leave again. At least, that's what Dat said first thing he saw me today," Leah replied with a smile. "Sol was nodding along."

"Can't blame them. Wish there was a way for you to work round here instead."

"That's up to Reuben. Oh, before I forget, Sol wants ya to show me the set of china he bought for yous."

"Sure. Come out to the kitchen pantry—the big box is in there. It's a practical yet lovely engagement gift."

Leah smiled. "Sol always seems to know what to choose, considering all the nice birthday gifts he's given me and our Mamm over the years."

In the walk-in kitchen pantry, Ellie showed Leah the pretty white dinner plates with a raised circular design along the rim. "It'll be perfect for special occasions."

Leah ran her finger over the lovely motif. "You're right. My brother *does* have *gut* taste!"

After their short visit, Ellie walked with Leah down to the end of the lane. "I hate to see ya go," she said.

"Oh, I'll be down tomorrow if ya need any help."

"Well, Mamm has everything assigned, but come. We can just relax and visit again." Ellie went on to say they expected up to three hundred and fifty guests for the wedding feast. "So Dat and my brothers'll be moving the partitions out of the house come Monday night to get ready. And Sol's gonna slaughter thirty-six chickens over at Aendi Miriam's house first thing Monday mornin'. Ain't the most pleasant task for the groom, but it's tradition, and Sol's been practicing with the ax—one chop, ya know."

"That sounds like him. Well, I'll see ya tomorrow." Leah turned to go up the road.

"*Denki* for comin'!" Ellie called, watching her almost-sister running now, skirt tail flying.

On the morning of her wedding day, Ellie rose very early and straightened up her room. She would soon welcome her darling there and wanted the place to look extra nice for their first night together.

Then she looked in the mirror at her eyebrows. They were still scarcely there, but at supper last night, Dawdi Hezekiah had tried to assure her, saying he doubted Sol would be fretting about her eyebrows today. *"Your husband-to-be will be interested in makin' his vows to you and God—and starting his new life with ya, Ellie."*

Later that morning, Ellie and Mamm headed up to her parents' room, where Mamm closed the door and reached for her hands. With tears glimmering, she said softly, "May this be a most blessed day for you and Sol, dear. Ever since you were born, your father and I prayed for the young man who would one day become your life mate, and now this wondrous day has come."

Ellie fought back happy tears.

Her mother kissed her cheek. "Remember who brought yous together." She glanced upward. "And always remember to trust Him daily as Sol's wife and, Lord willin', the mother of his children."

"I promise." Ellie still struggled not to cry.

"Sol's love for you is all over his face. 'Tis a beautiful thing to observe as your mother."

Ellie's heart swelled with joy. "*Denki* for prayin' for this day, starting all those years ago—you and Dat. Knowin' this is so precious to me."

"One day you'll tell Sol and your own children 'bout it." Mamm smiled tenderly.

"I can only try to be as kind and loving as you've been to me and my brothers and sister, Mamm."

Her mother gave her a pretty tatted hankie. "I carried this under my sleeve the day I married your father."

Ellie admired the pink roses. "You kept it for me?"

Mamm nodded. "You might want to give it to your youngest daughter someday."

Deeply touched, Ellie kissed her mother's cheek.

Mamm wiped tears from her eyes, then slipped out of the room.

I'm truly blessed, Ellie thought, placing the delicate hankie under her left sleeve.

The congregation began to sing the third verse of the familiar *Loblied* German praise hymn as Ellie walked single file behind her groom. Sol followed Leah and his brother Aaron ahead of him as the wedding party began the procession through the house and narrow passages of the crowded room. Close behind Ellie were Sol's cousin Jake and Ruthann, the other two atten-dants. Sol and his young men were clad in black suits and long-sleeved white shirts, just as they would wear to Sunday Preaching service, while Ellie, Leah, and Ruthann wore their new blue dresses, overlayed with white organdy capes and aprons.

It was the day Ellie had contemplated even as a young girl. Now she was delighted to see so many relatives and friends as she followed Sol to one of the six cane-back chairs set aside at the front, where the bishop and other ministers sat. And as instructed beforehand, she and Sol sat down in perfect unison, with Ellie, Leah, and Ruthann facing Sol, Aaron, and Jake.

During the second sermon, the main one, Ellie listened attentively as the bishop pointed out the well-known couples in the Old Testament—Isaac and Rebecca, Jacob and Rachel, and Ruth and Boaz. Then he read from the New Testament, "'Husbands, love your wives, even as Christ also loved the church, and gave himself for it,'" followed by another verse, "'Therefore shall a man leave his father and his mother, and shall cleave unto his wife: and they shall be one flesh.'"

When the time came for Ellie and Sol to stand before Bishop Mast, Ellie's heart was filled with love as Sol held her hand. Sol was to be honored and commended for his determination to be all he could be for her and for the Lord. And looking into his face, she felt truly grateful to be his bride.

After their vows were made and the bishop had prayed a blessing over them, Ellie felt her face warm as she and Sol returned to their seats. *God's presence is here*, she thought.

One of the preachers gave a word of testimony, and then the deacon was invited to make remarks about the sermon, both ordained men in agreement with the Word of God. Last of all, the brethren gave their blessings for Sol and Ellie's sacred union.

The service and the five-minute wedding ended with a prayer as all the People rose from their seats, turned, and knelt. Then after singing the final hymn, which referenced the glorious wedding of the Lamb—the Lord Jesus Christ—the official service was over, and the celebration of Sol and Ellie's marriage was to begin.

Upstairs, Ellie and Sol met privately, as was the custom for newlyweds, where Sol took her in his strong arms and kissed her for the first time. She smiled sweetly, and he gave her another kiss, more ardently this time, and she wished they could stay right there forever.

"My precious bride," Sol whispered. "I'm mighty happy."

She searched his beautiful hazel eyes. "I know that feelin'." Ellie remembered what Mamm had told her about praying with Dat for her husband. "God knew all along 'bout this day, *jah?*"

Sol smiled and reached to open the door. "He was leading us, every step we took, to each other."

Ellie followed him down the hall and to the stairs, looking forward to the wedding feast and greeting their kinfolk and friends.

The start of our new life, she thought, holding her husband's hand.

35

Three days after the wedding, Ellie rode with Sol and Dat to look at available land in two different locations. During the short trip to East Lampeter to survey twenty acres described in a newspaper ad, Dat revealed that a number of guests had privately approached him during the wedding feast and slipped him money.

"Mighty surprising," he said, mentioning that it was to be used toward preparing the burned acre for future replanting. "Some were quite sizeable gifts," Dat shared in hushed tones. "Many relatives and friends wanted to help."

"That's very kind," Ellie said, "and a little surprising when some had turned their backs on us."

Sol was nodding. "Maybe things are turnin' round at last?"

"Well, some former customers are still holdouts," Dat replied.

"By the way," Ellie interjected, "I made a sign that says *Cider by the cup or jug* and put it out front. We can make more money than by just sellin' by the jug. And we can sell cider by the cup at market, too."

Sol chuckled. "My dear bride's bound and determined to do her part."

Ellie laughed. "Mamm and I also made apple butter all day yesterday to take to Central Market tomorrow."

Dat gave an approving nod. "Well, I appreciate everything you're doin', Ellie."

"She's on a mission," Sol added.

"I just want things to return to normal," she replied.

They arrived at the property in East Lampeter, and immediately Dat pointed out that the lay of the land wasn't advantageous for planting lines of trees from north to south. "They need to be laid out that way to increase the amount of sun they receive each day. It's also too flat here—we need drainage for the trees."

"*Ach*, you're right," Ellie murmured, eyeing the spread of land. "I see that."

"Might also be too far away from our present orchard," Sol mentioned.

They traveled back toward Bird-in-Hand, a half mile northeast of their own orchard. This second acreage was so appealing that Ellie asked Dat if they could pull over and stop so they could look it over more closely.

Dat let Sol take over the driving lines while he and Ellie got out. "It's grazing land, so that's *gut*," Dat said as they strolled along the roadside. "How many acres did ya say?"

"Fifteen."

"Looks promising. What's the askin' price?"

"It's not listed in the ad."

Dat pointed. "I see a farmhouse and a few large trees toward the back of the property. I'll come back first thing tomorrow to talk to the owner."

They walked a bit farther, then returned to the buggy and Sol. Ellie couldn't help but notice the spring in her father's step.

Lyle felt the mattress move when Elisabeth rose the next morning. She'd told him she'd be up by four because she and Ellie planned to ride with a Mennonite woman to the historic Central Market in downtown Lancaster. They wanted to set up before the doors opened at six o'clock.

Rolling over, Lyle rested a while longer, the acreage he and Ellie had walked along yesterday very much on his mind. He was fairly sure the price would be higher than he could afford, but for Ellie's sake—and the family's—he would dicker on the amount with the owner, George Stewart, a man he'd never met.

After a cup of hot black coffee, he made his way out to the stable to hitch up Captain to the spring wagon, then headed down the road.

He soon learned that George was spending the winter in Florida, but his daughter gave Lyle a phone number where he could be reached.

"Might I have your father's mailing address instead?" Lyle asked the young English woman after she gave him the price for the land. "I only use the shanty phone for emergencies."

"Sure," she replied, apparently surprised. "But if it's the price you're concerned about," she added, "it's not negotiable."

"I see." Lyle thanked her and headed toward his waiting horse and wagon. *Well, I guess that's that.*

Three different groups of relatives—aunts, uncles, and cousins—stopped by with wedding gifts that Preaching Sunday after the fellowship meal. Ellie and Sol visited with each one, thanking them for their kindness. Invariably, someone mentioned the new sign out front, and Ellie kindly asked if they'd be willing to spread the word about her selling cider by the cup. "Mamm and I have apple butter now, too," she added.

"Have ya thought of sellin' door-to-door?" one of Dat's older cousins asked. "Maybe hot cider by the mug?" The man chortled.

Standing by Ellie's side, Sol clarified that she was working extra hard to earn funds to restore the burned section of the orchard.

Ellie looked up at him, thankful he'd defended her, even though she felt sure the cousin was just joshing.

In the midst of a chilly yet sunny day nearly a week and a half later, Ellie's father, husband, and brothers broke ground for the new *Dawdi Haus* near the one Dawdi Hezekiah lived in. Ellie and her mother donned their coats and went out to watch for the first little while, remarking how nice it would be for Mamm and Dat to move in sometime in early spring.

"The time'll go quick," Mamm said, glancing at her. "You and Sol should be comfortable for now, we hope."

"Sol loves our room high in the eaves." Ellie smiled, remembering how on their wedding night, he'd asked how cold it got in the winter up there. Then right away he shook his head, saying they would keep each other warm.

On the walk back to the main house, Ellie wished Dat would have at least written the owner of the land over northeast. If Mr. George Stewart wouldn't budge on the price, then so be it. But they couldn't know without trying.

Once Ellie had helped redd up the kitchen following supper on Thanksgiving evening, she went to see Dawdi, who was suffering from a flare-up of his rheumatism. "Weather related," he'd said during the noon meal as Lydia, Jonah, Rudy, and their families gathered around Mamm's long trestle table.

"You haven't been tellin' your family stories lately," Ellie said presently, sitting on the settee near Dawdi's chair. "I miss hearin' them."

"My tall tales?" He chuckled as he balanced a hot water bottle on his right knee.

"Oh, now. I wasn't ever the one to say that."

Dawdi smiled at her. "Married life seems to suit ya. You're like a fancy light bulb, ya know . . . always a-glowin'."

"Never happier," she said, smiling.

"From the first day Sol came to work for us years ago, I knew he was somethin' special. I daresay God gives us old folk a *gut* measure of wisdom."

"Can't argue that." Ellie paused, thinking that now might be a good time to tell him the thing that was pressing on her heart. "Maybe you can reassure me 'bout somethin', Dawdi."

"I'll give it a try, Ellie-girl." He frowned, eyeing her. "What's troublin' ya?"

She considered how this could affect him—all of them, really. "It's just that I haven't heard from Evan in quite a while." She sighed.

Dawdi shifted his weight. "Well, keep in mind there's no tellin' where he could be fighting." He looked toward the window. "Or what conditions he might be in."

Ellie hoped she hadn't upset Dawdi, who looked so solemn

now. "Mamm hasn't said anything 'bout not hearin' from Evan, either, so I'm not sure I want to bring it up to her. Surely she would've told Dat if she was worried, but that doesn't mean he'd mention it to me."

Dawdi sighed loudly. "My prayer continues to be that Evan's life will be spared so he gets a second chance."

A second chance to join church, he means. And if so, she hoped that, too.

They talked about other things, especially the relatives and friends who had visited bearing wedding gifts every weekend since the wedding. Even some from Somerset and out of state— Maryland and New York, mostly.

"Sounds like you'll have plenty-a household items once you and Sol take over the main house," Dawdi said.

"Combined with everything in my hope chest, we should be well set."

"Is there a bigger item yous might need?"

"Let's wait and see after all the gifts are brought, okay? You've already been very generous with your cash gift, Dawdi. Sol and I can't thank ya enough."

"That's what we do for our young ones startin' out," he replied, nodding. "After all, we can't take it with us when life is over."

Ellie offered to help him to the main house for Bible reading and prayer.

Dawdi shook his head. "I'll sit right here and pray. Need to go easy on this here leg."

"Okay," she said, heading for the door. "You'll be careful walkin' around, now, won't ya?"

"Ain't too bad off yet."

"Hope ya feel better after the storm comes through."

"Me too!" Dawdi chuckled. "Feels like it could snow a heap."

She hoped not, because that could hamper the construction of Dat and Mamm's new addition. But that was the risk involved with building this time of year.

"I'll see ya tomorrow, Dawdi."

A week later, Ellie was closing the family store for the day when the door opened and Cheryl Herr stepped inside.

"Hullo, Cheryl," she said, surprised to see her there. "What can I get for ya?"

"I came to see *you*." Cheryl leaned on the counter like she was suddenly fatigued. Then, touching her ponytail, she said, "I'm worried. Evan hasn't written in weeks." She looked toward the front window for a moment. "Have you heard from him lately?"

Ellie's insides tumbled. *She hasn't heard anything, either?*

Swallowing hard, Ellie tried to put on a brave face. "*Nee*, but maybe his unit has moved."

Cheryl nodded. "I've wondered that, too."

"I've read sometimes soldiers are sent to remote places where it's not so easy to receive or send letters."

Cheryl seemed to consider this. "In his last letter, Evan wrote that you were getting married. Has the wedding already happened?"

"*Jah*, November second."

"He really wished he could have been here for your wedding. He's talked of you, in fact, in every letter. And I know he worries that you and your family are anxious about his safety."

"We pray for him every day," Ellie replied. "I certainly don't like going this long without hearing from him."

Cheryl blinked several times, then looked down at the counter,

clearly trying to keep her composure. It was obvious how concerned she was, and it made Ellie feel sorry for her even though
she didn't like the idea of an outsider having a close relationship
with her brother.

"I apologize for barging in like this," Cheryl said at last. "But
I needed to talk to someone else who cares about Evan."

Ellie understood and told her so.

"I just hope he's not . . ." Cheryl stopped and cleared her
throat.

Ellie saw the fear in her eyes. "We'll have to look forward to
his next letters and give him to God's care," she replied, saying
this as much for her own peace of mind as for Cheryl's.

Cheryl nodded but couldn't seem to speak, her lower lip quiv-
ering. She turned to reach for the doorknob. "Thanks for taking
time for me, Ellie."

"It's okay," she said, taken aback. "Come anytime."

In that moment, Ellie felt sure of only one thing. Evan had
told the truth about Cheryl Herr—she was as nice as she was
pretty.

36

While Elisabeth and Ellie were hanging up the washing the following Monday morning, Lyle heard a knock at the front door.

Who could that be? He set his coffee mug on the kitchen table, then made his way through the house, mighty curious.

He opened the door to see two army men standing there, shoulder to shoulder. "Hullo," Lyle said, a lump rising in his throat. He'd seen these types of uniforms on military men in the newspaper during the past few years.

"I have an important message to deliver from the secretary of the United States Army," the older of the two men stated quietly. "May we come inside to talk with you?"

Lyle's heart pounded as he stepped aside to let them in. "Is this about my son Evan?"

Without responding, the men entered, and Lyle realized he was holding his breath. "Have a seat," he told them, then sat near the window, bracing himself.

"May I have your full name?" the younger man asked, not unkindly.

Dread crept nearer. "Lyle Hostetler." *Has Evan's terrible decision come to this?* Lyle wondered, suddenly feeling light-headed.

"The secretary has requested me to express his deepest regret that your son, Private Evan Hostetler, has been reported missing in action during combat."

"He's missin'?" Lyle asked with a small sense of relief. "Not deceased?"

The same man nodded slowly, his expression sympathetic. "You shouldn't give up hope. Your son may have been taken prisoner, and if so, the authorities will be notified directly once he's located. Are other family members at home that we should speak with?"

"My wife and daughter are here, but I'll break the news to them."

"If you're certain," the other man said.

"*Jah.*" *No telling how they'd react to knowing that men in uniform were waiting to talk to them.*

The men rose in unison, and Lyle went with them to the door, still feeling woozy. He closed the door behind them and trudged toward the settee. Sitting there silently, he stared out the window at the sky, reliving what he'd been told.

After a time, Lyle turned to kneel, folding his hands and asking God to keep Evan safe and out of the hands of the Viet Cong. He didn't know what that might mean for his son. He also asked for divine peace that passes all understanding, that it would guard his heart and mind as well as his family's.

Almighty God, grant Thy mercy to our lost son, and may we grow in faith through Christ our Lord during this trying time. Help me have strength to be a witness of courage and compassion to my family.

Here, he paused, wondering now if Evan had received his letter yet.

Lyle resumed his prayer, tears rolling down his face. *O faithful heavenly Father, give us all a complete and righteous compassion for our wayward boy. In the name of our Savior, Jesus Christ.*

After Lyle wiped his face and beard with his kerchief, he rose and plodded back through the house toward the kitchen, sustained by the living God.

Now, to share the news about Evan with his wife and daughter while attempting to pass along this heaven-sent sense of peace.

At the kitchen table with her parents, Ellie felt like she'd run into a rock wall. *This is dreadful news!* She felt even worse because Mamm was taking it quite hard. Yet Ellie understood, because she, too, felt thoroughly shaken.

"Let's keep in mind what the army men told me," Dat said, a solemn look on his face. "Evan could be found at any time."

Mamm nodded and pressed her handkerchief to her nose and mouth, eyes closed. "My poor, lost son," she murmured.

Ellie slipped her arm around her. "Dat's right, Mamm. And we'll pray that way, for Evan's sake."

No one was hungry for breakfast. Dat didn't even want coffee, nor Mamm her tea, even though Ellie offered to get them something to drink. Sol was out working in the orchard but would return any minute. She wished he was already here, then realized that he, too, would be shaken by this news.

Eventually, Dawdi Hezekiah came over as he usually did for breakfast. When he sat down, he looked round like he was wondering why Mamm wasn't cooking eggs, frying bacon, or making oatmeal. Dat got up from the head of the table and slipped over to sit next to him, then quietly told him that Evan was missing in action. "Two men from the army came a little while ago to tell us."

Dawdi showed little emotion, though he did say this was cause for even more prayer. Like Dat, he emphasized the fact that all was not lost. "The Lord sees exactly where Evan is, whether in a deep, dark trench or a rice paddy. And we must continue to be patient till he's found." Dawdi ran his hand through his long beard. "Sure ain't a *gut* way to start the mornin', son," he said, turning to look at Dat. "I'm sorry ya had to suffer through two strangers bearin' bad news."

Dat shook his head. "They were polite, even kind. I think they were worried I might pass out. I never imagined we'd find ourselves in this place."

Dawdi Hezekiah nodded. "Let's bow our heads and pray for Evan, wherever he might be clear across the world. But he ain't missin' to our ever-present Father above."

They did just that, Dawdi taking the lead, caring for and comforting Dat in that meaningful way. With her head bowed, too, Ellie silently asked God to help them through this grim time, grateful that her Dawdi and Dat were devoted to the Lord— sincere and faithful leaders for the family.

———

A short while later, Ellie watched as Dat and Dawdi Hezekiah hitched up Nelly to the family carriage before hurrying off to see Lydia, Jonah, Rudy, and their spouses. It would be a long and painful day for poor Dat as he retold the staggering news. But because he seemed to have a peacefulness about him, she believed he was wholly trusting God. And yet she sensed a struggle within him, too. Was he plagued with regret at how things were left with Evan before he went off to basic training?

After supper dishes were washed and dried, she donned her coat and warmest scarf. Even in wintry seasons, she'd always found solace and inspiration in the orchard—and divine peace, too. *Where God lives*, she thought, recalling her childlike perception.

But this twilight, Ellie felt anything but peaceful. It was easy to feel God's presence during spring's blossoming and summertime's harvest. But now? Now, when trees were spindly black sticks against the icy white snow and miserable gray sky, was God still there?

Ellie had a terrible time getting to sleep that night. She tried different positions—on her side, on her back, snuggled close to Sol—but nothing helped. She kept hearing her father telling them that Evan was missing in action, and she tried to comprehend what that really meant for her brother. Did it mean the other men in his unit just didn't know where he was or what happened to him? Had he been taken? Had Evan run away, maybe?

Over and over, she got bogged down in the trap of imagining what might be. It wasn't the first time this had happened. What was it about the middle of the night, anyway, when the house was stone still and the bedroom so dark? Why did nighttime cause her mind to wander and even trick her into thinking the worst thoughts about what Evan might be facing—if he was indeed alive?

Carefully, she moved the blankets and quilt back and rolled silently out of bed, fishing around on the cold floor for her slippers. She didn't want to awaken Sol, hard as he'd worked today—*every day*. Going to one of the windows and opening the shade slightly, she let the moonlight in.

She lit the lantern and carried it as she tiptoed downstairs to the second floor, making her way to Evan's room. Mamm had closed it off after his departure. There, Ellie opened the door and set the lantern on the floor, where she sat on the large rag rug she and Mamm had made. She leaned against the side of the bed, and in the stillness of her brother's room, she cried for her dear, lost twin.

Mamm said it herself early this morning, Ellie recalled. Evan was lost. At the time, she'd wondered if her mother might've been referring to Evan's spiritual state as well as his physical body. Surely Evan wouldn't have chosen war if he hadn't been close friends with Jack Herr, or tangled up in the world, dating Cheryl, spending time at the Herr home. Why else would Evan have pushed aside his plan to be baptized and abandoned that most sacred moment in life?

Ellie fought against the urge to be furious with Jack's family, especially Cheryl. She'd wanted to be kind, even friendly, when Cheryl came into the store. But now she wept angry yet sorrowful tears, letting them slide down her cheeks.

After a time, she rested her head against the mattress, fatigued as she was. *Please, God, keep my precious brother alive*, she prayed in the flickering lantern light. *Wherever he is.*

Sometime later, Ellie stirred in her sleep and found she was still sitting there on the rag rug. She couldn't be sure how long she'd been there, but her right leg was tingling with numbness, so it had been more than a short while.

Slowly, the bedroom door opened, and Sol knelt beside her. "Oh, Ellie, I wondered where you'd gone. I rolled over and found ya missin', so I went lookin' for you all over the house." He wrapped his arms around her, pressing his face against her cheek. "Have ya been cryin'?" He kissed her temple and held her close.

"I s'pose today's news caught up with me," she whispered, clinging to him.

"I'm surprised ya held it together this long," he said as he helped her up. Sol reached for the lantern and carried it while holding her hand. "Let's get ya to bed."

"I'm sorry for givin' ya a scare."

"*Nee* . . . no need to apologize."

Together, they made their way up the stairs, and he tucked her in as the sky was beginning to show a semblance of light over the eastern horizon. Sol pulled down the shade and dressed for the day's work, then said he'd let Mamm know Ellie needed to sleep a while longer.

Ellie gave in to slumber as he left the room.

Two days later, Ellie realized she must pay Cheryl Herr a visit. *She should know why Evan hasn't written*, she thought, telling only Sol where she was going with the two-wheeled horse-drawn cart. Ellie had told him all she knew about Evan's relationship with the young woman.

When she arrived at the Herr home a mile and a half away, a woman answered the back door, and Ellie quickly said who she was. "I'd like to talk with Cheryl if she's home."

"Yes, she's here." The woman was clad in a brown long-sleeved blouse and a short, tight-fitting vest with a pattern of brown, rust, and tan diamonds over a brown wool A-line skirt. She opened the storm door to Ellie. "Please, come in. I'm Cheryl's mother, Gladys. May I take your coat and scarf?"

"*Denki*, but I won't stay long."

"Well, have a seat while you wait." Then she pulled out one of the kitchen chairs for her and said, "I'll let her know you're here" before quickly disappearing from sight. Ellie sat down and leaned into the cushiony comfort of the chair, quite different from the hard wooden chairs at home. Across the room, a coppertone stove had a matching hood, and the windows near the table were adorned by two-tiered curtains with a design of apples and oranges. The room was as colorful as any she'd ever seen, overly decorated with equally bright plates hung on the wall.

An artificial ivy draped over the end of the far cupboard. On an apple-red corner table, framed family photos were on display, including one particularly large one of Cheryl in her high school graduation cap and gown. Ellie also noticed a photo of Jack wearing an army uniform.

What if we had a framed photo of Evan like that?

Ellie shook the thought away as she heard footsteps.

Cheryl appeared. "Hi, Ellie."

"Hullo," she replied, still feeling frustrated with Cheryl but no longer angry. "Will ya sit with me?"

"Sure." Cheryl frowned a little as she sat in one of the other kitchen chairs.

In that moment, Ellie knew how Dat must have felt telling her and Mamm the news after the army men left the house. "I thought you should know why Evan hasn't been writing letters."

Cheryl blanched white.

"It's not as bad as that, thank the Good Lord," Ellie said quickly. "But he *is* missing in action, so we still believe he may be found. We really don't know anything more."

"MIA?" Cheryl's jaw dropped. "That's exactly what they said about Jack!" She put her hand over her mouth as a wave of emotion appeared to overtake her.

Jack was listed as MIA, too? Ellie hadn't known that, and she wasn't sure what to say now. "It's hard . . . not knowin' what's happened to Evan. Ever so hard."

Cheryl's face was all scrunched up, like she was trying not to cry. "I feel sick. I can't bear to go through this again."

Ellie felt horrible. "I'm awful sorry to have to give ya such bad news."

"It's not your fault." Tears filled Cheryl's eyes. "But oh," she moaned, "it's happening all over again."

"We're prayin' Evan will be found," Ellie said. "Can't do any more than that."

Cheryl shook her head, then reached over and touched the back of Ellie's hand. "*I'm* the one who's sorry," she said softly. "You must be terribly worried about your brother." She paused. "I had no right to . . ."

"We all care for him."

"You're right. We do." Cheryl sighed. "Ugh, I hate this."

"It's quite a jolt, I know."

Cheryl offered her some coffee or tea, but Ellie simply wanted to head home. This visit had thrown her off-balance, and now, having heard Jack had been listed as missing in action, too, she felt more concerned for Evan than ever.

"I would be happy to drive you home," Cheryl said. "It's so cold today."

"*Denki*, but the horse and cart are waitin' for me, and it's not far." Ellie rose to leave.

"Thanks for coming over. I appreciate it." Cheryl went with her to the door, but Ellie noticed she didn't say anything about praying for Evan's safety. Given the circumstances, she didn't understand that.

For all the Decembers Ellie remembered, the days prior to Christmas seemed to move along quickly. Not this December. The hours slowed to a crawl, and every afternoon she bundled up and ran down to the mailbox, hoping for word from Evan or the military—anything to say he'd been found safe and sound.

As often as she prayed, Ellie had begun to wonder what would happen if Evan wasn't found. What if he were a prisoner of war? Or worse. She was especially haunted by Cheryl's admission that Jack, too, had initially been declared MIA. But by the time the army found Jack, it was too late to save him.

Each time she let her mind wander down that path, she rebuked herself. What Dawdi Hezekiah said after first hearing the news was the right way to think. No need to borrow trouble. Evan was said to be only missing, and that was a powerful hope to cling to.

When Christmas Day finally arrived, all of Ellie's siblings and their families came to celebrate. Every inch of the kitchen was filled with family members . . . except for Evan. Dat and Dawdi had set up three folding tables to accommodate the children, while a high chair was positioned beside the table, which had every one of its leaves in place.

Several times during the meal, Ellie noticed Sol looking at her from across the table, smiling as if to encourage her. And later that evening, before the two of them privately exchanged gifts, she breathed a prayer asking for strength to make it through till Evan was found. Yet what a struggle.

When Dat and Mamm headed upstairs early, Sol suggested they go and sit in the front room together. Ellie was pleased to have this time alone with her darling, and he made sure she sat to his right on the settee so he could hear her. Then he presented her with a wrapped box. Inside was a blue teapot with white trim and white cups and saucers. Her gift to him was a pair of thermal-insulated work gloves. "I noticed your old ones have seen better days," she said.

"Practical gifts are best, love. Just what I needed."

She nodded and thanked him for her lovely gift.

"You were so quiet today." Sol slipped his arm around her. "I was worried 'bout ya."

She gave him a smile. "Was remembering earlier Christmases when Evan was home."

"I thought you were prob'ly missin' him." Her husband kissed her cheek.

She nodded but still didn't want to share what Cheryl had revealed—that Jack had been declared missing, too. *Not on Christmas.* She hadn't said anything about it to anyone. There was no need to add to the family's anxiety. *We're all suffering enough . . . each in our own way.*

37

In mid-January, Lyle sat working in the barn office after looking at another land option with Ellie earlier that morning. Sol had remained behind to prune apple trees with the rest of the crew, since all the burned trees had been removed last month. Today's property had been a disappointment—too far away and too rocky for planting fruit trees.

Lyle recalled Ellie asking him weeks ago why he didn't write George Stewart in Florida about the property they'd been so fond of. *"What's the use since it's priced out of reach and he won't budge?"* he'd asked, though it did little to satisfy her.

Ellie had also filled him in on all she was doing to help Sol learn the key managerial duties for the orchard, including selecting the best varieties of saplings for the future replanting to be done late in the summer. She'd also set up meetings to introduce Sol to the local buyers, as well as to contacts at the Bird-in-Hand Farmers Market and Central Market in downtown Lancaster. Thankfully, handling the accounting ledger seemed to come easy for Sol, she'd said, seeming rightfully proud of her husband.

Together, they're an ideal team, Lyle thought.

Lyle made his way across the yard to visit Daed later that afternoon. Once inside, he removed his gloves, hat, and coat, then sat down on the sofa. "Thought I'd see how you're doin'," he said, rubbing his hands together near the heater stove. The January air was even colder than it had been that morning.

"Well, ya know, every day there's no more news 'bout Evan," Daed said out of the blue, "is a day for hope. 'Least that's how I see it."

"Sometimes hope's all we've got." Anymore, Lyle felt like he was holding his breath. "You an' I both know missing in action usually means the worst. I'm sure most of the family believes Evan's been killed, left behind enemy lines somewhere. But like you, I prefer to believe he's alive till we hear otherwise."

Daed leaned forward, his long beard touching his knees. "It could be he's even in hiding for safety from the enemy."

Lyle took that in, still feeling heavyhearted. "No matter what, I can always count on your listenin' ear, Daed."

His father's eyes searched his. "There'll come a day when you and I can't discuss things any longer, son." He glanced at the ceiling. "I'll be gone to Gloryland."

Nodding slowly, Lyle leaned back and sighed, thankful for each and every day he and his father had together. *A wondrous gift, indeed.*

Toward the end of January, Ellie took matters into her own hands. She went to talk to George Stewart's daughter, since she was the one who'd told Dat the price of the land wasn't negotiable.

291

She asked the young woman politely if the land was still available and was told it was. Then, bravely, she asked for her father's mailing address in Florida. That night, unbeknown to Dat, she wrote a letter to the man. Even if there was little chance of a reply, she felt she should do this. *What do I have to lose?*

> *Dear Mr. Stewart,*
>
>   *You don't know me, but I spoke with your daughter today about the acreage up for sale. My father, Lyle Hostetler, is an orchardist, and he's interested in your land. But our family's had quite a year. . . .*

Flurries were falling when Ellie's sister-in-law Priscilla arrived after breakfast the next morning, bringing some of her own recipes for Ellie's recipe box. While Ellie wouldn't think of saying it, she wondered what it would be like to be the only cook in Mamm's current kitchen. *Come spring, Sol and I will be in charge of this big farmhouse. How will it be, just the two of us?*

With Dat helping oversee the construction of the new addition, Ellie had been quite occupied with the business side of the orchard, so she was thankful when Priscilla and Mamm got busy making several loaves of bread and some pies. Ellie suspected Priscilla might be expecting their fifth child, though she hadn't voiced it. It wasn't their way to talk about a pregnancy . . . mentioned only very privately to adult sisters or mother.

And thinking about this, she wondered how her brother Rudy—eight years old at the time—had reacted to the surprise of twin babies when she and Evan were born. They were the only set of twins on both sides of the family.

Who could've known how very different Evan and I would become?

On the first day of February, Ellie smiled to see a letter from Leah in the mailbox. Leaning into the cold wind, she hurried up the long lane with Shadow at her side—Sol's father's wedding gift to him. Shadow scurried out to the barn, where it was warmer, as Ellie made her way inside the house. She stomped her boots on the rug in the kitchen hallway, then turned into the utility room and hung up her coat and scarf before blowing her warm breath on her icy hands. *Should've worn my mittens.*

Entering the kitchen, where Mamm was browning sausage for tonight's chili soup, Ellie breathed in the scent of savory seasonings—onion, garlic, and chili powder. A pan of golden cornbread cooled on the counter.

She held up the envelope. "Do I have time to read Leah's letter, or do ya need more help with supper?"

"Everything's in the chili pot just waitin' for the sausage. So go ahead, Ellie."

She went into the front room and curled up on one of the comfortable reading chairs in the corner. Because of the heavy gray clouds, she held the letter up toward the window, not bothering to light a lantern.

Dear Ellie,

I've been thinking of you and your family and praying for some word about Evan. It's good that Sol's so caring, especially during this troubling time for you. I miss both of you so much!

Did I tell you that Carolyn has met someone? Roger is a

young widower her age who works at the post office. She's been buying more stamps than ever before! I can only guess what will come of their growing friendship, but if it's worth her talking about him, she must be interested. That's all I know, but I'll keep you posted.

Ellie was suddenly excited. *If Carolyn gets married again, then Leah can return home. What good news!*

Now, as you know, Reuben's been courting me, and we're really fond of each other. In fact, he's proposed marriage, and we're looking to wed in November. Honestly, I've never been this happy, Ellie. You're the first I've written about it, and as soon as I finish this letter, I'll write to my parents and to Sol, then mail all three letters at once. Hopefully, they'll all receive them on the same day.

Reuben is eager to meet you and Sol and the rest of my family. We're talking of coming there for Easter, April second, when Carolyn's parents visit again. Oh, Ellie, I can hardly wait for you to get to know him. I think you'll definitely approve.

Ellie folded the letter, so delighted for dear Leah. *She's found love, just like I have,* she thought. *Life is certainly full of surprises!*

The next afternoon, while Ellie was in the office with Sol going over the schedule for spray and fertilizer applications, Dat poked his head in and waved a letter at Sol. "Hand delivery for Solomon Bontrager," he said, grinning.

Ellie was fairly sure it was from Leah. She'd had a hard time remaining tight-lipped about Leah's engagement but had reasoned that Sol should learn about it directly from his sister.

Sol thanked Dat, who headed back toward the construction site for the new addition.

Ellie kept busy working on her own while Sol read the letter. At last, he said, "Sounds like Leah's getting married."

"I know." Ellie smiled. "I received a letter from her yesterday, but I didn't say anything 'cause I knew she'd written to your parents and to you as well."

"So ya kept a secret from me?" Sol said, winking at her.

"It wouldn't have been right to tell ya beforehand."

"I'm just kiddin'."

"So how will we get down to Chambersburg to visit her?"

"The buses run on both sides of the road, ya know."

She nodded. "I've never ridden on one alone."

"We'd go together, so you'd be fine, love."

"Still, Leah won't be within walking distance or a buggy ride away." She sighed and shook her head. "Guess I took for granted that it'd be that way."

Sol looked thoughtful. "It won't be easy for my parents, either."

She didn't want to feel blue, but she did, and then she recalled Cheryl's truly painful words about her brother Jack.

"What're ya thinkin'?" Sol asked, reaching for her hand.

"Oh, somethin' Evan's girlfriend told me that day I visited her a couple of months ago." Then she finally shared what Cheryl said, that Jack had first been declared MIA.

"I'm aware that sometimes MIA soldiers don't return home," he said gently. "There's a lot we don't know, but remember, these are the times we must have faith in our Sovereign Lord. Do we believe He's with us, even when we don't perceive His presence?" Sol asked, sounding so like Dawdi.

Off and on the rest of the afternoon and into the evening, Ellie thought about Sol's wise remark. And when she was snug next to him that night, she thanked God for such a loving and empathetic husband.

Ellie had started to wonder if George Stewart would ever bother to reply when, two weeks later, Sol came into the barn office with an envelope addressed to her.

"Postmarked Florida," he said with a smile. "Might be from that snowbird landowner ya wrote to."

Surprised, Ellie tore open the envelope and began to read as Sol leaned over her shoulder.

"Goodness," she said. "He wants to meet with us when he returns home in mid-April." She handed the letter to Sol. "See for yourself."

Sol scanned the letter. "That's two months away. What's he waitin' for?"

"Maybe for someone to accept the price he wants 'tween now and then."

Sol returned the letter. "Guess ya'd better tell your Dat what ya did."

Ellie agreed. "I never really thought anything would come of my letter." She stood and looked out the window. "Have ya seen Dat around lately?"

"He was out in the orchard earlier with Titus and me."

Ellie stared at the letter. "I don't want to get my hopes up," she murmured. *O Lord, I trust Thee to open the door if it's Thy will.*

38

During peach tree pruning toward the middle of March, Ellie slipped off to market with Mamm for some loose-leaf black tea and needed food items. When they went their separate ways after Mamm spotted Aendi Cora, Ellie noticed Cheryl Herr holding hands with a young man. He was definitely an *Englischer*, wearing pressed brown pants flared at the ankles, a long-sleeved shirt with rust-colored designs, and a tan sweater vest.

In one way, Ellie was stunned that Cheryl had moved on from Evan so quickly, yet in another, relieved. But really, after Cheryl had taken the news so hard that Evan was missing three months ago, what was she doing already seeing someone else?

Ellie's first inclination was to wander over there, but she wouldn't embarrass Cheryl or herself. While she didn't approve of Cheryl's relationship with her brother, it was rather jolting to see her batting her eyes at this new fellow.

Just then Cheryl glanced her way and waved. Now she was coming toward her, leaving the young man behind to look at the hand-rolled soft pretzels.

"Ellie . . . wow. May I, uh, talk to you?"

Ellie hardly knew what else to say. "Okay."

"You must wonder what I'm doing with . . . him." Cheryl looked over her shoulder but didn't wait for Ellie's response. She lowered her voice. "I thought of coming to visit you but doubted . . . um, that you'd appreciate what I had to say." She looked sheepish.

"Why's that?" Ellie was very curious.

"After you told me Evan was missing, I lost so much sleep, crying and feeling the way I did when Jack was MIA. It's been rough . . . and I hated the constant not knowing." She paused, like she wasn't sure she could say more. "In the last weeks, I decided I would try to get out more to get my mind off everything. And . . . well, the guy I'm with today, I met only recently. I had no thought of being more than friends with him, but . . ." She cleared her throat, looking down at her feet for a moment. "As you may have noticed, we've become fond of each other."

"*Jah,* I did notice, in fact."

"I'm sorry you had to find out this way." Cheryl paused and frowned. "I realized I couldn't endure the waiting—not knowing—maybe never knowing. I decided I had to move on with my life."

You betrayed my brother, Ellie thought, wondering how Evan would feel if he knew. *What if just knowing she's waiting for him is what's giving Evan the courage to stay alive?*

Yet standing there, Ellie realized she couldn't blame Cheryl for any of it. Truth be told, Evan might have chosen the same path even without his interest in her, or her influence. After all, he'd become attracted to Cheryl once he was already running around with her brothers and other *Englischers.*

"Ellie, please excuse me," Cheryl said, seeing her new boyfriend waving her over.

Ellie bid her good-bye and watched her hurry back to him.

She assumes Evan's dead like Jack, thought Ellie somberly, then turned to find Mamm.

The following week, Dat and Mamm moved into their new house next to Dawdi's. Now two smaller homes sat connected to the big farmhouse, and it was a happy day for Ellie and Sol as they made the main structure their own. Ellie had suggested they move into her parents' spacious bedroom on the second floor, more comfortable temperature-wise during the winter and summer months.

All her parents' belongings had been hauled to the new house except the kitchen table and chairs and some of the extra bedroom furniture—including Evan's. Mamm and Ellie had agreed on that. *"It's for the best,"* Ellie had said, rather choked up at the thought of Evan's room remaining empty of his presence for the foreseeable future. Even so, she forced her greatest fear away and worked to set up the kitchen with items from her hope chest and numerous wedding gifts of silverware, glassware, essential cooking utensils, and the like.

Ellie worked tirelessly to make each room neat and orderly once Sol had placed their own furniture, most given to them by various relatives. Sol joked about all the bedrooms and how many children it would take to fill them.

That evening, after their first Bible reading and prayer on their own, Ellie sat with a cup of hot tea near the kitchen's cookstove, its embers warming the room. She couldn't help recalling her father's initial reaction when she confessed she'd written to George Stewart. But his startled expression had faded within a moment when she added that the man had replied and wanted to meet with Dat when he returned from Florida.

"*What could he have in mind?*" Dat had asked, then said, "*I'll write to him.*"

Ellie could see how pleased he was at her efforts.

The day before Easter, Sol and Ellie walked up to the Bontrager farm to meet Leah and her fiancé, Reuben Miller. Ellie felt nervous, wanting to be welcoming for Leah's sake, and Sol seemed to be on edge, too. Together, they sat at the kitchen table with Sol's parents—his father, Benjamin, sitting at the head of the table and nibbling on one of Nan's delicious crispy squares.

They were all waiting on what was surely a landmark day for Ellie's dearest friend. But Nan seemed less cheerful than her usual bubbly self, and Ellie assumed that she, too, felt a little disappointed that Leah would be permanently living so far away.

Soon, a taxi pulled up to the front of the house, bringing Leah and her beau home. Nan ran to the front room and peered out, but Ellie refrained from doing so, though she couldn't wait to size up the man who had captured Leah's heart. Sol fidgeted while Ellie rose and swept up the crumbs from her and Nan's side of the table.

"This is the moment we've been waitin' for," Benjamin declared, scooting his chair back to go welcome them.

Sol gave Ellie a curious glance before following his Dat.

It didn't take long for Ellie to learn that Reuben Miller was exceptionally outgoing and a good conversationalist, and the way Leah beamed at him while they all sat around Nan's table made Ellie joyful. With his open, friendly manner, it was easy to see why Leah had fallen for auburn-haired Reuben. He reminded her of her brother Rudy, who worked as their salesman at the family store and on market days. Reuben had a similar winning smile and apparent ease around people, strangers or not.

Ellie glanced at Sol as they enjoyed Nan's tasty goodies there at the table. As he interacted with Reuben, she sensed that her husband approved of his sister's choice. On the walk down the hill after their visit, Ellie asked Sol his thoughts on his future brother-in-law.

"I have no doubt Reuben will be a *wunnerbaar* addition to our family. In fact, he and your Dawdi Hezekiah would be a fine pair of storytellers, *jah?*"

Ellie laughed. "I thought of that, too, while Reuben was telling about his squirrel-catching days when he was a boy. I really think he and Dawdi would be fond of each other."

"I'm not sure when their paths would ever cross, though," Sol said, a ring of melancholy in his voice.

"True," Ellie said sadly.

Lyle scrutinized their much smaller kitchen while Elisabeth assembled ingredients for a carrot cake with creamy frosting.

"It'll be a tight squeeze tomorrow, even though we'll be hosting just part of the family for dinner," his wife said.

"But when everyone comes, like for Thanksgiving and Christmas, we'll still gather over at the main house, *jah?*"

"Makes sense, and Ellie and Sol will be happy to have us all."

"The women can pitch in with side dishes like before, ain't so?"

Elisabeth stopped her baking and gave him a quick hug. "You have no idea what all goes into these big doin's, do ya, love?"

"Doubt I could even cook a potato without askin' directions," he said, admitting the truth with a chuckle.

"S'pose that says it all."

"Well, it's just one of the reasons I married ya." He gave her a wink.

Elisabeth smiled and turned her attention back to the moist, delicious cake she planned to serve tomorrow when Lydia, Rudy, and their families came for Easter dinner, the celebration falling this year on an off-Sunday from church. Jonah and his family were going to Priscilla's parents' for Easter dinner, and Sol and Ellie would be up yonder with the Bontragers.

"I'm wonderin' when that landowner fella will tell me where and when he wants to meet," Lyle mentioned. This had been playing on his mind.

"I'm still wonderin' what Ellie wrote him to get this kind of response!"

Lyle laughed. "I wouldn't be surprised if she played on his heartstrings."

Elisabeth turned toward him, eyes wide. "You think she'd do that?"

"Maybe, but I'm also sure she meant every word."

"She must really want that land."

"We'll see what happens." Lyle pulled out the chair at the head of the table, eyeing the space once again. "This kitchen really is much smaller than what we had at the main house. What were we thinkin'?"

"To tell the truth, I'm happy for less work."

He nodded. "Might be 'bout time for us both to slow down some," he said, looking around him. "Getting moved into this house took some doin'. But I'm not ready to fully retire yet. Maybe in another year or so. Besides, it'll take that long for Sol and Ellie to be ready to manage the orchard on their own."

"True," his wife said absently, her expression more solemn now.

Lyle had forgotten again. Every time he mentioned the management of the orchard, it stirred up Elisabeth's thoughts of Evan. "I'm sorry, love."

She shrugged. "One of these days, maybe it won't hurt like this. I just wish . . ."

He stepped to her side and slipped his big arms around her. "I pray we can get through this."

"Some things only the eyes of faith can see," she said, tears brimming.

He nodded, holding her for dear life.

39

On Easter Monday—for Leah's sake while Reuben was off fishing with Aaron and Sol—Ellie and Leah leisurely rode around the neighborhood in the two-wheeled cart hitched up to Nelly. Amish businesses were closed for the holiday, so more buggies were on the road than usual.

Ellie had chicken salad with potato rolls and raspberry Jell-O planned for the noon meal following their little jaunt. She was still growing accustomed to Dat, Mamm, and Dawdi having their meals at her parents' new house, though sometimes Sol invited them all to supper for old times' sake. It was, of course, a big adjustment for everyone, but Ellie enjoyed having the big farmhouse to themselves.

"This is nice of you," Leah said as they rode past a number of her relatives' farms for the fun of it.

"Can't let ya forget your old stompin' grounds." Ellie smiled, holding the reins.

"Oh, trust me, I haven't. My kinfolk'll always be close to my heart."

Ellie nodded.

"By the way, Reuben told me something interesting this

morning. One of my uncles has invited him to work here in his woodworking shop once we're married."

"Such *gut* news! Do ya think Reuben will accept?"

"This just came up, but he seems interested."

"Well, I've been prayin' to get ya home somehow."

"Me too." Leah laughed softly. "A lot, in fact."

Ellie wanted to hug her, but she didn't dare let go of the reins. Instead, as close as they were sitting, she leaned against Leah. "Honestly, this could be our answer."

"We'd get to raise our future children together like we always wished—*if* Reuben accepts the job."

"*Jah*, and things could go back to what used to be." Ellie paused. "I mean, for our friendship."

Leah agreed, and Ellie refused to think of Evan then, focusing instead on the soothing sounds of Nelly's trotting as they rode past the bishop's farm. The fact that Reuben might accept work here meant he and Leah could return to Bird-in-Hand come November—or even earlier if they chose to have the wedding here.

Just knowing that's a possibility makes life a little more tolerable.

In the midst of a heavy drizzle after supper the next evening, Ellie took the family buggy to visit Priscilla and the children while Sol and Dat went over the accounting ledger. Then on her way home, she stopped in to see Ruthann.

Her cousin greeted her at the back door. "What're ya doin' out tonight? You ain't a single woman anymore, ya know." She chortled.

"Sol's tied up with Dat, workin', so I thought I'd come see what you're up to."

Ruthann led Ellie up to her room, then showed her two new dresses she'd recently made for herself. "I'll be sewin' my wedding dress this fall, too," she said with a smile.

"You're engaged?"

"Menno asked me right before Easter. He wanted to get things in order before he did—a place for us to live and full-time work for him."

Ellie hugged her. "You must be so thrilled, cousin."

"I truly am." Ruthann's eyes glimmered with emotion.

"Things are comin' together nicely for you and Menno."

"God's been so *gut* to us." Ruthann grinned. "I've been thinkin' of having a Sisters Day gathering next month. What do ya think?"

"It'd give us somethin' to look forward to."

Ruthann touched Ellie's arm. "Get our minds off Evan . . . if that's even possible."

"Well, not as long as we don't know where he is, but I know what ya mean."

"Everyone I know is prayin'." Ruthann sighed as the lantern in her room flickered.

It was cozy and so pleasant being there, and Ellie was heartened by her cousin's words. "We appreciate the prayers."

Ruthann nodded. "Ever since I was a little girl, I've been taught that God knows all things and walks with us through our trials as well as our victories." She reached for her Bible and opened it. "This verse is from Isaiah, chapter forty, verse twenty-nine. I bookmarked it so I can read it every time I think of poor Cousin Evan."

Ellie was deeply touched by this and listened closely.

"'He giveth power to the faint; and to them that have no might he increaseth strength.'"

Agreeing wholeheartedly, Ellie replied, "Sol says we must cast our burdens upon the One whose shoulders are big enough to carry them."

"He's right." Ruthann reached for Ellie's hand. "Our faith is in our heavenly Father alone."

On Friday afternoon, Lyle was mowing in the orchard with Sol when he heard rapid thumps on the grassy strip behind him. He turned to see Ellie running his way.

"Dat!" she called rather loudly.

He hurriedly met her, and she worked to catch her breath as she handed him an official-looking envelope. His heart pounded when he saw the return address.

Sol came over quickly to stand next to him. "Might be best to go to the house and sit while ya read it," Sol suggested.

"*Nee*," Lyle replied. "If it's bad news, the Lord'll give me strength."

Ellie had her hand over her mouth as Sol slipped to her side.

Ellie held her breath as her father opened the envelope and read. She and Sol stayed close to him as his hands began to tremble. Then he bowed his head, holding the letter to his chest, his shoulders rapidly rising and falling.

Sol stepped closer to Ellie as tears clouded her vision.

Dat started to weep, then sob, sounding as though he was racked with pain. Or was it . . . laughter?

Sol steadied him, and Dat turned and embraced him.

"Evan's been found . . . wounded but alive . . . and he's comin' home soon," Dat said between gasps. "He was in a landmine explosion . . . and because his dog tags were blown off and he couldn't remember who he was, they couldn't ID him. Must've been a lot of confusion."

Ellie wrapped her arms around both Dat and Sol, something she'd never done before. But this news was cause for the greatest gratitude.

"I must go an' tell your Mamm." Dat's face was streaked with tears.

"And Dawdi," Ellie added, her own joyful tears flowing.

"The Lord God be praised." Dat stopped to kneel right there in the orchard, his face raised toward the sky. "His merciful name be praised!"

Ellie and Sol stood on either side of Dat, giving thanks with all their hearts as well. And then and there, Ellie was sure that God was indeed present everywhere, both in the wintertime orchard when all seemed dormant and fragile and in the dire conditions of Vietnam's jungles.

40

The following Monday, Lyle rose before dawn, too fidgety to sleep. This was the day Evan was to arrive home, though Lyle didn't know the exact hour. So he kept busy hauling the last of the scratch brush out behind the barn for burning.

Midmorning, he walked around the main house and sat himself down on the front porch, not wanting to miss a minute of his son's return. *He doesn't know Sol and Ellie have taken over the main farmhouse, or that a second addition's been built,* Lyle thought, sitting where Evan could see him from the lane, and where he could witness with his own eyes that his son was home.

Word of Evan's impending return had traveled fast around Bird-in-Hand, particularly during the fellowship meal yesterday after Preaching. Relatives and other church members had been dropping by the house with casseroles, baked goods, and even packages of licorice sticks, a favorite of Evan's.

Ellie had freshened Evan's bedding on Saturday and thoroughly cleaned the room for his first night back. *He'll be exhausted from traveling,* she assumed, and she wanted to give him a chance to return to familiar surroundings, at least for now.

She stayed indoors instead of doing orchard work that morning, but it was almost impossible to focus on her housework. Mamm and Dawdi came over for the noon meal, as did Jonah and Titus . . . and Dat, who'd been sitting out front, waiting. Seeing her father out there, her heart had been drawn to him, and if she'd been finished folding clothes, she might have gone out there to wait, too.

Midafternoon, Lyle spotted a young man dressed in an army uniform and hat walking slowly up the road and carrying a tan army-issue bag. Lyle sprang to his feet and squinted.

He looks older . . . and thinner, he thought, making his way toward the porch steps. *Can this be my son?*

Heart in his throat, Lyle nearly lost his footing going down the steps. The soldier turned into their long, tree-lined lane and seemed to lean toward his left side at times. As Lyle walked farther to better see him, the young man began to quicken his pace, his right arm moving strangely—as if to steady himself.

Lyle's pulse was pounding now as he strode toward him. This was Evan, for certain, but the cuff at the bottom of his left sleeve was knotted shut, the sleeve hanging empty as Evan quickened his pace.

Dear Lord in heaven!

Lyle's heart dropped like a stone, but he opened his arms wide. "Willkumm Heem, son."

Evan stepped awkwardly into his big embrace. "At last," he said, his breath against Lyle's neck.

They walked unhurriedly now, without speaking, then Evan paused to set his canvas bag on the ground. He almost stumbled as he turned to face Lyle. "I'm guessing I look a little different to ya, Dat."

Lyle studied him, sincerity all over Evan's scarred face. "I'm just glad you're home."

Evan looked around, taking in the side yard, the meadow, and the orchard beyond.

"The family's anxious to see ya." Lyle took a step forward, but Evan didn't budge. He just stared at the house, standing stock-still.

Lyle saw tears welling up. "Son?"

Evan's gaze found his, and then he said with measured words, "There's something I need to say. . . ." His eyes were full of pain.

Lyle braced himself. "All right."

Evan took a deep breath. "I was wrong every which way, Dat. Will ya forgive me?"

This isn't the Evan who left to fight, Lyle thought, and he wasted no time in replying. "I certainly do forgive ya, son."

Evan sighed audibly. "And something else. I want to be baptized this September."

"That's music to my ears." Elated, Lyle searched Evan's face.

"I received your letter, but then the explosion happened, and I wasn't able to reply. But it came at the right time."

"We'll begin anew."

"I'm ready for that." Evan reached down to pick up his bag, then hoisted it onto his right shoulder. He surveyed the house, the cider shed, and the orchard beyond as if drinking it all in, his expression one of bliss. "Standing here . . . it doesn't even feel real."

Lyle glanced toward the house. "I daresay Ellie's peekin' out the front window, mighty eager to see ya."

"I sure missed her."

They resumed walking, and Shadow came bounding out to meet them, his tail whipping back and forth.

"Hey there, boy," Evan said, reaching down to rub the dog's neck, his left sleeve dangling.

Shadow whined almost sadly.

The door opened, and Ellie flew out. "Bruder!" she hollered, running toward him.

Evan stretched out his only arm, and instead of her being horrified, her eyes filled with tears of love. She smiled as Evan reached for her.

"Wasn't sure I'd ever see ya again," he said as Ellie clung to him.

Ellie and Evan headed up to the house. "Come inside and have some goodies," she said. "The neighbors, relatives . . . all the People have been bringin' food by. And I baked your favorite pie."

Lyle stepped back, realizing Evan would have seen the new addition by now and probably put two and two together. "I'll head over and tell your Mamm you've arrived," he said, leaving the twins alone for their reunion and choking back tears for his injured son.

Ellie had watched from the house prior to running out to greet Evan, and when she'd realized the extent of his injuries, she'd felt the first pricks of tears. Quickly, she'd wiped them away, exhorting herself to be strong for her brother's sake. *I have all night to cry. This is the time to rejoice.*

Now she observed him as he sat in his usual spot at the long table, though he'd struggled to be seated.

"No need to fuss over me." Evan jerked on his left sleeve.

"Little by little, I'm learning how to function again. The rehab doctor said it might take years, but I'll get there." He went on to explain that, after the explosion, he was flown by helicopter to a hospital, though he had no recollection of that. And because his dog tags were never found, the authorities had no idea who he was until his memory returned only recently. Soldiers from his unit who might have identified him were taken to other hospitals, and there'd been many fatalities.

"It was evidently total chaos," he said, "and I was an unrecognizable mess anyway. They wouldn't let me see my face until after the skin grafts healed." He shook his head.

"If anyone's determined, it's you," Ellie said.

"Well, I can only do it with God's help."

Ellie's heart lifted, hearing that.

"You wouldn't believe all the prayers going up in the trenches," Evan told her quietly. "And not just mine."

"Oh, Evan, what ya suffered." She didn't want to give in to tears again, so she focused on how thankful she was to have him back. She looked at her brother, his deep-blond hair so short it was practically shaved, his army uniform so strange to her.

Evan looked around the kitchen as though seeing it for the first time. He stared at the cellar door where Mamm's calendar had always hung. "A lot has changed since I left. I'm guessing you and Sol have taken over the main house."

"*Jah*, but not everything changed. I kept your room the way it was."

Evan opened his mouth to reply but merely nodded, his eyes moist. "Thanks."

She smiled. "But as you can see, I wanted to make this kitchen my own. Thankfully, Mamm let us keep this big table for family gatherings. Their new place is quite a bit smaller."

"I saw the new addition as soon as I got out of the cab . . . down the road a ways."

"Why'd ya come so far on foot?"

"Wanted to see the orchard up close and slow. I missed it dreadfully."

Ellie cut a large slice of the butterscotch pie for Evan and grabbed a cookie for herself. "Seems like you've been gone forever."

"A year and almost seven months," he murmured, eyeing the pie she set before him. "And, Ellie . . . I'm glad Sol's the man who won your heart."

"Dat is, too."

Evan picked up his fork. "I secretly hoped he'd be the one."

"God knew best," she replied. Then sitting across from him, she told him Menno and Ruthann had ended up together.

For the first time since he'd stepped into the kitchen, she saw a trace of a smile on Evan's lips. "So . . . Sol and Menno switched girlfriends?"

"It wasn't quite like that, but we're all happier. Oh, and Menno and Ruthann are getting married this fall."

Evan glanced out the window, his lips pressed together. "I missed your wedding, Ellie. Wanted to be there so bad."

She could hardly eat her cookie for wanting to look at him. *He's aged*, she thought, but maybe it was the unfamiliar uniform and the scars on his face. "I thought of you every day, and I prayed all the time, too. But the important thing is that you're here now, *alive*."

"The Lord heard your prayers . . . and got me this far," he said, sounding almost sad.

Ellie offered him coffee or milk, and he chose the milk.

"While I was at boot camp, I quickly learned it wasn't the

smartest thing to drink too much coffee." He seemed to force a chuckle, and there was a quiver in his lower lip.

Ellie was filled with so many thoughts and emotions. She appreciated this time with Evan. But she also wondered how long she should wait before bringing up Cheryl Herr—and her new boyfriend. Certainly not today.

She heard the screen door open, and Mamm soon appeared in the kitchen, wearing her pretty green dress and black cape and apron. Dat stood close behind. "I heard my boy was home." Mamm rushed over to throw her arms around his neck. "It's *wunnerbaar-gut* to see ya, Evan."

Ellie could tell that Mamm was trying to keep her composure, yet her face absolutely shone. *Dat must've warned her. . . .*

Her brother rose, wrapped his arm around Mamm, and told her how happy he was to be home. "Come, sit with us. Have some pie," he said as Dat patted him on the back.

"Dawdi and Sol are out runnin' errands together, or they'd be here, too," Dat said. "They'd hoped to return before you arrived."

Ellie slipped into the chair where Mamm had always sat, to the right of the head of the table. Now, though, Mamm sat next to Evan, her gaze fixed on him.

"I sure missed getting your cookies after I went overseas," Evan told their mother as tears sprang to his eyes. "To be honest, I missed *everything*."

Mamm reached up to pat his cheek, the room ever so still.

Evan broke the silence. "You're sitting on the wrong side of me," he joked.

"Aw, now," Mamm said, shaking her head and looking down-right *ferhoodled* for a moment.

"I can still shave my face and brush my teeth," Evan told her.

"It'll be nice to have some hair back on my head, though. You can trim it up once it's long enough for a respectable Amish cut."

Mamm's eyes brightened.

"I'm home where God meant me to be," Evan added, looking at each one of them.

Mamm was glowing. "You were always one of us, son. Ya just forgot for a while." She reached for a cookie and asked Ellie for some coffee.

Evan replied, "I know now why war is to be avoided at all costs. We Amish have it right—peace is always the thing to strive for. It's to be cherished, in fact."

Ellie listened as Evan shared more about his new outlook, as did her parents, Dat wide-eyed.

After a time, she poured more coffee for herself and Mamm and Dat, as well as more milk for Evan. "We'll have a nice big gatherin' for ya, Bruder. The whole family can come."

Evan bowed his head. "I'll need some time first."

"However long it takes." Ellie pressed her lips together to hold in the emotion. Life wasn't exactly back to normal, not with Evan suffering the trauma he'd endured. Her heart broke for all he'd lost, but he was home and actually talking about God, and that was a very good start.

I can breathe again, she thought, ever so thankful. *At long last.*

41

Ellie scurried out to meet Sol on the back part of the porch while Dat helped Dawdi unhitch their horse by the stable. She told Sol that Evan had been in an explosion before suffering through months of recovery and rehab all while not even remembering who he was until recently. And he'd lost his left arm.

"He lost . . . *what?*" Sol clenched his jaw, clearly stunned.

"It's a lot for him to deal with." Her stomach turned again at the thought. "Yet he seems to be taking it in stride. Doesn't seem like him."

"He may be coverin' up his real feelings, maybe for your sake and your parents'. I mean, how can ya lose a limb and not grieve the loss?" Sol sighed. "This is unbelievable."

Ellie nodded. "Thank the Lord he didn't lose his life. And there's some good news, too. Evan wants to make things right with the bishop first thing."

"Can you repeat that?" Sol said, pointing to his injured ear. She did.

Sol looked startled. "So I *did* hear ya right the first time. What a blessing!"

"And not only that," she said, glancing toward the side door, "but he's talking of joinin' church come fall."

"Glory be!"

"That's for sure. Evan's heart's been changed, Sol. I couldn't be more grateful."

Sol leaned down to kiss her. "Your face is lit up like a candle."

She hugged him tight. "Evan sounded eager to get out of his uniform. I wouldn't be surprised if he's upstairs changin' clothes right now."

Sol followed her around to the side door.

Ellie continued, "Honestly, I was uncomfortable seein' him dressed that way. He looked like he'd been plucked out of another world and dropped into an Amish farmhouse."

"I can only imagine," Sol said, opening the screen door for her.

Ellie stepped inside and yet again realized that both of these young men she loved had lost something in their stand—one for peace and the other for military service.

Recalling Evan's fondness for it, Ellie prepared macaroni goulash for supper while Sol read the newspaper at the table. Evan had slipped away upstairs to his room, and after a time, Dawdi came over and asked to see him before heading upstairs. Ellie was glad their grandfather was eager to visit with Evan. *He'll need all the encouragement we as a family can give him*, she thought as she browned the ground beef.

A while later, Dawdi came down the stairs and stood in the kitchen, sighing. "*Ach*, mighty hard to see Evan like that," he said, his straw hat in his big hands.

318

Ellie nodded, turning away from the cookstove. "How's he doin' up there?"

"Seems fine. Already talking 'bout packin' his uniform away. He looks like an Amish fella again—got his Plain clothes on."

"I wondered if he might want to change."

"He's prob'ly put on a brave face for yous, but he was weepin' when I went up there. Our boy's depressed, that's certain, and for *gut* reason." Dawdi paused, grimacing. "He showed me what little's left of his arm. It's still healing, but he said he knows what to do to take care of it. He told me a warm towel will go a long way when he gets phantom pains."

"I wish he'd said somethin' earlier," Ellie replied, wishing she'd thought to ask if he needed anything special.

"He's havin' to relearn how to do many things that used to be second nature." Dawdi shuffled to the hallway leading to the side door. "I invited him to come stay with me next door whenever he's ready, since I've got that spare bedroom an' all. He an' I, we'll look after each other."

Sol perked up. "That's just like ya, Hezekiah."

"You're welcome to have supper with us tonight," Ellie said, thinking it might be easier for all of them if Dawdi was around. He knew how to make the best of every situation.

"Your Mamm already invited me over there, but I appreciate it, Ellie-girl." Dawdi put on his hat. "Well, yous have a nice evening together." With that he headed for the hallway.

Ellie heard the door open and close, saying nary a word, wanting Sol to talk first if he was so inclined. *My brother's upstairs,* she thought with a somewhat contented feeling, in spite of her concern.

319

Sol was quieter than usual after they bowed their heads for the suppertime blessing. Ellie felt as if she had to carry the conversation, talking about everything except Evan's injury. She wished she knew what Sol was thinking at the head of the table she'd set with their good dishes.

"I'll be packing my uniform away up in the attic, out of sight. The Purple Heart medal, too," Evan shared. "They stir up memories I want to forget. Reminds me of everything I turned my back on. Other soldiers are proud of all that, but I was never really one of them."

"That's all up to you, Bruder," Ellie said, passing the big bowl of green beans to Sol as she considered what Dawdi had told them earlier.

A shadow seemed to pass over Evan's face. "Three of my closest buddies died in the explosion that nearly took *my* life," he said more quietly. "Sometimes at night, I see flashes when I close my eyes, reminding me of the nonstop horror we saw night and day. And then there are the nightmares. I wake up drenched with sweat."

A lump rose in her throat. "I wish there was somethin' I could do."

"Tying my shoes would be a start." Evan sounded embarrassed to say it.

Sol leaned forward at the table. "Whatever ya need, Evan, we're here for you, and we want our home to be a place of refuge. I know Hezekiah invited ya to move over there, but Ellie and I want ya to stay with us however long you'd like."

Evan looked surprised and frowned a little. "I appreciate this, comin' from you. You were the better man, Sol . . . choosin' the way of peace." His voice broke. "It means . . . more than I can say."

"We don't have to talk about any of that," Ellie said, seeing how grim and beaten down he looked. "You've had more than enough trouble for one lifetime."

"Ellie's right," Sol said. "Your family truly cares, Evan. Every one of us."

"*Denki*," Evan said, eyes glimmering.

"And we're brothers now, remember," Sol said, smiling.

Ellie's shoulders relaxed. *All will surely be well*, she thought, grateful for this generous welcome from her husband. It had made all the difference for their first meal together. But she also knew Sol would understand if Evan decided not to stay in his boyhood room, living in the same house with her and Sol as they began their marriage.

Still, she worried Evan was in more pain, both physically and emotionally, than he was letting on. *Like Dawdi said.*

That evening, Ellie, Sol, and Evan met in the front room for early Bible reading. Evan requested prayer for the families of his deceased unit buddies, as well as for the nurses who offered care and kindness to him, especially after his amputation.

"They were like the ministering spirits mentioned in the New Testament," Evan said before they knelt in silent prayer. "The medics and corpsmen on the battlefields need prayer for energy and stamina, too. So many soldiers are wounded and dying every day."

Ellie's heart was touched by Evan's sincere request, and she did as he'd asked. But she added a prayer for her brother's emotional and mental state as well.

Before Evan headed up to his room for the night, Ellie offered him a warmed towel, and he thanked her.

"I also have some aloe juice, if ya think that would help soothe the scars on your face and neck," she said.

"Wish I'd had that overseas. Might be too late now, but I'll try it."

Much later, as Ellie and Sol settled in their room for the night, she told him she had something to discuss before too long.

"Why not right now?" he asked as they sat in bed by the light of the lantern.

She moved closer to him. "I can't help wonderin' if Dat might be wishin' he'd waited to appoint us the orchard's future managers."

"That crossed my mind, too." Sol reached for her hand. "If it'll help, just know that I can get a job with my older brother. That was always my plan before we were engaged."

"You wouldn't have continued workin' here?" She was a little surprised.

"Maybe part-time. I would've missed workin' in the orchard, no question, but I knew I'd need a better income eventually." He paused. "About the time I was gonna tell ya, your Dat approached us 'bout takin' on his role."

Ellie sat there in the dim light and pondered that. "First I knew this."

"So now that Evan's back and lookin' to become a church member, are ya thinkin' of talking to your Dat 'bout changing the current plan?"

"If it'd free him up to follow his heart with this, *jah*." She leaned her head on Sol's shoulder, and he cupped her chin in his hand. "But only if you agree, love."

"Go ahead, but with Evan missin' an arm, I really don't know how he could handle everything," Sol said. "It could take him a long time to fully adapt. But your father will tell you what he's thinkin', and it'll be less awkward if you're the one to offer for us to bow out."

"You don't want to come with me to discuss it?"

Sol shook his head. "I'm in agreement with whatever's decided."

Closing her eyes, Ellie was relieved at Sol's kindhearted understanding. She tried to think what it'd be like not to be involved in the business side of things after all this time working alongside Dat and loving the orchard as she did. But Evan had made an about-face, and it was worthwhile to share with Dat how she and Sol felt.

"Sleep peacefully," Sol whispered, "knowin' that we'll be well taken care of either way—whether I work elsewhere or we continue on here."

She scooted down under the covers and let that sink in. *I want Evan to know how happy we are to have him home*, she thought before slipping toward sleep.

Lyle turned in bed and draped his arm over Elisabeth as she lay on her side. He'd dreamed Evan had returned home intact, not wounded at all and still hardheaded and distant, then headed straight for the Herr farm and his worldly friends. It was all Lyle could do to relax, and he had to remind himself that Evan was indeed severely wounded, yet his heart was in the right place.

"You all right, dear?" Elisabeth murmured.

"Just a bad dream."

"You were gasping."

"I'm fine now."

"Something 'bout Evan?"

He scooted closer and reassured her he was okay. "Our son has returned to us. There's no cause to fret, love."

"M-hm," she whispered, then sighed back into slumber.

Lyle remained awake, recalling the day's events and feeling wholly indebted to the Lord above. All the same, he felt certain that Evan's sense of self-worth was at stake, given the trauma and loss he'd endured and would suffer for some time. *Our son needs to find something meaningful to do, something that will give him a purpose.*

42

"H ope ya still like your eggs over easy," Ellie said to Evan in the kitchen the next morning as she finished making chocolate chip pancakes for him and Sol.

Evan nodded and smiled. "You're spoilin' me, Ellie—it's been so long since I had a choice."

Sol poured coffee for the three of them, mentioning that the peach trees would be putting on their pink dresses in another day.

"In time to celebrate Evan's return," Ellie said, wondering what her brother might say.

"The Lord sure knows how to throw a party," he replied, stirring sugar into his coffee.

Ellie laughed softly. Her brother must've had a good night's sleep, because he seemed a little more perky this morning.

"I'll be visiting Bishop Mast after breakfast," Evan said, taking a sip of coffee before setting down his mug. "Want to tell him how God changed my mind about a few things."

Ellie smiled as she carried over the platter filled with the eggs and pancakes, all piping hot, just like Mamm served them. She sat down as Sol bowed his head and folded his hands for the table blessing, and then Ellie realized that Evan couldn't fold his hands anymore. Tears came to her eyes.

After the prayer, Evan told them he wanted to compose a letter to Cheryl Herr, telling her about his change of heart toward being Amish and following the Lord. "But I'll break it to her gently."

"Might not need to be too gentle," Ellie said. She looked at him while salting her eggs. "I'm sorry to be the one to tell ya, but she's been seein' someone else."

Evan seemed to take this in. "Well, I quit writing to her weeks before the explosion. So I guess it isn't too surprising. I had no interest in the world any longer, but at the time, I didn't know how to tell her."

Ellie took a bite of her eggs and studied her brother. "'*When God changes our hearts, He changes our desires,*' Dawdi says."

"He's been sayin' that since I was little." Evan offered a smile.

Sol nodded. "Hezekiah's our resident minister."

Ellie agreed and was thankful Evan didn't have to suffer yet another hardship at the news of Cheryl's moving on. And relieved, too, that Cheryl wouldn't pose a problem for his return to Amish life and the faith.

As Ellie was working with Sol in the barn office, Dat came in and mentioned that the peach trees they'd planted three years ago were blossoming.

"They might actually produce fruit this year," he said, glancing at the ceiling as if deep in thought. "Planted them the year before Evan was called up for the draft."

Sol nodded. "I remember helpin' with that block of trees."

"Say, I'll be headed over to meet with George Stewart at his place this afternoon. Interested to know what's on his mind."

"He wrote ya back?" Ellie asked.

Dat shook his head. "Actually, he approached me at the post office this mornin'. He must've heard the postmaster mention my name—oddest thing."

"Well, just think of all the cherry and plum trees we could plant if ya make an offer and he accepts," Ellie replied, delighted at the prospect.

"I'm curious, though. Surely he's had other offers."

Ellie had a few ideas about why the man might have waited to talk with Dat, but she wouldn't say—not till everything played out.

She wondered if her father would bring up Evan's visit to the bishop and how that might impact his decision for future management of the orchard. But he just sat down at his end of the desk and began to work.

"The never-ending cycle of keepin' an orchard," he said to Ellie, who was contemplating what she should say to him about Evan's rightful place in the business.

After Sol left to run an errand, Ellie continued to work on the books. Then an hour or so later, Evan surprised her by coming into the office, grinning.

"How was your visit with the bishop?" she asked as he pulled one of the chairs toward him and then slowly eased himself into it.

"He was as kind as I remembered."

Ellie swiveled her chair around to face him. "I knew he'd be glad to see ya."

"His eyes lit up when I talked about taking baptism classes this summer."

"I think Dat's must've, too, when ya first told him."

Evan scratched his head, suddenly serious, then sucked in his breath hard. "Bishop Mast and I talked about Sol's attack last year—his hearing loss and all the weeks without the use of his right hand. Bishop was the one who first wrote to me about it, ya see."

She could tell Evan's heart had been pierced—either because of what Sol had suffered or that she hadn't been the one to tell him about the attack. Maybe both.

"To think Sol suffered so terribly right here at home, and for doin' the right thing . . ."

Nodding, Ellie said, "I didn't tell ya 'cause I didn't want to saddle ya with all that."

"I was knee-deep in the jungle at the time," Evan said pensively. "Maybe it's a good thing you didn't, but both the bishop and Jonah mentioned it later in their letters."

Ellie shared further about what had happened that horrible day and specifically how worried she'd been about Sol's concussion and his initial symptoms. "I realized then how much I cared for him. It was a clear turnin' point for both of us."

Evan's expression was still solemn. "Has Sol's hearing improved in that ear?"

"Not really. But he's learned to compensate over time."

"Like I have to," Evan said quietly, glancing toward what was left of his arm. He sat there for a moment, like a hundred thoughts were flying through his mind.

"Not to offend ya, Evan, but would it maybe help if I trimmed off the one shirt sleeve and hemmed it? Less to get in the way?"

He looked down for a moment, then nodded. "Thank you,

Ellie. It really would." He looked longingly out the window. "You know, I think I need to get back to work in the orchard. I can't do much, not like before, but I can do some things. Just slower."

"Speakin' of the orchard," she began, "Sol and I were talkin' last night, and I've been thinking 'bout something since you returned. You've prob'ly guessed that Dat's been training Sol and me ever since we married so we can manage things when he retires."

Evan nodded. "Wise choice."

"But since you're makin' plans to move forward with baptism and all, Sol and I are willin' to back out of the business agreement with Dat."

"Why would you do that?" Evan frowned. "No, Ellie. Even though it's just like you to offer, you and I both know I don't deserve it. And you must promise me not to approach Dat about it."

"Won't ya at least think 'bout it, Bruder?"

Evan shook his head. "You were the faithful twin. And with God's blessing, you and Sol will succeed." His expression grew even more serious. "I'll be perfectly content to work alongside you both, once that time comes."

She knew better than to argue with Evan. He was her elder brother, if only by several minutes. But even so, he was fiercely determined. And that was likely one of the reasons he'd survived in Vietnam. "All right. I won't say anything to Dat. And I'll let Sol know that you and I talked this over."

A satisfied smile appeared. "Just so ya know, I have decided to take Dawdi up on his invitation to move over there, but I'd like to stay in my old room for another few nights."

"Of course," she replied, glad she'd have him under their roof for a little longer.

Evan continued. "I'll be honored to look after Dawdi in his

twilight years. That will help Dat and Mamm, too," he said, his voice cracking. "I owe so much to my family."

"Only love," Ellie whispered, enjoying this precious time together.

"'The greatest of these . . .'"

The natural way Evan spoke the Lord's words brought joy to her heart. "I'll be glad to have both you and Dawdi over for meals, and I s'pect Mamm will, too. So yous might never have to cook," she said. "You could rotate between the two houses at mealtimes and never be lonely."

"Sounds like a wonderful-good life to me."

"For all of us, really." A lump rose in her throat, seeing him there beside her—a dream come true.

43

That afternoon Lyle took Sol and Ellie along with him to meet with George Stewart. It was rather surprising to be welcomed so heartily when the man invited them into his sitting room.

Lyle sat across from George, who—out of the blue—immediately began to talk about his youngest son's defection to Canada last year. "Being a veteran myself, I was horrified that my own son avoided the draft and ran off instead of serving this wonderful country. He was eventually caught—doing his time now."

Why's he telling us this? Lyle wondered, glancing at Sol.

"When I received your daughter's letter, she told me about your son Evan. I was sincerely moved." George smiled faintly. "What I'm getting to is that the trials your family went through, especially when Evan went MIA, made me do some soul-searching about the price."

Lyle realized that Ellie had indeed shared a lot with George about their family's difficulties, just as he'd privately speculated to Elisabeth.

"So, I'm prepared to offer my land to you at a reduced price," said George.

Lyle almost gasped. "Well, we sincerely appreciate that. But you should know that Evan has miraculously returned home—though permanently wounded in battle."

"All the more reason, then," George replied, smiling. "You and your family have truly suffered, and because of it, I'd like to sell my land to you at a third less than the asking price," he said.

"Are ya sure?" Lyle asked, astonished.

"Absolutely."

Lyle planned to stop by the bank later and make the necessary arrangements to purchase the land from George. The sale also included the area with the barn, though Lyle hadn't requested it.

With hearts filled with gratitude, he, Ellie, and Sol headed back home.

"Well, that was unexpected, ain't?" Sol said.

"Praise be!" Lyle responded, nodding.

"I'm beyond happy," Ellie declared.

"You were born happy, as I recall." Lyle chuckled, remembering what a joy both twins had been as babies.

"Easy to imagine that," Sol said, smiling at her.

"We certainly wouldn't be where we are at this moment if you hadn't stuck out your neck," Lyle told her.

"Maybe my letter to George was part of God's plan," Ellie said rather humbly.

Lyle glanced over at her. "I believe you just may be right."

When they returned from visiting George Stewart, Ellie walked down the lane and opened the mailbox. Right on top of the stack of mail was a letter from Leah, and without bothering to look through the rest, she hurried to the front porch and sat on the top step to read.

Dear Ellie,

I'm so happy to hear that Evan is coming home. Please tell him I can't wait to see him when I return to Bird-in-Hand—when I move back just before my wedding in November, if not before. I'm so glad Reuben decided to accept the job in Bird-in-Hand!

I've been excited to tell you that I've become good friends with Reuben's younger sister, Hannah Mae, and she's agreed to be one of my bridesmaids. Since you're married, of course I can't have you, but Hannah Mae will be a special choice since her brother's the groom. I'll probably choose one of Menno's younger sisters for the other bridesmaid, even though I'm not nearly as close to those cousins as I am to you.

I have something else to share. Carolyn is getting serious with Roger. The timing of this is perfect, Ellie. I mean, they might actually be married before Reuben and I are! Which will work very well, as I'll be giving my notice well in advance of my wedding.

"*Wunnerbaar!*" Ellie exclaimed into the air, then glanced around her on the porch, hoping she hadn't awakened Evan. He was resting upstairs. *Things are surely workin' out for Leah,* she thought, longing to see her friend again.

Sitting there on the steps, she glanced at the cloud-laden sky. Within a moment, rain sprinkled her bare feet. She recalled the time she knew Leah was to be her close friend. *We both loved sitting on the porch when it rained,* she mused. *Who'd ever have thought that would be a clue to our future as friends?*

Controlled though he usually was, Lyle could not stay away from the main house over the next few days. He checked on Evan morning and evening, realizing his son must be exhausted—though he sometimes found him on the floor of his room doing one-arm push-ups.

Surely his fatigue was a normal response to the radical surgery he'd had, even these many weeks ago. But was he also depressed? Evan's reluctance to talk might mean he was still processing all the adjustments he was making, and Lyle wouldn't think of pressing him. If anything, it was important to give him the time he needed to rest and heal, and Lyle was glad Ellie was keeping a close eye on him. Daed had mentioned that Evan would be residing with him soon, and both Lyle and Elisabeth agreed that was an ideal plan all around.

Ever since Evan's return, Lyle'd had fleeting moments of disappointment about his youngest son's future. He was no longer torn about the right path forward for the orchard, though. Sol and Ellie had been the right choice. His disappointment was related more to the fact that Evan's *Rumschpringe* choices had brought him so many difficult consequences.

He needs a routine, Lyle thought, wondering if Evan's living with his elderly Dawdi might become monotonous over time. Evan wanted to begin working in the orchard again in a few more days, but would that be satisfying enough in the long run?

Ellie made a point of helping Evan with his shoelaces every morning, double-knotting them so he wouldn't have to worry about them coming undone.

Today, she'd also agreed to stand by while he carefully climbed into his courting buggy. "We might need to dust it off," she said as they stood in the carriage shed doorway, looking at it.

"I'll never be able to hitch up on my own."

"Two can hitch up better anyway. Besides, you'll always have someone nearby to ask. Workin' together is our way, ya know."

Evan managed to get in on the driver's side, a flat expression on his face as he stared at the dashboard.

She waited, not interrupting his thoughts. This wasn't the first time she'd seen him like this. *Everything's different*, she thought, determined to encourage him, to offer him cheer and acceptance—and hope.

"Do you think Sol might take a ride with me?" Evan asked suddenly.

"Once his work's done tonight, he might. Dat's signing the bank loan for the new land this evening."

"I'd really like to go riding now," Evan said, rather insistent.

She thought about that. "Well, what 'bout me?"

"Better yet," Evan said, scooting out of the buggy.

Together, they pushed the open carriage out of the shed and then headed over to the stable. Evan led Nelly down to hitch her up. The mare nuzzled against Evan while he was trying to put the harness over her head.

"Aww, she missed ya," Ellie said.

Evan stroked Nelly's long nose and talked softly to her. "Wish I had a sugar cube in my pocket for ya, girl."

"You always liked spoilin' her and Captain," Ellie said, memorizing this moment. "I daresay you're a born horse lover."

335

"You got that right."

"Maybe someday you could assist the vet."

"I'd like that," Evan replied, a smile appearing. "I really would."

Ellie pushed the driving lines through the openings in the dashboard, wondering how Evan would manage to hold them both. But he must have thought it through, because he quickly grasped them in his right hand when Ellie stepped into the buggy. At the click of his tongue, Nelly moved forward, and they were off.

A mile or so down the road, Evan let out a holler. "Yahoo!"

Ellie laughed out loud, and meeting his gaze, she detected the old twinkle in his eyes. "I love seein' ya this happy."

"I'm finally back. And home is best."

Ellie sighed with contentment, the wind in her face, her twin by her side, enjoying their first ride together in ever so long.

Sisters Day the last Saturday in April began with pastries and coffee around Aendi Cora's kitchen table. Ruthann had put out pretty floral dishes and matching teacups and saucers. Ellie had brought her gooey cream-filled donuts, and Lydia had a baker's dozen of her wonderful sticky buns to share. Their offerings combined with all the others' goodies.

Altogether, eight sets of sisters were present, including Mamm and Aendi Cora, making the table chatter joyful. Ellie was happy to sit next to Lydia for once without the distraction of little ones vying for their attention.

Lydia whispered amidst all the noise. "Can ya keep a secret?"

Ellie nodded, wondering what this was.

"Priscilla thinks she might be expecting twins. She said I could tell you and no one else."

"That'd be just *wunnerbaar*," Ellie said, though a bit surprised Priscilla would mention this.

"She's told Jonah what she suspects, too, but she couldn't keep it from me when we were out picking rhubarb together yesterday."

Ellie so wanted to talk more about this, but she didn't want to call attention to them sitting there whispering. *The first set of twins in the family since Evan and me*, she thought gaily.

The rest of the morning, they worked to put up large quantities of rhubarb sauce and rhubarb juice. Mamm and Aendi Cora stood over near the sink, heads together as they talked. *Undoubtedly about Evan*, Ellie assumed. *His return to the People is on nearly everyone's lips.* But no one asked probing questions, and Ellie was relieved.

As she, Mamm, and Lydia were getting ready to leave, Ruthann asked to talk to Ellie privately. They slipped into the spare room, and with a smile, Ruthann told her Menno had signed the lease on a small house for them, less than a mile down the road.

"Such nice news!" Ellie grabbed her hands and smiled.

"Isn't it, though?" Ruthann twirled around like a schoolgirl. "I've never been so happy."

"I can see that," Ellie said, laughing.

Hand in hand, they walked back to the kitchen, and Ellie thanked her and Aendi Cora for hosting the get-together.

"We'll have the next Sisters Day at my house," Ellie said, making her offer as she glanced at Lydia. Her sister's eyes shone with their shared secret.

Two weeks later, Ellie prepared barbecue chicken sandwiches for the outdoor family gathering in honor of Evan's homecoming. The women of the family brought sides of homemade French fries, potato chips, five-bean salad, macaroni and cheese, and pickled beets and red beet eggs, in addition to an array of mouthwatering pies and cookies, plus date-nut pudding. The spread was impressive, and Ellie hoped it helped show Evan how happy they were to have him with them again.

The day was most pleasant in the low seventies, a warmth they rarely enjoyed as early as mid-May. But with the occasional breeze and low humidity, no one could possibly complain.

Evan gravitated toward Ellie, sitting with her and Sol and one of their young nephews—eleven-year-old Sammy. Sammy had wandered over and plunked down next to her brother, and Ellie wondered if he was curious about Evan's strange-looking shirt with its one short sleeve thanks to her tailoring and hemming. *Surely Titus and Lydia have talked to him and his siblings about their uncle's injury,* Ellie thought. Nevertheless, Sammy kept sneaking peeks at the empty short sleeve, then glancing up at Evan.

"Wanna arm wrestle?" Evan asked Sammy, grinning.

Her nephew shook his head right quick, looking a little scared.

"I've been practicing," Evan told him, raising his muscular right arm.

By now Ellie was trying not to smile, and slowly but surely, Sammy caught on. Then with a sad face, he looked up at Evan and said, "I'm sorry 'bout what happened to ya, Onkel. . . ."

Evan leaned next to him, then reached around with his right hand and tousled his nephew's light brown hair. "Remember, Sammy, life has its ups and downs. Ain't always gonna be easy."

Sammy nodded like he was thinking about something else.

"Was wonderin' . . . did ya ever fall off the swingin' rope in the haymow when you were little?"

"Nope. Did you?"

Sammy nodded again. "*Jah*, but I climbed right back up the ladder and got on again."

"Now you're talkin'," Evan said, bobbing his head. "Never give up. *Ever*."

"You sound like Dawdi Hezekiah," Sammy replied.

"Say now, I do, don't I?" Evan glanced at Ellie. "Don't I?" he said again, teasing her.

"I s'pect we all have a ways to go before we're as wise as Dawdi," Ellie replied, happy that Sammy and the younger generation were taking notice.

All during the rest of the meal, Sammy sat taller beside his courageous uncle.

When Ellie and her brother found themselves alone while everyone else was getting dessert, Evan said he'd talked with the local vet. "Lo and behold, he needs a part-time assistant. Doesn't even mind that I have some limitations."

Ellie was delighted. "Guess I had a *gut* idea."

"Sure did! I start workin' this coming Monday. And just so ya know, nothin' can pry me away from working in the family orchard, too." Evan chuckled.

Ellie remembered sneaking out of the house with him, in their nightclothes, scampering up and down the orchard rows in the moonlight. It seemed so long ago now, but she was encouraged to hear that Evan still thought so fondly of the place where she'd always felt God's presence.

"You're beamin' today," Ellie said softly, not wanting to be heard by the others.

"I made peace with my Maker in Vietnam," Evan said. "And

with myself here lately. Ya know, I sometimes wonder if I had to lose my arm to gain back my soul."

Swallowing hard, she looked at him across the long folding table. "What a thing to say, Bruder."

"I'm okay with it." Evan gazed around them for the longest time, taking in Mamm's vegetable garden, the cider shed, and the orchard beyond. "What a *wunnerbaar-gut* day to be alive!"

She nodded in agreement.

Evan headed over to talk with Jonah and his family, then slowly made his way to each table, visiting with every loved one present.

Ready for dessert, Ellie strolled to the serving table, smiling and rejoicing all the way. *God answered our hearts' cry.*

Epilogue

Seven months have passed since Evan's return. For me, the best day of all was sitting in the congregation on Baptism Sunday in mid-September, hearing my twin make his vows to God and the church. What a sight to see as the bishop's tears mingled with the baptismal water poured on Evan's flaxen hair. I doubt there was a dry eye in the house of worship that morning.

Tomorrow, another special moment will take place—Leah's wedding to Reuben Miller. *O Lord, bless them with a most special day.*

While waiting for the second seating at Leah's wedding supper, Mamm and I walked out to the little brook that ran through the Bontrager farm. Standing there with her, I stared down at the riffle of water, relishing the sound of it moving over rocks and twigs, the call of winter birds around us.

"Did ya notice how Leah's face glowed when she looked at Reuben during the ceremony?" I asked.

"*Jah.* Reminded me of you and Sol on *your* wedding day."

"I still can't believe Leah is home to stay."

"And your brother, too," Mamm said, glancing at me. "Such a long journey back to what he nearly lost."

"Evan wishes he'd never left."

"We all would want that for him if we could, but he's a much stronger Amishman now, with a deep faith." Mamm sighed. "We either learn from our mistakes or keep repeatin' them. It's human nature. But thanks be to God, who answers our call for help."

The supper bell rang, so we turned to head back to the house, arm in arm.

While waiting in line to go inside, I spotted Dawdi Hezekiah coming down the back porch steps, patting his middle. "Did ya overeat?" I asked, teasing him as he walked our way.

"Just wait'll ya see all the food, Ellie-girl." He described the usual wedding fare—roasted chicken pieces mixed with stuffing, mashed potatoes and gravy, and all the typical appetizing side dishes. "But the wedding cake—*ach, appeditlich!*" he said. "Melts in your mouth."

"How's Evan doin' paired up with Reuben's sister for the day?" I whispered, Mamm now talking with the neighbor standing behind her. I was curious, because Leah had told me how shy Hannah Mae was. Yet she hoped to move here to be closer to her newlywed brother.

Dawdi chuckled, then replied in an equally lowered voice, "Well now, I saw Evan lookin' at her just as they were seated at the table, a twinkle in those blue eyes of his. And Hannah Mae, why, she couldn't've disguised her big smile even if she'd wanted to."

"I wonder if this is the start of somethin' 'tween them."

Dawdi's expression grew mischievous. "I ain't a bettin' man, but if I was . . ." Now he was grinning.

A wave of joy washed over me at the possibility. I had to stifle my urge to laugh with delight, but it was ever so difficult.

That evening, Sol and I sat quietly in our bedroom after the day of celebration with Leah, Reuben, and all the wedding guests. I mentioned that Dat had seemed more energetic here lately, especially since Evan's return, and Sol agreed.

"A man's children are his responsibility under God, and when he learned that Evan was runnin' with a worldly bunch, it took a toll on him," Sol said while sitting in his favorite chair by the window.

"It wonders me if he might postpone retirement longer than he first thought," I replied, running my hands through my newly brushed hair.

Sol chuckled. "I've been thinkin' the same thing lately, and that'd be fine."

"We still have plenty to learn from him." I plumped our pillows, then slipped into bed. "And it's a *gut* thing, too, havin' Dat working with us every day . . . since our first baby will be comin' durin' the June peach harvest."

Sol quickly came to my side of the bed and kissed me. "Aww, love. I've been waitin' to hear such *gut* news," he said, looking at me tenderly. "My sweet Ellie's gonna be a Mamma *and* an orchard manager."

"A Mamma first and foremost," I said, leaning up to kiss him, too.

"We'll teach him or her to love the orchard as we do," Sol said, his eyes smiling.

I thought of Priscilla just then. "I wonder if we'll have twins someday."

"Twins *would* be a blessing," Sol said, nuzzling my nose with his. "Or triplets."

Now I was laughing and couldn't stop.

"What's so funny?"

At last, I said, "Mamm might have to move back in here if we have three babies at once."

"Well, she's right round the corner, remember."

"True. But no need to plan too far ahead. Let's just pray that our first little one will be healthy."

Sol went around the bed to outen the lantern, then raised the quilt to settle in. I couldn't help but reflect on the Lord's merciful kindness to our family—ever so many blessings, indeed—and thanked Him in my silent nighttime prayer.

Author's Note

As a child growing up in Lancaster County, Pennsylvania, I eagerly awaited the appearance of thousands of peach and apple blossoms each springtime. In the fall, I could hardly wait for the scent and taste of freshly picked apples, which I would help my mother core and peel to make apple crisp or baked apples. Naturally, with my lifelong love of orchards and everything about them, I decided to feature one in this book. The fictitious Hostetler orchard is inspired by the well-known Kauffman Fruit Farm, owned and operated in Bird-in-Hand for six generations by the Kauffman family. (As a side note, Sentry peaches were developed in 1980 in Maryland, but for the sake of this story, I altered their advent by ten years.)

The path of my research led to fascinating discoveries. And thanks to the wonderful help of my fine consultants—Dale Birch, Amish and Mennonite friends (who wish to remain anonymous), linguist and translator Hank Hershberger, and the writings of Donald Kraybill—I was blessed with knowledge of Plain-community happenings during the early 1970s.

Rochelle Glöege has been my editor for nearly three decades

345

now, and I am grateful to her beyond measure for many reasons! She continues to head up my excellent editorial team, which includes David Horton, Charlene Patterson, Jean Bloom, and Elisa Tally.

Bethany House Publishers' talented fiction marketing team, with Michele Misiak, Raela Schoenherr, Karen Steele, and Anne Van Solkema, as well as Rachael Wing, Chris Dykstra, and Lindsay Schubert, gave this novel a resounding launch.

My husband, Dave, smoothed out my writing days with fun-filled moments of brainstorming and by making delicious lunches and snacks. My sister, Barbara, added her in-depth proofreading skills to the mix, along with encouragement and prayer. Our grown children—Julie, Janie, and Jonathan—and granddaughter, Ariel, buoyed me along with their thoughtfulness and support. My prayerful family, friends, and colleagues were also my constants during the hardest days—sincerest gratitude to every one of you!

As always, I think fondly of my faithful readers and reviewers and offer my heartfelt appreciation.

To the Creator of us all, I am continually thankful for divine prompting and direction, so evident to me during this story journey. *Soli Deo Gloria!*

Beverly Lewis, born in the heart of Pennsylvania Dutch country, is the *New York Times* bestselling author of more than one hundred books. Her stories have been published in twelve languages worldwide. A keen interest in her mother's Plain heritage has inspired Beverly to write many Amish-related novels, beginning with *The Shunning*, which has sold more than one million copies and is an Original Hallmark Channel movie. In 2007 *The Brethren* was honored with a Christy Award.

Beverly has been interviewed by both national and international media, including *Time* magazine, the Associated Press, and the BBC. She lives with her husband, David, in Colorado.

Visit her website at www.beverlylewis.com or www.facebook .com/officialbeverlylewis for more information.

The Heirloom

The Next Novel From Beverly Lewis

When her widowed father remarries, nineteen-year-old Clara Bender feels at a loss now that she's no longer needed to run his household. But when she comes across letters from her Mamma's aunt Ella Mae Zook, she sets off to visit Hickory Hollow and decide where her future lies. The two women form a warm bond while restoring an heirloom wedding quilt and sharing about their lives, with Ella Mae confiding about a tragedy from her courting years. Then Clara's own life is upended by an unexpected incident and a young Amish man. Through it all, will she find where her heart truly belongs?

AVAILABLE FALL 2023

Sign Up for Beverly's Newsletter

Keep up to date with Beverly's news on book releases and events by signing up for her email list at beverlylewis.com.

More from Beverly Lewis

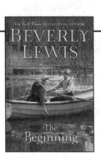

Susie Mast's Old Order life has been shaped more by tragedy than by her own choices. But when she decides to stop waiting on her childhood friend and accept another young man's invitation, she soon realizes her mistake. Will family secrets and missed opportunities dim Susie's hopes for the future? Or is what seems like the end only the beginning?

The Beginning

Also from Beverly Lewis

Visit beverlylewis.com for a full list of her books.

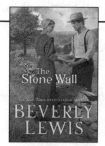

Eager to begin a new chapter as a Lancaster County tour guide, Anna searches for the answers of her grandmother's past and an old stone wall—both a mystery due to the elderly woman's Alzheimer's. And when Anna grows close with a Mennonite man and an Amish widower, she's faced with a difficult choice. Will she find love and the truth, or only heartbreak?

The Stone Wall

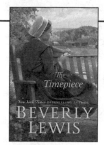

In this continuation of *The Tinderbox*, young Amish woman Sylvia Miller's world is upended by the arrival of Englisher Adeline Pelham—whose existence is a reminder of a painful family secret. Sylvia must learn to come to terms with the past while grappling with issues of her own. Is it possible that God can make something good out of the mistakes of days gone by?

The Timepiece

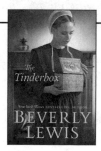

When Sylvia Miller finds her father's old tinderbox left unlocked, her curiosity is piqued. She opens the box and uncovers secrets best left alone. A confrontation with her father leads to a shocking revelation that will forever change not only her own life but also that of her family and her Amish community.

The Tinderbox

❖ BETHANYHOUSE

You May Also Like . . .

In the summer of 1951, Amish woman Maggie Esh is struggling with a debilitating illness and few future prospects. When tent revival meetings come to the area, Maggie attends out of curiosity. She's been told to accept her lot in life as God's will, but the words of the evangelist begin to stir something deep inside her. Dare she hope for a brighter future?

The First Love by Beverly Lewis
beverlylewis.com

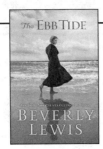

When a young Amish woman takes a summer job as a nanny in beautiful Cape May, she forms an unexpected bond with a handsome Mennonite. Has she been too hasty with her promises, or will she only find what her heart is longing for back home?

The Ebb Tide by Beverly Lewis
beverlylewis.com

Tally Smucker's quiet world is shaken when her neighbor Danielle—who grew up Plain but joined the Army—returns in need of a friend. Tally invites Danielle to join her quilting circle, and they are both inspired by a story told of a WWI soldier. But when disaster hits Tally's family and Danielle's PTSD becomes unmanageable, can they find the hope they need?

Threads of Hope by Leslie Gould
PLAIN PATTERNS #3
lesliegould.com

BETHANYHOUSE